Praise for *Family of Choice*.

"*Family of Choice* is an intimate exploration of relationships and the long work of healing. With compelling characters and nuanced prose, this book sweeps you up in its heartfelt journey. I couldn't put it down!"

—The Rev. Leah Romanelli DeJesus

"Overall, a funny, warm book that explores how the family we choose can be more important to our emotional and spiritual growth than the family we are born to. With humor, snappy dialogue, and a bit of spice, there are deeper messages of life's lessons, human growth and maturity, spirituality, and coping with grief and loss. Eminently readable, you'll enjoy meeting Micky, Brad, Lillian and Sally, and wish they were your family, too!"

—Kathleen R. Ashton, Ph.D., ABPP
 Psychologist

"I was captured by the depth of this story and the characters as well as the author's ability to draw me into this close-knit group of friends. I felt excitement, joy, and sorrow throughout and was pleasantly surprised by unexpected outcomes. Not only is the book a great read, it offers real insight into the complexities of love, faith, life, and death. I am eagerly awaiting the next book in the series."

—The Rev. Vincent Black

Family of Choice

Raising Each Other

Family of Choice

Raising Each Other

Corky Thacker

Tampa, Florida

This book is a work of fiction. The names, characters and events in this book are the products of the author's imagination or are used fictitiously. Any similarity to real persons living or dead is coincidental and not intended by the author.

The views and opinions expressed in this book are solely those of the author and do not reflect the views or opinions of Gatekeeper Press. Gatekeeper Press is not to be held responsible for and expressly disclaims responsibility for the content herein.

Family of Choice: Raising Each Other

Published by Gatekeeper Press
7853 Gunn Hwy., Suite 209
Tampa, FL 33626
www.GatekeeperPress.com

Copyright © 2023 by Corky Thacker
All rights reserved. Neither this book, nor any parts within it may be sold or reproduced in any form or by any electronic or mechanical means, including information storage and retrieval systems, without permission in writing from the author. The only exception is by a reviewer, who may quote short excerpts in a review.

The editorial work for this book is entirely the product of the author. Gatekeeper Press did not participate in and is not responsible for any aspect of this element.

Library of Congress Control Number: 2023950702

ISBN (hardcover): 9781662944383
ISBN (paperback): 9781662944390
eISBN: 9781662944406

The tagline GOD LOVES YOU. NO EXCEPTIONS.® (US Federal TradeMark Appln. No. 86-344,844; Registration No. 4,691,924) is used with permission from the Episcopal Diocese of Ohio.

Dedicated in loving and grateful memory of Felix G., who re-parented me.

CHAPTER 1

Micky McHale rolled over and tried to grab the pillow to shield her eyes from the vicious sun stabbing through the wooden slats of the shutters. Through the cocktail-flu throb of her head, she felt some confusion—the drapes in her stateroom on *Luxe of the Seas* should've been closed.

The pillow didn't budge. It was held fast beneath a dark head of curly pomade-greased hair that now shifted to turn and grin at her. "Hey, Gorgeous. Welcome to mornin'!"

She tried to hide her surprise as she took in the view of a bedroom in what looked to be a tropical bungalow. "What time is it?"

"Almost nine," he said.

"Oh, *shit!*" Her cruise ship was to have departed from Key West at midnight. Worse, her company's awards banquet for top account managers was scheduled in the Prime specialty steakhouse for 8:00—last night. She'd just stopped into Sloppy Joe's after her afternoon tour of Hemingway's house because she wanted to have a drink in the iconic author's favorite local pub. "My flight back to Cleveland leaves Miami at eleven! How the hell can I get to the airport?!"

"Sorry, darlin'. There *is* no way in hell," said the owner of the handsome face. "It takes over three hours to drive to MIA . . . and I don't have a car." He reached his arms toward her, but she was already on the other side of the bed, wrestling olive leggings over her long legs and slim hips. Diving into a jungle print tunic, she grabbed her jute bag and fled.

In the back seat of the Uber, Micky's lush black hair fell across her face, blocking her iPhone screen view, which also was impeded by what felt like a chunk of yesterday's mascara in her right eye. Her thumbs were flying wildly as she searched for an alternative flight home when the cell buzzed with a call from her boss. She thought about letting it go to voicemail, but answered. "Where the hell are you?" said Jack Benson. "And where were you last night? Some people thought you'd fallen overboard and wanted to alert the captain to call out the Coast Guard, but we were tied up with the ceremony—and I figured you'd just screwed up again. So I told them you were in your cabin with a norovirus. But now we're boarding the bus for the airport, and I need some answers."

"I'm on my way, Jack, but I'll have to catch a different flight. It took a while to find a ride."

"Great. Just great. I covered for you last night, but Mr. Cordero is concerned that our Top Dog honoree is missing, and the shuttle driver won't leave without a full head-count."

"I won?! First?! Wow, that's *fantastic!* Can't you tell them I'm in the infirmary getting checked out, and they won't let me leave the ship until I stop puking?"

Jack sighed. "That should work. And yes, you won. Your numbers are so good that I can't fire you—yet. But if they slip, I've got a problem. So, get your ass into the office Monday—on time. I'll set up an appointment for you with EAP in the morning."

*****

Mid-January's afternoon sun in Northeast Ohio wasn't as intense as Miami's, but it warmed Lillian Meadows' kitchen and her guest almost as well as her coffee. Brad pushed his six-foot-two frame back from the round oak table and stretched like a contented cat. The cat under the table dislodged by his foot was *not* contented and departed in a blur of calico. The blueberry pancakes and sausage had tasted like the best food he'd ever eaten, and he was finally feeling some peace after quitting smoking a week ago.

"That was fabulous, Lil! I feel like a new man," he said. "Now, if I could just stop wanting a cigarette to go with this coffee . . ."

She responded with a smile. "Just have the coffee. It's fine by itself—and you won't have to go outside on the porch. Still a bit chilly for that."

Her phone rang before he could reply. "Oh, my. *This* is a surprise." She held it up so Brad could see the caller ID before she connected. "Well, hello, Micky; it's been a while. How's everything?"

"I just won my company's top sales award . . ."

"And?" Lillian interrupted.

"And I missed the presentation. And the cruise ship. And my original flight home. And my boss is making an appointment for me with Employee Assistance and says he'll fire me if he gets a chance. I just want to go back to meetings and really get into the Twelve Steps this time—I'm hoping they'll let me do outpatient treatment. Would you please, *please* give me another chance and be my sponsor again?"

Lillian paused. "Well," she said. "I'll say yes for now, and we'll see how it goes. Where are you now?"

Micky brightened. "Waiting to board my flight in Miami. I should land in time to make Last Call . . . do they still meet at your church?"

"Yes, but I don't go to that one now; I can't stay awake for evening meetings anymore," Lillian said. "But Brad still goes there. You remember Brad?"

Shaking his blond crew-cut head vigorously, he mouthed, "NO! NO!" and stretched his arms toward Lillian with his forefingers forming a cross to ward off a vampire.

Lillian smiled. "Brad will meet you there. He'll be your co-sponsor. I'm seventy-seven now, so I think it's a good idea to have back-up these days. Call me after you've gotten your treatment plan worked out and we'll take it from there.

"And, Micky?"

"Yes?"

"It's good to hear from you. Welcome home."

Brad didn't think it was so great to hear from her. "How could you *do* this to me?" he cried in only semi-mock anguish. "You're my sponsor! And I thought you were this sweet, pancake-making little lady—but you're *evil!*"

"Methinks the lady doth protest too much," she replied.

"That woman is a *train-wreck*. She's a bigger drama queen than my *ex*, and I thought he *owned* the crown."

"Who's being the drama queen now?" Lillian's blue eyes twinkled.

They were interrupted by a knock on the back door. A tall red-haired woman walked through it, laughing. "I heard some commotion in here from out on the verandah," she said. "What's going on?"

"I'm helping Brad with quitting smoking, Sally," Lillian said with a grin. "He needs to get out of himself, so he's going to assist me as a co-sponsor. Micky's back."

Sally raised her eyebrows and nodded to Brad. "Oh, boy. She'll give you a run for your money!"

With a dramatic, pained expression, he shrugged and grumbled, "I was taught to always say 'yes' when asked to do something in A.A.— especially if *she's* doing the asking." He jerked his face in Lillian's direction.

Laughing, Sally said, "I'll pray for you, Brad!"

"Good," he said. "I'm definitely going to need professional help with this! Please light a candle while you're at it!" As he got out of his chair, he felt around out of habit, then remembered he didn't have a pack of cigarettes and lighter to restore to the pocket of his Merino wool shirt. Grinning, he said, "And I could use another candle for the smoking thing. Well, ladies, I have some shopping and errands to get out of the way before the tornado rips through my quiet life. Oh—that's right; it's already pretty tattered from Oscar, the move, and nicotine withdrawal. Like John McCain once said of bombing Afghanistan, this will just be making the rubble jump!"

As Brad made his exit, Lillian laughed and turned to Sally. "So, are you here for church biz, program or just a cup of coffee with a friend?"

The Reverend Sally Wise moved to the cupboard in the butler's pantry and retrieved a mug, then grasped the pot and poured. "Coffee, thank you; and the program sort of melds with my priestly duties. As your sponsor and spiritual advisor, I'm curious: Why would you let Micky back into your life?"

Lillian considered the question while her friend of fifteen years settled into a caned chair at the table. "Well, I don't know how much help I can be, but she needs all she can get. I knew her mother from recovery meetings when Micky was just a toddler. Her parents got her into modeling then—to pay for her future college education, she said. So, between having a stage mommy who was a sneak-drinker when her husband was traveling for business and a rage-a-holic pot-smoking daddy who was so emotionally abusive that his wife offed herself with pills before their child's tenth birthday . . . I'd say Micky never had a chance of turning out any other way but warped. And alcoholic."

"Very alcoholic," Sally concurred. "And impulsive, with terrible judgment."

"Aren't we all, when we come in?"

"True. But she's a standout. Why stick Brad with her?"

"I seldom take back a returnee who went back out while I was sponsoring her; I figure if a woman didn't get the message sufficiently from me to stay sober, perhaps she can better hear it from a different messenger," Lillian explained. "Brad needs to get out of himself right now . . ."

Sally smiled. "And she'll give him plenty to focus on instead! Plus, I'm guessing that you're not really feeling up to that level of challenge?"

"Maybe not; but I really think this match-up could be good for both of them," Lillian mused. "You know very well that God works miracles—often in mysterious ways!"

They shared a laugh, then Sally pressed on. "So, how are you—really? And how's the manuscript for 'Cat Hair' coming along?"

Lillian hesitated as she spoke, groping for honest words. "I'm feeling older . . . missing George more each day, not less, and it's been three years already. I thought this book . . . my new life as a widow, would help me work through it, but it hasn't." Slouching, she put her elbows on the table and rested her chin on clinched hands. "In fact, for the first time in my career, writing is hard; I can't find my usual humorous point of view about this particular woman's stage of life. Beyond the title, *Cat Hair in the Bidet*, there's little to give the reader even a mild snicker."

"How's your deadline?"

"My editor wants the first three chapters next month. I have two so far, but I don't like them."

"You may be too close to the work to judge," Sally suggested. "I'd be happy to give it a read, if you'd like another perspective."

Lillian smiled and straightened her slight figure back up in the chair. "That's a great idea—your insights were really helpful with *Hairs in the Sink and other Signs of Love*! And just sharing the work in progress with you removed that sense of isolation I get when I'm deep in a project."

A ray of strong afternoon sunlight broke through gray winter clouds and streamed in the window, illuminating newly etched creases added to the crows' feet and laugh lines that had characterized Lillian's face ever since Sally had known her. She also saw the fatigue in her friend's eyes, and reached across the table to touch her hand. "You know, Lil . . . you can't use humor to mask this. It can have its place, but you'll also have to allow yourself to feel the pain and to communicate that vulnerability with your readers—many of whom may be coping with the same thing. If you're willing to do this, I think it will be your best work yet and it can help a lot of women."

"Really?"

"Yes. And you won't have to do it alone. I'll be with you—and so will God."

CHAPTER 2

Micky shivered in the still-cold parka and boots she'd left in her car at the Cleveland Hopkins Airport parking lot. She turned up the Buick Regal's heater and kept driving west on I-480 until she found her exit and headed south.

It had been seven years since she'd driven this route, but she was pretty sure she remembered how to get to Lillian's house and the church next door where the meeting was. Yellow flashers marked an intersection that looked familiar. She turned left on Grace Avenue, toward Stromberg.

The new moon was rising over barren fields resting under a blanket of snow. The thin sliver yielded scant light, and Micky felt very alone and vulnerable on the isolated road. Yet, as she kept going, she began to see the vista as quiet and peaceful—a welcome change from the chaos of the rest of her day. *I remember someone once told me that this phase of the moon is a favorable time for new beginnings. Maybe things will work out...*

After 10 minutes or so, she saw the outline and lights of Lillian's house with its elegant turret, then another house with a tall, gabled roof next to the twin spires of Grace Church Episcopal. She turned left into the long driveway and found a space in the parking lot.

Keeping the heat blasting, she flipped up the lid on the lighted vanity mirror and fumbled in her bag for lipstick. She applied a swipe of red before giving up on her bedraggled looks and killed the engine. She got out of the car and walked carefully toward the church, aware that the four-inch heels on her designer boots made them a safety hazard on the ice.

Focused on her precarious balance, Micky hadn't noticed the tall man hovering by the side door of the church. She was startled when he extended his hand in greeting.

"Well, if it isn't *'Miss Thing!'* Long time no see, Micky," he said.

"Oh! Brad! Lillian said you'd be here . . . but I thought I'd find you inside."

"It's easier this way." He held the door open for her, and she followed him into a former gymnasium filled with noisy people and the smell of coffee. He guided her to the back of the room where two large urns offered regular or decaf and a box of glazed donuts glistened.

"You look like you need a donut," Brad said. "And a cup of coffee—high-test okay?"

She nodded. "I haven't had much sleep. Or much to eat—the pretzels on the plane were all I could get, and I just landed in time to come straight here."

Brad gathered the provisions and offered the napkin-wrapped donut to her slightly trembling hand. "I'll carry your coffee; let's go sit down." He steered her to a seat in the front row, just as everyone was settling in for the meeting to start. Handing her the coffee, he said, "Remember to stand up and introduce yourself when the secretary asks if there are any new people." She nodded.

When the time came, she stood and said, "I'm Micky, and I'm an alcoholic." It felt strange, even though she'd said it often a few years ago. She also felt a weird sense of relief that she'd never experienced.

Exhaustion and racing thoughts made it hard for her to listen to what the speaker was saying. She didn't think she had anything in common with the guy with bright green hair, tats on his neck and heavy piercings. She guessed he was about eighteen . . .

maybe early twenties. She hadn't done crack, or raided medicine cabinets for pills or—thank God—shot heroin. She didn't drink the things he was talking about, she'd never bounced around taking any gig she could find, she never got stabbed hustling on the street or got evicted.

Then he described himself as "an egomaniac with an inferiority complex." That hit her right between her eyes. It described her at her core. She was exactly like him.

If he's an alcoholic, I guess I'm one, too—really.

The rest of the meeting went by in a blur. After the Lord's Prayer at the end, Brad smiled and said, "Let me buy you a real cup of coffee, and maybe a burger. Dooley's is just up the street." Seeing her hesitation and footwear, he added, "I'll drive."

"Thanks, Brad! That donut made me realize how hungry I am!" She took the arm he offered and stepped gingerly across the slick blacktop a few yards to the Mini Cooper Clubman parked under the light. Brad opened the door and eased her into the passenger seat.

"We're just going up the street, so it won't warm up," he said. She nodded, and looked out at the town square on their right and the mix of churches and shops on their left. Brad turned into a small parking lot. "*Yes!* We cut out of the meeting fast enough to get a space."

He helped her out of the car and into the warmth of Dooley's. Yellow ochre walls supported an eclectic collection of paintings, old movie posters and antique porcelain advertising signs. A thin dark-haired man who looked to be in his fifties emerged from behind the forest of ferns and spider plants hanging in the front window, greeting them with menus and a big smile.

"Hey, Brad! Good to see ya! Who do we have here?" he asked, as he led them to a booth in the corner.

"Hi, Dooley! This is Micky. She's just returned from a few years of further research. I'm co-sponsoring her with Lillian. She needs a good meal."

"Welcome home, Honey! We'll get ya fixed up." Dooley turned and hailed a young waitress. "Bridgett! Bring some coffee and two waters to these folks." The thin girl with rainbow hair hustled to the booth and smiled as she served the beverages. "Bridgett just started yesterday, but she's catching on quickly. I'll keep an eye out for ya, too, so just grab either of us if ya need anything. We'll give ya a couple of minutes to decide whatcha want."

"What's the soup today?" Micky asked.

"Potato. And we always have French onion," Bridgett replied.

"Ooh, French onion, please; and I'd like a burger with Swiss and grilled onions and mushrooms," said Micky. "I'm too hungry to focus and read the menu . . ."

"Make that two onion soups, but I'd like the portabella burger with brie and an order of fries we can split," Brad added. He took a sip of his coffee while Micky doctored hers with creamer and Splenda. When Dooley and Bridgett had hustled off from their table, he said with a wry smile, "We're glad you're back, Micky—but we were *really surprised* you called *Lillian*, of all people . . ."

Her dark eyebrows knit into a confused frown, enhancing the directional line of the widow's peak toward her straight nose. "She was my sponsor. Why wouldn't I call her?" She leveled her deep blue gaze at him, looking for an answer.

"After what you *did* at her *party*, I'm just *amazed*, that's all."

"What do you mean? What party?" Micky's confusion was shifting to impatience.

"*Lil's* party celebrating her thirty-ninth anniversary of sobriety. Friday, October thirteenth, seven years ago last fall." Her blank, questioning eyes told him his prompting had not jogged her memory.

"You came to the party *late*, with an open bottle of *champagne*—then *threw your arms* around her *husband* and laid a *lip lock* on him!"

"*What?!* No! *No way!*" Her eyes were widened and flashed blue fire.

"Micky, I'm not making this up. You did it in front of *everybody*. Including *Lillian*."

"I don't know what you're talking about! I *never did* that—I would never do anything *like* that!"

"Um, I'm sorry to have to tell you, but, *you did*." Brad began to realize that she had no recollection, but thought he should get it all out in the open. He softened his tone. "You tried to unbutton George's shirt, then tried to get him to go outside with you. He used that as a way to escort you to the door, and once you were outside, he closed it. Then your car peeled out, and that's the last we heard from you."

Micky sat still, in stunned silence.

"You don't remember *any* of this?"

"No." She looked worried. "I don't think you're lying . . . but how could I not remember something like that? How could I *do* something like that?!"

"The bottle you brought was almost empty. And it may not have been your first of the evening. It *sounds* like you were in a *blackout*."

"Oh. My. God." Micky suddenly connected this with her rude entry into the beginning of this day. "Is that what happened last night? All I did was go into a bar for *one drink*—and I woke up in a stranger's bed this morning in Key West. I'd missed my ship, the awards ceremony on board and my flight—and now my *job's* on the line!"

She was surprised when Brad grinned. "Was he at least *cute?*" She nodded. "Well, I once came to in a similar situation. And I *really* had desert mouth, so when I saw a glass of water on the nightstand, I chugged it—and got hit on the mouth by the guy's *dentures!*"

Micky laughed so hard she needed to wipe her eyes. "*Oh, God!* I feel better now—thanks!"

"Not every alcoholic has blackouts, Micky, but you and I *obviously* do," he said. "And social drinkers *never* have them. It's one of the big clues that we are what we are: Powerless over alcohol, and our lives become unmanageable."

She nodded. "First Step, right?"

"Yeah. Normal people always remember what they do. But people like us can *look* perfectly normal—while we're *kissing* the wrong person, *picking fights* in public or driving the *wrong way* on the highway—and not have a *clue* what we're doing, or have *any recollection* of doing it."

"Oh, God! I don't want to *ever* do that again—I'm *scared!*"

"Good. Me, too; it keeps me working the program," he said, as their food arrived. "Including co-sponsoring *you.*"

"How can Lillian ever forgive me? An apology seems so lame . . ."

"I'm guessing she knew what she was looking at when it happened and forgave you back then," Brad replied. "Otherwise, she probably wouldn't have answered the *phone* this morning. We can go over to her house tomorrow afternoon, and you can start with your sincere apology, which I'm sure will be welcomed." He enjoyed a juicy bite of his portabella burger, wiped his mouth and paused.

"And you're *right,* that really isn't sufficient—for her or for *you.* The real amend will be staying sober, working the program and growing into a woman who really *doesn't* do things like that anymore."

CHAPTER 3

Early in the afternoon following church, Sally Wise had changed out of her collar and was sharing coffee in Lillian's kitchen. The bright sunshine warmed the butter yellow walls and walnut pantry cabinets, making Sally question her choice of the light sweater she'd thought was needed for the brisk day. Lillian's cat, Pretty Girl, basked in a sunbeam on the hardwood floor by the window.

Papers were spread out on the oak table in front of the two friends as Sally gave Lillian feedback on the two chapters of "Cat Hair" that she had reviewed last evening. She pointed to a few mark-ups here and there to tighten the prose, asked questions where she thought more clarity was needed, and praised the drafts overall, especially certain parts that moved or amused her.

Then she looked steadily into Lillian's eyes and said, "I think the reason you don't like these is that neither is good as an opening chapter to the book. They'd be fine as chapters two and three—but the book needs a stronger start."

Lillian nodded and sighed. "I know. I just don't know what that is."

"There's no hook, nothing to really draw readers in," said Sally. "I think you're assuming they've just finished 'Hairs in the Sink' and your relationship with George is fresh in their minds. But that book came out—what?—seven years ago?"

Lillian knitted her brows and pursed her lips. "Why is that important?"

"Well . . . you jump right into talking about this new life dimension you're in, but there's no emotion—nothing to bring the reader close to you, nothing to illustrate what you've lost." Sally shook her head. "And, you're right—there's very little humor. Despite the fact that widowhood and bereavement are not typically laughing matters, finding amusing sides to everything in a woman's life is what your readers expect from you; you certainly did it in *Never Date Your Divorce Lawyer*."

Lillian looked down. "I haven't found that yet."

Sally put her arm around her, hugging her close to her side. "I know, dear, I know."

The warmth of her friend's embrace was comforting. "So how do I do that? It's been three years and I haven't found it. How do I do it now—and on a one-month deadline?"

Interrupted by the oven's buzzer, Lillian leapt up to get the apple-cinnamon crumb cake out and put generous slices on two plates. Sally inhaled the sweet and spicy fragrance, held it, and smiled as she slowly exhaled. "First, you enjoy the moment. This is aromatherapy!" She picked up her plate and brought it close so they both could breathe in the bouquet like two connoisseurs. Then she enjoyed a bite and a sip of coffee.

"Now, back to your question. I think you need to both stay grounded in today, and revisit your past, your years with George, maybe re-read 'Hairs' to remember the fun. Then reflect on the later years, those after that book's scope. You might find something you can use to give a synopsis of your happily-married-at-last time, and a humorous vignette not yet shared in print that can engage readers—including new ones who may be reading this book first and don't know the backstory. That can provide the contrast needed to empathize with the magnitude and suddenness of your loss."

Nodding, Lillian said, "Yes. I like that idea—that could work. Thanks!" They both smiled. "I especially like that you've given me something to *do—actions* to take to get out of this dark rut."

"Or at least be able to peep out over the edge," Sally said. "Remember: We have to act our way into right thinking; we can't think our way into right actions."

*****

Brad took his eyes briefly off the road to glance at Micky in the Mini Cooper's passenger seat, appraising the turtleneck peeking above her parka collar and the fur-topped, knee-high Uggs. "Nice outfit, by the way—much better for Cleveland-winter comfort."

She answered with a wry smile. "I didn't have many wardrobe options yesterday." Waves of glossy black hair tumbled to her shoulders from her red cashmere hat, and her make-up was flawless, but it couldn't completely conceal a slight pallor underneath, and her blue eyes revealed fatigue when she looked at him.

"Did you sleep?"

"Not much. I thought I would, I was so exhausted. But I couldn't stop my mind—it was like a squirrel on an exercise wheel. No—more like a nest of squirrels running all over it!"

Brad nodded. "I know. When I got sober, I also had to get off of tranquilizers and sleeping pills, and I had the same problem."

"What did you do?"

"Reading in bed was my answer; still is. But not anything *at all* related to my job, classwork for school—or any kind of a page-turner like a mystery or even a novel I really enjoy."

"Sounds kind of limiting. What did that leave?"

"Michener was my *lifesaver*—I never did finish *Chesapeake*. Initially, I'd read two pages or so and fall asleep with the light on. It pretty quickly shortened to a couple of paragraphs, and I'd start dreaming . . . roll over, put the book on the nightstand and turn out the light. Reading something focuses my mind enough to keep the squirrels at bay, and I think the motion of my eyes following the lines of text lulls me to sleep."

Micky weighed this information. "I could try it. I need *something*—my brain kept skipping from one terror to another: Thinking my luggage must be lost because it wasn't delivered last night . . . losing my job . . . facing my boss tomorrow morning . . . facing Lil today . . ."

"But the important thing is that you're *sober*. When we stay sober, we can face *anything*. We might not *like* it, and it may be *scary*—but I've found when I actually *deal* with something that scares me *shitless*, it's never as terrible as I've *imagined!*"

Micky saw the Grace Church spires come into view. "We're almost there. I feel sick."

"*Good!*" Brad turned into the driveway and killed the engine. Seeing her perplexed expression, he explained, "If you didn't feel *anything* about going to someone you've wronged, you'd be a *sociopath*—and nothing that can fix that!

"Besides, Lil asked you to come today, and I called to give her a heads-up about our talk last night, so she won't be blindsided. You'll be fine." He climbed out of the low-slung car, walked around it and opened Micky's door. Helping her out, he turned her when she started toward the front steps. "We're family. We use the back door. She'll be in the kitchen, probably with Sally." Seeing the fear in her eyes, he smiled. "There will be great coffee. And I'll bet fresh-baked pie or something—it's Sunday!"

As they started up the verandah steps, Lillian threw open the door with a warm smile and gathered them both in a welcoming embrace. She hustled them inside and shut the door against the cold, then took their coats and hung them on hooks by the door. "Help yourselves to coffee," she said over her shoulder. "Mugs and fixings are in the butler's pantry, coffee cake is on the table; just came out of the oven!"

As they settled in around the table, Sally extended her hand. "It's good to see you again, Micky. Welcome back!"

"Thanks, Sally . . ." Micky blushed. "Were you there, too . . . that night . . . at Lil's . . . when I hit on her husband and ruined her party?"

"Oh, yes, I was there—but you didn't ruin it—just provided some unplanned entertainment. The open bottle provided context to the rest; we all just hoped you got home alright."

"I don't remember. I guess I must have. I don't remember *anything*. Brad told me last night." Micky's hand shook as she tried to lift her coffee cup. She set it back down. "I feel *terrible*. I am *so sorry!* I *can't believe* what I did, but I *do* believe it, because you were all there and *saw* it. And I'm *glad* Brad told me, and I'm glad he told me *last night*—because yesterday morning I woke up in a stranger's bed and had *no idea* how I got there. The two things together really shook me up . . . *now* I know I *really can't drink*."

Lillian asked, "How long had you been drinking, Micky? I noticed a definite drop-off in phone calls and meetings after about six months."

Micky nodded. "Somewhere around then, I think. My probation was over, no more proof-of-meeting-attendance papers to get signed. And work was really intense, so I didn't have time for meetings or *anything* . . . and I thought I was fine. I really just thought the DUI was bad luck . . . I never really thought I was an *alcoholic*."

"I'm sure your father never thought so, either," Lillian said.

"I never told him. I knew how he felt about alcoholics—like my mother—and I didn't think I was one, anyway. So when he'd want me to do something on a meeting night, I'd make up some work excuse about why I couldn't join him. Then, after my paper sentence was done, I felt I had to make up for lost time with him—and just went back to what I did before." She raised the coffee to her lips using both hands.

Lillian smiled slightly. "But you still kept in touch and went to some meetings until October. Why did you do that?"

Micky paused, trying to make sense of it herself. "I don't really know. On some level, I must have known that I did need the program . . . I also needed to keep up appearances at work. My boss knew about the DUI because I was driving a company car."

"The same boss who's threatening to fire you now?"

Micky nodded. "He's been doing that for the last couple of years, actually." Lillian's shrug and uplifted palms prodded her to continue. "There've been other . . . incidents."

"Such as?"

"At first, minor stuff like always being late to work or call reports being overdue," Micky said, looking down at her plate. "But I knew it didn't matter, because my numbers were always good, and . . . he *liked* me."

"Professionally, or personally?"

"Both. I was *always* over quota, so he relied on my production for his own job performance." She sighed, and sipped her coffee. "*And* I knew he wanted to be *more* than just my boss . . . and I let him believe that *might* be *possible*."

"And what's been different for the last two years?" Lillian cut a generous slice of coffee cake and slid it onto Micky's plate.

19

"I started missing client meetings. Jack would cover for me, and say I was sick . . . had car trouble, was stuck in traffic . . . you name it. He's been *very creative*. And we started working as a team on the excuses . . . he'd tell me the storyline, so I could play along if anyone brought it up. Then the threats got woven in . . . on *both sides*. After some time of this, *he* was as guilty as *I* was—and he knew it. Continuing my stellar performance was the glue that held it all together."

Brad spoke up. "That's an *incredible* amount of *pressure!* How can you *handle* that?"

"Jack sent me to a psychiatrist, who prescribed anti-anxiety and sleep medications."

"Please tell the nice people at EAP *what* you're taking and for *how long*, and ask for medical help in safely weaning off of them—*especially* since you've also just *quit drinking*," he said. "Do you agree, Lil?"

"Oh, yes!" Lillian put her fork down and looked at Micky and Brad. "I think you two need to work directly together. Brad, you'll be the sponsor and I'll keep close to both of you. Micky, I'm so glad you're back, and are accepting your disease. But you're going to need more support than I have to give right now." She paused to look at Sally. "I'm having a writer's crisis and have a tight deadline. Sally's seeing me through this, and you'll be in good hands with Brad. And we'll all get together on Sunday afternoons. Does that sound okay?"

Everyone nodded. Sally reached out and they joined hands around the table. She prayed, "Dear God, we give thanks to you for the return of our sister, Micky. Please keep her sober, as you do all of us, and strengthen and guide us all on our daily paths that we may better do thy will."

"Amen!"

CHAPTER 4

Micky was hustling back to her office after meeting with the EAP director, but she didn't move fast enough. Jack Benson was lurking in his office doorway and flagged her down.

"Come in and close the door." He motioned her into a chair at his round mini-conference table and sat down next to her. "How'd it go?"

She repositioned her chair to face him, pulling back slightly. "Okay, I guess. Alice was glad to hear that I'd reconnected with my sponsor and had already attended two A.A. meetings. She told me she understood how important it is that I can continue working and agreed that intensive outpatient treatment was appropriate for my case. She'll get paperwork over to Glenbeigh today to place me in their evening program at the Rocky River facility."

Jack stroked his chin. "What will your schedule be like?"

"Monday through Thursday from six to nine. I can go to A.A. meetings at lunch during the week and evenings on the weekends." Micky swept a stray lock of black hair out of her right eye and tucked it behind her ear.

Jack tapped his index finger on the gleaming table top, processing this information for a minute. "Well, I think we can work with that. If you have calls on outlying clients, you could schedule those on Fridays or Mondays to allow for extra drive time; might need to travel on Sundays occasionally and overnight in a hotel if necessary."

She furrowed her brow. "What do you mean? I don't *have* any clients outside of the Cleveland SMSA . . . nobody does."

A tight-lipped smile momentarily appeared on Jack's face. "I'm doing you a favor." He rose from his chair and walked to his desk to retrieve a manila folder, which he placed on the table in front of Micky. He leaned down, opened it and withdrew a white sheet titled "2017 Annual Performance Plan" and handed it to her. She looked at it and gasped.

"That's almost *twice last year's* plan! And last year, I set a *record* in *my territory!*"

"I know. And I know you can't expect to make this year's nut with the same clients." He leaned forward again, this time brushing his torso against her right shoulder and arm as he extracted a quarter-inch thick Excel printout that he dangled before her face. Now he grinned. "I told you I was doing you a favor. This is how you can make your numbers." The grin collapsed into a smug smile.

Micky's sapphire eyes widened in disbelief. Stunned, she scanned the pages. "These are just *companies* organized by cities throughout the *state of Ohio! No info at all!!*"

"You've always been great at prospecting and qualifying potential customers. I didn't want to pre-judge the list."

Trying to keep her cool, she sighed and said, "Well at least if I have to drive all over the state, I'll have a *really great car* to do it in."

"About that. It'll take a bit of time before you get the Cadillac."

Micky was furious now. "What do you *mean?!* I *won Top Dog!*"

"And didn't value the award enough to be present to receive it. So, I think some delay in getting the prize is in order. Don't you?" Jack moved behind her and put his hands on her shoulders. She flinched, and he tightened his grip.

"How *long* a delay?"

He began massaging her tight shoulders. "Take it easy, Micky. I'm sure we can work out a mutually beneficial solution. I'm thinking maybe three months, maybe six."

"Depending on *what?*"

"We've been through a lot together. We've helped each other out. You know, you really put me on the spot with this one, though. You owe me. Big time."

Micky stood up and walked away. "I need to get back to work now."

"Sure, you do that. As I said, I'm sure we can work something out."

*****

Lillian, curled up with Pretty Girl on the front window seat cushion, snuggled the calico tighter to her chest and stroked her long silken fur. Her gaze scanned the ornately carved walnut woodwork that defined the foyer and sweeping staircase. As her eyes traversed the view, her thoughts returned to George—as always. She couldn't help it. It had taken him the better part of the first year of their rehab to strip the five layers of paint to reveal the glowing grain of the wood, accented by sections of natural burl paneling. It was then that she had truly come to know and fully appreciate the wonderful man she had finally found and had had the good sense to marry at the tender age of 60. She still marveled at the steadfast patience and persistence he displayed, day in and day out, to properly execute the restoration. Every time she came through the area, she was awed anew by the depth of his talent and creativity when he occasionally had needed to replicate sections that had been too badly damaged to use. And how careful he had been to plan his work to avoid getting construction debris in their living areas during those initial three years of their marriage.

A ray of sunlight streamed through the stained-glass window on the landing where the stairs turned right to reach the second-floor mezzanine. She contemplated the dust swirling lazily in the light, then realized the morning was slipping by with no production. In the early days of her career, writer's block was documented by the number of crumpled copy paper wads surrounding her desk. Today, it was the lack of additional page and word counts in a unit of time.

Deciding that she needed a more disciplined approach, she moved the cat off and toted her laptop down the hall to her paneled library office. She had taken Sally's advice and reread her last book and some of her earlier ones. Now, she decided to do a stream-of-consciousness dump of memories, feelings and fun times as a warm-up that might yield something she could work with as an opening chapter.

How do I miss thee, George? Let me count the ways: I miss your sense of humor—especially your word games that provided us with endless free entertainment; I miss having you to depend on—you were the first and only man in my life (except my father) who actually did what you said you'd do and was competent to do it well! I miss watching sports with you (women friends are poor stand-ins for that). I definitely miss your cooking—much better than mine! I greatly miss your partnership in our rose garden; after all these years, it's really a bitch to have to do the spraying chores again (thank God we now have so many more easy-care specimens, including some of my own babies)! I miss your taking us out for Sunday drives in the '57 T-Bird (and I miss sitting in the church pew with you, too). I miss talking over the news, world events and local gossip with you; your amusing curmudgeon's point of view was always funny as hell!

And the sex. I especially miss our sexual union. We always said God had saved the best for last for both of us. Physically, it was always a thrill and we also experienced a special emotional bonding—that "mutual joy" that was mentioned in the Episcopal celebration of marriage. Whenever I looked into your eyes, I saw your love for me. And the laughter! We often laughed together before, during and after. Like when I had my first back injury, and couldn't lie down . . . I had to sleep half-reclined in the living room chair for weeks . . . and you engineered a way to place my feet on the two ottomans that would allow you access to give us both a really good time! And your later strategic use of the chaise lounge—the "ooh-la-la" for which that piece was no doubt designed! I swore at the time that we should create a "Kama Sutra for the Golden Years"!

"That's it!" Lillian cried out loud. "That's the title of the first chapter! I can rework some of this to be like I'm talking to the reader instead of George, and I can move into the bidet I insisted on when we remodeled the master bath . . . which in recent years has been commandeered by Pretty Girl for her personal feline water trough, hence the title of this book."

She picked up her phone and called Sally. "Hallelujah!"

*****

At 6:30 that evening, Brad was preparing to turn into the driveway of his executive temporary housing unit, but the outline of a black car parked there caused him to swerve out of his trajectory and park on the street in front. He double-checked the address, then got out of the Clubman to investigate. As he approached, a dark familiar figure climbed out of the Mercedes two-seater sports car.

"Oscar. What're you doing here?"

"I brought you a present, Bradley. For you to drive home."

"I *am* home. And I bought *my own* new car."

A sneer twisted the mouth framed by the perfectly groomed black beard and narrowed the sleepy, molten chocolate eyes. "Oh, *please.*

You can't be serious. Monopoly board houses have more character than *this*. And *what* is *that?*" A black-gloved hand swooped to point toward Brad's car.

"*That* is none of your business. Nor is my current address. How did you find out where I'm living?"

The sneer became a mocking smile. "I have my ways. You ought to know that by now."

Brad took a step back. "Get out of here before I call the police and tell them you're blocking my driveway. It will be good to start documentation on your stalking."

"You *know* you don't mean that."

"Like I didn't mean dialing nine-one-one when you were hurling statuary at me three weeks ago? The cops took pictures of my face and the smashed cherubs' remains all over the floor."

"Just a lovers' quarrel and my freedom of expression. We've been through this before. And my *gift* expresses the *depth* of my *sincere* apology. *Please* come home."

"No. Take it and leave. Now." Brad pulled his ringing phone from his coat pocket, saw that it was Micky and started toward his front door. "I have to take this."

Oscar walked up the driveway, fading into the darkness enveloping the black car, then turned to face Brad. "You'll come back. You always do."

"Not this time."

*****

Micky looked up as Brad joined her at a table next to the fire in the rear room of Panera's. "Thanks for meeting me here."

"No problem. I need to eat anyway, and I don't feel like cooking tonight."

"Me neither. I probably don't have anything in my kitchen anyway," she said. "I haven't gone shopping since I got back from the awards cruise, and don't have the energy to do it now."

"How did things go today?"

"The EAP part was okay. The manager was nice about everything, and she agreed outpatient treatment would be best . . . weekday evenings in Rocky River . . . weekends I can go to my regular A.A. meetings."

He observed her drawn expression, tension in her shoulders and fingers clenching the edge of the table. "That sounds good. So . . . what's *not so good?*"

"Jack. My boss. He's really out to get me."

"Are you *sure?* What *happened?*"

"He doubled my quota this year—after I set a record last year—and said he was *helping* me by making me responsible for cold-calling businesses across the entire *state*. Now I'm also expected to *travel* most weeks to make calls. That will make it harder to get to my meetings. On top of that, he's not going to let me get the top sales winner's award car . . . at least not for three months, or maybe *six* . . . *depending.*"

"Depending? On *what?*"

"Well, the way he *grabbed* me and told me I *owed* him for covering for my absence at the awards dinner . . . I'm thinking he's expecting sexual favors." Her gaze dropped to the table.

"Seriously?! Doesn't he know you can *report* him and sue him *and* the *company* for that?"

"There were no witnesses to our conversation. And between documenting my drinking problem through EAP and giving me an impossible quota so he can demonstrate poor performance, that will pretty much destroy any credibility I might have. Plus, I think he's setting all of this up so he can fire me—and I just *can't* lose my *job!*" She looked up at Brad with scared-rabbit eyes.

He reached out to cover one of her fists with his hand. "It's okay, Micky. You still have your job *today*. And even *if* the scheme you described *is* his plan, it will take some time for it to play out." As his hand lifted from hers, it instinctively moved to his shirt pocket. "*Damn!* I want a *cigarette* really *badly* right now. Let's get our food."

They got up and went to the front counter to order their dinners, which they brought back to the table. After a few minutes dedicated to eating, Brad asked, "So, Micky . . . how are you *feeling* about what Jack did this morning?"

She set her soup spoon on the plate's edge and looked up, puzzled. "How am I *feeling? Scared.* I just bought my condo last year. If I get *fired,* it will be hard to get another job that pays this much and I'd *lose* it—and maybe end up having to move back to my *father's*. And I *just can't* do *that!*"

"That won't necessarily happen—but I can certainly *understand.* When my New York restaurant career flamed out near the end of my *drinking,* I crashed at my parents' house back in Stromberg. Their constant shaming of me and my decision to study for a *third* career path drove me to make the *stupid* decision to allow my ex that I just left to sweep me off my drunken feet and *move in* with him while I was going to school at Oberlin. *Classic* alcoholic thinking!" Brad shook his blond head and reached again for the familiar pack of cigarettes that was no longer there.

"*Third* career?" Micky asked. "What did you do before?"

"Originally, I went to med school; my dad is a cardiologist, my mom's a nurse, my older brother is a dentist. It was the expected thing to do, I was accepted into the program, but I never *liked* it. So

I dropped out after the first year and went to the Culinary Institute, then studied in Paris to become a pastry chef—which I *loved!* Those credentials launched my start in the restaurant scene in Manhattan, where I *thrived* until the progression of my disease took it all away."

"And at Oberlin?"

"It was close by, and had a great architectural history program. I've always loved old buildings. I met Oscar there—he teaches interior design. Things quickly got crazy, I drank even *more* and finally realized that I had to stop drinking or I'd lose everything *again*. I met Lil at campus A.A. meetings, and I also got to know her and George through the Preservation Society, so it was a *no-brainer* to ask her to be my sponsor. After a couple of years of sobriety, the two of them suggested I transfer to Kent State, where I got my degree in architecture. I'm working now for a small design-build firm that specializes in rehab; like my previous profession, it combines *creativity* with hands-on execution—but *none* of my creations are soaked in *booze!*

"But back to feelings. Where I grew up, they weren't *permitted*. So in my teens, I learned that alcohol worked *wonders* in helping me stuff them *deep inside*—until they almost *killed* me. In A.A., it's *okay* to have feelings; they're part of being human. And if we don't accept them, feel them and let them pass through us, they can take us *back out*. But I didn't even know what they *were*. Lil had to *teach* me. So, besides *fear*, what else are you feeling about today's events?"

Micky's expression was blank as she shrugged. "I don't know."

"Well," Brad said, "If somebody gave *me* a nearly impossible objective and then put the moves on me, I think I'd be pretty *angry*."

"*Yes!* You're *right*." Micky sat up straighter, suddenly animated with blazing blue eyes. "I was *furious* in Jack's office. But I had to keep it together. I didn't want to add insubordination to the list of things he can use against me. I guess I *did* stuff that feeling."

"Good. If you leave anger stuffed, it becomes depression and makes you feel hopeless," Brad explained. "If you acknowledge it, without dwelling on it to become a resentment, it can energize and empower you to envision solutions and take action to protect yourself."

She smiled for the first time. "I like that! A feeling I can *use!*" She paused before continuing. "I didn't *dare* show any feelings when I was a kid, either. My mother and I both walked on eggshells around my father to try to avoid making him fly into a rage. And while he was out of town on business, my mom didn't want to deal with *anything* that would interrupt her drinking. A *lot* of things happened that I had to stuff.

"So . . . is it *just* nicotine craving that you're feeling tonight, or is there *more?*"

"*Touché.* I also had to deal with a warped man trying to control me with a car—just when you *called,* as a matter of fact. It provided a very timely exit, thank you." Brad smiled.

"*What?!* Who?" Micky prodded.

"Oscar. My *ex.* He found out where I'm living and was parked in my driveway with a new Mercedes that he thought he could *bribe* me with. I guess I shouldn't be *surprised*—we've seen this movie before—but he doesn't understand that this time is *different*. Emotional mayhem, infidelities, screaming fits and manipulation prompted me to leave a few times before, and those were patched over by apologies and virtuoso romantic gestures. But *this* time, it was *physical* abuse involving cops. And I have more sobriety now."

Micky's smile was teasing as she insisted, "So . . . *feelings?*"

Brad sighed. "I'm extremely *pissed*. And, yes, *scared*. Like, how did he *find me?* Am I going to have to look over my *shoulder* everywhere I go? Should I call the cops in *Strongsville?* Should I call a *lawyer?* So I guess I could add *confused* to my feelings list."

"Wow! What are you going to do?"

"I *won't* pick up a drink or a cigarette, I'm *helping* another alcoholic, I'll ask my *Higher Power* for help and protection, and I'll call *my sponsor* to help me stay sane and sort things out."

CHAPTER 5

The Reverend Sally Wise, sitting in one of the crewel-embroidered wing chairs by a crackling fire in the rectory's living room, was engaged in her favorite late-February activity. Surrounded by stacks of garden catalogs with dog-eared pages, she added notes to the list of plants to be ordered on a heritage cultivar of red bee balm from the open page of *Roots & Rhizomes* balanced on her lap.

As she finished her entry, a loud pop in the fireplace startled her. She put all of her materials on the floor and put her feet up on the ottoman. She looked through the diamond-shaped panes of the leaded-glass bay window to the snow-covered arbor at the garden's edge. A picturesque snow fell gently from the pewter-gray sky, illuminated by the waning four o'clock light of this blessedly peaceful Monday afternoon.

Sally treasured her days off as her time to rest, relax and recharge. *This is such a perfect time, the lull between Epiphany and Ash Wednesday . . . the opportunity to let go, just be with God . . . and allow Him to fill me with renewed strength to rise to the work I need to do during Lent, Holy Week and Easter.* She breathed deeply and slowly, focusing on the dwindling light and turning her thoughts to gratitude.

I'm so glad Lillian taught me the value of good hardscaping in the garden. She was right: Winter is a major season in Northeast Ohio! And this is so beautiful right now.

Family of Choice: Raising Each Other

I'm also very grateful that she was Senior Warden and leader of the search committee that called me here fifteen years ago! I love this place. This parish. These people. I'm so very blessed to live in this lovely, quiet home . . . such a refuge, a truly safe place . . . to have the freedom to create my wonderful English cottage garden . . . and to have Lil as a gardening mentor, program sponsor and best friend! She helped me heal and fill in voids untouched by my family's upbringing. A whole new kind of love!

Sally brought her attention back into the room, looked at the antique Oriental rug at her feet whose original reds had faded to soft orange and peach, and smiled. *I am grateful, too, for my family. My mother, God rest her soul, modeled how to live a happy, fulfilling life without a husband during the two decades after Dad passed. I think that helped her let go of her plan for me to have a socially appropriate marriage after my first one failed. We were never close, and I don't think I ever met her expectations, but I'm glad we achieved a comfortable relationship and that I could be there for her last spring during her final illness. I'm grateful to have this rug, and the china and silver that was hers and her mother's before her as a reminder of the advantages they gave me and the work ethic they instilled in me. And Mother was my original inspiration for finding joy in the garden.*

Sally picked up her pile of materials and put them in the built-in bookcase. She poked the fire and added another log, then settled back into her chair and stretched, reveling in the quiet at the day's end.

She had just closed her eyes when pounding on the front door shattered the tranquility. *What?! Who?! No one bothers me on my day off, unless we've made plans! And I'm not expecting any deliveries.*

Fearful of an intruder, she grabbed the poker as she headed to the door. Her careful opening of it revealed a painfully thin woman in an inadequate shrunken jacket and skinny ripped jeans with stringy strawberry blonde hair straggling out from a worn knit cap who said, "Hi, Mom."

*****

After helping her daughter lift her small battered suitcase over the threshold and hanging her snow-soaked jacket on the foyer's coat-tree to dry, Sally ushered her to one of the chairs by the fire. Replacing the poker in the tools caddy, she said, "I was just adding a log to the fire when you arrived, Shelley. Good thing, too; you look frozen!" She retrieved a chenille throw from the bay window seat and draped it over the young woman's lap. "I'll get you something warm to drink. I have a wide assortment of teas, coffee, or would you prefer hot cocoa?"

"I'd rather have a hot toddy."

Sally managed a tired smile. "Shelley, you know I don't have anything like that in my home."

"Oh. You're still not drinking?"

"Of course not! I've been sober for more than twenty-five years! Why would you think that would change?"

There was a shrug from under the throw. "Dad drinks."

"That's his business. It has nothing to do with me." Sally turned toward the kitchen. "So. Tea, coffee or cocoa?"

"Coffee. Black."

In the kitchen, Sally put the kettle on for some orange ginger mint tea for herself, and popped a pod into the Keurig for a mug of coffee. Returning to the fireside, she handed the coffee to her daughter and settled into the chair where she'd spent the afternoon. It didn't feel so comfortable now. "Well. This is quite a surprise. It's been a long time since I heard from you, Shelley."

"I've been away."

Family of Choice: Raising Each Other

"I'm glad to see you, but why didn't you call and let me know you were coming?"

"I don't have a phone. A friend was coming to Cleveland for business, so I asked for a ride at the last minute. I hope that's okay?" Her voice scaled up with the question.

"How long are you planning to visit?"

"A week? Maybe two?" The girl stiffened in her chair.

Sally paused, considering. "Let's see how the week goes. This one is fairly clear, but next week my schedule is pretty busy." She sipped her tea. "Are you still living in Columbus?"

"Nearby. Dublin. With my friend. For now, anyway."

Sally leaned forward slightly. "How are you, Shelley? What's been going on that you suddenly show up out of the blue—or, rather, out of a snow storm—after what, five years since we last spoke?"

Shelley looked down at her lap. "I've had a run of bad luck."

"Oh? What do you mean? The last I knew, you had a good job designing for the Limited. You'd just been recruited from the design firm in Chicago where you worked since graduating from Kent State's fashion program, and I was glad you'd moved closer."

"Yes. My twenties were great! This decade hasn't been, so far."

Sally waited in silence for more.

"A friend asked me to deliver a package for him. I owed him a favor, so I agreed. It was wrapped in Kraft paper and tied with shipping string, and I had no idea what was in it. But the recipient knew, and he was an undercover narc who arrested me. It was obvious that I didn't know what was going on, and since I had no prior record at all, I got a light sentence. But it was still two years in Marysville, and I lost my job."

"Shelley! Why didn't you tell me? I could've gotten you a good lawyer!"

Shelley's head hung lower. "I didn't want you to know. And my friend took care of my legal bills."

"And after that?"

"I couldn't go back to the L Brands companies, and no one would hire me as a designer with my record. I did eventually get a job as an assistant manager in a TJ Maxx store. That was going okay, until another friend called me during work and kept me on the phone while she signed my name to a receipt of merchandise and intercepted the goods. So, it was back to Marysville for another three years for felony theft. I just got out last week, and I need some time to get myself together so I can start over."

"Well, it sounds like a good place to start is to get some better friends." Sally looked at her watch. "It's time for dinner. I was planning to have leftover spinach casserole; there's enough for two."

"You know I never liked that."

"Well, I do like it. If I'd had advance notice of your visit, I could've laid in other supplies. As it is, this is what I have to eat in the house. I do my grocery shopping on Tuesdays, so we can go together tomorrow and I'll buy some things that you'd like."

*****

After dinner, Sally got Shelley settled into the guest room and went downstairs to her study. She picked up her phone and called Lillian, who answered on the first ring. "Lil! Thank God you're there! Shelley just showed up on my doorstep this afternoon—unannounced. Now I know why she was out of contact for the past several years: She was incarcerated at Marysville penitentiary a couple of times!"

"Oh, Sally, I'm so sorry! Sorry . . . but not too surprised."

"Really? Why not?"

"Well, when members of an alcoholic family cease communications, it's usually not because they're just too busy. They *have* been busy . . . busy making a mess of their lives. Then they resurface when they want someone to fix things for them, dumping their chaos in their 'loved one's' living room."

Sally sighed. "That's exactly what happened. Just as I was serene and relaxed, counting my many blessings and joy in the moment watching it snow from the warmth of my fireside, the Prodigal Daughter returned—and I'm sorry, but I don't feel like rounding up the fatted calf and the village for a feast."

"What did she ask you for?"

"She wants to stay for a week or two to get herself together. I told her we'd see how it goes."

"Good thing you're in Al-Anon. It's working!"

"Yes. I still feel like a bad mother, though; however, not so much that I failed to notice how she treated me like an inn-keeper. She expected me to have booze, and complained about the food."

"Thanks for letting me know . . . I'll keep you in my prayers," Lillian said. "And Sally—watch yourself."

CHAPTER 6

Brad was grateful for his Mini Cooper's GPS as he tried to find his way to Micky's condo in the labyrinth of look-alike row-houses in the Strongsville development. The evening's darkness and snow piles plowed from last night's storm obscured crossings that separated one block from another, so her vague "it's the end unit of the middle row" description was useless. He was relieved when the calm voice informed him that he had reached his destination.

He extracted the Panera carryout bag from the passenger's seat, confirmed the address on the porch railing post and carefully ascended the stairs. Handing the food to Micky as she opened the door he said, "You really need a bench on this porch to create a landmark. And you could put things on it when you come home and need to open your door."

"Why? I'm never out here; I go in through the door in the garage." Following her to the kitchen, he observed stark white walls, neutral gray carpeting, limited non-descript grey furnishings and empty white built-in bookshelves. When they brought their food out to the black glass-topped dining table in the great room, he noticed that the bowls of tomato basil chowder provided the only color in the space. A black 56-inch TV screen was the only item mounted on the walls.

"How long have you been here?"

"A little over a year." She sipped her soup. "Why?"

"Well, it looks like my temporary quarters and I just moved in. I can't *wait* to get some of my things out of boxes so it feels more like *home,* even though I *hope* I won't be there for long. I'm leaving most in storage while I'm house-hunting, but there won't be much on the market until spring." He took a bite of his turkey avocado sandwich. "So, didn't you have an apartment before buying this? What about your stuff?"

"My father didn't want me to waste money on rent, so I lived there until he told me I earned enough that I needed a mortgage-interest tax deduction. And I've never spent much time at home anyway . . . still don't."

"Don't you have some things from your childhood that are special to you? Pictures? Books? Vases? House plants?"

Micky shook her head. "My mom killed herself when I was ten. My father emptied the house of anything that reminded him of her, including decorations and things in my room. I learned then not to get attached to things . . . or to people. He had a succession of girlfriends who moved in, some that he married. Each one would try to be nice to me, but they didn't stay long. Couldn't take his temper fits when he'd come back from his business trips. And each one would redecorate and get rid of everything that was there before."

"How *awful!* I'm *so sorry!*" He paused and looked around. "Well, now you can buy things that *you like!*" Brad said with enthusiasm that made no impression on her blank expression. "You know—make it your *own home!*"

"I have *no idea* what I like. All I've done is *work* and *drink.*"

Brad nodded. "Actually, that's not unusual. Most of us really don't know *who* we are when we're drinking; it takes *time* to discover that. My self-esteem was so battered when I met Oscar that it was easy for him to dazzle me with his flattering attentions that I willingly moved into his Italianate Victorian mansion with its expensive, period-correct antique furnishings that made me tiptoe around in stocking feet for fear that I'd *damage* something. I was *never* comfortable there, and I *never liked* the look, but of course *he* was the tenured *professor* of interior *design*. *And* it was *his* house. I didn't count.

"But I do now! And I can't *wait* to start hunting for a nice Arts and Crafts house that I can rehab and furnish with stylish, functional pieces that I'll *enjoy living* with."

He reached in the shirt pocket where he used to keep his cigarettes and produced a bronze-colored metal medallion that he handed to Micky. "Speaking of *time* in the program, I believe you've earned *this*—congratulations on your one-month anniversary of sobriety! And Happy Valentine's Day!"

Micky looked at the round, flat object that was about the diameter of a silver dollar. She recognized the engraved faces of A.A.'s two founders, Dr. Bob and Bill W., and the 1 MONTH designation was self-explanatory.

Micky smiled and said, "I don't remember getting anything like this before."

"Lil only counts anniversaries in years," he said. "That's how it was done back when she got sober, and most groups around here still do it that way. But a gay discussion group I've attended since I was new recognizes initial months as well, and these really meant a *lot* to me in *my* beginning. The medallions emphasized the *importance* of my *sobriety date* as something to *treasure* and *protect*—my *flag* that I planted in the ground from which I continue to move forward in recovery.

"Your anniversary date is January 14, 2017. Make that *your flag* and honor it and your medallions as they add up each month in your *first* year—and the annual ones in the years *to come*."

Brad grinned again. "And since you're in the *incentives* business, I thought you could relate to *achievement* awards!"

Micky laughed. "Yes, you're right. And I didn't realize a month had already gone by . . . *thank you* for the reminder and the *award!*" She slipped it into the right front pocket of her jeans.

"You're really doing *great*, Micky—especially with treatment and your pressures at work!" Brad finished his sandwich and stuffed the wrapper, bowl and napkin back into the bag, which he then pushed aside on the table. "So. To keep the good stuff going—*and* increase your ability to cope with the stuff that's *not* so good—you need to move forward in the steps. It's time to get into the Second Step, where we come to believe that some power greater than we are can end our insanity."

She nodded. "We've started talking about that in IOP . . . a lot of people in the group are hung up on the word 'sanity,' but after digging up all of those examples of unmanageability in my life for my first step list . . . I see *so much* that's *just nuts!*"

"Yeah. Me, too," Brad said. "We work the first step every day, and that one puts me up the proverbial creek without a paddle—*I'm powerless* and my *life is unmanageable*—which is *way* too *uncomfortable* for me! My *Higher Power* is the paddle I need to shoot the rapids of my life and avoid going over the falls. *Really reduces* my amount of insane behavior!"

"Well . . . that's the problem I have with this," Micky confessed. "I don't get the whole Higher Power thing. My parents didn't go to church, so by the time my father sent me to a Catholic girls' high school (probably to keep me away from *boys*), mass was just something I had to go to . . . I had *no idea* what was going on, what the *Bible passages* meant or what the *priest* was talking about . . . they might as well have been speaking in *Swahili.*"

Brad nodded. "That's okay. This is a *spiritual* program—not a *religious* one. You don't even need to believe in *God,* just in a *power greater than yourself* that *can restore you to sanity* and keep you from drinking. Some people use the *group;* these are people who are *staying sober together* who can show you how to live a saner life *without drinking* or using other substances. Others say G.O.D. stands for *Good Orderly Direction.* I'm more in *that* camp—I use the principles of the program and of various religions or belief systems, which all share many similar *concepts*."

Micky sighed. "That all sounds really complex . . ."

"Try reading the Big Book chapter addressed to agnostics and the Second Step in the Twelve and Twelve. We'll discuss those. You don't need to believe in anything specific right now, just be open-minded and *willing to believe.*"

"I already *do believe* in God . . . but I have no *real concept* of how that relates to staying *sober* . . . keeping my *job* . . . and staying out of *trouble,*" she explained.

Brad smiled. "You've been asking God to keep you sober every morning and thanking Him at night for another day of sobriety—right?" Micky nodded. "And that's kept you sober for a *whole month* now. Have you gone without drinking for a month during the last seven years?"

She shook her head.

"So, keep doing that, and it will *keep working.*"

Micky pondered that. "It's that simple? I can *do that!*"

"Yes, Micky—it's a *simple program.* The readings will explain it more," Brad said. "And if you think you'd like to learn more about God and the Judeo-Christian *underpinnings* of the program—and get some additional fellowship and *support*—you might try attending Grace Church on Sunday mornings. I'm *sure* Lil and Sally would be happy to see you there, and to answer any questions you may have." He grinned.

"*Besides*—you can get the first slice of hot coffee cake when it's fresh out of the oven!"

CHAPTER 7

Micky slowed her car as she approached Grace Church Episcopal, a Gothic building set well back from the road. The 18-degree temperature and brilliant sunshine on this February Sunday morning made the snow covering its expansive lawn sparkle like the glitter on a Christmas card, while its twin spires reached toward the cloudless crystalline blue sky.

She pulled her parka's zipper closer to her throat as she exited the car, and found her way to the red front door. A smiling man inside handed her a folded booklet and extended his right hand in greeting. "Hi, I'm Bob Dolan. Welcome to Grace Church!"

"Thank you! I'm Micky McHale... I'm a friend of Lillian Meadows and Reverend Wise."

Gesturing toward the center aisle, he said, "Oh, Lil's a few pews from the front on the right." She paused as she moved through the open double doors, dazzled by the intense colors of stained-glass windows all around the church: upper and lower rows of them filled the walls on both sides and a huge round one was above the altar. The morning sun blazed through the windows on the right wall, so blindingly bright that she had to shield her eyes to see Lillian, who stepped out of her pew to give Micky a hug and lead her to her seat.

"I'm so glad to see you, Micky! Brad told me you might be with us today."

Micky smiled and sat down next to her, still enthralled by the surrounding beauty. She admired the elaborate, carved wooden seats on the upper level and the similar ornamentation behind the altar that guided her eyes up to the colorful round window above it. She delighted in the soft glow of these well-tended furnishings and thought of how many people had been praying here over the past century, since the time when the craftsmanship to create such a church was still available. She'd been in beautiful churches before, but they had always seemed cold, remote . . . untouchable. But Grace Church was different, somehow. Despite its grandeur, this felt warm, cozy . . . and safe. Micky experienced a unique sensation . . . a kind of prolonged tingling, and then she felt her face relaxing into a wide, involuntary smile.

Organ music began. Lillian leaned into her and whispered, "Don't worry about what to do. I'll guide you through the service." Still smiling, Micky nodded.

*****

The sun was still bright as it poured through Lillian's kitchen windows after the service. Micky basked in the cheerful light and inhaled the incense of warming apple-cinnamon crumb cake and freshly brewed coffee as her co-sponsor handed her a mug of it and asked, "So, how did you like it?"

"It was wonderful! I really like this church!"

"You seemed to follow along with the liturgy pretty well," she observed. "Some newcomers find it a bit confusing."

"Well . . . it's been a *long time* since mass at my Catholic high school . . . but the basic *structure* seemed similar," Micky said. "But other than that, this was *totally* different."

"How so?"

"Well . . . besides having a *woman priest,* Sally actually talked *to* us, not *at* us. And she made *sense* of the scripture she read and talked about how it related to our lives *today.* She even gave examples of her *own* behavior and how she often *fell short* of what the passage was telling us! The Catholic priests I experienced at school *never* did that! They just pointed what I called 'the loaded finger' at us and yelled about what *we must* do."

Lillian laughed. "You're right; Sally would never do that."

"And that's another big difference . . . *laughing,*" Micky said. "Lots of people this morning laughed along with Sally as she admitted her chronic failures of patience while driving, nodding their heads like *we* do when we identify with the speaker at an A.A. meeting. At school, *nobody ever* laughed during mass! The nuns would've made them *really sorry!*"

The timer's chime summoned Lillian to remove the coffee cake from the oven. She cut two pieces, put them on plates with forks and brought them to the table. She looked at her watch as Micky enjoyed her first delectable bite and said, "I wonder what's keeping Sally? Her daughter, Shelley, is visiting; maybe she's bringing her along."

Her phone announced Sally calling. She swiped to answer and put the phone to her ear. "Oh, God," she said. "We'll be right there!"

Lillian nearly fell over the cat in her rush to pull her coat off of the rack by the door. To Micky, she said, "Grab your coat and purse. We're going next door. Sally found Shelley on the floor of the guest bathroom with a syringe next to her; looks like she OD'd."

When they arrived, Lillian selected a key from her ring to let themselves in and told Micky, "Call Brad and tell him to meet us at the rectory. He should park close by in the church lot; we need the driveway clear for the ambulance, and we need Brad to drive us all to the emergency room. I'm going up to the third floor to be with Sally and Shelley. You and Brad should wait here to let the EMS folks in and send them up."

*****

Sally had been quiet during the whole ride in Brad's Mini Cooper to the Cleveland Clinic Jacobs emergency department in Avon. She had gripped her sponsor's hand all the way, white-faced and tight-lipped, silently crying. Lillian had done all of the talking when they arrived, and Sally just followed her and the nurse, with Micky and Brad trailing after.

Now, in the waiting room, she was distraught. "Why didn't I see this coming? I had no idea she was using heroin! How did she get into that life?! She wasn't raised that way!" When her expressive hands stopped flying around, Lillian reached over and covered one of them with her own. Sally blushed and managed an apologetic smile. "Thanks. I'm just tortured by so many questions—like, why is she doing this? Where did she get it? Did she bring it with her—bring it into my home? And if she has no job and no money, how the hell could she buy it?" She paused for breath. "I'm just *so pissed!*"

"At her? Or at yourself?"

"Both." She closed her eyes and furrowed her brow as she said, "I just hope to God she'll be okay. I shouldn't have left her alone!"

Lillian squeezed her hand. "I know you feel responsible, Sally, but she's pushing forty—way too old for babysitting. And like you said, you didn't know what she was up to. Plus, you've had work to do; counseling appointments that had been set up long before she surprised you with her visit, and the service this morning. Where you may have gained a new parishioner," she said, looking at Micky, who smiled and slightly raised her hand.

Sally brightened and smiled back. "Oh, Micky, I'm so glad! Welcome to our parish family!"

A woman in scrubs and a white coat who looked barely older than Shelley entered the small waiting area. "Reverend Wise?"

Sally, who had changed out of her clericals, stood and replied, "That's me."

"I'm Doctor Weber. Good news. The Narcan EMS gave Shelley worked, and we were able to get her stabilized. She's still pretty out of it, but you can see her for a short visit if you like."

"Oh, thank God! And thank you, Doctor Weber!" Sally hesitated. "I'm not sure I really want to see her right now; I don't know if I want to kiss her or kill her."

The doctor said, "I understand. Sadly, I've delivered this message many, many times, and I assure you that your reaction is pretty typical. Your daughter needs to rest now anyway, and she'll be here for a few days while she detoxes. I'll tell her you're glad she made it, okay?" Sally nodded, looked at the others and added, "And please tell her we're all praying for her."

*****

The next day, Sally tried her usual day-off puttering about the house, but was too restless. She couldn't even focus on reading the Stromberg weekly paper. *I need to do something, some simple chore to calm down before I even think about going to visit Shelley. Oh—I know! I can polish the sterling flatware Mother left me last year. I've been meaning to do that since I got it.*

She went to the kitchen and retrieved the Wright's silver crème from under the kitchen sink, setting it and a soft rag on the counter. She walked into the dining room, but the walnut silver chest wasn't on the sideboard. Even though she knew it wouldn't have fit into the sideboard's cupboards, she opened the right door anyway, expecting to see the silver trays stacked in their anti-tarnish wrappings—but it was empty. With a sick feeling, she opened the other door and discovered that the hollowware was gone, too, as were the serving pieces that should've been in the drawers.

She called Lillian, who was at the door within five minutes.

"Sally, do you have any photos of the stolen pieces for insurance?"

"Yes, I'll get them from my office."

"Good. Bring them here and then put on your collar and your coat," Lillian instructed. "We're going for a short ride. I have an idea where we might find your silver."

Lillian drove Sally to a side street off of the town square to a pawn shop. Inside, Sally asked the balding gray-haired man who appeared behind the chipped counter, "Hello, are you the owner here?"

"Yes, ma'am."

She pointed to the open silver chest and sterling serving pieces in the display case and said, "Well, I'm the owner of those." Seeing his face go white, she pulled out the photos of the rest of her goods. "And I'm guessing you have all of these items, too. Am I correct?" He nodded. "Bring them here, please. We're taking them home. If you give them back right now, I won't call the police and charge you with receiving stolen property." He made a few trips into the back room and placed everything on the counter.

With her hands shaking a bit, Sally accounted for all of the pictured valuables. She then produced an old photo of Shelley. "Is she the one who brought these things in and sold them to you?"

"Yeah."

"Was anyone with her?"

"Not that I saw."

"Thank you." She and Lil began gathering the goods to take to the car.

"Hey, what about my money? I paid a couple thou in cash for that stuff!" the man whined.

Sally drew herself up and fixed a cold stare on him. "Must I really remind you that you're not going to jail and paying legal bills? I'm forgiving you for your sin of larceny."

Lillian, who had returned from the car to take the last load chimed in, "You'll need to forgive yourself for your sin of stupidity."

They made the short drive back to the rectory and restored the silver pieces to their rightful places in the sideboard, then Lillian lit a fire in the living room while Sally made tea. The two settled into the wing chairs by the fireplace.

"I'm glad I'd already planned to polish the silver; I can't bear the thought of using any of it until I've cleaned the filth of that place off of it!" Sally said. "But that will have to wait for another day. Right now, I need to figure out what to do about Shelley. And I need to call a locksmith, since she may have taken my keys while I was in the church office last week.

"I feel really bad for her almost dying, and I'm sorry she's made such a mess of her life. But I'm also *furious!*"

"Of course you are! You're human, Sally—despite being ordained and having decades of sobriety," Lil said. "Speaking of sobriety, are you foregoing pressing charges because you think she might be ready to try recovery?"

Sally shook her head. "No. I just don't want to pile on any more trouble for her. But I can't help her now; she's not interested. Any time I tried to bring up subjects like treatment, writing her resumé or parole requirements, she either snapped at me, bristled or rolled her eyes."

"It is hard to muster any sympathy for her. And we both know that wanting recovery for anyone won't do a thing," Lillian agreed. "She'd need to want it for herself, and it doesn't sound like she's even interested."

"I wouldn't even have tried to talk about it, except that she'd said the reason for her visit was to try to get her life back together. But I'm afraid that was just a ruse for robbery, rather than a genuine desire," Sally admitted. "And I'm scared of her now. I really don't want her back in my home, especially since it's church property!"

"What are you going to do?"

"I'm going to pack up her suitcase and take it to the hospital. This evening—before they try to discharge her. First, I'm going to call our Junior Warden and ask him to get a locksmith today. Can you be available to let them in if they don't come before I head out for the hospital?"

*****

Sally knocked softly at the half-open door to Shelley's hospital room. "May I come in?"

Her daughter rolled over in the bed to see who was there. "Mom. Hi."

Sally said a silent prayer for guidance as she looked into the wan face and empty brown eyes of this shell of a person who only vaguely resembled her once-vibrant, confident child. She touched her on the shoulder, carefully avoiding the IV line and monitors. "How are you feeling? You gave us quite a scare."

"Sorry. I'm okay. It's not a big deal."

Shocked, Sally exclaimed, "Not a big deal? You almost died!"

"It's happened before. A couple of times. I just forgot that I couldn't do as much since it'd been a while since the last time I got high."

"You're already detoxing, Shelley. Would you like to go to treatment, and really start your life over? I'd pay for that."

Shelley rolled her eyes. "No, Mom. We've been through that. I'm fine. Really. They say I'll probably be out of here tomorrow afternoon."

Sally winced. "Well, the offer stands if you ever decide you want to go to treatment. But that's the only assistance I'll provide." She paused. "In any event, you'd better find another line of work—you're a lousy thief!"

"Oh. You found out. That was fast."

"Of course I noticed! And dumping your stolen goods at a pawn shop five minutes away from the scene of the crime was really stupid! Thankfully, it made them really easy to find. And I showed an old picture of you to the owner, who identified you. So, just to be clear: You've worn out your welcome in my home. I can't trust you. And the locks have been changed."

Shelley turned her face away.

Sally put Shelley's suitcase and jacket on the visitor's chair. "Tell your 'friend' to pick you up tomorrow, and to take care of the hospital bills. He has a few thousand dollars from the sale of the silver, I believe. Good-bye, Shelley. And good luck; you're going to need it. I'll pray for you."

Shelley turned her back to her mother, who walked out of the door and closed it behind her.

CHAPTER 8

March had come in like a lion with yet another snow storm, and the cold front had stalled over the region. Temperatures had remained in the teens all week, so by Friday, Lillian was in the mood to make comfort food. Knowing that her dear friend was in need of some comfort, she'd invited Sally to come for dinner and share it.

As Sally came through the door from the back porch, Lillian hung her outerwear on the rack and steered her toward a large pot on the stove. "Help yourself to a bowl of pasta and follow me to the dining room."

"This smells heavenly! What is it, Lil?" Sally asked as she ladled creamy shell-shaped pasta with vegetables into an elegant flowered china soup bowl with scalloped edges and placed it on a matching plate. "Your grandmother's Spode is so lovely. And the dining room—if I'd known we were going formal, I'd have dressed up and come to the front door!"

The hostess, serving herself, replied, "It's cavatelli, spinach, sun-dried tomatoes and roasted garlic with an asiago cream sauce. The dining room is much cozier than the kitchen in this weather. And seeing your silver on Monday reminded me that I might as well enjoy using mine!"

Lillian had set two ivory lace placemats with sterling flatware on the Jacobean table, which showed off the ornate inlaid woods of the tabletop. The lily-themed art nouveau chandelier was turned down low, and dark green candles in crystal candlesticks on the table and matching sideboard calmed with their soft warm glow.

She sat down at the head of the table. Sally sighed. "Ah, this is so wonderful! Beautiful and peaceful. And—celebratory? Do we have an occasion?"

"Do we need one? Well, let's pray," Lillian said. "Lord God, thank you for the gifts of our very full lives. We especially thank you for guiding us to the restoration of Sally's family silver, and for strengthening and supporting her in the difficult times with her daughter this week. We thank you for saving Shelley from death, and we pray for your continued protection of her and for her eventual acceptance of your ever-available grace in recovery.

"We thank you for Micky's new openness to that grace, for her first month of sobriety, and especially for her joining our faith family in seeking to know you better.

"We celebrate Brad's first month without cigarettes and his courage to leave a dangerous relationship. We pray you will keep him safe, and guide him to the home you know will be best for him now.

"And we thank you for Sally's help with my new book and for my editor's enthusiastic response to my first three chapters. We pray for your continuing guidance in further developing this work. Thank you for this food, O Lord. Bless it to our use and us to your service. Amen."

"Amen. Thank you for offering that spot-on blessing, Lil," Sally said as she picked up her crystal stem of water for a toast. "To all our blessings and our friendship."

They clinked glasses and Lillian asked, "How are you feeling, Sally? You had quite a week."

Sally smiled as she savored the pasta. "Lil, this is superb! I'm blessed to have a friend with so many talents, especially cooking!" She took another bite to give her time to process the question.

"To be honest—I don't know. Exhausted. Like I've been wrestling with the devil."

"You were," Lillian said. "That's why I thought you needed some TLC and serious sustenance. Have some Italian bread."

Sally complied, delighted that the bread was still warm enough to slightly melt the butter. After further rumination, she continued, "I'm relieved. That she didn't die—and relieved that she's gone. I did make one last-ditch effort to interest her in fully-paid treatment, but, as we suspected, she scorned the offer. Still, I'm glad I extended it, and that I made it clear she's not welcome in my home again without treatment first."

Lillian nodded.

"But it hurts. And baffles me. She's nothing like the young woman I raised and—well, that's not true. She always *was* defensive, curt and self-absorbed. But she was also animated, talented and ambitious. She insisted that she was fine, that she'd been through this before, that almost dying was no big deal. *No big deal!* And Lil, her eyes. Her eyes were totally empty. Vacant. Soulless. You're right—I did wrestle with Satan in that room. I'm glad I'd prayed for God's guidance, which was to offer the grace of treatment, and to quickly leave when it was refused. And yes, I'm totally spent. Somehow, God gave me the strength to counsel people this week; actually, he spoke through me. I had nothing left in the tank. I'm so very grateful that you invited me into this warm, safe cocoon and are feeding me this wonderful meal!

"Now—enough about me. What did your editor say?"

"She *loved* the first three chapters I sent; especially the first one titled, 'Kama Sutra for the Golden Years'. I'm so glad you suggested reminiscing about the good things I lost for the book's opening!"

Sally smiled. "So, what does she want next, and when does she need it? I noticed your prayer for guidance tonight."

"She wants the outline with working titles for the rest of the book, plus the fourth chapter draft. By the first of next month."

"April Fool's Day," Sally noted.

"Yes, and I'd be a fool if I didn't send them by March thirty-first!"

"Any ideas?"

"Sort of, but I'm not sure," Lillian said. "The second and third chapters were about things I had to deal with right away: 'Purgatory is the Living Room Mantle' and 'Death and Taxes: The Final Deduction.'"

Sally laughed. "Oh, I remember. You rode that contractor mercilessly until he finally produced an acceptable extension of the columbarium in the chapel since there was no more room in the original one and the initial cabinet they installed didn't match at all!"

"And I felt so guilty about George gathering dust, but it felt creepy to use the feather duster on him and I never was much for doing housework—but I didn't trust anyone to do it for me! I mean, what if they'd spilled him?

"Those were easy, because I'd lived them," Lillian continued. "But since that's all I've really done, I'm at a loss for material. So, please ponder my problem while I clear. Hopefully, you'll have some thoughts by the time I return with carrot cake and your favorite tea, Constant Comment."

"Deal." Sally slipped into a semi-meditative state while staring into the flame from the closest candle. By the time Lillian returned, she was smiling and alert. She gave her friend time to settle back into her chair before speaking.

"My dear, I offer an approach to all of your immediate problems," she said. "And it's really quite simple: First, brainstorm and list all of the moving on chores you've put off until now. Next, give them your clever names for their chapter titles and put them in the order in which you can or need to do them to create your outline. Then do each chore and write about it." Grinning, Sally picked up her dessert fork and attacked the generous slice of cake with buttercream frosting.

"Wow. For a woman of the cloth, you kick butt like a drill sergeant." Lillian laughed. "I know I'll need to make my own list, but can you suggest one as a thought-starter?"

"Thank you. Remember, I began my career as a schoolteacher, then moved into counseling," Sally replied. "As your thought-starter and first project, I suggest that you get all of George's clothes out of closets and donate them. Your working title could be 'Spring Cleaning, Twelve Seasons Late.'"

*****

Lillian, now facing deadlines from both her long-time editor, Ann, and Sally, sat at her walnut custom-made desk in her paneled office at 10:30 the following morning even though it was a Saturday. She'd bribed herself with an extra mug of Costco's Nicaraguan-grown coffee that now rested on her right, safely away from her computer. No laptop for this work, with its built-in temptation to wander in search of inspiration; no, this to-do list/outline commitment was going directly into the tower machine.

She indulged in a deep swig of coffee before plunging into her task. Pretty Girl, curled up in a nook of the desk between its built-in pigeon-holes and filing shelves that had fit her much better as a kitten, regarded her with the narrowed eyes of feline judgment. "All right, all right!" Lillian replied. She restored the mug to its spot and pulled the keyboard toward her.

There's a reason I've procrastinated so long; I never wanted to even think about all of the things I should do. I justified ignoring everything other than the immediate legal and social requirements on the grounds that they were all-consuming at the time and hard enough in the wake of losing George. After that, I thought I deserved to rest and pamper myself. But Sally's right; it has been three years and this editorial deadline is really the divine two-by-four God's using to whup me upside the head and tap me on the backside to get in gear and stop wallowing.

With a sigh, she put Sally's suggested chore on the page and began to randomly add other things that needed doing. She studied the list. Then, she prioritized the items and added a couple more. She finished with creating the chapter titles:

- Clean George's things out of closets/donate (Spring Cleaning, Twelve Seasons Late)
- Get T-Bird tuned up/reconditioned/detailed to resume pleasure drives in spring (Kicking the T-Bird Out of the Nest)
- Return to Preservation Society meetings/go with Brad? (Septuagenarian's Social Début)
- T-Bird Part Two, Actually Driving It (Flying Solo)
- Resume Entertaining (Open Garden: A New Spring Flush)
- Inventory/Organize George's workshop in barn garage/decide what to keep, sell or donate/Brad (A Toolbox of One's Own)
- Clean out George's office in upstairs of barn garage (Artifacts of Memories)
- Hire Brad to Finish apartment in garage loft that George started (Creating a New Space)

Lillian reviewed the list and the working titles of the chapters, deciding it was good enough for this stage. She rewarded herself with a brief rest to finish her coffee. Then she said a quick prayer for God's strength and guidance, grabbed a legal pad and pen to record donations, and headed to the pantry for a box of large trash bags to take with her to George's dressing room upstairs.

CHAPTER 9

By early March, Brad had been residing at the Redwood Apartments for about two months, and had completed unpacking and arranging what he was able to fit into the fully furnished suite. This included his go-to cookbooks, favorite professional stainless-steel cookware and utensils, two sets of everyday placemats, flexible silicone flame-proof non-slip pot holders and gloves and stainless flatware. He had swapped them for the minimal gear that was provided, which he put into the boxes he'd unpacked and stowed away in a utility closet. He did likewise with the hotel-style pictures, replacing them with a few of his paintings by local artists—many of whom were friends—from his fifteen years of living in Paris and New York. He also replaced the table and desk lamps with treasured Arts & Crafts antiques he'd found in shops in Brooklyn and Queens.

This had made his initial entry into his new life tolerable for the short-term. At first, it was a safe haven from the escalating chaos he'd fled—and while the bland modern décor was not his taste, it was way better than his ex's stifling prison of French and Italianate antiques.

But he missed his furniture, books, dishes, glassware, and the rest of his paintings that were in storage. He'd thought perhaps he could put some of his rugs over the carpeting, but they either clashed with the colors or didn't fit into the spaces here.

And since the confrontation with Oscar in the driveway, he'd grown increasingly anxious. This haven was no longer safe.

So, on this Saturday, Brad sat down at the desk, opened his laptop and went shopping on Zillow. He entered the basic specs he wanted: Arts & Crafts bungalow, 1900–1939, 1-1/2 stories, 1 bath, kitchen, dining room, living room, fireplace, 2 bedrooms in Stromberg or Strongsville. He left the price range blank, hoping to find a good rehab prospect but also wanting to check out the whole market. He also wanted to check his preferred communities first, planning to expand into Lorain and Cuyahoga counties if necessary. He would avoid Wellington and Oberlin, both home bases of Oscar.

Two properties came up in Strongsville. The one with the lower price was definitely a fixer-upper; most period appointments had long since fallen victim to what he called "remuddling" and the overall appearance of the property showed decades of neglect. He couldn't tell the condition of the bones of the house from the photos, but thought it might be at least educational to see it. The second was on the opposite end of the continuum. It was at the upper end of his planned price range and was already fully restored including craft tiles on the fireplace surround and stenciling on some ceiling beams. It had radiators with hot-water heating, and high-velocity air-conditioning. There wasn't much left for him to do to put his personal stamp on the home, however, he might want to do a kitchen makeover. And its move-in condition would be a plus at this particular moment.

His search for contact information showed the same listing agent for both properties, a great convenience he thought, and possibly useful for his hunt if neither of these worked. He tapped the info into his contacts list and called.

It was promptly answered by a melodious high tenor. "Baxter James, at your service. How may I help you?"

"Hello, Baxter. I'm Brad Mueller. I'm looking for an Arts and Crafts bungalow, and I see you have two listed in Strongsville on Zillow. I'd like to see both of them, please, tomorrow morning if possible?"

"I'll get back to you shortly with times," he replied. "You know they're *very different* properties?"

Brad laughed. "I'm an architect at a design-build contracting and renovations firm. Originally, I was planning to look for a bungalow to rehab and then move into. But I'm in temporary quarters now, and I'm itching to get out of here after just eight weeks."

Baxter laughed, too. "Understood! By any chance, do you work at Classic Homes Construction?"

"Yes."

"I've used your firm for some projects and have referred several clients. You can ask Rob Weber about me, if you'd like a reference. Or Sue Stern; we've known each other since our days at Baldwin-Wallace."

"You know, I *thought* your name seemed familiar, Baxter. I designed some of those projects. The paperwork always listed you as B. James, though; I *definitely* would've remembered Baxter."

"Yes, people often tell me I'm pretty memorable."

"I'll bet you are! I look forward to meeting you tomorrow."

*****

The first showing at ten o'clock was the low-priced property. It would need a gut-rehab and had foundation issues. They didn't waste much time there.

"I *would* like to do a rehab," Brad told Baxter. "But only if the original architectural details are still intact, or at least *most* of them. And the location needs to be somewhere pleasant enough to make the work *and investment* worthwhile."

"I agree. I think you'll like the next property much better."

This bungalow was in excellent condition. Brad admired the craftsmanship of the original builders and those who'd made minor updates. He even liked the color scheme. The kitchen, however, was all electric, which he hated, and the boiler was oil-fired. The house was in Lorain County, almost in Columbia Station and gas lines had never been run in this farmland area. Water and sewer lines also didn't exist, so it had a septic tank and its own well. Brad also hadn't noticed in the listing that it was on 20 acres.

"Love the house; I *am* hoping to find this level of details, even if they're not finished like these are," he said. "But I think we need to refine our search criteria to incorporated areas with good services and utilities. Also, I'm not looking for acreage (sorry, my bad, I overlooked that in the listing). I grew up in Stromberg, and if anything comes on the market there, it would be *ideal*."

"This is all really good information," said Baxter. "Initial showings typically are more about getting to know you and fine-tuning what you want and need. I'd love to work with you in your home search, if that's okay?"

"Yes, I'd like that—unless, of course, Sue or Rob vote thumbs down tomorrow," Brad said with a grin.

*****

It was a short drive from the bungalow with too much acreage to Lillian's house, and Brad was at her back porch door at noon sharp. "Come in out of the cold," she said with a welcoming hug. "Micky's here, and Sally will join us as soon as she changes out of her clericals."

He greeted Micky, "Well, you're here early! What got you out of bed on this chilly Sunday morning?"

Family of Choice: Raising Each Other

"Church!" she said, smiling. "As you suggested, I tried it and liked it so much that I came back."

"And we're glad to have her with us. It's nice to have company in my pew," Lillian said as she handed a mug of black coffee to Brad. She joined them at the table and filled them in about the events of the week regarding Shelley and Sally.

Micky was shocked. "I can't believe she stole from her *own mother* . . . I *am* glad she lived . . . but it doesn't sound like much of a *life*. And how can *anyone* think they're okay after *almost dying* . . . and not accept *treatment*?"

"I guess that's why people who use heroin and fentanyl talk about being 'in the life,'" Lillian said. "Those who aren't can't understand it. But it's really not too different from us; 'The Doctor's Opinion' in the Big Book says that our alcoholic life seems so normal to us that we need a total psychological change to recover—which is beyond human power to achieve."

"Which is why I'm coming to church . . . I want to get closer to my Higher Power . . . God."

"It is important, Micky. And make no mistake—many, many people die from alcohol. If not from alcohol poisoning directly, which does happen, then from related conditions such as esophageal hemorrhage, cirrhosis, heart disease and others, or car wrecks. It's also a leading cause of suicide," said Lillian. Changing the subject, she asked, "So, what's new with you, Brad?"

Before he could answer, the timer chimed and Sally entered. After serving slices of hot apple pie and topping off coffees, she prompted, "Sally, Brad was about to fill us in on what he's been up to."

"I've started house-hunting. Despite my best efforts to add a few personal items to my extended-stay quarters, there's just no way to make them feel like home," he said. "And ever since I found *Oscar* camped on my doorstep a few weeks ago, that place just doesn't feel *safe* anymore. I saw two properties this morning. Neither were right for me, but the listing agent offered to work with me on finding others that might be."

"Are you planning to do that?" Lillian asked. "If so, beware of buying one of his listings. An agent who represents you is supposed to be protecting *your* interests, suggesting strategies and prices to get you the best deal. But if he's also representing the seller, that's not possible—so the agent usually defaults to serving self-interest. I learned that the hard way!"

"I probably will use him. Apparently, he has a niche in historical real estate; he's hired our firm to help him get some homes ready to market. In fact, I did some of the drawings for his projects. I will ask Rob tomorrow if he's good to do business with, and maybe Sue—she's known him since college."

Lillian nodded. "Good idea." She paused. "If he's focused in that specialty, I'd think we'd know him in the Preservation Society. What's his name?"

"Baxter James."

"Hm. Never heard of him. Although I have to admit I haven't been to any meetings for three years; he could've joined in that time frame and I wouldn't know it," she said. "Speaking of which: Going back to Society meetings is on a list I just made yesterday, thanks to pressure from Sally and my editor. I needed to create an outline of the rest of the chapters for my book, which turned out to be all of the things I've put off doing since George died. Brad, I'd appreciate your help with some of them, like going with me to the next meeting, or sorting through George's tools in the workshop."

"Sure," he said. "I'll be happy to help."

She looked at Sally with a triumphant expression. "I already did the first thing on the list. I cleaned out George's clothes from the closets. And I'm taking them to the Salvation Army in the morning."

"Atta girl!" Sally grinned. "Keep up the good work!"

CHAPTER 10

For the first time in what seemed like forever, Micky was in a good mood and looking forward to her day as she drove to work on this mid-March Monday morning. It helped that the sun was now up by the time she got into her car, and the early spring thaw had raised temperatures into the forties—balmy compared to the recent deep freeze.

The reason for her new outlook was that her weeks of research were on the verge of fruition. She had found an automotive business with multiple luxury brands, one of which was a Cadillac dealership. Further digging gave her the data she needed to draft an incentive program that would make him a big winner in the national contest and be a major win for her, too.

There was a spring in her step as she walked from her car into the office building. She hung up her coat and stepped into the ladies' room to brush her glossy black hair. She also checked her red lipstick and her outfit, slim gray wool slacks over black ankle boots topped by a Kelly-green cashmere/silk blend tunic with a cowl neck. With a slight frown, she leaned toward the full-length mirror and extracted a small emerald that had dropped inside the neckline and positioned its fine gold chain to dangle the gem over the rolled collar. Satisfied, she stopped by her office, transferred her portfolio-size purse to a hook on the door, took a folder from it and strode down the hall.

Knocking lightly on the partially open door, Micky enlarged the opening and smiled. "Happy Monday, Jack! Have a few minutes? I've got a plan I'd like to run by you . . . it could make us some good money . . . possibly a major score."

"Oh?" Jack Benson looked up from his desk chair with raised eyebrows. "Come in, Micky. Have a seat. You're looking lovely this morning—is that sweater and necklace representing the color of this prospective money? Saint Patrick's Day was last week."

She laughed. "Both. I was brought up to celebrate Saint Pat's for at *least* a week . . . the necklace was my father's gift for my thirtieth last August." She put the folder on his desk.

The motion caught Jack's eye. "And the matching ring?"

"My birthday present to myself . . . bonus money put to good use." She smiled. "I want *more* of that . . . and with your ambitious *goal* for me, I focused my prospecting on mid-sized businesses large enough to afford us in industries that can most benefit from our services."

"Smart. And?"

"Midway Fine Motors in Elyria," she replied. "Paul Price owns the Cadillac dealership, and I checked with our rep in the Detroit office who has a national program for Cadillac . . . Paul's registered as a participant. The in-house plan I've roughed out would make him a winner, and be a nice win for us as well."

"Great idea!"

"Thanks. I thought you'd like it." She paused. "Midway Fine Motors also includes *four more* luxury brands, all grouped together in separate facilities . . . BMW, Volvo, Lexus and Infinity. My plan includes them, too. You know, so the other salespeople and managers don't feel *left out* . . . and they can all compete against each other for additional, *larger team awards,* which will further push the Cadillac team and *ensure* Paul's personal national trip award . . . and put him in the running for Cadillac's *Top Dealers Council* honors."

Jack's jaw dropped. "Micky! That's genius!"

She flashed a bright grin and handed him her folder. "My draft plan has the program details and numbers. It includes travel and merchandise. Estimated cost is two hundred thousand for Cadillac only . . . a million-plus if he goes for all five brands. Please look this over and let me know what you think." She stood up, then added, "The numbers include a possible trade agreement for the cost of my Top Dog award lease . . . if you *approve,* of course."

Jumping up from his desk, Jack exclaimed, "Babe, if you sell this you certainly deserve it!"

In his excitement, he gave her a congratulatory hug, which she accepted without flinching.

*****

Micky had no trouble getting a meeting with Paul Price. When she spoke to him on the phone, she got his attention immediately by tying into the Cadillac trip incentive program and asking if she could come and present a plan for his people that would ensure he'd be basking in the Tahitian sun next January.

Three days later, she pulled her Buick Regal into a parking space in the row outside the dealership's front showroom floor-to-ceiling windows. She and Jack walked to the door. Before Jack could open it, an auburn-haired fortyish man with slightly graying temples wearing a sharp brown tweed sport coat did it for them. As he quickly appraised them—particularly Micky's long slim legs with black heels, royal blue fitted suit and red silk blouse—he welcomed them inside with a movie-star smile and extended his hand.

"Paul Price. And you must be Micky; truly a pleasure to meet you."

Returning the smile, she met his gaze while shaking his hand. "Likewise . . . and this is my boss, Jack Benson."

"Pleased to meet you, too, Jack," he said with a quick nod and a handshake. "Let's meet in our conference room. Please follow me."

Micky noted the casual elegance and comfort of the light warm gray-carpeted showroom and the soft but abundant lighting that caressed the four vehicles featured in it, and cherry-stained round tables with charcoal leather captain's chairs for informal conversations or waiting for visitors, as Paul had just inhabited. Six sales offices with doors lined the back wall. As they followed Paul through the hallway, she saw wood-framed photographs on the wall opposite the managers' offices that depicted historical milestones of the dealership, founded in 1913 by John P. Price, and iconic Cadillac models from each decade. It appeared that Paul was the third-generation leader, taking the helm in 2009.

The conference room had complementary décor. The 14-foot oval table had the same cherry finish, surrounded by 16 charcoal mesh-backed adjustable swivel office chairs with ergonomically padded seats and arms. Its walls were decorated with regional sales awards, annual dealership sales winners for new and used cars, and monthly winners for the current year. A presentation screen was at the far wall, flanked by a podium. The projector was mounted on the ceiling.

Micky started to extract her laptop from her briefcase, but Paul stopped her. "If you have your presentation on a thumb drive, I'll put it in the system's computer for you. Everything's wireless, so you can present from the podium or the table. Your choice."

She smiled. "Oh, I'd rather talk *to* you than *at* you. Where would you like us to sit?" she asked as she placed the USB drive in his open palm.

As she and Jack settled in where Paul had indicated, Micky put three maroon folders in front of her. When he returned, she handed one to him and one to Jack, then opened hers and took out a stack of pages secured by a binder clip. "The folder has copies of the slides we'll discuss today. Some people like to use it as we go along to note questions . . . I'll make notes on any issues you raise, changes you'd like or corrections to data I used in preliminary budget calculations. Full descriptions of proposed program rules, budgets and paybacks are in the folder's other pocket . . . we'll discuss those after you've had time to review them, if you decide to move forward."

Impressed, Paul smiled and said, "Thanks. Show me what you've got in mind."

Micky clicked to bring the title slide to the screen: Paul Price's Ticket to Tahiti, with a subhead of Sales Incentive Proposal for Midway Fine Motors.

"Okay, that should be Price Cadillac," Paul said.

"It can be," replied Micky. "And as a stand-alone Cadillac store program, it will definitely help you win the trip . . . but if you leverage extra effort from *all five* brands and throw in some team competitions, it will *further drive* your Cadillac participants to *secure* Tahiti . . . and also put you in the running for the national Top Dealers Council." She paused. "I notice that you've won lots of *regional* awards . . . but this would move you to the *highest* level. And besides the recognition, which is great, as I understand it, the top national dealers also get special opportunities from the factory like price rebates, floor plan discounts, first choice of colors and extra allocation of highly popular, limited production models."

With a bemused smile, Paul remarked, "Well—you've certainly done your homework."

"As much as I could from public data and our company's national Cadillac incentive program's awards and rules structure," she said, returning his smile. "The program details and budgets in the leave-behind are based on the national average figures on unit sales and margins. It will be important for you to replace them with your actual data . . . when the figures are correct, our incentive awards are structured to pay for themselves from the increased revenue they produce."

"Don't you have my information from your national program?"

"Of course not! We *never* share confidential business information used to develop or operate our programs with *anyone*—not even with each other."

Paul looked to Jack for confirmation, who said, "She's absolutely correct."

"Okay. So how does this work?"

Micky advanced to the next slide that showed a bell-shaped curve. "In any group of employees, dealers, distributors or manufacturers' reps, sales performance falls into your basic bell curve. Your top performers will always succeed and make their plan, and your least productive ones will always struggle." She pressed the advance button and dotted vertical lines marked the points where the curve flattened out near the ends. "An incentive program can reward and spotlight your top ones . . . even inspire them to beat quota by a greater percentage. Over time, with regular programs, it can help retain your top talent and as word gets around, attract other top people to seek positions here, possibly replacing the ones who are dead wood. But that doesn't pay for the program or increase your bottom line very much."

She advanced again, and two more vertical lines the same width apart appeared farther to the right of the original, and a new bell curve, filled in with green appeared between them. "Our programs are designed to significantly increase the production of the *majority* of your participants. That's where the required increase to win results in enough additional *net profit* that pays for the cost of the program *and also* leaves more that adds to your bottom line." She paused for Paul to take this in. "It's also why it's in your best interest to involve all of the people who are part of each deal . . . your sales reps, sales managers and finance managers in *all five stores* to participate. The greater the total dollars in the middle of your bell curve, the greater the program's profit impact. For example, if your program rules pay out awards for a ten percent increase in net, and your baseline performance is a million dollars, you'll get an additional hundred thousand dollars. But if it's *five* million, you gain five hundred thousand dollars. You can also see why using your correct figures is vital for defining the rules so your winners get something meaningful and your business wins financially."

Micky noticed Paul was making notes and doing a rough calculation, so she waited for him to turn his attention back to her. He looked up with a slight smile and nodded. "Midway Fine Motors it is."

The next slides showed pictures of activities of a Carnival Cruise Lines five-day sail from Miami to Cancun, Cozumel, a private island and Key West. Young and middle-aged couples and singles frolicked in the ship's pools and hot tubs, parasailed, rode jet skis over waves and snorkeled. Cocktails were consumed on catamarans, and dining rooms on board showed people laughing and talking. Palm trees were everywhere. Sunsets dipped into the sea's horizon as couples looked romantically into each other's eyes. Other shots showed dancers enjoying live music, people drinking at thatched huts on the beach and gambling in the ship's casino.

"Sun-and-fun is the best incentive for your employees' demographics and likely travel experience. It's also very cost-effective and creates instant excitement at the program kick-off, which we maintain through monthly communications reminding participants of what they can win and their progress or standings to date . . . you've seen that for your Tahiti trip program. We make it clear: Do this, get that. The trip will be for your top ten overall sales winners, your top sales managers for new and used cars, and your top finance manager. They'll earn points along the way based on a combination of dollars and gross margin, with minimums to qualify for consideration."

She then showed slides of items such as golf clubs, jewelry, watches, designer sunglasses, luggage, cameras, smart phones and apparel, as well as a catalog. "All participants will also earn points based on units sold, awarded each month, which can be used for Awards merchandise from our program catalog. In addition, we'll have monthly team competitions between the dealerships based on units with an extra one hundred points to each member on the winning teams for new and used sales. This keeps everyone involved, even if they're not in the running for the trip awards. And it pushes full participation from each store, with some friendly competition. People really get into this; we recommend sending communications featuring each month's winners.

"The whole program injects *fun* and personal *recognition* to your workplace and makes people feel valued. That's a big part of what makes them consciously work harder and smarter—and makes more money for your business."

She pulled out the details from her folder. "The preliminary budget is on the first page of the executive summary. This is based on my generalized, publicly available numbers and an initial rules structure. Your investment would range between a million dollars and one-and-a-quarter million. We'll adjust that based on your actual figures, and we can tweak the rules to limit the cost or increase it if your profitability allows and you want to reward more people. Do you have any questions?"

"I can work with this range. I'll plug in my numbers to your calculations, and will let you know if we need any changes," he said, looking at Micky. "But I do have one question: Why isn't a brilliant, beautiful woman like you driving a Cadillac?"

"Yes," she replied. "About that . . . I won our company's top sales award for last year. My big prize is a one-year lease of a Cadillac, and I don't have it yet." She dipped her chin slightly and looked up into his hazel eyes. "I'd like to get it from you." As Paul blushed, which gave away his quickening pulse, Jack added, "I'm thinking we could work a trade agreement for the car to lower your program cost. No cash has to change hands. We can select the vehicle and handle the paperwork when we come back with the program letter of agreement."

"Sounds good," Paul said, never taking his eyes off of Micky. As they stood up and shook hands to conclude the meeting and their verbal business agreement, he held onto Micky's and placed his left hand over their clasped ones. "I look forward to working with you," he said with an ardent expression, which she rewarded with a dazzling smile.

CHAPTER 11

The last Saturday in March was sunny but chilly. Brad was glad he'd put on a warm turtle-necked sweater under his tan goose-down jacket as he drove to meet Baxter James at a showing in an older section near Strongsville's town square. It was adequate per his criteria, but the house was dark inside despite the sunshine and lack of leaves on the overhanging trees. He made similarly short work of looking at the next house, which was nearby. This one lacked any of the Arts & Crafts detail that he prized and the rooms were cramped.

"That's okay," said Baxter with a twinkle in his eyes. "I saved the best for last. It's in Stromberg; it's on the northeast side, about three blocks from the square. Follow me."

Brad was familiar with the neighborhood and streets lined with tall, graceful elm trees. As he climbed out of his Mini Cooper, he paused to admire the green exterior of the home, which had marvelous leaded- and beveled-glass sidelight windows flanking the front door, topped by a second-floor alcove balcony framed by carved facia trim. He couldn't help saying, "Wow."

Baxter smiled and blinked in mock apology. "I know you'd said one-and-a-half stories, but I didn't think you'd want to miss this one."

"Oh, you're definitely right!" Brad liked the curved front walk and the weeping cherry it embraced as he made his way through the generous yard and up the steps to the wide full-length covered porch. Its roof was supported by round columns and sported a small gable with carved trim mirroring that of the balcony. The chiseled stone foundation looked sound, as did everything else. A wicker porch swing with yellow, pink and dark green floral-print cushions, antique umbrella-stand and hanging potted ferns extended a well-staged welcome.

"Wow," he repeated. "This must be early Arts and Crafts, with hold-over decorative flourishes from Queen Anne."

"Indeed. Built in 1903," Baxter said, handing him the sell sheet and opening the door. "You'll see those touches throughout the home. It's definitely transitional."

Another transitional element was the small vestibule inside the front door, a bit of a nod to Victorian, while the coat closet in the vestibule's left wall provided functionality more typical of Arts & Crafts, as did the 15-light door of dark wood and clear glass. That door opened to a center hallway. Through a pair of graceful round columns to Brad's right, the living room featured a coffered ceiling and a fireplace at the end that had an artisan-tiled surround and a simple mantle, flanked by built-in bookcases with leaded-glass doors. Small casement windows were on either side of the fireplace, and art nouveau bronze floral wall sconces book-ended the wall. Another pair of sconces were on the wall opposite the porch view, where they had no doubt illuminated artwork above a sofa or chairs. The soft chamois-colored walls made the room feel warm and comfortable, complementing the dark-stained Douglas Fir woodwork while keeping the space light, assisted by a bank of four double-hung windows that formed a bay looking out onto the porch, topped by an arched transom leaded-glass window with the design that echoed the bookcases' doors. A cushioned window seat offered an inviting spot.

To his left, a matching pair of columns marked the transition to the dining room, which had windows that matched those in the living room plus two individual ones on the outer wall.

The dining room was of equal size and beauty. It had the same gorgeous fir woodwork, which included a bay window in the same style and proportion as the one in the living room, but without a seat. Brad thought that would be a perfect place for a decorative table that could be used to display dessert or coffee. Most of the long wall opposite was a built-in sideboard and china cabinet, again with the leaded glass doors. In the middle was a beveled mirror that reflected the small garden in the front yard. More sconces and a similar-themed chandelier provided lighting, along with two windows on the short wall.

Brad, entranced, admired the white oak flooring of both rooms and the dividing hallway as he walked to the swing door past the sideboard. Baxter followed as he pushed open the door and entered a large butler's pantry with a small sink, counter and leaded glass cabinets with shelves for dishes and cups above with closed cupboards below for cookware. The opposite wall showed the side of the refrigerator and a bank of deep pantry shelves. Flooring was period linoleum, in good shape, which extended into the spacious kitchen.

The flooring was a soft gray with a six-inch wide burgundy accent stripe around the outer edges. Bead-board wainscoting and all of the woodwork in the kitchen had been painted white, probably to go with the fruit motif wallpaper on a white background. "Not exactly my style, but it's not terrible," Brad said to Baxter. "The kitchen's big enough to eat in, which is good, and there's enough room to even add an island." He looked back toward the pantry, and saw the refrigerator door. "I like the recessed refrigerator. The space would allow for one much larger, if I decide I'd need it." On the opposite side of the pantry door was a small laundry. He walked in, and saw an opening in the ceiling. "Cool! A laundry-chute!"

Returning to the kitchen, he walked to the backdoor and looked through its window at a small porch with steps to the driveway and to a patio, which bordered a fenced backyard with an evergreen in the far-right corner and two crabapple trees along the fence leading back to the house. On the other side, the fence connected to a converted carriage house garage. The back fence had a small strip of garden; the rest of the yard was a grass lawn.

Brad and Baxter left the kitchen by an arched doorway to the hall that led to the living room and the stairs to the second floor. Brad opened a small door that revealed a powder room under the stairs.

Across from the staircase landing, a fifteen-light stained fir glass door like the one in the foyer revealed a sunroom, with the opposite wall of double-hung windows and matching French doors on the end that opened to the backyard. "Wow—this would make a *fabulous office!*"

Brad walked toward the doors, then paused and looked around. "I'd line the solid wall on the hallway side with bookcases. Center a library table on the other wall, with two leather chairs with ottomans—or maybe trim recliners—on either side with reading lamps. My desk would be in front of that, facing the view of the yard."

"That sounds *perfect,*" said Baxter.

Brad grinned, and turned to the doors, checking their condition, which looked excellent. They opened easily, and he stepped down to a flagstone patio large enough for a small dining table and chairs. A grill mounted on a gas-line connection column was by the steps to the back porch and kitchen door. "Wonderful! This will be *great* for entertaining—and just grilling for myself," Brad said to Baxter. "Do you know if it's functional?"

Consulting the sell sheet, he replied, "They say it is. Of course, your home inspection should check all appliances and fireplaces."

"Fireplaces—plural?"

"Oh yes. Apparently, there's a second one in the master bedroom."

Brad grinned again. "Let's go see it!"

They returned to the sunroom and walked through its door to the staircase across the hall. The newel post and spindles had subtle vine-and-trumpet flower carving, and the post had a flat top that would be large enough to support a statue or flower arrangement. Wall sconces provided plentiful lighting.

The upstairs hallway also had many sconces, but this morning, a large beveled- and leaded-glass window at the end to their left flooded the space with light embellished with rainbows from its prisms. Brad was mesmerized. He just stood there while a slow smile grew larger and larger. When he approached, he saw that the window had a simple flower framed in the design. Smiling, he said, "I'd *really enjoy* starting my days like this."

Turning to his left, he opened the door to a white-tiled bathroom with black-and-white basket-weave floor tile. The claw-foot tub had a shower with a curtain, and the sink appeared to be vintage. He noticed a door from the bathroom and moved through it into a bedroom. The outer wall had a sloped ceiling, allowing for the roof gable. A short hall led back to the main hallway. "I like that the bedroom is accessible from here, yet is also directly connected to the bath."

Immediately to the right of the stairwell was a large built-in linen closet with double doors at the top that covered a very deep space divided by a shelf. Three drawers were below, which all opened and closed easily. A nearby trap door in the ceiling pulled down a folded ladder; Brad climbed it for a quick look in the attic, and turned on the light. "Everything looks good. No evidence of any leaks. And the attic fan should provide sufficient cooling with all of the cross ventilation in the design."

Finally, they came to a door at the end. "I guess this must be the master," Brad said as he opened it and saw a pair of French doors in front of him and two archways on either side. "Wow. *Excuse* me, I mean the master *suite*—which is *really sweet!*" The French doors led to the balcony. "This is *so cool*—a really private spot with a view of this entire, *beautiful* neighborhood! And it's larger than it appeared from down below. A *perfect* way to check the temperature to decide what to wear—very helpful with our changeable weather."

He stepped back inside and looked through the arch to his right. "Ah, *there's* the second fireplace! And a beamed, *cathedral ceiling!*" The room was cavernous, with lots of light from a pair of double-hung windows framing the sandstone mantle and a triple bank of casement windows facing the front yard.

The second arch led to another room of equal size, also with the same beamed ceiling and windows. Baxter, consulting the specs, explained, "This is described as a dressing room; not uncommon in homes of that time." Indeed, the far inside wall opened into a gigantic walk-in cedar closet with hanging racks on both sides plus a shoe shelf in a small portion of the right side.

A door from the main part of the room went to the master bath, which shared a wall with the closet. Its walls were white subway tile, including the baseboard tile, which topped white hexagonal unglazed floor tiles. A three-foot-wide oval white porcelain enamel sink under a frosted glass double-hung window had a deep basin and wide sides that eliminated any need for a vanity and counter. This commode looked original, or at least period sanitary ware from the 1920s or '30s. The bath was a much larger claw-foot, also with a shower and curtain ring. Brad furrowed his brow a bit. "I *love* the huge tub for soaking. But I *really* would want to add a shower—I think I could take enough from the closet on the other side of this wall to make a nice three-by-four-foot shower."

"Oh, I agree," said Baxter. "That's a great idea, and there's certainly room to carve that out of the closet without much sacrifice."

"This room is large enough to be my bedroom *and* dressing room. I'd rather sleep in here, steps away from the bathroom, and make the fireplace room into a cozy private sitting and TV room. The cable will already be coming into my office below it, so the line could easily run up the outside wall to a flat-screen above the mantle."

"So, what do you think, Brad? This was just listed; I'd move fast if you want this house."

"I do want this house. I *have to* have this house. Please write up an offer at list price—nothing has to be done to it *immediately*, and I'm pre-approved for more than this by Key Bank."

Baxter took a form out of his portfolio and quickly completed the paperwork, putting down two-thousand dollars for earnest money. Brad made out the check and signed the offer. "I'll take this right over to the seller, and will let you know as soon as I get an answer."

Brad grinned and shook his hand. "Thanks, Baxter. Fingers crossed!" They got into their vehicles. Brad waved as he drove off; Baxter picked up his phone.

"Hi, it's Bax. The showing was a slam-dunk. You may want to call our mutual friend to say that I'm about to present you with an offer at list."

*****

Brad smiled all though his usual Saturday errands of going to the bank, grocery shopping and picking up his laundry from the cleaners. He pulled into the garage and carried the afternoon's procurements into the residential unit. Looking around, he nodded to the bland walls with a satisfied smile. "Not much longer, thank God, not much longer." After putting everything away, he grabbed his phone and called Lillian, but it went to voicemail. "Lil, great news! I've made an offer on a totally *fabulous* house in Stromberg—I'll tell you and everyone about it tomorrow! Cheers!"

As he was putting the phone on the desk, it announced an incoming call from his agent. "Baxter! Did the seller accept my offer?"

"Not yet, Brad. Turns out another buyer wants it, too. So, we're in a multiple-bid situation."

"What does that mean?"

"It means that you and the other party need to submit revised offers by noon tomorrow. You'll need to increase the price and make it as simple as possible if you want the house."

"I'm bidding against someone else—like an auction?"

"Yes. And no. You're bidding against the other person, but there won't be any back-and-forth like an auction. You just have one shot at it, and you're bidding blind. The seller will accept the bid that's in his best interest. It's not necessarily just who goes higher over the asking price, although that's important. But streamlining the deal can also be a factor. So, you'll want to remove as many contingencies as you can, such as the home inspection or financing approval."

"I can skip the inspection. I didn't see anything questionable, and I have good resources for repairing anything that may need it. And I'm pre-approved by the bank."

"Okay, I'll change the offer to as-is condition. Pre-approval will help, but there's still a time lag of up to six weeks before closing. Plus, banks can require inspections beyond what's in the offer. Cash is better, if you're able to do that," Baxter explained.

"No, I'll need to finance. I could pick up closing costs, if that would help."

"That's a good idea. Those can run up to a couple thousand dollars, but you can roll those into your loan. I'll put that in. Now, how much over asking price do you want to offer?"

"I don't know, Baxter. How much do I need to do?"

"There's no set amount. Generally, if you want to bid—and some buyers decline—you'd go at least twenty-five hundred over. But the market is better than the last couple of years, and properties are selling quickly. Plus, this is a unique home."

"It certainly is—and I *really* want it."

"How much can you afford?"

Brad hesitated. "Give me a minute. In fact, can I check some costs on the immediate updates I'll want and call you back in a few?"

"Of course. In the meantime, I'll start writing up the rest of the offer. And remember, you can probably roll those improvements into the loan, too."

"I know, I was planning to. Thanks." Brad disconnected, and looked up some commercial-grade stove prices as well as the larger refrigerator-freezer he wanted. Then he made some notes on prices for materials and labor to create the shower. He'd need to buy some additional furnishings, and those wouldn't fly with the bank. Some he could do without until he could afford them, he decided.

He called Baxter. "I can go five thousand over asking, and pick up the seller's closing costs. Or, if you think it would be better, just make the offer seven thousand over."

"Let's do seven over asking price. It's an easier comparison to another bid, and no one knows those costs until just before the deal closes. I'll be right over with the new offer for your signature."

*****

Sunday at twelve-thirty as they sat around the kitchen table with their coffees, Brad was telling Lillian, Sally and Micky about the house's many design gems and how much he loved it when Baxter called. Brad put the phone on speaker mode. "I'm so sorry, Brad, but the other bid was ten thousand over asking, and it was a cash deal. The seller went with that one. But we'll keep looking, okay?"

"*Shit!* Sorry, but I'm just in *shock*," Brad replied. "I have to process this before I'm ready to look at anything else—*nothing* could compare to *that* house. I really thought it would be *mine!*" He disconnected and silenced his phone.

Lillian reached out for his hand. "Oh, Brad, my poor boy! You look like someone just died."

"Not some*one*, but some*thing did*—my *vision* just died." He grimaced and hung his head. "Now I have to keep living in limbo. Stuck in that blah utilitarian so-called 'residence'. I don't know how much longer I can *stand* it. I was *so excited* about packing up and leaving it for a new start somewhere *really special*—and that *paradise* was just snatched away. It's like a *bad dream!*"

Sally silently handed him a tissue, then Lillian handed him a change in perspective. "Brad, I know this is a blow. Of course, it hurts. It's hard; but we can do 'hard'. My sponsor, Sebastian, taught me that. And to start by looking at a hard situation in a different way. I just started applying that to losing George, and I'm feeling better than I have for three years. You don't have to waste that much time; I've done that for you."

Brad looked up, his eyes still moist. "Yes. I *do* see you're more like yourself now. What am I not seeing here?"

"Well, first off, the house you were describing was nothing like what you'd had in mind before. It's much larger, and is really more ornate than the type of property you'd originally said you were looking for. So, this is a *new* vision. Now that you've seen it, maybe you'll want to redirect your search along those lines, or at least expand your criteria to include Victorian. There really are many homes in that era that were transitional, and properties are easily categorized as Victorian or Arts and Crafts, so if you include both, you'll see more properties."

He nodded. "You're right. I really didn't know I'd respond *so intensely* to that style."

"You may have shut down about the more decorative styles because of your years of negative experiences in the Italianate house you just fled. Understandable. Now, since you're an architect and design period rehabs, you can note the specific details from the house you tried to buy and look for a property that either has them or would lend itself to your *adding* them. You do this for clients all the time, and you have all of the resources to find things like that glorious window you told us about."

Micky spoke up. "Brad, if you design things like that, how could you not know how much you like them?"

He thought for a moment, stroking his chin. "I guess when I work for a client, I'm detached—it's professional, not *personal*. I can spec things and find them in the salvage stores, knowing they're right for the space. But when I check the installation, I'm looking at our workers' quality and if the final project works. I'm not *experiencing* it—or seeing myself living there. It's *their* home, not mine."

Lillian smiled. "Brad, you'll be fine. You may be wise to take a break from chasing listings for a bit, and just keep your eyes open and network to find properties that might be available to someone like you before the owners put them on the open market." She turned to

Micky. "You mentioned before church that you had some good news to tell us?"

Micky blushed, and decided to downplay her good fortune. Now just didn't seem right for a victory lap in light of Brad's deflated expectations. "Well, it isn't a *done deal* yet . . . but I created a program plan for a new client that would run this year and give me about *half* of the *obscene* quota increase I'm saddled with. I pitched it last week with my boss . . . and the owner *really* seemed to like it. He *verbally* agreed to go with it . . . and called me on Friday to schedule lunch to discuss some questions and details so I can write up a formal letter of agreement. And Jack is being *much nicer* to me now."

Brad smiled for the first time since the devastating phone call. "That sounds like *great* news, Micky! And I'm especially glad to hear that Jack's laying off—does this mean you'll get your Cadillac soon?"

With a mischievous smile, Micky bobbed her head yes. "*Actually,* that's part of the deal. The client is a Cadillac dealer, in addition to Volvo, BMW, Lexus and Infinity . . . all five are included in the sales incentive program, and a trade agreement for my Cadillac lease is part of the budget. Our company won't have to make any cash outlay for it . . . I knew Jack would *particularly* like that, and wouldn't pass it up!"

Brad whistled. "You *are* good! I'm *impressed*. And, *see*—you *can* do your thing sober; I knew you were *worried* about that."

"How did you *know?*"

"We *all* experience that when we come in," he replied. Lillian and Sally nodded in agreement. "Look at me; I even changed careers—although mine was more about avoiding the booze-soaked restaurant biz. I still enjoy cooking and baking. But I've always *loved* old houses, so I got the training to make my living pursuing *that* passion."

He looked at his sponsor. "Lil, the Preservation Society's April meeting is Saturday evening. May I take you to dinner first?"

CHAPTER 12

March was going out like a lamb in the month's final week, and Micky celebrated the warmer spring weather by wearing a long-sleeved light green dress with low-heeled pumps. Paul Price admired the dress's fit as he followed her to his favorite table by the windows with vistas of the Club's patio and golf course.

"Order anything you want," he said as Micky studied the menu. "I'm having the strip steak. Everything here is always excellent."

"The salmon sounds good to me."

Their waitress reappeared with the iced teas they'd requested and he said, "I'd like the strip steak, medium, and the lady will have the salmon."

Micky looked around the elegant dining room with its beamed ceiling, then out at the forested, park-like fairways. "This is beautiful," she said. "And very quiet . . . a great place to talk."

"Yes. I do a lot of business here, as well as socializing and, of course, golf," he said. "My family was among the charter members when the club opened in 1905. We had a large hardware business at the time; my grandfather got into the automobile business in 1913 as one of Cadillac's early dealerships in Ohio."

"So, you grew up in the dealership . . . is that what you always wanted to do?"

"Oh yes. I'm a car guy. I've always loved cars—and business," he said. "I love selling them and working with people. That's mainly why I don't have any general managers at our stores; I prefer to handle that role myself. It also means I can keep an eye on everything." He paused as their meals were served.

Micky said, "I can understand that . . . but it sounds like *a lot* of work . . . I'm amazed you can find time to play golf!"

Paul grinned. "Well, a lot of my golf games are business. But you're right. There isn't much time for anything else, which was a big reason for my divorce five years ago. That and my two children moving out as they launched their careers. My son, an attorney with a large firm, is twenty-five and my twenty-three-year-old daughter works for an interior design company. They both went to Northwestern, and decided to stay in Chicago after graduation. So, what about you?"

She took a sip of her iced tea. "My father is managing partner for a national media representative firm. He has always spent most of his time on the road . . . when he was home, he focused on bringing me up to be successful, steering me toward a sales career. I remember when I was five or six, I'd made a bunch of loops on paper with a crayon, pretending to do cursive writing . . . he picked it up and declared I *had* written a word: it was *selling*."

Laughing, Paul said, "Well, you're certainly good at it! What about marriage? Any kids?"

"Never even close. My parents' marriage and my father's subsequent ones didn't make it look appealing," she replied. "I'm happy to focus on my career . . . actually, I started working when I was four . . . as a model for ads selling bread, cereal, ice cream, kids' clothes, you name it. I was always happiest when I was working."

"A kindred spirit—that's refreshing!" Paul smiled as the server refreshed their tea. "I reviewed the information you left with me. Very complete, thank you, and the cost figures all look appropriate. I do believe this program can give my people an exciting challenge to up their games and be rewarded. I'd like to increase the budget to give

Family of Choice: Raising Each Other

trips to the top *two* winners at each store for new and used. In all cases, there are two reps who're always ahead of the pack, so I want to make sure they're all rewarded. They're always competing against each other anyway, and the program's recognition aspects will increase that drive. But I also want something to give the others a shot at some kind of runners-up prize, without going to ten more trips. Any ideas?"

"Sure . . . what about putting the names of the third-place winners from each dealership into a drawing for *two more* trips, with the rest of them earning three thousand more merchandise award points? The extra points *look* significant, but the cost is about five hundred apiece, or an extra four thousand to your program cost for both new and used. The two extra trips for that level plus your additional ten top winners adds another thirty thousand . . . so thirty-four thousand total additional spend."

"Let's do it. We need the extra winners."

Micky smiled, but looked puzzled. "That's great, I'll make the changes to the program rules and budget . . . but I'll admit, this is a first for me. Usually, clients look for ways to *cut* costs . . . will the new numbers still work for your payback?"

"Of course. All of our people are good, and they're very competitive. They'll all put the pedal to the metal and will produce the payback gains and then some."

Paul put his napkin on the table beside his plate. "Unless you'd like dessert, let's go drive some cars so you can pick out the trophy for your victory-lap year."

As they approached the dark blue CTS sedan he'd driven to the club, he handed Micky the key. "This is the model and trim level leased by most companies. See if you like how it drives."

Micky adjusted the seat and started the engine. The car smoothly glided out of the parking lot, and Paul interspersed driving directions with descriptions of its features. Micky said, "Thank you for lunch . . . the club is so lovely, and the salmon was delicious."

"I'm glad you enjoyed it. I also belong to the country clubs in Westlake and Avon, where I live. Many of my customers come from those areas."

"That must keep you busy."

"Again, it's business. I try to maintain a regular presence at all three."

The road went from two lanes to four and the speed limit increased to fifty-five. Micky accelerated, noting that only the speedometer revealed a faster speed. "Wow . . . I'll really have to watch it to avoid getting a ticket!"

"Take the ramp coming up to get on Ninety-East, and press the switch behind the gear shift for sport mode. It's great for accelerating into highway traffic."

She did, and the car leaped forward when she stepped on the gas. "This is like a Thoroughbred coming out of the starting gate! And it's still smooth, yet it feels more responsive."

When she was in her lane and at sixty-five, Paul told her how to engage the cruise control. He had her take the next exit and return to the dealership. She easily pulled into a parking spot in front of the door, as directed. "What do you think?" he asked.

"It's very nice . . . *obviously much* better than the Regal."

"What kind of driving do you do for work and commuting?"

"Well, it *has* been mostly city driving with some urban and suburban highways. I live in Strongsville near our office . . . but with my new territory expansion, I'll be doing *a lot* more interstate driving and will be out of the office *much* more."

"What about color, exterior and interior? Do you like this one?"

"The blue is nice, and very corporate . . . but kind of boring. And the interior is kind of funky . . . not sure what color it is, but it's very dark."

"Yes, Dark Adriatic Blue Metallic is a very popular fleet color," Paul confirmed. "The interior color is called 'Carbon Plum'. It's new this year, and people either really love it or hate it; it sounds like you're in the latter group. What's your favorite color?"

"Red. But since all of my cars except my first one, a used Camaro, have been company cars, they've all been blue, gray or silver . . . those were my only choices. And most had black or charcoal interiors, which were always hot any time the sun was out."

Inside the showroom, he invited Micky to sit at the round table next to the door and proceeded behind a counter holding a laptop. He consulted the screen and texted a request through the inventory system.

Joining her, Paul said, "I think you'll like this one. It's more suited to what you want, and your boss will be happy, too. Its sticker price is about six thousand less than the CTS you just drove. And it takes regular gas."

Micky's blue eyes widened and her face lit up as a rich, bright red, slightly sporty four-door midsize car with slim lines accented by chrome-look trim pulled up by the door. "Oh my! It's *gorgeous!*"

Paul smiled. "Red Passion Tricoat outside, Maple Sugar interior. This is new this year. Come take a look."

As they walked around the vehicle, Paul explained, "It's an XT5, which stands for 'crossover touring' five-seater. Plenty of room and comfort for passengers. A three-point-six-liter V-six engine gives it plenty of power. Like the first one, it's a Luxury All Wheel Drive, similar interior appointments plus a lot more electronics. Its 4G LTE, wireless charging, built-in wi-fi hotspot and four USB ports give you an office on wheels, and OnStar along with the map and compass display will help you find your way in unfamiliar areas. OnStar also gets you help if you ever have trouble on the road. Heated seats and steering wheel, and a Bose Premium eight-speaker sound system will make your travels more comfortable."

"That sounds wonderful! It almost makes me look forward to traveling." Micky, who had examined every nook and cranny of the car, completed her inspection. "I like that the rear hatch cargo space is ample for luggage and anything else I'm likely to need without having to fold down the rear seats."

She got into the driver's seat. "Nice . . . I can get into it in a skirt without having to *climb* like most SUVs, but it does give me enough elevation that I can see the road better." Paul, now in the passenger's seat, gave her time to explore all of the controls, answering any questions.

They took the same highway route as before, but returned by a two-lane road skirting the Black River Reservation until they turned off toward Midway. When she had parked by the showroom, she turned to Paul with dancing eyes and an excited smile. "I *really love* this car!"

Smiling back, he said, "I thought you would. I'll email you the lease numbers and details for your boss's approval, and the bottom-line deduction from the new budget. Can we get this written up and signed by Friday?"

*****

Jack drove when he and Micky returned for the contract signing, as her early-return clause for the Regal's lease required turn-in to the originating Buick dealer. Since she had emailed the letter of agreement to Paul the previous day for him to study, he just needed a quick look-over before signing.

Then he asked, "Micky, I'm planning to have a kickoff meeting in two weeks. Could you come and present the program to my team? I'd rather have you explain the rules and answer any questions, and you can use your previous slides to create excitement—it certainly did with me!"

"Of course. I already have our creative team working on the program theme and literature. I'll talk with them this afternoon to get the materials ready by then," she said after an approving nod from Jack.

"And, maybe a couple of weeks later, I'd really appreciate it if you'd share ideas on finding research sources for prospecting at our May staff lunch-and-learn. My people can use a fresh perspective to improve on what they're already doing," he asked. Looking at Jack, he added, "If that's permissible?"

Jack hesitated. "That's not usually in the scope of services we provide. But you're a new client and this is a substantial program. We want to do whatever we can to make sure it's a success, and hopefully, the beginning of an ongoing relationship. Micky, is this okay with you?"

"Yes, I think it's a great idea!"

Jack stood up to conclude their meeting. "Sounds good." Shaking Paul's hand, he said, "Thank you for your business. We look forward to working with you." He also shook Micky's hand. "Congratulations, Micky. Enjoy your Top Dog award—hopefully enough so you win it for another year! See you back at the office."

After he left, Paul told Micky, "Due to the size of the group, we'll be using a conference room at the Club. I'll reserve the dates and let you know. Both will include lunch. Now, let's get you into your first Cadillac."

He walked her out to the gleaming red vehicle, its chrome sparkling from its delivery wash and polish. "Red Passion! Such a perfect name for this color . . . and for the car. I haven't named a car since the one I got for my sixteenth birthday, but this one is special!"

He handed her the key fob and opened the driver's door. She got in, adjusted the mirrors, buckled up and started the engine. Then she put the window down. "Paul, I'm really glad you've invited me to be a part of the program. Thank you for everything! This is going to be really fun!"

"You're more than welcome. I greatly look forward to working with you. See you in two weeks!" He smiled, and was still smiling as he watched her drive the XT5 out of the lot.

CHAPTER 13

Lillian sat on the side of her Art Deco guest-room bed, surrounded by heaps of dresses thrown in disgust when she'd discovered they no longer fit. Pretty Girl, who'd appeared when alerted by her feline instinct of the sudden opening of a long-closed door, also abandoned the closet and jumped up beside her. She reached out to shoo her away, then petted her instead.

"I guess it doesn't matter if you shed on them now, Pretty. A little cat hair won't reduce their donation value."

She shook her head in dismay, and continued talking to the calico. "Some coming-out event. I forgot that April's meeting is the Oberlin Heritage Center's Annual Meeting and community awards ceremony. Like most of the women, I've always dressed up a little; not a cocktail dress, but one that I'd wear to an evening wedding or a writers' conference awards dinner. I had no idea I'd gained that much weight over the past three years—this old debutante has nothing to wear!"

Sighing, she rose and went to the second closet, where she kept the outfits she wore to church or book signings. Rifling through the hangers, she paused at a dark blue tweed suit that had a skirt. She took the jacket to the gaping door, pulled a few lustrous silk blouses from the corner into the light and selected a light blue one with attached streamers for a bow. "With my good pearl earrings, this should pass."

She hung the blouse with the suit, restoring the jacket to its hanger. Then she sat on the bench of the bedroom set's vanity in front of its large round mirror. "I've just been using powder and lipstick for so long—do I have any blush and eye makeup left?" She fumbled through the top drawers and found a Dior pressed powder eye-shadows compact in shades of blue as well as her old stand-by Clinique peach blush. More digging produced bronze highlighter powder. However, all three mascara tubes she opened produced nothing but dried crumbs of color. "These are all toast," she declared as she tossed them into the waste basket. "Oh, well, we go to war with the army we've got—praise the Lord and pass the ammunition!" She paused, then added, "Wow, Pretty, that really dates me: that saying came out of World War Two!"

She did a creditable job of applying the goods, surprising herself, although she found that aged eye shadows didn't blend very smoothly. Mercifully, the blouse fit and the bow was easy to tie. Then she sucked in her breath as she pulled up the skirt, holding it as she successfully zipped up. "Hooray! Oh, now, where are the pumps that go with this?"

Finding them in the back of the closet, she stepped into the navy shoes and promptly realized she'd forgotten how to walk in three-inch heels as she nearly fell over the indignant cat. "Shit! I can't make it down the stairs in these—and now Brad's here!" She had the presence of mind to sit on the vanity bench to remove them, then hurried to the closet for her go-to black ballet flats, grabbed her usual black Sunday service purse and remembered to put on the jacket, swipe on her lipstick and add the pearl earrings. She hustled down the hall and staircase, making it to the front foyer just as Brad rang the bell.

She opened the door and joined him on the wrap-around porch. "Brad, Brad, Brad! You did *not* give me enough time for this!" she chided.

Confused, he consulted his watch, but Lillian shook her head. "No, you've arrived at the agreed time. What I mean is that I needed time to shop for a whole new wardrobe—none of my nicer dresses fit anymore!"

*****

Lillian had never heard of the restaurant Brad had selected, nor had she ever envisioned this sleek modern décor of gray tones and stark white tablecloths as Italian. "I appreciate your remembering my favorite cuisine, Brad, but I'm feeling a bit like Rip Van Winkle awakening after twenty years," she said. "Doesn't anyone use red-and-white checkered table coverings anymore?"

"Um, not much! But the food here is *outstanding*—I'm sure you'll enjoy it, despite the less-than-cozy atmosphere."

Their waiter appeared, handed them book-like menus and rattled off several specials before departing. "I'm sure it's all good, but the choices are overwhelming; I think I'll go with the pasta special. It sounded delicious!" Seeing his slightly disappointed expression, she added, "I'm so glad we're doing this, really. But it's harder than I thought. I realize that I haven't dined out except at Dooley's and I'm there so often it's like my second kitchen. I know the entire menu by heart!"

He managed a sympathetic smile. "Happy to help, Lil. You've been there for me through *lots* of rough times—it's nice to have a chance to return the favor!"

"Speaking of which, how are you coping with the house that got away?"

The waiter returned for their orders, which gave Brad a chance to consider his reply. "Honestly? Not very well. I still can't erase the images of it from my mind, and the reality of the void is just one fathomless pit."

"Oh, Brad, I'm so sorry that didn't work out." She reached across the table to touch his hand. "And I'm glad you're willing to try networking tonight, taking some action that might move you toward your goal. I'm thinking we should split up during the social hour before the program; we can cover more ground that way, and it will give me something to say and a reason to move on before anyone starts talking about George. I'm not sure I could handle much of that."

"That sounds like a plan. I *hope* this will help—I'm not sure how much longer I can *stand* living in *limbo* in that hateful *hell-hole*."

"Well, tonight is just a start. I have another idea, too, if you're interested?"

"Sure. What?"

"Would you consider rehabbing George's office in the barn loft into an apartment? I'd pay for materials and any subcontractors you'd need. In return for your design and hands-on labor, you could live there rent-free in a more suitable temporary haven. It would be large enough for you to get your things out of storage, too."

He brightened. "Yes, I like that idea! I remember George talking about doing that—the longer he was retired, the more he realized he really didn't need an office anymore. He was planning to convert the whole loft, which is a *great space!*"

"Of course, if you find a house you want quickly, I'd pay you for your work," she said.

"No need, Lil. It's kind of you to offer—but, again, it's *the least* I can do for you!"

*****

Due to the expected number of attendees, the Annual Meeting was being held in an auditorium-style lecture hall at the university's history department rather than at the Heritage Center's headquarters, and the pre-meeting social hour was in the building's lobby. Brad led the way into the crowd. "Lordy!" gasped Lillian. "There must be over two hundred people here!"

"Do you still want to split up? We don't have to, you know."

"Thanks, Brad. But it's time I take the plunge. As my first sponsor used to say, 'Feel the fear and do it anyway!'" She scanned the edges of the crowd, since she was too short to look over it. "Oh. I see a familiar face! Meet me back here in forty-five minutes?"

He nodded, and she made a beeline for Dr. Ingles, the history professor who'd helped her with background facts when they created educational character sketches for the Center. "Troy! Wonderful to see you here! It's been ages since we worked on that project together; have you retired yet?"

"Lillian! Great to see you again, too!" He greeted her with a big smile and a quick hug. "Yes, I retired last year. Wish I'd done it sooner, like you! Keeping busy, I trust?"

"Of course; you know me! Working on another book. And I'm trying to help my young friend, Brad Mueller, find a Victorian or Arts and Crafts house, preferably one he can buy directly from the owner. He's looking for a lot of original design detail, and he's open to doing restoration; he's an architect for that vintage-properties design-build firm, Classic Homes Construction. Do you know anyone with that type of home who may be thinking of downsizing, or moving out of the area?"

"Oh, Classic Homes is a very good company! I'm sure people would be pleased to have their home go to someone like Brad, but I don't know of anyone planning to sell right now. I'll ask around though, and will call you with any leads I may find," he offered.

"That would be greatly appreciated, Troy, thanks," she replied. "It's been great chatting; hope to see you again soon!" She moved on, so pleased to realize that she had enjoyed the brief visit with her former colleague that she dove into repeating the process until the crowd began moving toward the auditorium. Like a salmon swimming upstream, she deftly threaded her way against the flow of humanity and joined Brad at the front doors.

"Do you mind if we make our getaway and skip the meeting and awards?" she asked.

"No problem. I'm not really interested in all of that," he agreed. "Let's head for the car."

"Did you have any luck with your networking?"

"Not really, but I talked to a lot of people who said they'd help get the word out. How about you?"

"Pretty much the same. But a couple of recent retirees from the university said they have friends with homes of the era who may be thinking of downsizing or moving to be near kids and grandchildren. They'll check that out and will call me with any leads," said Lillian. "In the meantime, do you have any plans for this Saturday?"

"Nothing other than the usual errands. What do you have in mind?"

She grinned. "When you're free in the afternoon, why don't you come over and we can start with cleaning out George's office, and we can kick around ideas for the remodel over dinner? I'll cook!"

"Deal!"

"Great! This will give me material for two more chapters of my 'Cat Hair' outline! And tonight's outing makes that three!"

*****

Brad was up early on the last Saturday in April, as he'd been for the previous three. He and Lillian had moved mountains of boxes containing the contents of George's office from the barn loft to her home's attic and had brainstormed about the renovation that same evening. Both were eager to move forward with the project, and their intense focus helped them cope with their emotions. A week later, Brad had drawings to review with her and had created a final set and budget that she approved.

This morning, he was reviewing the bill of materials he'd ordered, which were to be delivered that afternoon, when he was surprised by a knock at the front door.

He was shocked when the opened the door revealed a contrite-looking Oscar on the stoop, holding a nine-by-thirteen white envelope with a royal blue bow on it.

"Hello, Bradley. I'm sorry to bother you, but I owe you a profound apology for all of my past behavior and want to make things right between us, if that's possible," he said, extending the envelope toward Brad. "This is for you. May I please come in for a moment?"

CHAPTER 14

Too stunned to speak, Brad invited Oscar in with a curt nod and a gesture toward the living room. Oscar sat down on the small couch. Brad pulled over the desk chair to be close enough to accept the large envelope without sitting beside his ex.

"Thank you for letting me in, Bradley. I want you to know that the last eight years with you were the best of my life, and I deeply regret that they weren't as good for you. You made it clear that you're not coming back to our—rather, *my*—home, and I don't blame you. You want a fresh start in a home of your own. I just want you to be happy, and to help with that," he said, handing the beribboned offering to Brad. "I wanted to do this sooner, but it took a bit of time to pull everything together."

Puzzled, Brad opened the envelope and pulled out two sheets of paper. The top one was a quit claim deed and official property description, notarized and signed by Oscar with another blank for his own signature. The second page was a copy of the sell sheet for the house he'd tried to buy.

"*What* the *fuck? Is. This?! You—you* were the successful bidder on *my house!!* How the *hell* did you even *know* about it?"

"Bradley, Bradley, please. We both grew up in these small towns, you know how people talk. And the gay community here is even smaller. Everyone knows us, many wanted to help." Oscar shrugged with upturned palms and dark eyes pleading his case.

"Baxter."

Oscar looked down and away.

"That *sneaky bastard*. His name was familiar, but I didn't recognize his face. And he really has done business with our firm—I handled some work on his properties. I thought *that* was the connection."

"Yes. I've known him for years. He was at a couple of our parties, the larger ones where you may never have talked to him," Oscar admitted. "Please don't be mad. After my misjudgment with the Mercedes, I wanted to be sure to give you something you actually wanted, and you'd said you were house-hunting, so I called Bax. You just happened to engage him as your agent."

"Oh yes, I *really wanted* that house. Do you have any *idea* how *devastated* I've been since I lost out on buying it?"

Oscar, crestfallen, said, "I do now. I'm *so very sorry*, Bradley; the *last* thing I wanted to do was to cause you any pain. Once again, my intentions seem to backfire with my clumsy execution. Please accept my *additional* apologies for that, and please accept my parting gift."

"Thank you, Oscar, but I'd rather *buy it* from you."

"No need. Please? I already paid a premium price for the property, had the inspections done, closed the deal, recorded the deed, and hired an attorney to create the quit claim deed giving you the house. I won't take your money for it. If you can't accept my gift now, I'll rent it out in case you change your mind down the road."

Brad hesitated.

"At least please consider it," Oscar begged. "I understand how hurt and angry you are right now. You can set any conditions you want—any. Including my leaving you totally alone and never seeing you again. That would be hard, but I'd do it. I've never loved *anyone* like I love you."

Looking at his watch, Brad said, "I have to leave in a minute. I need to be present to sign for a delivery of materials at a job site. I'll think it over this afternoon."

"Could we discuss your thoughts over dinner? My treat, of course, anywhere you'd like."

"Fine. I'll meet you at seven—at Hyde Park in Crocker Park. I'm in the mood for steak."

*****

Brad arrived at Lillian's just in time to open the large double doors of the upper level of the classic bank barn's hay storage area and position himself to direct the lumber truck's driver past the house and up the short grade. He then ran into the garage section and up the stairs to guide him to back into the barn to make the delivery. Brad checked off everything on the bill of materials as the driver and helper unloaded the order, stacking specific items per his instructions. Smiling broadly after all the goods were in place, he shook their hands and thanked them for their excellent work, giving each a twenty-dollar tip before they departed.

"Impressive," said Lillian, who'd come up to watch. "I've never had the opportunity to see you in action, Brad. No wonder you're doing so well in your job; in addition to inspired designing, you're a meticulous project manager! George would be so proud of you!"

"Thanks, Lil—that means a lot to me."

"I made a fresh pot of coffee. Do you have time for a cup?"

"That would be great! These doors need to stay open for a bit to air out all of the exhaust fumes before I close up anyway. And, um, there's something I need to run by you."

Lillian kept silent as they walked down the driveway and through the back porch door to her cozy kitchen with its inviting aroma of ground and brewed beans. Seated at the table, Brad closed his eyes and inhaled the fragrance. "Jamaican?"

"Close," she replied. "Costco labeled this as Nicaraguan." She handed him a mug, and put a plate of cookies on the table before sitting down with her own. "I didn't bake this morning. I did my Saturday errands; picked up some Walker's Shortbread for us. So, what's on your mind?"

"Oscar paid me a surprise visit this morning."

"Oh?" Lillian tried to keep her expression and voice neutral.

"He was the other bidder on my house—and he presented me with a quit claim deed to it. I offered to buy it from him, but he refused. He insists on giving it to me, says if I don't take it, he'll rent it out in case I'll change my mind later."

"Oh!" Her brows shot toward the ceiling and her widened eyes betrayed her dismay. Struggling to return to impartiality, the best she could manage to say was, "And?"

"And I said I'd think about it." Brad sipped his coffee and reached for a shortbread cookie.

"Ah. So, what strings are attached to this gift house? One is tempted to think of the Trojans."

He couldn't suppress a smirk. "Not my *brand*, but I'll be sure to stay safe. Actually, there are no strings from *him*—he said he'll accept any conditions *I* might want. We're meeting for dinner to talk about that. I know I'll need a lawyer to review the deed and advise me on any legal considerations or obligations connected with this. Do you know anyone?"

"Wouldn't your agent know attorneys who specialize in real estate matters?"

He scowled. "That *double-dealing son*-of-a-*bitch!* Sorry! But *he's* the one who told Oscar about my offer to buy the property."

"I'll call my lawyer and see if he can help you, or recommend someone who can."

"Thanks, Lil! I won't do *anything* until I can check this out thoroughly. That will be at the top of my list for tonight's discussion. I'll also have a number of iron-clad boundaries for Oscar, some of which I'll ask the attorney about possible legal means to enforce, if necessary," he said, adding, "And don't worry—I'll move forward with *our* project, no matter *what* happens with the house."

"I'm not worried about that, Brad, I'm worried about you. This just doesn't seem like a good idea."

"Yeah, well—returning to your horse analogy, I'm reminded of a news article I once read about Jacqueline Kennedy when she was First Lady. The President told her that recently-passed ethics rules meant that they couldn't accept the gift of two Arabian horses from the emissary of a middle-eastern nation's ruler. She reportedly replied to her husband, 'I understand. But there's a problem with that: You see, I *want* the horses.'"

*****

Oscar was already seated at a corner table when Brad arrived, and stood to greet him. Impeccably yet casually dressed, his camel jacket and brilliant white Egyptian cotton shirt, open at the collar, showcased his flowing black hair, slightly olive complexion with perfectly groomed beard and large, deep brown liquid eyes topped by expressive dark brows. He still conjured up images in Brad's mind of a cover illustration on a steamy romance novel, or maybe a snake charmer.

Brad extended his hand to avoid an embrace, and sat down across the table.

"Thank you for coming, Bradley," Oscar said. "I know this is hard, at least it is for me, and I'm guessing it's no picnic for you either."

"No, no picnic. More of a steak dinner—where I'm hoping the knives will be restricted to cutting the meat on our respective plates."

Oscar relaxed a little with a slight smile and chuckle. "I've always loved your sense of humor, among many other things. I'm so sorry I didn't demonstrate that better when we were together, and I really do want to do the best I can to make things right between us. Even if it's just for peaceful closure. Have you given consideration to accepting my gift of the house?"

"Yes. And yes, I'd very much like to accept the house—with conditions. First of which will be reviewing the quit claim deed with a qualified attorney. While it appears straightforward, it's just due diligence to check. And I'd appreciate copies of any inspection findings and the contacts—these usually have a number of items that the new owner should take care of, even if they aren't violations, and that would be very helpful to me in keeping the house at its best."

The waiter appeared. Both chose to start with lobster bisque. Brad ordered the bone-in ribeye, rare, with jumbo crab, asparagus and bearnaise sauce and a side of roasted Brussel sprouts with bacon marmalade; Oscar went with the Chilean sea bass with crystal citrus sauce and sautéed spinach and mushrooms.

"I'll send you copies of all paperwork concerning the property, and a legal review certainly makes sense," Oscar said. "Do you have any other concerns or conditions around this?"

"Oh yes—it needs to be agreed that this property transfer is in *no way* conditional upon resuming our relationship. I'll ask the attorney if there's any *legal* need for language to that effect, but in any event, you need to be *perfectly clear* on that," Brad insisted. "You're a most *handsome* and *charming* devil—but the *devil* part now outweighs your attributes. The *verbal* abuse was bad enough, but the escalation to *physical* was a wake-up call. I don't feel *safe* with you, Oscar—and I didn't get sober or develop my career to *live* like that. I now have a *zero-tolerance* policy for abusive behavior of *any* flavor from *anyone* in my life—*especially* from someone who *claims* to *love* me."

Oscar hung his head. "I know, I know. That's why I believe I owe you a major form of restitution. If we'd been married, I'd owe you half of our house and contents; but we weren't, and you never liked my house or décor, so this method makes sense to me."

The waiter arrived with their bisque. When he departed, Oscar continued, "I'm so ashamed of my behavior; I don't want to live like that, either. It woke me up, too, and I've been working with a therapist since you left. And I'll continue in therapy whether you accept the house or not, and whether we get back together on any basis or not." He looked up, and Brad saw a new vulnerability in his eyes.

"I'm glad to hear that," he said. "I'm living proof that with *work*, people *can change*—sometimes a *lot*. I'm *not* the *same person* I was when we first got together, when I was a broke student, still drinking after swilling away my career. I believe you're still *in love* with who you *think* I am—but you don't *really know* me now. You may not even *like* me—but *I do*."

They finished their soups in silence.

Oscar said, "You're right. I *don't* really know you; you've grown up over the last seven years. You've grown into a strong, principled and admirable man, whom I'd like to *get* to know better. *If* and *when* you decide to let me."

Brad saw earnestness in his facial expression and forward-leaning body language. And he felt an uncharacteristic sincerity from Oscar.

He chewed on these observations as well as his steak when their meals were served. Perhaps the therapy was working. Gone was the typical arrogance displayed in their previous life and during their last encounter after he'd moved out. Maybe there was a chance?

"Okay," he said. "Pending a green light from the attorney, I'll cordially accept your gift of the house. Honestly, I don't know about anything else right now—but if there *is*, it will need to be *very slow* and *not* start immediately. *I'll* call *you*."

"Thank you, Bradley. You deserve the house, and to live in it happily and peacefully."

"If we *do* start seeing each other again, you will need to *call before* coming over, and I can say 'no'—no more surprise visits."

"Agreed. I will remember basic manners. If you like, I'd be happy to help with any redecorating or furnishings; you can get my twenty percent trade discount," Oscar offered.

"This may come as a *news flash* to you, but I've been in the trade *myself* for the last several years—and I have my own resources. But thanks," Brad said. "And thanks for dinner. Hopefully, I can clear things with the attorney in the next week or so, and I'll courier your copy of the signed quit claim deed."

Oscar smiled. "And I'll send you the keys."

CHAPTER 15

Micky loved the spring, especially when the flowering trees were in bloom, and this mid-May Sunday morning was perfect. She'd reveled in the fresh morning air and the fragrance of the white crabapple blooms in the gardens by the Grace Church parking lot upon arrival, and now admired the soft, clear colors of the east windows that were illuminated by tender sunlight. She was glad that Lillian preferred to sit on the aisle, because it gave her the full view of the prophets depicted in the stained-glass portraits.

She was becoming more familiar with the liturgy, and enjoyed participating with the help of the service bulletin. Now she was able to focus more on the messages. Today, three words of a hymn particularly caught her attention, and she repeated them in her mind: God is love.

That theme was also in the Holy Gospel that Sally read, John 15:9-17, and she built on it in her sermon.

"In the first sentence of our Gospel reading for today, Jesus tells his disciples that he has loved them just as his Father has loved him. And while Jesus was *directly* God's son thanks to the Holy Spirit and the Virgin Mary, we, too, are *all* children of God, and he loves us, too. As our Episcopal Diocesan slogan proclaims, 'God loves you. No exceptions.®'

"Yes, you. And me. Despite our many sins, imperfections and mistakes, God loves us. He does *not* love our sins, but he does love *us*, his human children, sinners all, with the exception of Christ Jesus, whom he sent to show us how he would have us live and to take our sins with him to the cross to save us.

"As mere mortal humans in this world, we can't perceive how *much* God loves us. But we can try. In last week's Gospel, Jesus compared his love for his disciples to that of a mother hen, gathering her chicks under her wings to shield them from danger. This being Mother's Day, that's a timely image. Happy Mother's Day to all of the mothers in our congregation this morning! And we all have or have had mothers; so, take a moment to reflect on the strength and intensity of your mother's love for you . . . then try to imagine that magnified to be a trillion times greater! Then believe that God's love is even greater than that."

Sally paused for a moment, then continued. "Unfortunately, for many people, that's not where they experienced anything like God's love. For many of us, our source of unconditional love and support was elsewhere—perhaps a grandparent, an aunt or uncle, a sibling or other family member. Or maybe we had to find that kind of love outside of our family of origin.

"For some of us, our experience is more like Jesus's love for his disciples, which he tells them to give to each other. He tells them *twice* in this short passage. 'Remain faithful to my love for you. If you obey me, I will keep loving you, just as my Father keeps loving me, because I have obeyed him. Now I tell you to love each other, as I have loved you.' In fact, Jesus made it a commandment in the last line of the passage: 'So I command you to love each other.'

"Christ also reminded his disciples that he chose them and sent them out to produce fruit that will last. And that fruit is sharing the good news of God's love. As Christians, we are charged with that mission: To see Christ's love in each other and to share it with more people.

"I see it and feel it here in our parish family. We genuinely care about and support each other, and live that out in our ministries and in our community. I see it in our kitchen.

"I see it also in our former gymnasium, in the many recovery groups that meet there. And beyond the food and the sobriety that people find here, the real fruit is the welcome, fellowship and feeling of connectedness that develops in these settings. Some of us find our main source of sustaining love in these ad hoc families of choice and the deep friendships and trust that they foster.

"The refrain of the hymn we just sang sums it up: God is love, and he is with us wherever true love is.

"In the name of Christ. Amen."

After the service was over and most people had exited the church, Micky approached Sally, who had changed out of her vestments. "Today's service was very special to me . . . *especially* your sermon. *Thank you* for talking about families where there's no love available, and *alternatives* where we can find it. I feel it in this church . . . in our sponsorship family, and in my talks with Brad. But the *best* thing for me this morning was that description of God . . . God is love. That's *simple* enough for me to use . . . *really* use to move forward in my program. Brad and I have studied Step Three in the Big Book and the Twelve and Twelve, but I wasn't comfortable enough to formally take the step . . . I mean, how could I *seriously* turn my will and my life over to a God that I knew *nothing* about? Now, I know as much as I need to do that!"

Sally smiled and hugged her. "Oh, Micky, I'm so happy for you! Would you like to do that now? Or would you rather take it with Brad?"

Without hesitation Micky replied, "Now would be great! Brad had suggested I come to this church to develop my understanding of

God, and in addition to being my friend, you *are* my *priest*. And I'm hoping you'll be guiding me to learn more over time."

"Me, too. Would you prefer the chapel? It's more private."

"That sounds good. Thanks!"

She followed Sally into the chapel, where she knelt at the small altar rail and invited Micky to join her. "I'll say the prayer first, then you will. Do you know it, or did you bring your Big Book?"

"I think I know it . . . I've been reading it a lot lately."

"Would you like me to hold your hand?" Micky nodded. Sally recited the Third Step prayer, then gave Micky's hand a gentle squeeze.

Micky then repeated it. She offered herself to God to use her for his purposes, and asked to be released from her prison of self-interest to be freed up to do God's will. She also prayed for God to remove her problems so that she could help others by showing how she benefits from God's power, love, and way of living. She concluded by asking God's help to follow his guidance always.

Sally hugged her. "There! You're on your way!" she said, then stood up.

Remaining on her knees, Micky told her, "When I just finished that prayer, a warm, sort of tingling feeling wrapped around me like a blanket . . . and it's still there. I've felt it before in this church . . . but this is *much stronger*."

Smiling, Sally sat on one of the front chairs. "I feel it, too. Many of us have experienced it here."

"What is it?"

"I think of it as the palpable presence of God with us, or perhaps the Holy Spirit." They lingered in silence for a few minutes before Micky rose from the altar rail.

"I'm sure Brad's stressed that this step is just making a decision," Sally said. "The big part is putting it into action! I say this prayer every morning to remind myself of that. After all, our problems or sins are usually a result of our unrestrained will running amok."

Micky laughed. "Oh, I can relate to that!"

Sally said, "You also seemed to relate to my talking about troubled families. As you already know, I was speaking from my own experience. I have plenty of experience, strength and hope to share in that area, and I do a lot of counseling in my vocation, if you'd ever like to talk."

"Thanks, Sally . . . I have a feeling I may need that . . . especially as I get into Step Four."

"You can call any time as an A.A. member in a crisis or with a question. To dig into your past or for therapeutic help for problems or deep issues, we'll schedule sessions. I had a counseling practice prior to seminary, and I've maintained my license," she said. "Now, let's go see what Lil has baked for us!"

When they arrived at the back porch door, Brad opened it. "There you are! Lil wouldn't let me cut into the blackberry cobbler until you got here—I was getting anxious! And *hungry*."

"Sorry, Brad," Micky said. "I wanted to talk to Sally after the service . . . and then I ended up taking Step Three with her!"

Brad enfolded her in a bear hug. "Wonderful! Congratulations, Micky!" Over her shoulder, he silently mouthed "Thank You" to Sally, who nodded and smiled.

Lillian emerged from the butler's pantry with plates of cobbler. "I heard your news from the kitchen, Micky. Good for you! You two know where the coffee is, so help yourselves. And there's cobbler plated up there for you, too."

When they were all at the table, Lillian said to Brad, "So. Is your move still on for tomorrow?"

"Yes, thank God! I met the locksmith at the house yesterday, and got my new keys. I confirmed with the mover—they'll meet me at my storage locker at nine. They'll load the furniture, books and crated art on their truck, and I'll put delicate things like lamps in my car. Then we'll clean out the few things I have at the rental and head for home!"

"I am happy for you, Brad. I know how much this house means to you," she said. "I just hope there aren't any, shall we say, complications that arise down the road from it."

"All of the paperwork is properly filed, Lil, and your lawyer checked everything. He saw no potential problems," he replied. "By the way, thank you for recommending him."

"I wasn't thinking of legal pitfalls. I just can't help worrying about Oscar. It's hard to believe someone would give anyone a house—without expectations. Let alone the hurtful way he orchestrated this 'gift.'"

"Wait," said Micky. "*Oscar* bought the house out from under you . . . and then *gave* it to you? Why would he *do* that?"

"He's been working with a therapist, and said he realizes how badly he'd treated me. He feels he owes me restitution—like an amend. But since I didn't want the Mercedes he'd bought for me, he needed to find something I *did* want. And he *apologized* for causing me pain in the process."

Micky sighed. "While that sounds pretty *twisted* . . . it also sounds like something my father would do. It never really made up for his actions, but I realized a long time ago that it was probably the best he could do. Maybe Oscar's like that."

Brad smiled at her and joked, "I like that thinking—remember it when you write about your dad in your Fourth Step list!"

"Okay, I will. Still . . . how can Oscar *afford* gifts like a Mercedes or a house? I didn't think college professors made that much money."

"They don't," Lillian said.

"Besides his salary, Oscar has a pretty lucrative interior design business," Brad explained. "And beyond that, he has a very large trust fund from his grandfather's estate, along with the house he inherited, which is fabulous but just never was my taste. And *now*, I have a fabulous home of *my own!*"

*****

Moving day dawned brightly, and Brad was up at first light. He'd spent the previous day and evening packing up his minimal belongings and restoring the rental's furnishings to their original places. He dressed and loaded his personal items, laptop and his two lamps in the Mini Cooper Clubman. Breakfast was coffee and two Egg McMuffins from the McDonald's drive-through, consumed en route to the storage unit.

He parked near it, careful to allow room for the moving truck. He unlocked and raised the overhead door, then took all of the small, delicate items and stowed them in his car, using the rolled throw rugs and a few decorative pillows wrapped in trash bags for padding.

While he waited for the movers, Brad surveyed the locker's remaining contents, some of which he'd recently added from his parents' basement where they'd been stored. There'd been no space at Oscar's for his bed and dresser, dining room set and the nine-by-twelve Oriental he'd used with it. Ditto for his dishes, china, stemware and flatware.

The movers arrived, and made short work of loading while Brad returned the lock and key to the office and closed out his account. Likewise, he didn't have much for them to do when they packed up his temporary quarters. He'd kept the crates for the two paintings he'd hung there, so they had only to add the paintings and reclose them. And his clothes only required two wardrobe boxes and two large square cartons. He'd already packed up kitchen goods in their previous labeled boxes. While they worked, he put the contents of the refrigerator into a small cooler and took it plus two bags of grocery items from the cupboard to the Clubman.

When the truck was loaded, Brad locked the door for the satisfying last time and nearly skipped with joy as he took the key to the office. The middle-aged woman with dry hennaed hair checked his signed paperwork terminating the rental and asked, "How was your stay with us?"

He replied with a tight-lipped smile. "I guess you could say it was inspirational."

Brad led the way to his new home. With glee, he nearly danced up the front steps and opened the front and foyer doors, then came out on the porch to direct traffic.

Unloading seemed even faster than loading the truck. The crated paintings went into the living room for now, as he only knew at this point where three of them would go. Most boxes went into the large corner of the kitchen, the ones with table linens and china in the dining room for the breakfront, towels and bedding upstairs into the hallway near the linen closet, clothes in his bedroom along with his Craftsman double bed and dresser, and a five-by-seven Turkish rug. His antique oak desk, chair and bookcases went in the first-floor sunroom, and they placed them as he had planned when he first saw the house. They fit perfectly. His other five-by-seven rug also worked well in the office, where he added his two antique table lamps, one on his desk, the other on a bookcase. A pair of Craftsman cushioned chairs with ottomans were carried upstairs to the front bedroom with the fireplace, soon to become the TV den—once he bought a flat-screen.

"That it?" the driver asked. "You got a lotta empty rooms."

"Yes, that's it," Brad said, tipping him. "I've got a lot of shopping to do."

It was just after one o'clock when the truck departed. Brad went into the kitchen and unpacked his cooler, leaving out the turkey, leaf lettuce, muenster cheese, Dijon and mayo to make himself a sandwich on whole wheat bread, which he consumed while unpacking the kitchen essentials boxes and minimal groceries that moved from the temp quarters. Next, he went upstairs to unpack bedding and towels. Now that he had two full baths, the only things left to go into the linen closet were his flannel sheets and heavy blankets. He decided to steal the face towels from the second bath to use in the powder room under the stairs for now, mentally adding hand towels to his shopping list.

Returning to the master suite, he made his bed and unpacked his clothes, then took a breather out on the balcony. The temperature had risen to the low seventies, and he saw a few gray-haired retirees busily mowing their lawns and tending their gardens, which were full of iris and azalea blooms. He smiled, enjoying the view of his new community—and noticed that his own grass badly needed attention. Not owning a lawn mower or any gardening tools, he'd need to find a service to handle that, at least in the short term. Another list entry.

That brought his mind back to his current tasks. Withdrawing from the balcony, he went downstairs and completed the kitchen boxes, deciding which things to put in the cabinets over and under the counters and which to store in the butler's pantry. His maternal grandmother's china, crystal stemware, sterling flatware and serving pieces were displayed in the dining room sideboard's leaded-glass cabinets, cupboards and drawers. He thought of her fondly, remembering how she had stuck by him when he came out, and that she bequeathed these things to him when he broke with his family's medical tradition, knowing that in his culinary career he'd be the one most likely to use them.

Unpacking his books and desk items in the sunroom office was quick work. When he finished, it was four-thirty and he realized he was hungry and didn't have anything for dinner on hand. He grabbed his phone and texted Lillian: Hi Neighbor! I'm starved. Meet me @ Dooley's in 20? I'll buy!

Sure! See you there.

It was rare for her to reply instantly, and he was grateful. He was even more grateful when he realized that his go-to restaurant was just three blocks away, so he set out on foot. Lillian was already seated at a table when he arrived, since she had driven there.

"Walking through these beautiful tree-lined streets made me really feel part of the neighborhood—*home*, at *last*," he explained. "And then I realized that I haven't felt that—haven't really *had* a home of my *own* since I left New York almost *ten years* ago! First, I stayed at my parents' house, then moved in with Oscar."

"Oh, Brad! Now I better understand your urgency to find a house, and the depth of your pain when you lost the bidding for the one you loved so much."

"Thanks, Lil. I hadn't connected the dots myself until now," he replied. "Can you also understand why I was even willing to accept it from Oscar?"

"It does put that in a different perspective." She paused while the waitress took their order, then looked into his eyes and asked, "How do you feel about Oscar?"

He sighed. "I really don't know. I perceived a very different man across the table when we met for dinner a couple of weeks ago. I'd like to believe therapy is helping him change—but who knows if it's real? The only way *to* know would be to see how he *behaves* and how he *treats* me over time. But I don't know if I even *want* to see him—and I *also* don't know that I *don't*."

Their onion soups and burgers arrived, and they turned their attention to eating. "I'm glad Dooley's is so close—I let my food stock dwindle to nearly nothing before the move. After the cable gets installed tomorrow morning, I'll lay in proper provisions. Then I plan to peruse Amazon to order a TV and a microwave. That's all I can handle before I go back to work on Wednesday—there are *so many* things I need to buy!"

"I'm sure you'll end up getting a lot of home maintenance items, but you can take your time choosing a lawn mower; I've spoken to my yard guy about you. Here's his number. Also, my housekeeper's contact info."

"Thanks—I'll call him tomorrow! My grass is pretty long." He took the check from the waitress and handed her his credit card.

"So, do I get to see chez Mueller now? I drove here so I could save my steps for the tour!"

Lillian was delighted by the house, and enthusiastically endorsed Brad's ideas for adding the shower stall in the master bath and the phased remodeling of the kitchen. "Don't worry about having empty rooms for a while," she advised. "Just get things as you need them, and have fun browsing antique shops and shows, auctions and yard-sales for the rest. I had very little in my house when George and I got together, which was good since we needed to do a lot of rehabbing. At least you don't have to do much of that!"

Micky called shortly after Lillian departed. "Hi Brad! Just checking in . . . how did the move go?"

"Quickly! I don't have much stuff—yet. I'll have *a lot* of shopping to do."

"So how do you feel, finally being there?"

"Tired, but really happy! I can't *wait* to wake up to the morning sun rainbows lighting up my upstairs hallway! Thanks for calling, Micky. I need to turn in, though—good-night!"

The rigors of moving and his walk to the restaurant caused him to fall asleep as soon as his head hit the pillow, and he slept soundly until eight the next morning. It was a joy to wake up in his own bed, in his own home. Excited, he got up and went into the hallway.

But no rainbows were dancing there. He went out on the balcony and saw an overcast sky. It felt like rain.

CHAPTER 16

Micky was just settling in at her desk as her phone rang; caller ID said it was Paul Price.

"Good morning, Paul! What can I do for you?"

"Actually, you've done so much for me that I'm calling to return the favor," he replied. "You've gone the extra mile to help my entire sales team understand our incentive program and even shared prospecting tips to find more business. So, I'd like to help you get some more business as well."

"That's very nice of you, Paul! But certainly not necessary!"

"I've already been telling some friends at the Elyria club about what you're doing for us. They'd like to meet you. I know it's kind of short notice, but the Memorial Day barbecue would be a great opportunity for some low-key networking, if you're interested. Are you available?"

"Oh! I don't have any plans . . . so, sure. Thanks!"

"It will be outside on the patio, weather permitting. Otherwise, the buffet will be in the dining room. Dress is casual."

"Like, business casual?"

"Sort of. Guys will be in khakis and golf shirts, maybe a sport coat if it's not hot. Ladies usually wear nice slacks and blouses or dressy tee-shirts. You live in Strongsville, right?"

"Yes. I'll text you my address and cell."

"Great! I'll pick you up at five on the twenty-ninth."

Micky hung up the phone, somewhat stunned by this offer out of the blue. She was glad to have a business event on the holiday, though, since she could avoid spending it with her father. Seeing him in short doses was her most reliable strategy to dodge his temper fits. She decided to suggest a late lunch that day, noting it on her calendar.

She looked up to see Jack Benson waiting in her doorway, who now stepped inside. "So, when are you going to take that fancy red trophy car on the road for some new business calls?"

She stiffened slightly. "Actually, I've been *getting another* four-hundred-thousand-dollars of new business add-ons to my existing accounts' repeat programs in the past few weeks, as well as getting the Fine Motors program off to a fast start."

"Yeah. I've been meaning to talk to you about the excessive amount of time you've been spending on that *one* new account."

"As you recall, it's more like *five* new accounts and the numbers are great. I even sold an add-on to *that* program before it even *launched!*" She smiled. "And that extra time you think I've been *wasting* is paying off. Paul Price just called to thank me for my extra help and wants to reciprocate. He's been telling friends about his program, and several are interested. He's taking me to meet them and do *more* networking at his country club at the end of the month."

"What?"

"Yes. Serious, pre-qualified leads, Jack. You know those lead to *much* faster sales. And lower costs *without* travel expenses means more *profit* . . . and more *bonus* for *you*."

*****

Brad was finishing painting the barn's wide oak-plank floor of the bathroom in Lillian's apartment expansion when she peeked in the doorway. "Oh, I really like this brick red! It'll look great with the white bead-board you have planned for the walls," she told him.

"Good—glad you like it! After it dries, I'll add a couple of coats of clear, matte polyurethane to protect it from water." He looked up at her, and thought that her smiling, twinkly-eyed expression suggested something more exciting than a paint color. "What's up, Lil?"

"Do you have any plans for the rest of the day?"

"Other than the Saturday meeting at Grace, no. Why? What do you have in mind?"

"Another experience for a book chapter; the one about my maiden joy-ride driving the T-Bird," she said. "Would you be willing to ride shotgun? It would be much more fun to share this with you, and I'm not sure I'd be comfortable going by myself the first time."

"Sure! Where do you want to go?"

"I thought we could take the backroads to Medina. Kind of a town square-to-square trip; maybe grab a late lunch," she suggested. "George's mechanic friend went over the car thoroughly. It's all tuned up with fresh fluids and belts, plus a new set of tires. He delivered it with a full tank of gas, too."

"Sounds good. Can you give me thirty minutes to clean up, and pick me up at my house?"

*****

Brad relaxed while he waited on his front-porch swing. His face lit up with the grin of a smitten teen-age boy as he watched the Flame Red '57 Thunderbird convertible drive into view with Lillian driving, her blonde hair blowing in the breeze from under a red paisley head scarf. The car's bright color intensified as it emerged from the street's shady canopy and pulled up in his driveway, sunbursts popping off of its polished chrome bumpers and wire wheel covers.

He bounded down the steps and approached the passenger's door. Lillian looked decades younger as she looked up at him over her rose-tinted round wire-framed sunglasses and said, "Hey, Handsome! Wanna go for a drive?"

"You bet, Sweetie!" He winked and dropped into the white pleated vinyl seat inset into the red interior. "I know it's a *cliché*, but you look *great* in this car! And the *car* looks great, too—we should be taking it to a *car show!*"

She backed out of the driveway with ease and headed toward the square. "Thanks, Toots," she said. "No shows today, but you know, I just might look for one soon." She turned left onto Grace Avenue and headed toward Route 83. Giving the 312 Supercharged V-8 engine some gas, it flew forward, pressing them back into their seats. "Wow! I never realized how much fun this car is to drive!"

"You never drove it before?"

"Oh, no," she replied. "This was George's baby, his pride and joy. I was always the passenger, which was fun, too; but *nothing* like *driving it!*"

They drove south and then east, past neatly planted fields—some showing rows of green already. The speed limit dropped as they neared Medina and the fields gave way to residential real estate, then slowed to twenty-five as they entered the historic district. Brad rubber-necked to admire the beautiful homes on both sides of the street, then the fine old commercial buildings around the square. Lillian pulled into a parking space in front of the Swine BBQ.

"I saw this place online," she said as she cut the engine. "There are things on the menu I've never heard of that I just have to try!"

Seated inside, Brad studied the menu and agreed. "You're *right—lots* of *unique* dishes: Candied Pork Belly; Smoked Cabbage; Street Corn; Oatmeal Pie! *Five* house-made sauces—including one called Bama White—*what* is *that?*"

"Let's each get three-meat samplers with trios of sides and share," she suggested. "That way, we can try most of these!"

The waitress answered a few questions and took their order. "How's your writing going, Lil? It's great to see you doing all of these new things—along with *resuming* things you *used to* enjoy."

She took a sip of the blackberry iced tea the waitress delivered. "Ann, my editor, is pleased. Both with the speed of progress and apparently with what I've written—no rewrites so far, and only minor edits."

"With each thing you've done on your list, you seem to be more and more *rejuvenated*—more like *yourself*."

"At first it was really hard. Especially going to the Historic Society event; thank you so much for taking me to that! And for your wonderful work on the barn loft renovation—as well as coming with me today!" She paused while the barbecue feast was spread before them. "I do feel more like myself, but not exactly the same; more like 'Lillian MacAllister Meadows two-point-O'. Each task from my list is becoming easier and more enjoyable. I'm really looking forward to my next one: please put my Take Time to Smell the Roses open garden on your calendar for Saturday, June tenth!"

"Wonderful! I wouldn't miss it," he said, dabbing his lips with his napkin. "So, where to next?"

"We'll cruise to Brothers Antique Mall and see if we come across anything that might look good in your home! Or maybe something I just can't live without."

They were there in about ten minutes. She almost drove past the building's unassuming white exterior, but Brad saw the simple black-lettered sign.

The inside was a delightful maze of vendors' connected rooms filled with everything from primitives to museum quality antiques. A friendly man at the main desk near the entrance welcomed them. They scanned each booth for anything that caught their attention and quickly passed through if nothing did. "Lots of rustic and collectibles that are interesting, but those wouldn't fit in my house," Brad said. Lillian nodded, then darted into the next dealer's area. Brad followed.

"I have to have this," she exclaimed, pointing to an antique typewriter in a travel case. "The nameplate on it says it's a Remington Noiseless Portable. This will look great in my office bookshelves!"

"Yes, that *is* cool. But could you lift it off of this little stand, please? I'm thinking it could be *perfect* between my two Craftsman chairs in my TV room." He examined the top, which had only minor wear. "I really like the angled corners—it will set it back a bit from the chair arms. And this cabinet has two shelves—great for storing the remote, coasters, a notepad and pen."

They settled up with the dealer and took their finds to the front counter, then continued to shop. They were getting tired after wading through figurines, old campaign buttons, vintage clothing, shabby chic pieces and mid-century modern when Brad stopped in his tracks and pointed to the booth across the aisle.

"*Oh. My. God.* Look, Lil—what a *wonderful* sofa for my living room!" The object of his fixation had gracefully curved arms on either side of a solid seat cushion that was six feet long with a tufted back. The upholstery was a good quality heavy satin in a warm gold hue. The back had a camel rise in the middle, and had a dark walnut frame that featured carved roses in the center and in the center of each arm's face. "The rose details will pick up a bit of the leaded glass designs in the bookcases, dining room cabinets and transom windows in both rooms. I couldn't have designed *anything* more appropriate than *this* if I *tried!*"

"You're right, Brad. And the color is spot-on for that lovely warm chamois of your living room walls. What a find!"

He didn't attempt to dicker with the dealer, as he thought the price was very reasonable, and much lower than he'd have to pay for anything new of comparable quality. She gave him the receipt with her booth number on it, and suggested he speak to the manager to arrange delivery. He also had the dealer deliver the small cabinet table, as it wouldn't fit in the T-Bird.

After Lillian put her typewriter travel case in the car's trunk, they headed for home.

*****

Micky glanced around Sally's wood-paneled office, trying not to appear nervous. The fireplace they sat by in their needlepoint armchairs imparted a feeling of comfort, even though it wasn't lit on this warm late-May evening. Her eyes swept past the shelves of books, photos and religious symbols to the bay window and redbud tree blooming outside it.

"It's okay to feel a bit apprehensive, Micky," said Sally, who saw through her attempt at composure. "You're beginning a journey. And you're not sure where you're going, or what you'll experience along the way. Does Brad know we're starting this tonight?"

Micky nodded. "He's glad I'm doing this before and while writing my Fourth Step. He said that step can be tricky; we *have* to take it to stay *sober* and to grow . . . and looking at things we buried long ago because we couldn't deal with them at the time can drive some people back out to drinking. They *still* can't deal with them and feel an overwhelming need to medicate the *pain* . . . but even if we *don't look* at them . . . they're still there, and they'll deal with *us* . . . and we won't be able to stay sober."

"He's right. By the way, I won't share any of our conversations with *anyone*. That's a ground rule for all counselors and priests. But please feel free to tell Brad or Lillian anything you want; you may need to reach out for extra support at times. And remember to turn things you find hard to handle over to God's care. Let's invite him into our session with prayer.

"Almighty God, be with us now as your daughter Micky begins to acknowledge events of her earthly life's past, and help her to gain perspective on them that will enable her to grow into a new life in accordance with your will for her. Amen."

"Amen."

"Now, Micky, let's take three deep breaths. Hold your breath until I strike the gong, then exhale. Breathe in slowly."

After the three gong strikes and extra oxygen, Micky did feel some release of tension.

"Have you had any counseling before, Micky?"

"No. This is my first time . . . and, you're right. I have no idea what to expect."

"That's okay, we'll take things slow. To start, I'm going to ask you about some key areas of your life and I want you to answer with one to three words or phrases that describe them. I do this with everyone; it gives us a snapshot of your emotional roadmap and where you are on it at this point. We'll go back in our following sessions to discuss each in detail. If you feel you need to use a few more words, that's fine, but we want to avoid dwelling on any one area this evening. Any questions?"

Micky shook her head.

Sally smiled. "Okay, here we go: Your childhood."

"Lonely. Scary. Sad. Modeling was my escape."

"Middle and high school?"

"Chaotic. Rootless. Empty and bored. Started drinking at thirteen. Achievement, especially acting, was my only salvation."

"Your mother?"

"Emotional. Terrified of my father . . . when he was home on weekends. Loaded most of the time when he wasn't. Killed herself with pills when I was almost ten."

"Father?"

"Volatile. Demanding. Rages inexplicably . . . then remorseful and over-generous, trying to buy forgiveness. Hates drinking, but uses weed himself. Inconsistent. Very handsome and can be extremely charming—to *other* people."

"Siblings?"

"None."

"Extended family?"

"Not really . . . I was a late baby, so I never knew any of my grandparents . . . they died before I was old enough to remember seeing them."

"Any aunts, uncles, cousins?"

Micky sighed. "Back in St. Louis, where my parents were from . . . but they'd moved to the Cleveland area before I was born, and my mom told me my father didn't like their relatives. I guess they didn't like him either, so I never met any of them."

"They didn't come to your mother's funeral?"

"No. I don't even know if my father told them when it was."

"So, if your father traveled during the week for his job, who took care of you?"

"He hired a live-in nanny when he was between women. But it wasn't the same one . . . I liked the first one, Miss Morris. She was nice . . . and she felt sorry for me. But he discharged her when he married my first step-mother."

Sally looked up from taking notes. "First step-mother? How many have you had?"

Micky furrowed her brow and closed her eyes, trying to remember. She opened her eyes and counted on her fingers as she replied, "Jennifer was the first one . . . he married her when I was twelve, it was her first wedding and they had it at the Cleveland Botanical Garden, and I was a bridesmaid. She divorced him when I was fourteen. Then Amy moved in with us a few months later. She tried to be friends and drank with me when my father was on the road . . . he caught her when he returned on a Friday morning, and kicked her out. Bridgette was next. She only stayed about four months . . . left after the second rage attack, guess she saw it wasn't an isolated event and got out fast. He married Amanda when I was sixteen . . . I liked her, she taught me to drive, and also came to see me when I performed in school plays. She followed my lead in dealing with my father during weekends to side-step setting him off, and hung in there until I graduated and turned eighteen. We stayed in touch for a while after she moved out and divorced him. I lived in the dorm during college at Kent, and he no longer thought he had to have someone around for me. So, in total, there were four. Sorry, that was a lot more than three words!"

They laughed together. "Don't worry," Sally said. "I can see why you had difficulty keeping track! But let's move on: College?"

"Wanted to study theater, my father wanted me to major in business . . . we compromised on communications. First taste of freedom. Loved it! I partied, but still got great grades. Summa cum laude."

"Friends?"

"Acquaintances. No close ones. We moved so many times that I never had a chance to get to know anyone. Plus, girls were always jealous of me because of my looks, and guys were intimidated. I think that's why Brad is such a great friend . . . there's no competition between us for mates, and he'll never try to get into my pants!"

Sally smiled. "That's what Lil's said about her late sponsor, Sebastian. So, speaking of that: Boyfriends?"

"None really. Went to an all-girls high school, so just dates for dances that I met at mixers. Worked during college . . . internships at an ad agency, a radio station and a practical class at the journalism school's TV station. Briefly dated some guys I met there."

"Love?"

"Not sure I know what that is."

"Marriage?"

"No thank you! What I saw was hell. There was no physical violence, but having to be perfect according to shifting standards and walking on eggshells is *not* how I want to live!"

"Children?"

"I didn't like being one and I don't know how to relate to them. Not interested in having any."

"Work?"

"Independence. Money. Goals and achievement. Makes me happy . . . especially when I'm helping clients."

"Home?"

"Security. Safe place. *Mine*."

"Money?"

"Security. Independence. Ability to live my own life, get and do what I want."

"Authority figures?"

"Scare me. Can't trust them. Have to be careful around them and keep on their good side."

"Recreation?"

"Reading. Movies. Spa time. Swimming."

"Hobbies?"

"Never developed any . . . no time these days!"

"Health?"

"Grateful mine's good. Worth working to keep it that way . . . keep weight down, stay fit. And especially, stay sober!"

"Spirituality?"

"Not sure what it is. I want to learn more and grow into it through the program and church."

"That's it for this evening, Micky. On Thursday, we'll begin discussing your childhood and mother; you really can't separate the two subjects. And they're key for all of us, so we may spend several sessions on them. Your father will inevitably be part of this, but we'll also focus on him primarily later. Take my hand, and we'll close with prayer."

Micky reached out to Sally's outstretched hand and bowed her head. "God, thank you for guiding us here through your Holy Spirit. Please bless Micky, and keep her protected in the palm of your hand. May your son Jesus Christ walk with her this night and in the days to come. In his name we pray. Amen."

Sally held on to her hand and said, "Micky, from our brief talk I see that you've had to deal with a lot of very difficult things in your young life all by yourself, and you've survived. But life can be so much *richer* and *joyful* than just surviving, as you're beginning to see. Always remember that you're *not* alone anymore; Brad, Lil and I are here to love and support you in any way we can. *Please* call us any time you're in distress! And you can call on God, too—lean on him, hang onto him, let him carry you when you feel you can't handle things. In my experience, God will never let us down!"

CHAPTER 17

Micky's thoughts on Memorial Day morning were like a high-speed freight train blasting down the single track of her childhood memories. She had never traveled this way before, and now was aboard a non-stop express. Incidents or partial recollections rudely intruded as she struggled to pray and read her program meditation books, derailing her attempts to thwart them.

She had been okay during her second therapy session with Sally on Thursday evening, when she had matter-of-factly talked about how her mother had routinely left her with commercial photographers—mostly men—for photo shoots from the time she was four years old, and how nice they'd been to her. They'd taught her to look up at them slightly sideways and smile, and they'd give her a cookie or a toy. They'd also let her keep the outfits she modeled. She'd loved the attention—as well as seeing her picture in the newspaper ads for department, grocery or clothing stores.

She also told Sally about her mother's slurred confessions of regret at letting her father make her give up her career to be a mom. He said her salary was so low, they'd pay more for daycare than she'd earn, and he wanted a family more. She was being considered for a promotion that would've paid her enough to leave him and support herself, but she was already pregnant. The modeling, she said, would give Micky a good start at learning the importance of having a strong work ethic and pleasing a boss. It would also help pay for the college education she'd need to be independent and have a good life—*without* needing a man. "Don't ever get married," she'd tell her repeatedly. "You'll wind up with a husband and kids who don't give a damn about you!" And how she'd reply, "But Mommy, I *do* give a damn about you!" without a clue about what "damn" meant.

Her mother constantly lamented to her, "Children are a sacrifice!" and "I was perfectly happy and successful in my career, but your father *insisted* we have a child." And all she could think of to say was, "I'm *sorry,* Mommy!"

She told Sally that one of her father's favorite rage rants that he hurled at her mother was, "You used to be so cute! *Now* look at you—dumpy and ugly! You *really* let yourself go—*never* took off the baby weight, *won't* work out. I hate you! I never *want* to look at you. Why do you think I stay out on the road *every week?!* You *lazy bitch.* I think it's time to *dump* your miserable ass and get a divorce!" Her mother would just stand there, hang her head and cringe. And cry. Micky would cry, too, but out of sight. Her father, six-foot-four and a buff one-ninety pounds, red-faced, glowering and screaming, scared the shit out of her. One of her main childhood memories was running and hiding. The first thing she'd do when he moved with his subsequent women to a new house was to find herself a hiding place.

In the session, she told these stories like a reporter, detached and impersonal. The next day, she immersed herself in work, then went to a meeting. Saturday, the incidents began to percolate in her brain, and she shared that with Brad after the Last Call meeting and with the group during Sunday coffee. That had calmed her at the time.

But now, the memories had a life of their own, and they were spawning additional ones. Worse, they were cracking open long-frozen feelings: Deep, bottomless guilt at ruining her mother's life by being born and ultimately causing her suicide; terror, rage and loathing toward her father; and indescribable despair at being unwanted. She'd been standing in her hallway, heading to take a shower when this hit. She slid down the wall to the carpeted floor, curling into a ball and hugging her knees as she wailed and cried until her eyelashes crusted with salt.

Suddenly, she heard a still, small voice say very clearly, *"Mary McHale may not have wanted you, but God certainly did—and does."*

Her tears and keening ceased. She felt a strange but welcome calm and peace, surrounded by warmth and light. Exhausted, she rested quietly there for a while before trying to open her eyes. Their lids were stuck together, so she remained seated a bit longer.

"Thank you, God. Thank you! Thank you! Thank you! I love you, too! Now, please help me through this day." She rubbed her eyes gently, then licked her salty fingers to try to melt the crust on her lash lines. When she was able to see again, she slowly rose and made it to the bathroom, where she drank a full glass of water. Then she took a long, hot shower, dried off, wrapped her hair in a towel, and collapsed on her bed for a nap.

It was nearly eleven when she woke. She called Sally's cell number and told her about the overwhelming barrage of memories and feelings, and about the voice she heard.

"Oh, Micky, I'm so glad you called me! I expected something like this was very likely; when you shared a few of your childhood memories with me in our last session, it was as if you were describing things that had happened to somebody else. You were telling me about many very painful events with a perfectly straight face and normal, modulated voice. The dam on those feelings *had* to burst—and it's great that it happened so quickly. You'll make much faster progress in healing this way."

"I guess that's good," Micky said. "But will I have to go through things like this morning every time? I don't know what to do with all of these feelings!"

"You feel them. You accept that they are *perfectly normal and appropriate* feelings for those things that you experienced. The intensity that you felt today is how you felt as a small child, completely dependent on your parents and helpless to change what was happening. You hug that brave child who was smart enough to hide and to know not to show her fears and tears because that could stir up more trouble. That was her only means of protecting herself then. But those feelings that she froze stayed inside of you, and you've *been* feeling them subconsciously. The pain from that required alcohol and perhaps other things to numb it or distract you from it. That kind of relief was only temporary, so you had to keep repeating it over and over.

"Now, you're a grown woman. You're sober. You can look at your past from a new perspective. You can acknowledge things that happened, feel the feelings, accept and express them and let them pass through you and be released. You've been talking to all of us, and you'll be okay and grow through this as long as you hang on tight to us and to God."

"You were right, Sally . . . God *did* carry me through that this morning . . . I still can't believe how I just stopped crying and felt such peace. And the perfect clarity of that voice and message! Have you ever had that happen to you?"

"Not spoken words, no. But I frequently have thoughts or ideas suddenly presented to me in my mind; sometimes answers to problems I'm wrestling with, other times things I should do are just dropped right in the middle of my general prayers or while I'm doing things like gardening or taking a walk," she said. "That was a very powerful spiritual experience you had, Micky. God knows how much you needed to hear that truth *clearly* stated. Hang onto that! Repeat it to yourself any time you're feeling unable to cope, attacked or unwanted. You may never hear the voice again, but if you stay close to God you can expect guidance through thoughts, nudges, or seeming coincidences piling up that lead you to—or from—something or someone. How are you feeling now?"

"Better. But I'm still tired, even after a nap . . . and I'm supposed to meet my father for lunch at one, but I *just don't want* to *see* him right now!"

"Then don't. I agree that with the justifiable feelings toward him that have just emerged, that wouldn't be good for either one of you. In fact, it would be wise for you to steer clear of him during this phase of our counseling work. Some of my clients are upfront with their families about stepping back while they're in therapy, others find it safer to make excuses for not being available."

"That would be me," Micky said. "I'll text my father that I have a bad headache and need to rest until my business engagement this evening . . . he knows I have that scheduled, and *always* understands prioritizing business over everything."

"What are your plans?"

"A client has been telling his friends at the Elyria Country Club about the program for his sales reps I created for him, and some want to meet me. He's taking me to the holiday barbecue to introduce me to them."

"That sounds very nice," said Sally. "And an excellent way to get out of yourself and focus on others. Have a good time!"

*****

Heads turned as Paul Price escorted Micky through the open white French doors from the Elyria Country Club's main ballroom onto the rear patio. The electric blue silk short-sleeved blouse brought out her indigo eyes, and the modest pearl choker and pearl tear-drop earrings complimented her slim white slacks and low-heeled white sandals. Paul's navy sport coat over a light blue polo shirt with dove grey casual trousers made it look like they had coordinated their attire.

An attractive woman with well-coiffed steel grey hair quickly approached them with a warm smile. "Hello, Paul! Good to see you as always. And are you Micky? Our mutual friend, Lillian, said you'd be joining us this evening; I'm Betty Eldridge. My husband, Bill, is club president—welcome!"

Puzzled, Paul gave her a quick hug and asked, "Hi Betty; how do you know . . ."

She cut him off with a cordial socialite smile and fluttered her eyelashes. "Oh, Paul, you know how I know just about everybody!" To Micky she said, "Lillian and I belong to another club, we've known each other for years! She said I had to meet you; she speaks very highly of you."

"Great to meet you, Betty," she replied. "Lillian is one of my favorite people!"

Betty held up the nearly-empty glass in her left hand. "I'm going to the bar for a refill, may I order for the two of you? Micky, I recommend my Betty's Special—Diet Coke with a squeeze of lime and a shot of grenadine."

"Yes, please! That sounds very refreshing!"

"Paul, what would you like?"

Family of Choice: Raising Each Other

"Vodka and tonic, please, with a twist. Thank you, Betty. We'll be over there; I see some people I want to introduce to Micky." As Betty moved off, he asked, "Who is Lillian, and how do you know her?"

"She goes to my church, I sit with her every Sunday and have coffee with her and other friends afterward," she explained. "She's also a well-known author, who used to teach creative writing at Oberlin; maybe that's how Betty knows her . . . or maybe through historical societies, I know Lil belongs to several in this area."

"That's probably it. Betty has given programs here at the Club about its history as one of Ohio's oldest."

They reached two men who were kidding each other about their scores from the Opening Day Scramble the previous Saturday. Paul clapped the closest one on the back. "Now, Chet, let Howie enjoy his bragging rights. He lucked out drawing into a foursome with two previous Club champions. But revenge will be sweet at the Classic coming up in a few weeks!" They all laughed. "Allow me to introduce Micky McHale. She's the woman who created the incentive program for my people that I've been telling you about. Micky, this is Chester Gorman and Howard Matthews."

She shook their hands firmly. "Pleased to meet you!"

The younger one with the dark brown hair grinned. "I don't know about him, but please call me Howie," he said. "And speaking of bragging, Paul keeps telling us how your program's lit a fire under his whole sales organization—and that it will even *pay* for itself! Is that for real?"

Micky nodded and grinned back. "Yes, it *is!*"

The man with the salt-and-pepper thinning hair said, "Never mind the Chester business; I go by Chet. And Howie's right—Paul hasn't talked about anything else for the past month. I have a manufacturing business, and I don't have my own sales force. I'm at the mercy of manufacturers' reps. Are you able to do anything to get them to put more attention and energy into selling my products?"

"Of course! Many of our clients have the same problem . . . we do *a lot* of programs aimed at manufacturers' reps, distributors and distributors' sales teams," she said. "We've also done programs to reward customers for referrals, employee suggestion programs to cut costs, and ongoing programs to reinforce specific employee actions that help a business in other ways."

"Such as?" Chet asked.

"Well, for example, my company is always looking for top talent in a wide variety of areas . . . account executives, of course, but also writers, graphic designers, web and social media experts, programmers, travel professionals and production people. So, we earn award points to use toward merchandise or travel rewards for every resumé we submit."

Paul stepped in. "This really is working, guys. We're just wrapping up our first month, and the numbers are definitely up over last year already, with two more days to go. We'll have a company cookout at Cascade Park this coming Saturday to announce and celebrate our monthly winners, and everyone is really excited—and hustling to get in some last deals," he said. "Micky, we'd love to have you join us and present the awards. Are you available?"

"Of course! I'd be happy to do that!"

"I'd like to learn more about this, Micky," said Chet. "Is it okay if I get your contact info from Paul and call you to set up a meeting?"

"Me, too," Howie said.

Micky smiled. "That would be wonderful. I look forward to seeing you soon!"

Family of Choice: Raising Each Other

The waiter appeared with their drinks. "From Mrs. Eldridge." They retrieved them from the silver tray, said their goodbyes and moved on to mingle more before dinner.

After filling their plates at the buffet with pulled pork, barbecued chicken, bow-tie pasta salad with colorful vegetables and potato salad, Paul looked over the four-top tables with green-and-white checkered cloths and saw Bill and Betty Eldridge hailing them. Micky learned that Bill had been best friends with Paul's late father, and had known Paul all of his life. The families remained very close, even after the elder Price's passing. She answered their questions about her background, and how she knew Paul.

Between dinner and dessert, Micky followed Betty into the ladies' lounge. While brushing their hair and refreshing make-up, Betty told her, "You made quite an impression this evening—a good one."

"Why is that?"

"Because this is the first time Paul has brought anyone to the Club since his divorce five years ago." Betty blotted her lipstick.

"Oh . . . Paul said some people he'd told about our program wanted to meet me . . . it's just business!"

Betty nodded, smiled and said, "Of course."

CHAPTER 18

Lillian and Brad had worked since sunrise of June 10 to do final cleaning and set-up for the resumption of her annual Open Garden, the first without George. At nine-thirty, in fresh casual attire, they relaxed in the swing on the front porch.

"I hope people come," Lillian worried. "I wonder if they even remember me?"

"Lil, of *course* they remember you—it hasn't been *that* long!"

"Yes, but I haven't been to any meetings of the garden clubs I invited for three years. I haven't even been to any rose society events or shows!"

"Well, you *have* been to church regularly, and it's right next door—I'm *sure* your friends in the congregation will be here," he said. "It's nice that you're allowed to use the church's lot for parking."

Brad looked toward the sidewalk and saw Micky, who had paused at the junction of the walkway to the house to smell the fragrant old garden roses that lined either side of it. She slowly zigzagged and sniffed her way to the porch steps, continuing as she ascended with the crimson one tied along the railing to her left, then the vivid deep pink one on her right, which brought her to them.

Her greeting was an awestruck smile. "I *swear* I haven't been drinking ... despite my staggering ... but I *do* feel *intoxicated* by all of these *incredible fragrances!*"

"Good! That was exactly my goal when I planted them," Lillian explained, pointing to the pink rose. "This is 'Madame Isaac Pereire', and that's 'Souvenir du Docteur Jamain' on the other side. Both are among the most fragrant roses ever."

"I came a little early in case you needed any help," Micky offered. "And to make sure I have *plenty* of time to see your garden . . . as many times as I've been here, I've never had a chance to do that . . . and I had *no idea* it was so *huge* until I looked at the map on the back of your invitation!"

Lillian chuckled. "It grew as my interests in roses expanded; fortunately, I have a lot of land," she said. "And I *am* an *alcoholic*—anything worth doing is worth *overdoing!*"

"You've *certainly succeeded* at that, Lil!" Brad said with a grin. "Micky, we're all set up for now, but we could use a hand once things get going and people are all over the garden. Would you please keep an eye on replenishing the cookies and lemonade in the gazebo on the far hill in back? Supplies are in the cooler. I'll take care of the refreshments under the big arbor between the house and the barn."

"Sure! Happy to help," she said. "Lil, which way should I go? There's so much to see . . . I don't want to miss anything!"

Lillian pointed toward the path from the walkway that led toward the church. "You'll see the most quickly along that. When you get to the arched arbor over the path that leads into Sally's garden, take the other fork. Formal paths end at the greenhouse and shed, so just walk on the grass to the other beds and the gazebo. Have fun exploring!"

Soon after Micky set out, other guests arrived. They trickled in at first, then became a steady stream. Lillian and Brad left the swing, each grabbing a handful of maps. She stood at the bottom of the steps to greet and direct traffic; he assumed the post under the pergola. By noon it looked like a firehose had blasted people all over the vast garden.

A small group of ladies who were wearing dresses with straw gardening picture hats met her on the walk. "Lillian, how delightful to receive your invitation! We *loved* your presentation to our society when the Rose was named 'Herb of the Year' and just *had* to come see your garden!"

"It's wonderful to see you all! Besides the roses, there's a kitchen garden of herbs around the patio behind the house. Also, some of the main paths are lined with lavender, salvia, catmint and others. And a giant Bronze Fennel is a focal point in the front garden along the sidewalk near the church—if you like it, please take one of the small pots on the table under the tree near the potting shed. It self-seeds abundantly, so I'm always weeding them out and hate to let them go to waste!"

As they moved off, she welcomed many friends from the several local rose societies and the Northeast Ohio Perennial Society, and even managed to remember many of their names. Everyone seemed glad to see her again, and she accepted several invitations to give programs or put her place on their September garden-tour schedules. She was flattered that some long-time friends from the American Rose Society's Buckeye District had traveled from central or western Ohio to visit.

She accompanied many people who had questions about roses in various parts of the garden, and was about to sit down and rest when an old friend whom she hadn't seen in years appeared.

"Why, Gus! What a pleasant surprise; I would never have expected to see you here! Did you really drive all the way from Michigan?"

The dapper gentleman with a shock of gleaming white hair and well-trimmed mustache gave her a quick hug. "Well, there aren't that many rose hybridizers in the Great Lakes District, and I wanted to see what you've been up to in the last few years," he said. "I was so sorry to hear about George, he was such a grand gentleman. And I understood why you laid low for a while; I did the same when I lost Maggie. I was happy to see your invitation in our spring newsletter, and I've never seen your garden, so here I am! Now, which way to see your babies?"

"I'll take you to them. But first, let's have a cold glass of lemonade in the shade behind the house; it's a bit of a hike to that part of the garden."

He followed her, examining and inhaling the fragrance of the old garden roses along the front walk. "What a fine collection of OGRs," he remarked. "They look perfect with your gorgeous Queen Anne home. Do you use any of them in your breeding program?"

The dry-set sandstone path brought them to a patio under a nine-by-sixteen-feet pergola, buried by an explosion of purple-and-white striped blossoms at one end and a blanket of silvery pale pink blooms, portents of the full glorious sprays to come. "I'm trying pollen from 'Souvenir du Docteur Jamain' on 'Purple Splash' here in hopes of retaining its purple color and climbing habit and adding fragrance—but you know how hard that can be!"

He nodded as he sat down in a director's chair and accepted the glass of lemonade she poured for him. "Yes, fragrance is a very elusive trait. It pops up when you least expect it, and seems to defy line-breeding of fragrant pedigrees." He looked up, and noted, "This structure is a great support for this magnificent plant!"

"George built it. He insisted that it would overwhelm the porch railings so he put in the patio and built this before I could plant the rose. I put 'New Dawn' at the opposite end, it's just coming into bloom now. Between the two of them, it's created a nice, shady spot to rest and it also separates the backyard garden from the barn."

After lemonade and cookies, Lillian escorted him up the hill via the gravel path from the driveway, past a bed of Hybrid Teas shielded by the barn from bitter west winter winds, and took him into the greenhouse. Gesturing toward rows of black plastic 72-plant seed-starter trays that showed intermittent green growth, she said, "Got a decent yield this spring, but not stellar. I'll move them to slightly larger pots soon, then hopefully into gallons by fall. They'll stay here over the winter to plant in the first test bed next spring—provided they survive culling, of course."

Gus admired the desk and file cabinet in the corner, then noticed a pipe coming through the far wall. Following his gaze, she said, "That brings in water from an old livestock well. George built a pump house over it, and designed a watering system in here for the seedlings and outside for the test beds and mother plants garden. He did the same for the gardens near the house, but they use the home's city water. Most of the roses up on the hill are on their own."

"Impressive!"

"Yes, George was a mechanical and aeronautical engineer. He designed systems needed to operate spacecraft for NASA."

"Ah, a fellow engineer—no wonder I liked him so much!"

"I never knew you were an engineer, Gus. What discipline?"

"Electrical. And I worked in similar industries: aeronautics and defense. I'm surprised our professional paths never crossed; some of the firms I worked for were suppliers to the space program."

They had moved into the pump house so Gus could view the equipment. He approved it with a quick nod. "Very elegant. Versatile and extremely efficient; these valves and the digital timing system are superb!"

Lillian laughed. "Would you like to see the roses this system supports?"

"Of course! That's what I came to see; the beautiful engineering is an unexpected bonus!"

"These seedlings were last spring's germinations that passed muster and were just planted over Memorial Day weekend. We'll see how they do. My mother plants are in the next garden, up the rise and next to the shade tree."

They arrived at a large garden where all of the roses were planted in neat rows with gravel work paths between them. Most of them had at least a few white paper hats fashioned from the corners of envelopes and affixed to the stems with rubber bands. Plastic strips with code initials and numbers dangled from each.

"You've been busy," Gus observed.

"Yes, I did more this spring than in the last couple of seasons," she said. "When I could find time away from my writing."

"You're working on a new book?"

"Yes, about this new widowhood phase I'm in. I was totally blocked, until a dear friend told me I'd have to actually *do* the things I needed to do to get on with my life in order to *write* about them; resuming my annual Open Garden is one of them."

Micky, who had seen them from the gazebo, came out to join them. "Lillian, what is this garden about? And what're those things all over the roses?"

"I like to try creating new roses by hybridizing, or breeding, parents selected from my existing ones. This garden is full of my best mother plants—my broodmare barn, you might say. I collect pollen from roses whose traits I think would improve on specific seed-bearing mother plants here and put it on each bloom when the time is right; then I cover them immediately to keep bees or wind from contaminating the cross with pollen from other roses," she explained. "Micky, this is Gus MacGregor, a longtime friend who lives in Michigan. He's the Great Lakes Director of the Rose Hybridizers Association, to which I belong. He came to see if I've come up with anything interesting."

"And to see you and your garden, Lil." He extended his hand to Micky, who smiled and shook it. "In all of these years, I've never been here before. Our association meetings are always at American Rose Society National conventions."

Micky laughed and said, "I'm a friend who lives nearby and sees Lil every Sunday at church next door . . . and visit her *house*, too, and this is the first time *I've* ever seen the garden . . . which is *fantastic!*"

"Indeed, it is," he agreed. "Which way to your second- and third-year plants, Lil? And where are the ones you've introduced?"

"The introduced roses are in the gardens beyond this tree," she said, leading the way. "The gazebo is totally covered by my climbers." The gazebo consisted of an octagonal deck, with the front opening up two steps from the ground. The structure was made of six-by-six-inch pressure-treated posts that connected the upper framing that supported cross beams and the roof. The seven sides were made from lattice, barely visible through the lush, vigorous roses.

She led them around, describing each rose. "We decided to plant these in the raised-bed boxes attached to the structure, because of the roots of the nearby trees and to provide additional strength to prevent wind damage to the gazebo and the roses tied into it. The watering system is incorporated into the boxes, because losing any of these plants would leave gaping holes in the design."

The first side to the right of the entrance was engulfed by fragrant purple blooms with light pink stripes. "Wow," her guests exclaimed in unison.

"Thank you! This is 'Jumpin' Jack Splash', a cross of 'Purple Splash' and 'Thérèse Bugnet'. Both are extremely vigorous growers; the Hybrid Rugosa Thérèse adds more winter hardiness, disease resistance and fragrance plus a slight color twist to 'Purple Splash'.

"This yellow blend is 'Leapin' Lil'; George suggested the name. I love the Kordes climber 'Golden Gate' for its disease resistance, color and hardiness, so I crossed it with the OGR 'Stämmler' for fragrance; it also added some pink to the deep yellow."

Micky buried her nose in a spray, inhaled deeply then exclaimed, "That's *fabulous!*"

Gus followed suit and agreed. "This is even more intense than the first one."

Lillian laughed. "All seven are very fragrant, with variations of scent. When you're inside the gazebo, it's like shopping at a perfume counter!"

"That's why I just stayed in the gazebo," Micky admitted. "I only needed to replenish the refreshments once . . . but it was so pleasant and relaxing there!"

"I think she's falling under the magical spell of roses, Lil," Gus declared with a wink.

"Ah, there are worse spells one could fall under! Now, this deep pink is 'Polka Queen'. The apricot climber 'Polka' is the seed parent, providing these large ruffled blooms and disease resistance, 'Stämmler' contributed the color and fragrance.

"The next three are all single-petalled, thanks to their seed parent, 'Altissimo'. This light pink, 'Reach for the Stars' and the red one, 'By George!' have 'Thérèse Bugnet' as the pollen parent, which made them tougher and healthier with fragrance than their mother. The white one, 'Star Steps' is from a cross with 'Alba Maxima', I love it, but like its father, it just blooms in the spring."

"This one smells different," Micky said. "It's a much lighter fragrance . . . and the white petals with the yellow center do look like a staircase to the stars."

"Yes, that's characteristic of Alba hybrids. They smell a bit like baby powder," Gus said.

"The last of my introduced climbers is this light yellow, 'Close to Heaven'. The cross is 'Golden Gate' and 'Conrad Ferdinand Meyer'. In this case the pollen parent contributed the fragrance and reinforced the large, climbing growth habit."

Micky asked, "Do you have a rose named for you, Lil?"

"Sort of," she replied. "It's in a bed of miniature roses, in front of the potting shed. She led them down the hill to the east side of the small building next to the greenhouse. She pointed to a thriving short bush in the middle of the front row that was covered in dainty soft yellow single-petaled roses with dark gold stamens. "This is a cross of 'Grace Seward' and 'Baby Love'. George insisted that I name it 'Lovely Lillian.'"

"It is indeed quite lovely," Gus said, looking into her deep blue eyes. "Do you have any pots of it available?"

"No, but I can root a cutting for you, if you like."

"That would be grand! And perhaps this fall you might bring it to Grosse Pointe? And use it as a live example of your work for a presentation you might make to our rose society?"

She hesitated a moment, then decided, "You know, that could be fun. I haven't gone anywhere for ages!"

CHAPTER 19

Micky had been pleasantly surprised when Paul Price invited her to a gala after the Elyria Classic Golf Tournament. She already had meetings scheduled for the following week with the two members she'd met on Memorial Day to present proposals these new clients had requested.

Howie owned boat dealerships adjacent to his five marinas spanning Ohio's north coast, and he wanted to invest around three hundred thousand in a four-month incentive program to push late-season sales that would be likely to get all of the marinas to full capacity for winter storage.

Chet asked for a five-hundred-thousand-dollar plan for a travel incentive lavish enough to really get the attention of his manufacturers' reps and their spouses in the second half of the year, plus a full-year follow-on program for a million or more if the first one bore fruit. The current-year additional business increase was enough to shut down Jack's harping on her to hit the road and expand her geographical territory—at least for now. Maybe she'd meet more prospects tonight.

Micky stood in her walk-in closet, pondering the cocktail dresses she owned. Most of them were suitable for business occasions or weddings, her primary need for dressy clothes. She chose a short-sleeved deep red jersey classic wrap design with a tulip hem that reached the middle of her knees at the longest lengths and was slightly above them in the front.

She slipped on her black patent-leather pumps. Their pointed toes and three-inch heels were surprisingly comfortable; she had worn them to many events that required being on her feet for most of an evening. Simple jet earrings and her black clutch purse tied the accents together, along with the waves of her glossy black hair. A simple teardrop ruby pendant and ring completed the outfit. She applied a dark red lipstick, slipped it into the clutch and walked into her living room just as the doorbell chimed.

She opened the door and smiled in greeting. But Paul was speechless.

He just stood there, stunned and frozen on the small porch.

Finally, he managed to say, "You look sensational!"

"You look great, too. Are we ready to go?"

"Almost. You'd better grab a sweater, though. It will cool down this evening."

"Oh, I'll be fine," she said. "This dress isn't designed for that . . . I really don't have anything that's appropriate."

"Please, you must have something black that would do. I'll worry about it if you don't have a wrap with you, just in case."

Not wanting to upset her client who'd been so nice to her, Micky sighed and said, "Give me a moment." Paul remained on the porch and waited until she returned, a black chiffon unconstructed jacket from another dressy outfit folded over her arm.

When they arrived, they stopped to chat with Howie and Chet.

"Wow! Micky, you look great," Howie said, then jokingly, "Paul, you look okay."

"Gee, thanks."

Chet mocked him. "Price, we see you all the time. In fact, we saw you all afternoon—in the rough, the woods, the sand-traps. Micky is a welcome vision of loveliness!"

"Thank you," she said. "So, who won the tournament?"

"None of us," Howie replied. "Paul wasn't alone in falling victim to hazards. The ten holes with water seemed to have magnets that steered my shots into the drink. And Chet did well until he got near the greens; chip shots overshot, putts went everywhere but in the hole."

"Did you at least have fun?" she asked.

"Always!"

Paul steered Micky toward the bar, and brought her the Betty's Special she requested. Before working the crowd to make more introductions, he suggested she put on the jacket she'd brought. "You look like you're struggling to balance, with that over your arm while you hold your purse in one hand and your drink in the other."

"You're right, she agreed. "But actually, I'd rather put it down in a chair with my purse under it . . . it's too warm out here to add layers."

"It's just that . . . you need to cover up a bit."

"What? This dress is not risqué," she declared.

"But the neckline . . ."

"Doesn't show any cleavage, and I've never had a wardrobe malfunction." Her blue eyes flashed with annoyance.

"We'll be eating soon. When you sit down, I'm afraid men standing nearby will have a view I prefer they not have, especially if the wrap should gap," he explained, then tried to lighten the mood with a bit of humor. "And if I should see anything, I might not be able to restrain myself!"

She acquiesced, then excused herself to go to the ladies' room and see just how bad it looked.

As she contemplated her ad hoc ensemble in the mirror, she saw Betty behind her. "That jacket doesn't go with your gorgeous dress at all. I'm guessing this was Paul's idea?"

"Yes. What's *with* that?"

Betty smiled. "Don't take offense, dear. He's just making it clear to the other men here that you're *his*."

"But..."

Betty threw up her hands and stepped back, saying, "I know. It's just *business*—and I must admit that it's none of mine!"

When Paul took her home at the end of the evening, he apologized. "I'm sorry that I overstepped tonight. It's just that I'm crazy about you, Micky—and I acted like a crazy man!"

"Thank you, Paul. And thank you for a lovely time!"

"Would you do me the honor of accompanying me to the Fourth of July cookout and fireworks? I promise not to tell you how to dress!"

She smiled. "That sounds like fun. Sure!"

"Wonderful! And, I really don't want to wait that long to see you. Could we go out this Friday, just the two of us, on a real date?" he asked. "Dinner at a non-club restaurant, maybe Don's Pomeroy House, near here? I'd really like for us to get to know each other better—without business or other people involved."

She hesitated. "I've *never* dated a client before... I was brought up to believe that *wasn't* a good idea," she said. "But then, I'm realizing that a lot of things I was brought up to believe weren't necessarily true. And... I really like you, too, Paul! So, yes, I'll look forward to dinner with you on Friday!"

He smiled and gave her a light kiss on the cheek.

*****

Paul had correctly guessed that Micky would feel at home in the Pomeroy House, and that the library was her usual choice for dining. "I love this place," she said, as they settled into their booth. "The bookshelves surrounding us create such a cozy, private niche for conversations . . . and the wait staff is always very prompt but never hovering."

"You've brought clients here?"

"Occasionally, if their business is in the area. The food is always wonderful, and I love the feeling in this old house."

"It really is relaxing here," he agreed. "It does feel like a place where you can let your guard down, and not feel like you're on display."

Micky smiled and nodded.

"But that being said, you look particularly beautiful tonight! I like that light green dress, and your emeralds add a simple elegance; you really do have excellent taste."

As she thanked him for the compliment, their waiter introduced himself, handed them menus and asked for their drink orders.

"I'll have a glass of your house Chardonnay, please," Paul replied.

Micky asked for a Diet Coke.

As the waiter withdrew, Paul asked, "Why aren't you drinking? This isn't business tonight. Do you have a problem?"

"Not since I got sober in Alcoholics Anonymous."

"Ah. So *that's* the connection with Betty. Well, Betty's good people, and so are you. So, good for you," he said. "That's fine with me—as long as it won't bother you if *I* drink?"

"No . . . you've seen me at the club. The fact that booze doesn't agree with *me* has *nothing* to do with you or anyone else." Micky was pleasantly surprised at how comfortable she was in discussing this. "I'm anonymous in business . . . but since we're getting to know each other *personally*, it's important that you know that."

Their waiter returned with their beverages, and recited the specials. He left them to study the menu.

"I love the seafood here," she said. "Lots of great options . . . but that crab-and-lobster casserole special is irresistible! And the voodoo shrimp appetizer is intriguing."

"I usually stick to the classics. Shrimp cocktail, then the surf-and-turf," said Paul.

They repeated their orders to the waiter, who appeared as soon as they made their decisions. Paul asked for a second glass of wine to be brought with his meal.

"Betty told me the reason everyone was looking at us when we arrived at the Memorial Day barbecue was that you hadn't brought anyone to the club since your divorce. Did you even date during that time?"

"No. No time," he said. "And after going through all of that, I had no interest in it. You?"

"Pretty much the same . . . minus a breakup. Since I was working all the time, and people in my work life were off-limits, that kind of limited opportunities."

"Did you try online platforms?"

"I looked at a couple of them . . . but it all seemed so contrived . . . and I *really* didn't think *any* of the profiles were plausible!" They both laughed.

"Yes, that's why I've never bothered; it's hard enough to connect with someone in person!"

In their conversation over their entrées, they discovered many things that they had in common. Neither of them did much cooking; were members of a political party or intently followed politics; spent much time on social media; liked opera or the current popular music. Micky preferred classic rock, which Paul also liked, but his broader tastes included Doo Wop, blues, Mo Town, and even some country.

Both agreed that it wasn't fair to an animal to have a pet if you didn't spend much time at home.

Paul watched or listened to sports games, while Micky preferred sit-coms and movies. Her favorite movies were old classics, especially *It's a Wonderful Life* and *The Wizard of Oz*, as well as romances and dramas. Paul liked action movies and spy thrillers.

During dessert, he asked if she had any hobbies.

"In high school, I was in the drama club and the choir. I was also in a few plays when I was at Kent State . . . but I haven't had time for that since I started working," she said. "How about you? Besides golf, of course!"

He grinned. "What else is there? Have you ever played golf?"

"No. The closest I've ever come was miniature golf occasionally in high school or college . . . which I know doesn't count," she replied. "Still, when I did play, I usually won . . . my dates didn't like that!"

They laughed. "No, that doesn't count. But it does indicate you have the aptitude to develop a strong short game in golf. And you're competitive. I think you'd enjoy it—and it's a big asset in business," he said. "Would you be interested in trying it with a few lessons? My treat."

"Maybe . . . I'm worried that I won't have much time to practice, though. And what if I'm terrible?"

"My club in Westlake would be closest for you, probably about twenty minutes from your condo. The head pro is a great teacher, and there are several other instructors on his staff who are good for follow-ups after he grounds you in the basics. There are ample practice areas, which minimizes wait times," he said. "And don't worry, most people are terrible when they first start. And any of us can be on any given day—you heard about our woes in the Classic! But we still had a great time!"

She smiled. "Okay, I'm definitely interested! Thank you!"

When they reached her door at the end of the evening, she looked up at him and smiled. "Thank you for dinner, Paul. I had a wonderful time . . . I really enjoyed talking with you!"

"Me, too, Micky. I really enjoy being with you." He put his arms around her and kissed her lips, then pulled her closer and held her gently for a long, lingering moment before releasing her and saying goodnight. She relaxed into his embrace and rested her head against his chest, then whispered in reply, "Goodnight, Paul."

*****

Micky was already hard at work at nine sharp, proofreading the leave-behind for the next day's presentation to Howie when her phone rang.

"Happy Monday," said Paul. "I have things set up for you at the Westlake club—which is actually named Lakewood Country Club. Is this Saturday morning at eleven okay for your first lesson?"

"Good morning, Paul. Wow . . . that was fast!" She quickly checked her calendar. "Yes, that would be great. Thanks!"

"Good, I'll confirm it. And may I take you to lunch after? Or dinner?"

"Lunch would be better . . . I have a prior commitment for dinner with a friend."

"No problem. I'll hit some balls on the driving range during your lesson, then we can eat in the Grill."

"What should I wear for my lesson? And I don't have any clubs or anything."

"I've taken care of that," he said. "If you can go to the pro shop at the club sometime this week, just give them your name and tell them you need golf shoes and some starter outfits. They'll put them on my tab. During weekdays, late afternoons usually aren't busy and you won't be rushed. You won't need any equipment during your initial lessons. They'll provide clubs and putters."

"Thank you so much, Paul! See you on Saturday!"

*****

After Micky's first golf lesson and lunch with Paul, she took a shower and drove to Brad's house in Stromberg for dinner, to discuss Step Four and the Last Call meeting. She was also eager to see his home; he had waited until his kitchen updates were completed before inviting her.

He was wearing a white apron when he opened the front door, and quickly guided her through the dining room to the butler's pantry and kitchen. "I'm putting together a *super*-simple recipe for chicken cordon bleu—it's so easy *you* might even want to try it, so watch what I do. Then I'll give you the nickel tour while it bakes."

"Oh, Brad . . . this kitchen is *gorgeous*! What did you change in here?"

"Thanks! The linoleum is vintage, likely installed in the original build in nineteen-O-three. I keyed my colors to work with its grey background and the darker grey and maroon perimeter accent stripes.

"Cabinets and woodwork in here had already been painted white. I decided to keep them to brighten up the light grey walls—my change from the *hideous wallpaper*—and the dark soapstone countertops I chose to replace the existing ones. I put in this nice large white porcelain enamel farm sink.

"The island is new—I designed it and had it built. *Loads* of convenient storage. I used a lot of stainless steel—I'm used to it from my commercial life. Since I had to paint the new island, I went with this bright maroon that picks up the linoleum's accent and also adds a *nice pop* of color!"

"It's great," Micky agreed.

He grinned and shrugged. "So, time for your easy cooking lesson."

Micky paid close attention while he demonstrated how to cut a pocket into each boneless chicken breast, then folded Swiss cheese slices in half, wrapped them in a couple of pieces of ham and inserted them into the pockets, which he secured with toothpicks. After coating the breasts with Dijon mustard and mayonnaise, he covered them with toasted Panko bread crumbs, sprayed them with cooking oil, placed them in a baking dish and put them into the oven.

"There! Now you can see the rest of the place!"

She thought the lavatory tucked under the stairs was clever, and she'd never seen an old-fashioned water closet before. She loved his office, particularly the view of the backyard. She admired the living room's bay window and seat, coffered ceiling, fireplace and built-ins, and thought his antique sofa was a great find that looked perfect with the Impressionistic-style oil painting centered above it. He told her of the things he hoped to find to complete the seating options.

Upstairs, Micky was captivated by the secluded upper balcony and the TV room. At the end of the hall, she gasped at the leaded- and beveled-glass window. "Oh, Brad . . . this is *so beautiful!* Is this the one you told me about . . . that makes the rainbows in the hall on sunny mornings?"

He smiled and said, "Yes. It's a *very special* way to start the day—weather permitting!"

"This *whole house* is very special . . . I can see now why you'd do *anything* to get it!"

Back in the kitchen, he showed her how to make the Dijonnaise sauce in five minutes, then deftly put together several kinds of lettuce plus cherry tomatoes and pistachio nuts on salad plates topped with balsamic vinaigrette. He plated the chicken, ladled on the sauce, added a garnish of fresh tarragon along with toasted baguettes and led her to the dining room.

After they were about halfway through the meal, he asked, "How's your counseling going? Do you feel like you might be ready to start writing your Fourth Step list—or at least parts of it?"

Micky dabbed her lips with the linen napkin. "Maybe... I've been working with Sally twice a week for the last six weeks... and some things are feeling more... *settled* in me now. Other things, though... memories... are popping up out of the blue. Some are kind of neutral, like which woman was my father's partner when I was a certain age or when certain events took place. Others are just fragments... mostly when I was modeling as a kid... I'm not really sure what they mean or totally what happened. Sally says I'll remember more when I'm ready."

"Have you had any more traumatic episodes, like the one on Memorial Day?"

"No. *Nothing* like that... still, I'm really *glad* that she advised me to avoid my father as much as possible for a while. I'm not ready to deal with him."

Brad thought for a minute while he chewed a bite of baguette. Then he suggested, "Why don't you try starting with resentments concerning non-family members or institutions, such as work or college? Or start listing your fears? General ones, not part of specific resentments. And, of course, there's always sexual conduct—the Big Book notes that some of us needed to revamp that part of our lives. I know *I* certainly did!"

Micky put down her fork. "Yeah . . . about that . . . I just started dating someone last weekend."

"Oh? Who?"

"Paul Price. My *client* from that major new deal that's saving my bacon with my huge quota. He's taken me to one of his country clubs twice . . . to do networking and introduce me to friends who were interested in programs like his . . . *I thought* it was just *business* . . . and, in fact, *both* of those guys signed *contracts* last week!

"But he said he wanted to *date* and get to know each other *outside* of business. We went to the Pomeroy House last Saturday, then he bought me golf clothes and is paying for lessons at another country club . . . I had my first lesson today, then he took me to lunch. He'd already invited me to the Fourth of July bash at the first club, so I'll see him again on Tuesday."

"Do you like him?"

"Yes. It's just . . . *besides* the fact that I've never dated a *client* before . . . I *really* haven't, well, *dated* much at all! I'm not really sure what to do . . . or what's *expected*."

"This does all seem to be happening pretty fast," Brad said. "But maybe not—how long have you known him now, as your client?"

"A little over three months."

"What's he like as a client?"

"Very professional, and very nice . . . very *appreciative* of all of the extra help I've given him. That's why he said he wanted to help me get additional business, like I did for him. And it's paid off! It *wasn't* just an empty gesture."

"Have you slept with him?"

"No. That hasn't come up yet . . . actually, we've never been inside each other's homes," she told him. "The night he asked me out, he kissed me on the cheek. When he brought me home after the dinner date, he did hold me and kiss me on the lips. Just once. On my porch. Today, when we parted in the club's parking lot, it was back to the peck on the cheek."

"A public place. Lots of guys don't like making a display of affection—gay or straight," Brad explained. "It sounds like he's trying to take things slowly. But don't be surprised if things speed up soon—guys tend to go by a three-date rule."

"What's that?"

"On the third date, they expect to get laid."

"Oh! I guess the golf stuff and lunch at the grill counts as a second date . . . so the event on Tuesday would be the third one. I'm not sure what I'd want to do . . . or what I know *how* to do."

"What do you mean?" Brad asked. "We *know* you're *not* a thirty-year-old *virgin*."

"No . . . but I might as well *be* one. All of my experiences have been *bar* pick-ups . . . people whose names I didn't care to know, and who I never intended to see again. And with the *blackouts*, I don't even *remember* a lot of them! Brad, I've never had sex *sober!* I'm not sure I'll even know how to *do* it!"

He couldn't help laughing. When he stopped, he recounted a story of going to his first dance sober, stubbornly remaining at their table on the sidelines until Oscar literally dragged him out to the floor. "When I swallowed my fear and *tried it,* I joyfully realized that although I had learned to dance *drunk,* I *had learned!* I'm guessing you'll be the same regarding the horizontal bop."

"Really?"

"Pretty sure," he said. "Still—don't feel pressured to do *anything* you don't *want* to do. And remember, the Big Book suggests we look at each relation and weed out selfish motives. It reminds us that God gave us our sexuality, which is inherently good if respected as the gift that it is and is not exploited. And it advises that we pray about doing the right thing, and we'll be guided. You might want to try that."

"That's a good idea, thanks," she said. "Speaking of which, how're things in *your* life? Specifically, regarding Oscar?"

"Totally non-existent—until this morning, when that lovely floral arrangement on the sideboard was delivered to my front porch. Oscar's card offered congrats on my move, which he assumed had happened by now. Said he didn't confirm that with anyone, and that he was standing by our agreement that I'd be the one to call first, if I wanted to."

"And did you?"

"Yes. I called to thank him for the flowers."

CHAPTER 20

Even though Paul had promised not to tell her how to dress, Micky was careful not to wear anything that could be considered revealing to the Fourth of July bash. She chose a red-and-white striped pullover top with capped short sleeves and a demure boat neckline over dark blue Bermuda shorts and her white sandals. She also carried her new white cardigan golf sweater. Checking her outfit in the mirror, she smiled, thinking the image was suitable for a Doris Day movie. However, she did put on a new delicate pink set of silk undies that featured a bit of lace, just in case Brad's third-date rule was true. She also walked through a mist of Angel perfume.

When she and Paul arrived at the patio, they looked like they'd stepped out of the pages of a Land's End catalog. They went straight to the bar, where he got their usual beverages, then joined Howie and Chet.

"So, Micky, we heard you've started golf lessons. How's that going?" Howie asked.

"I had the first one on Saturday . . . and I liked it! The pro starts with putting, and amazingly, I was pretty good at it," she replied. "Of course, it was just short, straight puts on a level practice green."

"She made them all, though. No overshooting. And he did increase the distance a couple of times so she'd learn to vary her stroke," Paul said. "She made those, too."

"Paul! You said you were going to hit balls on the driving range," Micky protested. "I'd have been nervous if I'd known you were watching!"

He grinned. "But you didn't know, and you did great! You really show a lot of promise!"

"How often are you having lessons?" Chet asked.

"Just Saturday mornings . . . it's all I have time for. I'll try to go there to practice some evenings, if possible."

"Basic putting is easy to practice at home, too," Paul said. "I'll ask Tim to fit you with a putter and an indoor target. And clubs, of course, when you get to the point where he can see which would be best for your swing."

"Thanks, Paul . . . that's so kind of you!" Micky exclaimed, blushing as she looked up at him. "I just hope I don't disappoint you!"

"Micky, I'm thrilled that you're willing to try it. That means a lot to me," he said, meeting her eyes with a tender look of longing. "It's important."

Howie noticed a quizzical look on her face. "Paul and I have played a lot together over the years, because neither of our wives wanted anything to do with the game," he explained. "You may have heard the term 'golf widow?' Well, ours didn't like the role. But when they saw that complaining didn't change anything, they found other things to do with their time, and we grew so far apart that Paul and I both wound up divorced. Not the only reason, of course, but it set things moving in the wrong direction."

"On a positive note," Chet said. "My late wife and I had so much fun with golf in our time together, not only playing with each other, but also developing friendships with other couples on the course and individually with the men and women we played with. I'm a real widower now, and I miss my beloved partner every day. These guys have been great, though, inviting me to play with them."

"That sounds nice," she said. "I look forward to being able to play with people!"

Paul laughed. "I'll bet these guys would let us join them for a foursome when the time comes. What do you think?" he asked them.

"Absolutely!" Chet agreed.

"You'd be a welcome addition, Micky," said Howie. "And we'll promise not to razz you about bad shots—at least, not until you get good enough to beat us! Then, look out!"

They all laughed, and Micky said, "I don't think I'll need to worry about that for a while!"

The group moved to the bar to refresh their drinks, then headed to the buffet line for gourmet burgers, fries, potato and pasta salads and a wide selection of desserts. When they finished eating, the sun was approaching the horizon.

Micky noticed that some people had picked up blankets and were carrying them out to the course beyond the patio. She asked Paul what they were doing. "Some of us prefer to sit on the ground to watch the fireworks. I feel sitting on chairs for that seems unnatural," he said. "What would you like to do?"

"Oh, I agree! That was my favorite thing to do as a kid," she said.

Paul looked at the others. "Oh, it's been too long since I was a kid," Chet said. "I'd be too stiff to get up if I tried that now!"

"I'll stay with Chet here on the patio," said Howie. "Closer to the bar, anyway."

Micky excused herself and went to the ladies' room, where she ran into Betty. "Having a good time, dear?"

"Oh, yes," she replied, laughing. "And you were right, Betty . . . turns out, this *isn't* just business!"

"I'm happy for you, for both of you. And I'm relieved to know I haven't lost my powers of observation!"

Micky rejoined Paul, and followed him into the gathering dusk. When they were past the trees—beyond the bugs, he said—he spread their blanket near, but well behind, the rest of the ground-sitters.

He sat down first, and offered his hand to steady her as she kicked off her sandals and sat beside him. While she made herself comfortable, the last twilight was extinguished as if by the turn of a rheostat. In the privacy of darkness, Paul put his arms around her and kissed her deeply. She returned the kiss, and warmth flooded her whole body. She snuggled against him and rested her head on his shoulder. As he stroked her silky hair, she looked up at him and smiled. Then a shrill whistle pierced the night, followed by a loud boom that thrust an array of bright orange gems arcing across the sky and concluding in smoky jet trails as they fell to earth. The show was on.

A constant barrage of detonations and beautiful bursts were applauded by oohs and ahs from the crowd. Micky and Paul echoed those sound effects, sometimes elicited by the colors above them, but mostly in response to their kisses and caresses. As the din of the finale faded away, Paul kissed her again and asked, "Why don't we go and make some fireworks of our own?"

She looked down for a moment, then into his eyes and smiled. "I'd like that."

"Would you be more comfortable at your place?"

She nodded.

Using the flashlights in their cell phones, they made their way to the parking lot. Paul opened the passenger's butterfly door of the electric blue BMW i8 sport coupe for her, then got behind the wheel and tuned into SiriusXM Satellite Radio's channel five for 1950s classic rock. "If this were a classic fifties sports car, we could sit close together and keep the chemistry going," he said. "But this is probably safer for driving!"

She smiled and reached over the console to touch his arm, and rested her hand there until they arrived at her condo.

Inside, she asked, "Do you want anything? Coffee?"

"Just you." He took her into his arms, kissed her, then whispered into her ear, "Are you using any kind of protection?"

"I'm on the pill for medical reasons . . . it's been a long time since I've needed it for this." She led him to her bedroom, and left the door open so the hall fixture could provide dim illumination.

He held her and kissed her again, with a more deeply penetrating tongue. Then he gently ran his hands up underneath her blouse and lifted it off over her head. She moved to remove her bra, but he stopped her. "Please, let me. It's like unwrapping a beautiful gift," he said. "I wanted to do this during the fireworks so badly I could hardly stand it!"

"Me, too!" Her words gave way to soft moans as Paul lightly stroked every part of her body as he undressed her.

Then he lifted her and placed her on the bed, quickly took off his clothes and climbed on, too, hovering over her for a long moment. "You're so lovely." He explored and stimulated erogenous zones she didn't even know existed until he touched them with his fingers, his lips or his tongue, the pressure and urgency increasing as her breath quickened and her body writhed with pleasure. She'd had countless orgasms before he even entered her. Then another place deep inside that she'd never felt before produced such an intense sensation and overwhelming climax that she saw stars behind her closed eyes. And for a moment, a strange dark circular image appeared, then retreated. She felt like she was floating, outside of her body, yet very much a part of it.

She remained in this afterglow, immobilized and quiet, and she couldn't stop smiling. Paul held her this way, keeping her warm with his body until she turned her head to look at him. A novel feeling of attachment glowed within her, along with trust, safety and belonging. "You're incredible, Paul . . . and . . . I think I love you."

"You are, too, Micky. And I've loved you since the day I met you," he said. "I don't want to rush anything, but please know that my intentions are honorable."

CHAPTER 21

Oscar had wasted no time in launching into courtship once Brad called to thank him for the housewarming flowers. He had taken Brad the next evening to see the Cleveland Orchestra perform, and the two of them had watched the July Fourth fireworks from a mutual friend's boat on Lake Erie.

Now, just four days later, Brad climbed out of the black Mercedes sports car onto the main parking lot at Stan Hywet Hall & Gardens and watched Oscar extract a large wicker picnic basket and a small rolled-up rug from its trunk. Seeing Brad's puzzled expression, he smiled through his neatly groomed black beard and explained, "Our picnic blanket," as he tucked it under his arm. Since he grasped the wicker basket in his other hand, he nodded toward two folded canvas beach chairs remaining in the trunk. "Would you mind carrying those, please?"

"Of course." Brad closed the trunk lid after removing their seats, and set out following Oscar along a paved Macadam path that led down a hill, past the conservatory, and through a wooded area that opened to a grassy clearing with small lagoons aerated by fountains. Farther down the path, green plastic seats placed in rows faced the stage, where they would later watch the Ohio Shakespeare Festival perform *A Midsummer Night's Dream*. But they continued past that until they reached a secluded patch of lawn beside another lagoon with a picturesque arched footbridge.

Oscar set the wicker hamper down and unrolled an old Oriental rug. He arranged the low beach chairs on it, then sat in one and opened the wicker lid. Brad joined him in the other chair, and gasped in amazement as Oscar unpacked a silver champagne bucket that he filled with ice from a gallon Ziploc bag. Extracting a wine opener from the row of tools in the hamper lid, he opened a bottle of Pinot Noir grape juice, already chilled by cooler blocks. "As I recall, you were once very fond of this," he said as he poured some into a crystal long-stemmed glass that he handed to Brad.

"Oh my God—you *remembered* this? *Thank* you! I don't even know if The Greens restaurant *still exists* in San Francisco!" He took a long sip and savored it.

"I found a source. I'm glad you like it." Oscar poured a glass for himself, and placed the opened bottle in the icy silver bucket. "I remember when you first quit drinking, it was important to you to find something non-alcoholic that would still be *special*." The stemware balanced well on the stiff surface of the rug, where it rested while Oscar produced a charcuterie board with imported Brie, Camembert and dill Havarti along with hard salami, Genoa salami and prosciutto. A linen napkin was neatly folded over a basket of French baguettes and rosemary focaccia bread.

He liberated two china plates from the strapping in the basket's lid, and handed one to Brad with a napkin.

Brad raised his glass in a toast. "To a very elegant feast!"

Oscar's glass tapped his with a melodic clink. "We can enjoy a picnic without having to rough it."

"Very fitting for an evening of Shakespeare."

"And it will be so refreshing to enjoy the comedy of other people's romantic dramas on the stage, where they belong!"

"Huzzah!" cheered Brad. "Did you read the play before tonight?"

"Yes. It's been a long time since I studied it in college! But I was able to find my old text book in our library at the house; an advantage of never having moved."

"I wasn't so lucky," Brad said.

They discussed the play and memories of some characters while they dined, then had slices of lemon pound cake for dessert. Before packing up the hamper, Oscar handed Brad a Wash 'n' Dry packet. "I almost brought finger bowls, but decided that would be a bit over the top," he said.

Brad laughed. "Yes—that would've been over the top—even for *you!*"

They decided to take their picnic gear back to the car, since it would be very dark along the path after the show concluded.

When they returned, a friendly usher pointed them toward their seats. As they approached, Brad realized that the stage backed up to a sheer rocky cliff that was topped by a stone and masonry balustrade with twin roofed towers at each end. Behind and beside it loomed old-growth oaks and assorted varieties of pine trees. Ferns and small laurels sprouted from crevices in the cliff. "This certainly is a magical setting for staging this play," he said.

The natural light began to dim. Actors climbed down stairs to the stage, followed by other members of the troupe who ran and danced down the aisles between the seats. Bawdy songs and jests kicked off the warm-up entertainments, which invited audience participation. Brad and Oscar joined in.

After a very brief pause, the play began with a sporting contest between a nobleman, Theseus, Duke of Athens, and a powerful woman in leather hunting garb, Hippolyta, Queen of the Amazons. Theseus was armed with his short sword, and seemed outmatched by Hippolyta's long spear until he removed his cloak and rolled it to flick at and parry her weapon. Then she ran at him, leading with the spear, but he ducked and she tumbled over him, landing with her back to him. Theseus quickly threw the rolled cloak over her head to bind her arms and chest, and drew her against him.

She surrendered, and he bemoaned the four days that remained before their nuptial hour, lingering his desires. She replied that four nights would quickly dream away the time. He then charged his master of revels to go and plan merriments to celebrate their wedding.

Three story lines then unfolded alongside each other: Four young Athenians ran away to the forest, where Puck the fairy made both of the boys fall in love with the same girl; Oberon, the King, and Titania, the Queen of fairies had been feuding with each other for months, and Puck helped his master play a trick on his wife, causing her to fall in love with an ass; and a group of bungling tradesmen struggled to stage a comical tragedy where both lovers kill themselves, which Theseus chose for the entertainment following his wedding to Hippolyta and the weddings of the two Athenian couples. The tradesmen's production was mercifully brief, and the newlyweds all went off to bed.

The lights went down when the stage was clear, and the night's blackness closed in. Then, illuminated headdresses and other costume parts appeared to be magically floating through the aisles toward the stage. Puck appeared first, and announced the time of the fairies. Oberon, Titania and their courts joined him and danced as Oberon described their duties to bless each bedchamber for bonds of fidelity, safety, and flawless children. The fairies used all levels to exit the stage, going off to do their tasks. Puck, alone on the stage, bade the audience, if offended, to think that they had slumbered here, and that all of the visions they'd seen had been a dream. He then wished them all a good night, and disappeared.

Family of Choice: Raising Each Other

Brad and Oscar joined in the enthusiastic applause when the troupe returned to take their bows, then stood up, stretched and looked for the path to return to the parking lot. The stage lights enabled them to see clearly the way out of the seats and the beginning of the path. But once underway, it was dark. "I *love* the way the strands of white lights on either side of the path are draped in scallops," Brad said. "Since that's really *all* I can see, it maintains that *magical feeling* of the play!"

"Yes," Oscar agreed. "It really is too dark to see. Here, take my hand." As Brad grasped the firm, warm hand that brushed against his, he felt a jolt of electricity that shot up his arm spread throughout his body. Between feeling consumed in an enchantment and needing to focus on his footing, he followed Oscar along the path in silence.

Once in the car, the spell lifted enough for him to talk. "I'm glad *you're* driving—I never have the patience to deal with the after-event *exit*-jam."

Oscar smiled. "I know we'll all get out of here eventually. It's easier if I just relax and let the traffic carry me along. What did you think of the play?" He eased the Mercedes into the line headed toward the gate.

"I *loved* the setting for the stage—and the actors all did a great job. Costumes were equally wonderful—*especially* the *lighted* parts for the fairies," he said. "And *speaking* of fairies—the multiple characters, lovers' quarrels, triangles, unrequited love, plots for revenge, and use of deceit, magic flowers or plain old *manipulation* to win someone's heart along with masochistic devotion and cat-fight insults topped off with *much drama* and the *absurdity* of sudden infatuation just seemed like your typical gay *house-party* to me—*particularly* back in my drinking days!"

Oscar laughed as he turned onto the rolling road. "Sounds like some of the parties we had, even after you were sober. After all, you might not have been drinking, but most of our guests were!"

"And we never *intended* them to *be* house parties—but there were always some who wisely chose not to try driving home."

"And others who passed out on the sofas," Oscar added.

"Or, the ones who availed themselves of a guest room for a fling—often with someone *other* than their *partners*—and then fell asleep!"

"Oh, yes. Those were the most embarrassing. And then, of course, both wronged partners seemed to think we were somehow to blame. Depending on how drunk they were, or if they wanted the dramatic spotlight, they'd make a big scene as the party was winding down."

Brad nodded and laughed. "Oh, yeah. But the *worst* were the ones who created a major, *ongoing* narrative afterwards, recruiting people to their side and cutting the philanderers—and *us*—socially dead, at least until everyone grew *tired* of it."

"Or the next party when someone else was the next irate cuckold."

"There's been much less of that in recent years, though," Brad observed. "AIDS had a way of enhancing the importance of committed relationships. Things were still pretty wild when I came out in the early nineties."

"Indeed! And we were much younger then, too." Oscar said. "Everything was new and exciting: Dressing up to go out; exploring the gay bars and dance clubs; the thrill of the hunt, and the rush of closing-time conquests and after-parties."

Brad grimaced in jest. "Oh—those *were* best treated as ships passing in the night. *Everybody* looked cute at *closing time*—but dawn's early light was *not* kind!"

"True. But I tired of that scene rather quickly. Once initiated, the evening became routine. There was no sport to it; it was like shooting fish in a barrel. And jumping in bed with someone when shaking hands would've been more appropriate was just too meaningless, a total emotional void."

"I agree," Brad said. "But I've always loved this quote from Woody Allen's character summing up his life's wisdom at the end of *Love and Death*, 'Sex without love is an empty experience. But, as empty experiences go, it's one of the best!'"

They shared a laugh. When it passed, Oscar said, "When all you've known is that empty experience, it's good enough. But after experiencing the emotional bonding of a physical and loving union, you can't go back to that; at least, I can't." He turned his head to look at Brad in the yellow flashes of light from the caution signal at the intersection of Route 83.

Brad looked into his eyes. "I can't, either."

He took Oscar's hand and held it for the balance of the drive to his home. When they arrived, he asked, "Would you like to come in? I can make coffee."

"I don't need coffee at this hour," Oscar replied. "But I'd love to see what you've done with your kitchen, and the shower you added to your master bath. If that's okay?"

"Sure. Follow the drive past the house, and we'll go in the back door."

Motion sensors turned on the lights over the steps to the back porch and the door. Brad unlocked it, and they entered the kitchen, which also was illuminated by a sensor.

Oscar's professional eye absorbed the overall look and feel immediately, and he smiled, nodding approval. He then lingered over the details, admiration warming his expression. "It's wonderful, Bradley, really! I especially like how all of the colors work with this fabulous vintage linoleum. And the surprise pop of burgundy on the island that echoes the flooring's accent stripe."

"Thanks, Oscar!" He motioned toward the empty corner. "I'm having fun antiquing in search of some kind of round table and four chairs to go there. It would be more comfortable than the dining room for solo meals, or for hanging out with friends over coffee. I'm not narrowing the specs on type of material or style—this house allows a great flexibility of design. I'll know it when I see it!"

"I'm so happy for you, Bradley. The joy shows in your face!"

"I *do* feel joyful here! I'm *really* enjoying creating my *own space*—especially since I'm constantly doing that for others in my work," he said. "I've really not had much opportunity to express myself this way."

He moved toward the archway leading into the hallway. "The shower build just got done upstairs—would you like to see it?"

"Of course," Oscar replied as he followed Brad out of the kitchen.

They climbed the stairs and walked to the end of the hallway. Brad opened the door and led him into the bedroom. He quickly moved past an uninstalled curtain rod and swag fabric, explaining, "A few things aren't finished yet—the contractor just finished the shower yesterday, and I had to clean up that area."

In a few strides, he opened the door to the master bath and invited Oscar in, who said, "I still marvel at all of the original tile, fixtures and frosted glass window. And, oh! You've used the same glass for your shower door; wherever did you find it? Most people would've done the currently fashionable clear glass, but this makes it look like it's always been here!"

"Thanks, that was important to me. I found this in an old office door at one of the salvage houses I use a lot. I had to get the shower door made custom, and then finished the shower's opening to fit it—I think it was worth the delay."

Oscar opened the door. "It was! And another hard-to-find item: these period white baseboard tiles! The subways and hex tiles are easy to match, but not these."

Brad grinned. "An architectural salvage business in East Liverpool, south of here, specializes in tile. They bought out all of the ancient inventory years ago when the manufacturers in the area closed. I correctly guessed that the tile used when the house was built probably came from there."

"I'm impressed! I'm sure the chrome grab bars and shower fittings are new, but their designs are compatible with the period."

"Another benefit of the frosted-glass door—you don't see that they don't exactly match the ones in the rest of the bathroom, but they translate the feel of the times when I'm in the shower stall."

"So, show me where you found the space for this," Oscar wondered.

Brad led him out of the bath and around the corner to the walk-in cedar closet. "See that four-foot-wide shoe rack? That used to have shelves that went back as deep, topped by a bar for hanging shirts or sport coats. I have ample space for my needs in the *rest* of this closet—so I cut the shelves down to keep the cedar finish and just made them deep enough for shoes and accessories."

"Very well done!" Oscar left the closet and moved to the front windows, where he picked up the bronze curtain rod with its pineapple finials and the hunter-green swag of blended cotton, linen and polyester for inspection.

"Those will go over the windows there," Brad said. "There's another set in the same location in the TV room through the arches."

An inviting smile appeared on Oscar's face, along with sparks in his deep brown eyes under suggestively raised brows. "For now, though, we can use these to play a game of Theseus and Hippolyta. Which do you want?" He held them out toward Brad, who hesitated a moment, then remembered that the pale sea-green roller shades were down and had black-out backing for privacy.

"I'm trying to remember the *play*—got to consider the best weapon and *strategy*." His green eyes gleamed back at Oscar, who suddenly tossed the rod to him.

"Here, this gives you a greater advantage; you could do some real damage with those pineapples!" He then snapped the swag material at Brad like a towel in a locker room.

Brad blocked the fabric whip with the rod, then advanced with a lunge. But he stumbled from the weight extended in front of him, and went down on one knee.

Oscar quickly drew the fabric back, grabbed the loose end and tossed the snare over Brad's head, pulling him to the floor. He then pounced on Brad's back, pried his hand off of the rod and attempted to flip him onto his back, but Brad broke the hold and slipped out sideways, taking advantage of Oscar's shifted weight.

Brad was on his hands and knees by the time Oscar tried to sit on his back, so he just raised up on his knees and dumped him. A former wrestler, Brad spun around and straddled the prone Oscar. But instead of pinning the man's well-muscled shoulders in victory, he grabbed his open collar and ripped the sides apart. Oscar did the same thing. Buttons went flying, and the two reached for each other's belts.

Wrestling holds gave way to embraces.

Eventually, they moved from the rug to the bed. Later, they held each other, sweaty and spent. Oscar sighed and said, "I don't know how Theseus was able to wait for four days to do this."

"I'm glad *we* didn't!" Brad replied, and kissed him again. Then he fell deeply asleep in his lover's arms.

He awoke the next morning to the delightful smell of bacon frying. He turned on the light to see that it was after eight, then looked around the disheveled room with a mixture of shock and satisfaction.

Brad said softly, "*Now* what've I done?!" Then he laughed, looked to the ceiling with a shrug and quoted Puck, exclaiming, "Lord, what *fools* these mortals be!"

CHAPTER 22

Lillian poured herself a second glass of lemonade after putting her lunch plate in the dishwasher, and sat back down at the kitchen table. It was just too hot to go back to work on this sweltering mid-July afternoon. Though just five weeks after her Open Garden, the weeds, roses and companion herbs had experienced rampant growth; all required attention.

The congealed sweat under her damp tee shirt and cut-offs felt clammy in the air-conditioning. She got up and headed to the back door to enjoy her beverage in the shade of the verandah when her phone rang. She grabbed it from the table and took it out with her, sliding her thumb to answer without checking caller ID.

"Hello?" She set the glass on a table and sat down in a canvass director's chair.

"Lillian! Gus MacGregor! How are you on this fine afternoon?"

"Oh! Hi, Gus! I'm just taking an after-lunch break, waiting for it to cool down before round two of dead-heading and summer pruning. I spent the morning doing that, and I can't say which has grown more: The roses, or the weeds."

"In my garden, the weeds are winning that contest," he said. "You haven't done your gazebo roses yet, I hope?"

"No," she answered. "Why?"

"I am really impressed by them, and have a few ideas I'd like to propose to you concerning those climbers."

"Oh? I'm glad you like them, Gus, but what are you talking about?"

"I'm talking about taking some steps toward commercializing them," he said. "I know you don't care about making money from your hybridizing, which is fine. But there are so few climbing roses that thrive in our climates like yours—and none that I know of that combine all of their attributes—that I believe they should be made available to others."

"Oh! Well, I'm flattered," she said, hedging. "But I'm really not up to starting a new career as a nursery."

"Hold on, Lillian, that's not what I have in mind. And I know you're busy with your book, so I'd be happy to do all of the initial propagation required to start the process," he explained. "If this goes as well as I expect, commercial nurseries would grow the plants for retailers who would license them from you. But that would be down the road from now."

She took a big drink of lemonade. "Okay, so what *do* you have in mind?"

"For openers, I've drafted an article about them to hopefully run in the fall issue of the *Rose Hybridizers Association Newsletter*. If you're willing to review it, I'll email it to you with the photos I took in your garden. They're stunning."

"That would be very nice," she said. "Yes, please send your manuscript and the images. I can look at them tonight or tomorrow; I have a bit of a lull while my editor reviews the chapters I just sent to her. What else?"

"I'd like to come on Monday and help you with your deadheading and cutting back. I'd like to root enough cuttings to distribute plants next spring to RHA members in other areas to trial—and also to send to ARS for the national rose trials. You'd just need to approve things and sign paperwork; I'll take care of the rest."

"I'm not sure about all of this, Gus. I'll need to think about it. Is there anything else?"

"I'd also like to draft the patent applications for each of the roses. That's critical before we send cuttings to anyone," he said. "Again, you'd review everything and make any corrections before signing and mailing the applications. I'd prepare the whole package for you. You've already registered the roses and have ARS exhibition names for them, correct?"

"Yes, those are all registered," she replied. "And I understand the importance of patents, if I decide to move forward. And that's a big IF."

"I understand."

"What *I* don't understand, Gus, is why you would want to do all of this work for me—for my roses?"

"Because those are some of the best damn roses I've ever seen. I've never created any that are even close to their quality. I'm not even envious; I just want to help you share them with the world," he replied. "And, because I want to see you again."

She let this sink in for a moment.

"Why, Gus! Are you flirting with me?"

"Yes."

She laughed. "You know, most men would just *send* roses."

"I'm not most men. The manuscript should be in your in-box."

"I'll read it tonight. I'll think about the rest, and I'll call you Sunday evening. And Gus—thank you."

"My pleasure, Lillian. I know I've thrown a lot at you; thank you for considering my ideas."

Family of Choice: Raising Each Other

*****

Micky followed Brad into his living room, both carrying mugs of freshly brewed coffee that they set on a trim coffee table with an inlaid rose on its top before sitting down on the gold-upholstered sofa. "Is this table a recent find? I don't remember seeing it the last time I was here," she said.

"Fairly recent," he replied. "I still have *so* many things on my list that I need to buy to really settle in, but haven't had much time for shopping lately."

"I'm glad you suggested coming over here after Last Call tonight . . . I've been meaning to talk to you about something, but didn't want to do it over the phone . . . or even at Dooley's," she began.

The pause dragged on, so Brad prodded. "Okay—what's on your mind?"

"Well . . . you know what you said about the third date? You were right."

"Yeah? How was it?"

"Fabulous! And . . . different. Each time, I've felt this deep *emotional bond* . . . in addition to the physical part . . . I'm really feeling very close to Paul now," she admitted. "I think I'm falling in love with him. I've *never* felt that way before, and . . . it's *scary!*"

Brad smiled. "That's wonderful, Micky! And new love is *always* scary. Which also makes it *exciting*. No one knows if it's *for real*, if the other person feels the *same way*, if it will *last*. The *danger* to *sobriety* comes from *dwelling* in the fear—of *not getting* what you *hope for* or *expect*, or of *losing* what you think *you have*."

"So how do we deal with that and not drink?" Her questioning gaze was intense.

"Like everything else—one day at a time." He took a big swig of coffee and put the mug back on the table. "Are you enjoying being with him, doing things *out* of bed?"

"Yes. And learning to play golf is fun."

"Then just focus on what you do in each moment. Your Higher Power will take care of the rest—and at any point where you need to make any decisions, trust that you'll be shown what to do." He thought for a moment, then suggested, "Be sure to talk to Sally about this, too. Everybody has their *own version* of 'scary' concerning love, often involving *deeply* buried background issues. Those can do *a lot* of damage."

"Oh, I will bring this up in our next session! And some of my fear is right up on the surface," she said. "Based on my parents' marriage and my father's other attempts at it, I decided early in my teens that I did *not* want to be married. But maybe I'm wrong . . . anyway, after we first slept together, Paul told me he wasn't going to rush anything, but that I should know his 'intentions are honorable.'"

"Most people would find those words reassuring—but how do they make *you* feel?"

"I'm not sure . . . it's nice to know I don't have to worry about whether he'll call or not, but I do worry about a declared destination of marriage," she said. "But I'll try to focus on the 'not rushing' part instead. Because, honestly . . . I don't know for sure what I *do* or *don't* want."

Brad nodded. "I'm in *exactly* the same place."

Micky laughed. "Ah, so you *are* seeing Oscar! I *knew* that would happen as soon as you said you called him about those flowers! No *wonder* you haven't had time to visit antique shops lately!"

Family of Choice: Raising Each Other

*****

The next morning, Brad waited until everyone had finished their cinnamon rolls and Lillian was topping off the coffee mugs before putting his personal news out on the table. "This may or may not be a surprise to anyone—I've been seeing Oscar."

Lillian didn't spill a drop, but asked, "What do you mean, 'seeing' him? As in, across the produce department in the grocery store or at a restaurant? Or has he started stalking you again?"

"We've started dating, Lil. I don't want to keep that from my sponsor," he explained.

"Oh! Everything okay?"

Brad recounted their dates in the last two weeks, including the play. His face lit up as he spoke of the last activity.

Lillian noticed it and frowned slightly, but didn't say anything. Sally smiled and said, "You look happy, Brad."

"I am," he said. "He seems very different now. Very considerate. And *vulnerable*. He shares his feelings and owns his previous behavior. The therapy seems to be *helping*—but time will tell," he said. "And I have *no* agenda in mind. I really don't know *where* this may go, or what I might even *want* it to become. I'm just enjoying the moments when we're together."

"That sounds like a wise, balanced approach," Sally said. "Enjoy getting to know each other on this new basis, and watch what he shows you."

Micky spoke up. "I'm sort of in the same place with Paul, my client that I'm dating. I'm *really* starting to care *deeply* for him . . . and I've never done *any* of this *sober* . . . it's exciting and *fun*, but . . . *scary*, too. Brad and I talked about it last night. But Sally, can we get into this in detail in our sessions this week?"

"Of course! I think that's an excellent idea."

"Ah, youth!" said Lillian. "It's great to be head-over-heels in love; but just be careful that you don't end up in over your heads."

After Brad and Micky left, Sally turned to her friend and said, "I know you're a wordsmith, Lil, but where did that parting comment come from? What's going on with you?"

Lillian filled her in on Gus' call and his ideas for her roses.

"The article sounds very nice, and well-deserved," Sally said. "And it would be good to make your roses available to more people. It sounds like minimal risk or effort required of you, which is important with the demands of your book."

"Yes. Ann has the final chapters now. I expect there will be some revisions, and then galley proofs after that."

"So, what are you afraid of, Lil?"

"Gus also has ideas about, well, *me*. As in, *courting* me."

Sally laughed and winked at her. "Maybe your editor *doesn't* have the final chapter yet!"

"No! I'm not ready for that."

"I don't think any widow ever thinks she'll be ready for that. But, you have to admit, it *is* something many will have to deal with, eventually," Sally mused. "Why don't you try to keep an open mind about Gus? Like Micky and Brad are doing. Just enjoy the attention and have some fun. You can control the pace of things, and let God direct you."

"I'll think about it."

Shortly after five o'clock, she called Gus. "The article is wonderful; no changes needed. What time should I look for you tomorrow?"

CHAPTER 23

On Monday morning, Jack Benson intercepted Micky in the hallway as soon as she entered the building. "Good morning, Micky. We need to talk before you get caught up in your day. Let's go to my office for a few minutes." He ushered her there and into the chair in front of his desk. He sat behind it.

"I know you've been busy with your three new accounts, getting their programs launched," he said. "Which is wonderful. Great work! The heavy lifting on that should be winding up now, and it's time you focused on serious prospecting elsewhere—specifically, the greater Columbus area. I want a detailed list of at least fifty companies to review on Friday."

"What?! *Why?*" Caught off guard, she struggled to regain her composure. "I mean, why Columbus, specifically? And why the urgency? My business on the books operating this year will surpass my quota."

Jack smiled. "Yes, it will. Again, that's wonderful. But now is the time to find new customers for programs that would start on January one, twenty-eighteen. Planning and budgeting gets going in September, with allocations finalized in the fourth quarter. You'll need to be meeting new people next month.

"Also, I'm hearing that all regions in the company will be getting large increases in our plans for next year. Everyone will have to look at expanding territories to make their numbers. I want us to have programs in development or at least relationships building with a lot of Columbus businesses before the Cincinnati office tries to annex it."

"That makes sense," she said. "There *is* a lot more growth in Franklin County and the surrounding ones than in Akron-Canton or Youngstown. And is Toledo already handled by the Detroit office, or should we also get a jump on it, too?"

"I like the way you're thinking, Micky," he said. "I'm not sure if Detroit is handling that. I'll quietly explore whether there are any programs operating out of that area, and if so, who's handling them. In the meantime, we know Columbus is open to us—so far. So go get 'em!"

*****

Gus arrived promptly at eleven. Lillian met him in the driveway, and guided him into the empty space in the garage. When he got out, he opened the hatch of his dark blue GMC SUV and retrieved a large vase of multicolored roses with a wide green ribbon around it, finished in a bow.

"I *brought* you roses, Lillian," he said as he presented them to her. "These are some of my hybrids; you can root them when they fade, and try them in your garden, if you like." He gave her a gentlemanly peck on the cheek.

"They're beautiful, Gus! Thank you! But how will I know who they are?"

"They're all tagged, down on the stems behind the ribbon. And the details on each are in here," he said, handing her an envelope.

She laughed. "Form and function: Perfect design! Come on inside, I've made us lunch."

They climbed the stairs to the verandah and went into the kitchen. Lillian set the flowers on the round oak table, behind a bountiful bowl and a cutting board with fresh bread and a knife.

"Help yourself to chicken salad and Italian bread," she invited. "I'm having half lemonade-half iced tea; would you like that, or something else?"

"That would be grand," he replied. "I think I'll make a sandwich with the chicken salad."

She set the beverage before him and took a closer look at the bouquet before sitting down to eat. "Have you registered and patented these roses, Gus?"

"I've registered them, but not patented them. Frankly, they're nice but offer nothing unique. No point in bringing plants to market these days that aren't strongly resistant to diseases." He took a bite of his sandwich.

Lillian served herself and buttered a piece of Italian bread. "What information will we need on my roses to apply for patents?"

"A lot! The average application form is six pages long. I've brought an example for you to review, along with blank forms for us to make notes for various questions," he replied. "Our work today will be measuring, photographing, and discussing descriptions. We'll want to do that at the gazebo before we start taking cuttings."

She nodded. "You're welcome to stay a few days, if you like, Gus. There's a guest room with a private bath."

"Thank you, Lillian. We may need that," he said. "But I'll be careful to not overstay my welcome! Your chicken salad was delicious; where shall I take my plate?"

While Lillian did the dishes and put away the left-overs, Gus brought his bag and briefcase in from his vehicle. He put the briefcase on the table, from which he produced a folder. "Here, Lil. Take a look at this patent application for 'Fourth of July.'"

She took the document from him, quickly scanned the first couple of pages and gasped before going further. "Oh, my! Volumes of meticulous details about every aspect of the rose. No wonder so many breeders don't bother to patent their roses!"

"It's only important if you want to commercialize a rose," he said. "But even if they don't patent it, they often do trademark the name, which actually gives longer-lasting protection. Trademarks can be renewed indefinitely, while patents are good for ten years and only renewable for another ten.

"Since you'll be looking for a grower/retailer to take your roses to market, you should do both. You can license or assign your rights to that enterprise, which protects both parties."

She sighed. "I can see that it probably will take several days to gather all of this information. Oh, well! Shall we get started?"

Gus put the papers and folder back into the briefcase and took it with him to the back door. Lillian grabbed a clipboard, camera case and her gloves from a table on the verandah, and they headed to the gazebo.

"How will we go about this, Gus?"

"I'll spare you the drudgery of taking the measurements, but it would speed the process if I can call out the numbers for you to record. It's best if we record measurements from at least five blooms and then average the results.

"You'll need to provide the data on each cross, the year of registration and registered names. You'll probably know more about how the roses grow and how the blooms develop, open and age than I can see on the plants, as well as how each differs from its parents. We can collaborate on the overall descriptions and unique features of the various cultivars. I sort of generalized them in my newsletter article, but those might serve as a starting point for us."

They entered the gazebo and set their things on the table. Lillian sat in a chair, thinking to save her feet for what promised to be a long afternoon. Gus did, too, but he pulled his chair up to the table and unpacked a metric ruler and laser for their task, as well as blank application forms to collect notes in the proper places.

By four o'clock, they had completed measurements and photos of just two of the towering climbing roses: 'Jumpin' Jack Splash' and 'Leapin' Lil'. Lillian had also made preliminary notes on both for the Comparison with Parents section and the ten sub-categories required for Description of the New Variety.

She looked at her watch and declared, "Quittin' time!"

Gus wiped his brow with a white handkerchief and gave her a grateful smile. "Thanks be to God!"

Catching the familiar liturgical response, Lillian asked, "Are you an Episcopalian, Gus?"

"I am. And I noticed you live next door to an Episcopal church."

"Where I spend much of my time," she said, laughing. "I served as Senior Warden for six years, and headed the search committee fifteen years ago that called our priest and now my best friend, the Reverend Sally Wise. I currently chair the finance committee."

"A vital and thankless job," he said. "And I speak from experience—vestry, too. Well, at least you don't have to go far for meetings!"

"True! I think God led me to my house and to that church; in fact, the builder and original resident of the house carved out a portion of the property as a gift on which to establish the parish in the late eighteen hundreds," she replied. "I'm just the latest steward of the home and of the church."

"And God has blessed your labors abundantly." His blue eyes twinkled and a sly smile formed beneath his neat white moustache. "Now I understand how you could breed so many uniquely superior roses—the Holy Spirit worked through you!"

*****

Micky entered Sally's office for her Thursday counseling session and settled into one of the two armchairs by the fireplace. "I'm glad you suggested that I change into comfortable clothes rather than come here straight from the office," she said. "You're right . . . I *do* feel more open . . . more really *me* . . . than when I'm in business attire. When I'm in *sales representative* mode, I shut down my personal feelings and opinions . . . because I'm representing the *company* . . . and they can get in the way."

"Just as representing the company can get in the way of your personal life, such as dating Paul, whom you met through your business dealings," Sally observed. "And while business will remain something important that you share with him—and likely will in any future you may have together, since he owns the dealerships and you're already involved in them—your growing physical intimacy that we discussed on Tuesday is creating deeper feelings for him as you begin developing a stronger relationship that may perhaps lead to marriage."

"Which I *never* thought I *wanted* . . . and now . . . I don't know."

"And you don't have to know," Sally said. "There's been no proposal, and there may not be. And even if there is one in the future, you'll get to choose whether or not to accept it. Our work in the here-and-now is to identify and address any things from your past that may discolor today's reality, causing you to misinterpret things, to misunderstand, and to over- or under-react."

Micky was confused. "Under-react? What does *that* mean?"

Sally explained, "It can take various forms. For example, do you remember your assessment of Oscar's actions a couple of months ago, when Brad told us that he had outbid Brad on the house he wanted so badly, then offered it to him as a *gift*?"

"Yes. I thought maybe he was like my father . . . that even though it was pretty *twisted*, it might be the best he could do."

"Right. And while on one level, that viewpoint is a very insightful, forgiving and accepting attitude that is perfectly appropriate for an existing situation that one is powerless to change. But on another level, when one is discerning whether to get closer to or to stay with someone who acts like that, it can excuse seriously unhealthy behavior. It's important to call things by their right names—and to choose to put up boundaries to keep people like that out of your life, or at least on the periphery of it. Can you remember some times that you or your parents acted like that?"

"My father always said he couldn't remember the things he said or did when he went off on us . . . usually on my mother, but sometimes on me. If we told him, he'd say he didn't mean it. If he did it to me, he usually bought me something expensive to make up for it. My mother *wanted* to believe he didn't mean the things he said, but she knew he really did . . . drinking herself into oblivion was her solution."

Sally nodded. "Yes, I tried that approach. But nothing changed until I got sober and we divorced."

"Did your husband get sober, too?"

"Just long enough for us to both realize we didn't like each other and to agree on how to sort things out to end the marriage and provide for Shelley," Sally replied. Changing the subject back to their session, she continued, "Another survivors' coping mechanism is denial. Like battered women who believe that all men beat their spouses or girlfriends, and that it's normal in a relationship. Or thinking someone is sober when, in fact, they're drinking or using. Does that ring any bells?"

"My father claimed moral superiority because he didn't drink, and apparently thought his daily dope-smoking didn't count," Micky said. "My mother thought he didn't know she drank when he was out of town . . . so did one of his girlfriends who lived with us. And my mother must've thought it was normal to drop off a toddler or elementary-school daughter alone with a photographer so she could go to a bar. I don't *think* most parents would do that . . . but I don't *know?*"

Sally couldn't keep a professional poker face, however, her scowl and tone betrayed her anger. "You're right, Micky—most parents would *never* do that, nor *should anyone!*" Recovering her composure, she explained, "We take that very seriously in the Episcopal Church. Everyone in any form of parish leadership is required to take a course on recognizing signs of and stopping sexual abuse of children here, and correcting situations that might enable it. All parishioners are encouraged to do so as well. I'll let you know the next time the Diocese offers the class, in case you're interested."

"Yes . . . I think that might be helpful," she said, then paused. "I think some things might've happened at some shoots that shouldn't have . . . but I'm not sure."

"Why do you think that, Micky?"

"After my mom killed herself, my father called someone . . . I think one of the photographers who booked me a lot . . . and screamed a lot of ugly things and threats into the phone about pictures. I only heard part of it, but it *really scared* me, so I ran and hid. And he told me afterward that I wouldn't be modeling anymore."

"How did you feel about that?"

"I thought I must have done something wrong," she said. "And I missed it. I had fun doing it. I liked getting the clothes and the candy. And . . . I liked the *idea* that I was earning money . . . not that I ever *saw* it, but my mother always said this would pay for my education. So then, I was also scared when the modeling ended that I wouldn't be able to go to college."

"You were just ten then, right?"

Micky nodded.

"All of those feelings and reactions are perfectly understandable from a ten-year-old's perception. Do you remember anything sexual happening at any of the photography studios? Any touching? Or pictures being taken when you were naked?"

"No . . . but I only remember the modeling *generally* . . . I don't really remember *specifics* about any of the shooting sessions.

"Do you have any idea of how often you went to shoots?"

Micky sat in silence for a couple of minutes, trying to recall. "I can't be sure . . . but I think I did *at least* one every month . . . there were several photographers and a lot of different things I was being used to sell. Actually, there were a couple of years near the end where we were shooting every week for newspaper ads for kids' clothing for a local department store.

"And I think some of the other shoots were for general images. Sometimes, we went to playgrounds. Those usually had other kids, too."

"It sounds like more memories are coming forward as you talk about your modeling experiences," Sally said. "You might try journaling about it a little bit each night before you go to bed. And also note in your journal any dreams you may have about those times."

"Is this important?"

"It may be. It might reveal some emotional landmines that could affect your relationships with people, particularly with men and sex. But if not, at least it could fill in a lot of blanks you have about something that was once important to you."

*****

Micky was ready with her preliminary list of greater Columbus prospects for her meeting with Jack on Friday morning. She walked confidently into his office, handed him a copy of the document and sat down across from him at his desk. After the brief pleasantries, she kept quiet while he reviewed her information.

He looked up after finishing. "Good work, Micky. As I thought, there's very fertile territory there. Now, get on the phone and pitch some initial meetings. I want you down there by the third week of August to make at least five new business calls."

This caught her by surprise. "I thought we were going to *discuss* this list... narrow it down to determine the best prospects to research further so I could develop a preliminary proposal, like I did with Midway Fine Motors."

"You can use your initial meeting to get some of that background, after explaining in general how we help our clients," he said. "Remember, we're looking for programs to operate next year, so you don't need to walk in the door with a pitch. Go and find out what they need; some may be more interested in cost-savings or customer loyalty programs than incentives for sales reps."

"Fine," she said, trying to keep the irritation out of her voice. "Do you want me to just go down the list alphabetically? Or call everyone in a certain industry? Or different industries? I'm not sure how to best go about this."

He smiled. She realized he was enjoying making her uncomfortable. "Be efficient. Make the best use of your time—try to group your calls in geographical areas to minimize drive time. Then find a hotel that's convenient to most of them to use as your operating base."

Trying to play along, she said, "That sounds good. But that will still require a bit more research."

He made a shallow magnanimous gesture of open palms. "Okay. Take today to do that. On Monday, I expect you to be working the phone."

*****

On Saturday morning, Lillian and Gus were busy in the greenhouse, packing up the clear plastic-domed flats of rooted cuttings that he would take back with him. They'd decided to leave a 72-plant flat of each variety with her to grow out for local gardeners to trial as well. Even so, the four-by-eight-foot table was covered with stacks of flats destined for the cargo space in his SUV.

"Whew! What a week," she said. "I can't believe we got so much done! Thank you, Gus, for all of your help with this." She looked up at him, and he smiled.

"Very productive," he agreed. "The time flew by, though. It was truly a pleasure to work with you, Lil. We team up very well, don't we?"

"Yes, amazingly well," she admitted, laughing. "Although I do feel a bit guilty handling the online patent applications in the air-conditioned comfort of my office, while you were pruning all of those climbers' laterals in the heat and then cutting them into pieces with four bud-eyes and rooting them."

"Now, you did your bit with that. You filled all of the flats with dampened ProMix-BX and provided the labeling materials for me before you went inside to your computer."

"I really had thought we'd do that part after we'd hacked back my jungle of climbers and done the rooting," she said. "But this did work out better."

"It felt good to be so busy. And by doing that entire part of the task myself, I could get into a rhythm that felt so comfortable it didn't seem as fast as it was," he said. "And you certainly fed me well!" He picked up a stack of flats and headed for the door.

Lillian followed suit. "We were so busy and tired that we went to Dooley's twice, and two of the meals were frozen pasta I'd made in June. And you grilled the steaks we had last night!"

"Thanks for letting me cook with you, Lil," he said. "I haven't done that with anyone for a long time; it was fun."

She began to feel her eyes tear up, and struggled to focus on her footing, lest she put her armful of cuttings at risk. "Yes, Gus. It was. I've missed that."

"Well, we can do more cooking together when you come to Grosse Pointe for your presentation to our rose society in September," he said. "I'm holding you to that, you know!"

She laughed. "Of course! Although, I'm in a lull right now with my book. The calm before the storm of pre-publication work; any chance we could move that up to August? I can easily create a PowerPoint from the patent application material and photos."

They reached the garage and loaded the flats into his vehicle. "That would be grand! I'm sure we can arrange that!"

After several more trips up and down the hill, they had secured all of the flats for travel. He faced her and put his hands on her shoulders.

"This has been wonderful! Thank you again for your hospitality, Lillian."

"Call me to let me know you and the babies made it safely home?"

"Of course." He put his arms around her and kissed her lips lightly. Then he reached for the button to close the hatch.

"Wait," she said. "I have one more for you." She handed him a pot that she'd put by the garage door.

He looked at the rose's tag and smiled. "'Lovely Lillian'. Indeed you are!"

CHAPTER 24

The five-thirty central Ohio sun made the blacktopped Westin Hotel parking lot feel like a sizzling griddle as Micky wheeled her bag across it to check in. Mid-August heat typified the dog days of summer, and this Monday had been a bitch. Up at dawn, she'd driven to Dublin for new business calls at ten, one-thirty and three-thirty, and she could hardly wait to get into her room and collapse.

Automatic doors welcomed her into the hotel's air-conditioned lobby. Sadly, she wasn't the only business traveler who'd put in a full day before arriving here, so she had to endure a line. The sudden cessation in activity allowed her feet to scream their discomfort after twelve hours in pointed-toed high heels.

It was nearly six when she inserted the electronic key to enter her room. She locked the door behind her and put on the safety chain. Then she stepped out of the painful pumps, carried her bag to the bed and put her briefcase by the desk. She quickly scanned the room service menu, then picked up the phone and ordered dinner. She unpacked her garment bag, hanging the blue dress she planned to wear tomorrow and laying her jeans and pullover on the bed to wear after she showered before her food arrived.

She had just removed her pantyhose and unzipped today's dress when she was startled by a knock at the door. Thinking it might be housekeeping with fresh towels or something, she peeked out of the security view.

"Jack!" Micky cried through the closed door. "What are you *doing here?!*"

"I decided to accompany you on your calls tomorrow. May I come in?" Jack Benson used his most authoritative voice.

"No, you may *certainly not* come in! This is *totally unplanned.* I'm exhausted and was just about to get in the shower before room service arrives. Then I'll prep for tomorrow and turn in early. This is my *personal time.* Please go away and leave me alone now!"

"But we'll need to prep together for tomorrow," he insisted. "Let me in; I can wait while you shower."

"Absolutely not! If you insist on going on my calls tomorrow, get a room and meet me in the restaurant at six-thirty. I can bring you up to speed over breakfast," she said. "But it really makes more sense for you to attend when we have a proposal to pitch. Having the boss along on a first meeting makes prospects tense, they feel out-numbered."

"I can ride with you anytime I want," he replied loudly. "And I can *fire* you, too. Remember, you *owe* me!"

"I don't owe you anything more than my *call reports* on Friday!" she snapped. "And just go ahead and *try* firing me. I was last year's top sales person, I've already exceeded your punitively *huge* quota for this year, and I'm obeying your order to expand the territory. So whatever game you have in mind here—I'm *not playing!*"

Another face appeared in the door's lens. "Miss McHale? I'm José, I have the dinner you ordered."

"Thank God! José, would you please call security to help with your delivery? This man is trying to force his way into my room, and I don't feel safe!" José complied. Within minutes, two men with badges appeared in the dull yellow hall beside him.

Jack attempted to control the situation. "The woman in this room is my employee. I just want to give her some documents she needs for business tomorrow."

"Hand them over, sir, and we'll make sure she gets them," the taller, heavier man told him. "If you're also a guest at the hotel, we'll walk you to your room now. If not, we'll take you to your car. You're creating a disturbance. Do we need to call for police back-up?"

Defeated, Jack said, "No, that won't be necessary. I'm parked in the lot." The men escorted him from view.

Micky, who had slipped into her jeans and top as the confrontation unfolded in the hallway, opened the door so José could wheel in the cart with her dinner. He uncovered it and asked, "Are you okay, Miss McHale? My sister had a boyfriend like him. He was bad news. And is everything still warm enough, or would you like me to bring a replacement order?"

She was relieved, but realized she was shaking. "I'm all right . . . just shaken up. Thanks *so much* for your help, José. And the food will be fine." She signed for it and tipped him twenty dollars.

Her mouth was dry as she chewed her steak. She washed it down with a lot of water; the salad and French fries were easier. Afterwards, she stretched out on the bed, called Brad and reported what had happened.

"Micky, I'm *so sorry* you had to go through that! But I'm also *so proud* of you!"

"Proud? For what?"

"For standing your ground. For being wise enough to *look first* before opening your door—and then *refusing to open it.* For being able to think under that ambush pressure and *ask for help* when you saw the opportunity. And especially for calling his bluff about *firing* you— I'm glad you're *recognizing* your *value,*" Brad gushed. "You've grown so much in the past seven months—and I think your work with Sally is helping."

"I was in *shock* when I saw him," she admitted. "And I was *so mad* that I just told him off. I *was* careful to avoid profanity and tried to be polite in *asking* him to leave. No point in handing him an insubordination excuse. But after it was over, I was so *scared* that I was *shaking*."

"Confrontation is usually scary. But excess adrenaline can also cause shaking. How do you feel now?"

"Wrung out. More peaceful. And, somewhat concerned."

"About?"

She snorted. "About having to keep working with Jack after this! Now that he's shown his stripes, I won't feel comfortable working late at the office. Or driving anywhere with him," she replied. "And he'll probably think of some new pay-back for my defiance."

"Definitely keep your eyes open, and reduce those kinds of vulnerable situations," he advised. "Have you considered reporting him for sexual harassment? You should document this, at least in notes and use the names of the witnesses—get them from the front desk—and do the same if there are any other incidents."

"Well, I'll check out early tomorrow and will find a Bob Evans for breakfast . . . I *won't* be in the hotel's restaurant, in case he stays around," she said. "And I'll go *home* to write up my call reports in the afternoon. I'm still too mad to see him, and I may not be able to control my mouth in another encounter so soon . . . I think I may have inherited the McHale temper after all!"

"You know, Micky, with your current level of success, this *would* be the perfect time to look for your next job," Brad suggested.

"That could be awkward right now . . . with my dating Paul . . . and the new programs with two of his friends," she hedged. "Also, I'll be due for some *serious* bonus money after the end of this year."

"*Money* isn't everything. You don't really want to live with the pressure of this threat *long-term,* do you?"

"No . . . but I think there *may* be a better solution than a new job."

*****

Micky looked lovely on Friday evening in a red-rose printed dress with a slightly scooped neck and cut-out shoulders, perfect for dancing on the ECC patio after dinner. She was relaxed and laughing at Paul and Howie teasing each other when Chet returned to the table bearing a full golf bag and a box.

"I have a few things for our birthday girl," he announced. "Paul asked me to bring the clubs in. Pings. He has good taste—but then, we knew that, because he's with you."

She clapped her hands with glee. "Oh, Paul! *Thank* you! My very own clubs and bag . . . now I can practice more! Awesome!" She leaned over and gave him a kiss.

Paul put his arm around her with a satisfied smile. "You deserve them, Micky. You've been working hard at your lessons, and you're really progressing very well! Happy early birthday; I didn't want to wait until tomorrow. You can try them out then!" He kissed her again.

Chet handed her the box. "From me and Howie."

She smiled and said, "That's so sweet . . . you guys didn't have to give me anything!" She tore off the wrapping paper and opened the box to find four sleeves of golf balls and a bag of tees. "Thank you!"

Howie grinned and said, "If you're like us, you'll need plenty of balls!"

She laughed. "I'm *sure* I will. Thanks!" Then she saw a small envelope and opened it, expecting a birthday card, which it contained, along with a gift certificate for the pro shop designating a putter of her choice. "Oh, wow! Thank you! Thank you!"

Chet said, "Paul's right. You deserve it. You've helped all of us a lot, and we're looking forward to your joining us out on the links. You two can pick out your putter tomorrow."

"I thought you and I could play nine holes in the morning," Paul said. "I reserved a tee time for ten, if that's okay." He looked at her for confirmation.

"That would be great! My first time out on the course! Thank you, Paul!"

*****

Paul Price woke around six the following morning, with Micky's back snuggled against him. He inhaled the intoxicating fragrance of her thick, lustrous black hair, exquisitely flowing across her pillow. He leaned into her, nuzzled her ear and kissed her lightly on her neck. She stirred slightly and sighed.

"Happy Birthday, Beautiful," he said softly into her ear, and then kissed her again. She turned over to look at him, opening her deep blue eyes that were stunning even without makeup.

"Good morning, Paul . . . is it time to get up?"

He smiled. "Not quite yet. Reach under your pillow."

She looked puzzled, but slid her hand under the ivory satin pillowcase. Her fingers stubbed against a very small box.

"Find anything?" he asked.

She smiled and nodded as she retrieved it, then sat up in bed to remove the gift's matte gold professional wrapping, revealing a rich brown suede jewelry box.

"Open it."

Micky complied and gasped, "Oh, *Paul,* they're *gorgeous!*"

He grinned. "They'll go perfectly with your emerald ring and necklace—same cushion cut, and I think the color is close. You can wear them all tonight for your birthday dinner at Pier W."

She threw her arms around him and gave him a deep kiss. "Thank you, thank you, *thank you,* Paul! You're right... they'll match *perfectly!*"

"There was another pair at the jeweler's that I liked even better, but they had diamonds on either side of the emerald, and I thought that wouldn't look right since neither your ring nor necklace have any," he said, gazing into her eyes. "We'll have to put diamonds on you elsewhere one of these days." He kissed her, got out of bed and headed to the shower.

Micky lingered on the bed for a couple of minutes, admiring her new earrings from Paul and contemplating the last thing he'd said. Maybe she *wouldn't* have to endure Jack Benson much past the end of the year, nor need to look for a new job.

CHAPTER 25

The following Tuesday evening, Micky was back in Sally's office for her twice-weekly counseling session, and was feeling much more relaxed than she did the previous week.

Sally asked, "How's it been with your boss since Thursday?"

"I've been able to avoid him so far," Micky replied. "I was only in the office Friday morning long enough to turn in my call reports and let him know I'd be back in Columbus yesterday and today . . . he wisely didn't ask, but I stayed in the same hotel as before. I feel safe there since they have an incident report of Jack's conduct on file."

"And how was your birthday? We missed you on Sunday."

Micky told her about the emerald earrings Paul gave her that matched her ring and necklace, and his comment about putting diamonds on her. "I think he really *is* moving toward proposing . . . I'm *glad* he's not rushing it . . . Paul makes me feel safer and I feel like my *attitude* toward marriage is changing . . . I'm beginning to see *positive* possibilities."

"I think we should explore relationships and marriage at a deeper level," Sally said. "And you should start writing your Fourth Step inventory, if you haven't already. Since you're involved in what may be a long-term relationship, you'll want to get it off to a good start. Look at it this way: If you take clean water and pour it into a glass that already has dirty water in it, that clean water will become dirty. You owe it to both of you to get rid of your old baggage first, and this step helps you identify what that is."

Micky nodded. "I like that visual . . . going into the basement and dragging out old beaten-up, moldy suitcases . . . then taking them up the *steps* and out to the curb!"

"As we probe your early relationships, don't worry about trying to fit things into the format of the Fourth Step," Sally told her. "Just think of some things that you did—good or bad—why you did them, what you expected or hoped for. Think of any actions you took that were self-serving; were there any harmful consequences to you or to others? And were there harms others did to you?"

Micky took a deep breath and looked out of the bay window to Grace Church's peaceful trees and garden to calm herself. She exhaled slowly, and began. "My mother: When my father went off on her and I ran and hid . . . I did it because I was afraid of him . . . and I felt *guilty* for abandoning her; I felt like I *might've* been able to protect her somehow by staying . . . because he seemed to *like* me *better* than her, maybe I could've made him stop. But I didn't try.

"And, as I've said before, I *already* felt guilty for ruining her life by being born . . . when she'd do her usual lament about motherhood killing her career, nothing I said helped at all. I think that's why it was so important to me to do *really well* in modeling . . . it was *important* to her, so I thought maybe my success would make up for that."

"Has your journaling brought forth any more memories about the details of your childhood modeling? Or have you had any dreams?"

"No dreams," Micky said. "But the journaling brought back a few memories. Like, the clothing ads were usually shot at the department store's in-house studio. By Mrs. Woods. She was about forty. When she had finished, she'd page my mother over the loud-speaker . . . she always stayed in the store, either shopping or having lunch in the Grille. That was the main regular gig. Several male photographers had specific clients: One had a local dairy; another had a bakery; and a third one had a day-camp . . . I didn't see them very often.

"The other regular gig was with a guy who did shoots for a national toy company's advertising, a cereal brand and a lot of other things—some clothing, ice cream . . . and some general stock image houses."

Sally paused after Micky finished. "Any memories come up with the black circle you've described seeing?"

Micky shook her head.

"Let's go back to that last photographer," Sally suggested. "The man you worked with on a regular basis. First, close your eyes. Take a few moments to go back there in your mind."

Micky closed her eyes and sat quietly.

"Tell me where you are. What does the studio look like?"

"I think it's in the city . . . downtown Cleveland. Bare brick walls . . . industrial-looking, with exposed ducts, rafters . . . hoists with big hooks . . . lots of tripods with lights or cameras . . . backgrounds."

"Good. Now, where are you in the studio? Tell me what the photographer does and tells you to do. Walk me through it, if you can," Sally prompted.

"There's a portable clothing rack against the wall . . . he's taking a hanger from it and bringing it to me . . . I stand up and he takes off my shorts and tee shirt and puts on my next outfit . . . it's a yellow sundress, I think it's pretty. He spreads a beach towel on the floor and tells me to sit down on it . . . I don't like it, it's really hard, he tells me to pretend it's on sand, that this won't take long. He climbs up a short ladder and looks through the camera . . . it's up high on a tripod, pointing down at me . . . he tells me to sit cross-legged, facing across the room . . . then says to turn my head toward him, look over my shoulder and up at the camera . . . he says that's good . . . then tells me to lie on my stomach facing the camera, bend my knees and put my feet in the air, crossing

213

my ankles . . . then to look up at the camera . . . there, like that . . . it's fantastic, I'm beautiful . . . keep looking at the camera . . . that's it for now. He comes down the ladder and helps me up . . . then he goes back to the rack and brings back a bathing suit. This is for the next shot, let's get you out of the dress . . . I put my arms up, he pulls it over my head then pulls my panties down. Let's take a short break first . . . I'm glad, I don't want to go back on the hard floor right away . . . he picks me up and sits down on a chair behind the towel, puts me on his lap . . . he hugs me and says what a good job I'm doing . . . I'm the best model he works with . . . that makes me happy. He strokes my hair as usual . . . tells me I'm beautiful . . . has one arm around me and strokes my arm and my back with that hand . . . I see a ball or something in his other hand, he tells me to look at the camera . . . then he's touching me all over, in new places . . . I've never felt anything like that before, but it feels good . . . he says keep looking at the camera . . . the feeling is getting stronger and stronger . . . I can hardly stand it . . . I'm making sounds but not words . . . keep looking at the camera, keep looking at the camera . . ."

Sally said, "You're looking at the camera; what does it look like, what do you see?"

"The lens," Micky said. "I see a black circle."

"What happens next?"

"It stopped."

"Why?"

"The door just opened. A woman is screaming."

Micky opened her eyes. She looked at Sally and exclaimed, "Oh my God! It was my mother! She saw me naked on his lap, in front of the camera. She was crying, crying and screaming. She put my clothes on me . . . my clothes, not the dress from the shoot . . . and we left, got in the car. I don't remember any more."

"You don't remember going home?"

"No. I guess we did . . . but I don't remember."

They sat without speaking for a few minutes in the quiet office. Then Sally gently said, "Micky, the black circle you've been seeing during sober sex is no doubt the outline of the camera's lens; I believe you just described your first sexual encounter, and that image was imprinted with the experience."

*****

Sally greeted Micky with a hug when she entered the office. "How are you feeling, Micky? That memory you recalled in our last session contained a major revelation."

As they were settling into their chairs, Micky replied, "Okay . . . I really do feel okay about it. I'm not shaken up like I was when I learned about my behavior during my blackout at Lil's party, for instance."

"I'm glad you're okay. It is important information, though, and it may link to and explain other things, including your behavior during blackouts," Sally noted. "Like at Lil's party, and missing the awards dinner because you met a guy in a bar. You also may have a tendency to attract emotionally unhealthy men because of this initial experience; just be aware of that, and watch how individual men treat you."

Micky rolled her eyes. "Well, that might explain my boss, Jack."

"Yes. And you were able to handle that encounter very well."

"Brad told me he thinks I was able to do that as a result of our counseling work," Micky said. "And I *do* feel different . . . *stronger* somehow."

"Our work is part of that, but mostly you're growing from staying sober, working the steps and developing a trusting relationship with God," Sally said. "And speaking of the steps, we particularly regain our emotional health and strength when we face troubling events and feelings from our past and put them into a new, more accurate perspective in writing our Fourth Step inventories."

"I *have* been thinking about it," Micky said. "I've even started the first column list of people or things I resent, but I'm not sure how much or what to put in the middle column of what they *did* . . . let *alone* what goes into the *last* column."

"Well, let's try walking through an example," Sally suggested. "Let's start with Jack: What things has he done that you resent?"

"He lied to cover for things I messed up when I was drinking, then told me I 'owed him' sexually, but he never pushed it until now."

"What part did you play in these situations?" Sally asked.

"Well, I *was drinking* . . . and I *did* accept his help. But he never was upfront about his expectations, he'd just bring them up *after the fact*. And nothing happened, so I didn't take that seriously. I guess I *should've* . . . but I'm not sure what I should've done. And, to be honest, the game was working for me, until now."

"And you did what you should've done the first time he made the statement about owing him," Sally said. "Any other resentments concerning Jack?"

"Saddling me with the insanely *huge* quota for this year, and delaying arranging for me to get the Cadillac lease prize for the Top Dog Award. That time, he put his hands on me, rubbed my shoulders and said we could work something out about when I'd get the car."

"Your part in these things?"

"I put him in a *really bad* position when I missed the awards dinner *and the ship*. I guess I can't blame him for wanting to fire me, and it would've been really *hard* for him to do it, right after I'd won. I guess it probably really *pissed him off* that I worked getting the car into the program I pitched, successfully. Although I did tell him upfront, and he approved it. And now that I've made my *impossible* numbers, even *that* punishment didn't work. So, I guess I shouldn't be *surprised* that he's trying to get back at me," Micky said.

Sally replied, "The Big Book points out that many things we do to others out of our self-interest actually put us in a position for them to get back at us. So, can you see from this example what goes in the middle and in the last columns of your inventory?"

Micky nodded. "But do I need to write out all of the details I just said?"

Sally smiled and explained, "Just notes to guide you when you talk through your inventory in the Fifth Step. But be sure you are thorough enough in your part that it's clear what you did, so you don't blank out looking at illegible shorthand."

"Okay, I can do that," Micky said. "This one was pretty simple, but what about the photography incident? Can one event involve resentments against more than one person?"

"In my experience, yes," said Sally. "Especially where family members play roles. My Fourth Step included something similar to the incident of your question.

"My parents belonged to an exclusive, invitation-only society in Cleveland that originated the debutante ball in that city, where eighteen-year-old girls were presented into adult society: Formal gowns, long white gloves, the whole bit. In 1971, I didn't think anybody did that anymore, but my parents insisted that I had to 'come out.' They also insisted afterwards that I should date someone who also came out in the bachelor's ball held in conjunction; it was imperative that I quickly find a suitable mate from one of the three-hundred-fifty leading families, supposedly to protect our heritage and familial assets.

"Despite my objections, I saw no way around doing as I was told. I wore the white gown, attended the ball, and began dating a boy who was the son of one of my father's wealthiest clients; our fathers had arranged it. On our second date, he took me to a party at his friend's house where there was a lot of drinking, but after only my first drink, I don't remember the rest of the party. I believe he slipped that date-rape drug into it, because I came to later that night in a bedroom at that house in a pool of blood, undressed. That was how I lost my virginity.

"I told my mother what had happened. She didn't want to believe me, but I showed her the blood on my clothes. She told my father, who was angry about it, but insisted we couldn't confront the boy or his family. He said we didn't have any proof of who had spiked my drink or who had raped me—and without it, he wasn't going to risk his important business relationship by making any accusations. They did agree I didn't have to see him again, and dropped the whole deal of my needing to date people from that group, most of whom had been at that party.

"Instead, as soon as I recovered enough to date anybody, the pressure was on to get married to whomever would have me, as I was now, as my father put it, 'damaged goods.'

"That event spawned items on my resentments list about my mother, my father, that boy, that exclusive society, as well as society in general and the way women were still being treated as chattel."

"*Wow . . . thank you* for sharing that with me, Sally . . . I don't feel so *alone* now, about what the photographer did . . . or about my *seriously* messed-up family," Micky said. "But help me understand, please . . . what was *your* part in those situations? Or *my part* in mine?"

"Sometimes, Micky, our *actions* weren't at fault. Please be clear: Victims of sexual abuse or violence are *not* to blame for the wrongdoing of others. However, it *is* of value to us to examine our beliefs, values and attitudes associated with such events that put us in harm's way. That enables us to change and grow so we either don't attract bad actors or can deal effectively with situations that arise.

"In my example, I *did go* to the ball and on those dates. I didn't want to risk being disowned, which was threatened any time I disobeyed. I *valued* the financial security of paid-for college and future retirement trust-funds more than my personal beliefs or my self-esteem. Because I didn't change my perspective until I got sober, that knee-jerk obedience got me married to a guy I met in a bar in college whom I really didn't know. Then I put up with his verbal abuse and allowed him to bulldoze me into motherhood. We got divorced when I'd been sober for a year."

"So . . . my part with the photographer . . . I loved the attention I got, and the praise. I liked getting the new clothes. I believed I *had to* do anything he wanted me to do . . . that if I didn't please him, I wouldn't get any more jobs, and my mother would be mad at me," Micky said. "And that *last* part goes in the middle column of my resentments about *her*."

Sally thought for a minute. "Yes. And that last part also played into your going along for a few years with Jack's banter about owing him. Since you've been sober and in therapy, your childhood attitudes have been retreating. Not too long ago, you might very well have let him into your hotel room."

"You're right . . . I would've been too worried about losing my job. I couldn't see anything else."

"When we look at our past and what *we* did or didn't do, it identifies what we *can change*; it's empowering. We can learn from our mistakes," Sally told her. "We'll make mistakes in sobriety, too, but if we continue to look at them and learn, we don't have to keep repeating them."

CHAPTER 26

Lillian wiped the sweat from her dripping brow. The late August heat was unrelenting; she was glad she'd limited her time weeding and had strategically worked in the shade beneath the Black Maple trees near the gazebo, but she was drenched by perspiration nevertheless.

She entered the greenhouse to check on the new seedlings and the cuttings of her patent-pending climbers when a call jangled her cell phone. She extracted it from the hip pocket of her blue jean cut-offs.

"How are the cuttings doing?" Gus asked.

She laughed. "You must be psychic! I just walked into the greenhouse to look." She walked over to the tables with the domed trays. "Whew! They still look green and fresh," she said. "It's hotter than hell here, so I opened the windows for ventilation this morning and deployed the shade awning. Looks like it worked!"

"Good, good. We're a bit cooler up here," he said, stroking his white mustache. "How's your yield looking?"

"I'm pleased. I'd say success is about eighty-five percent with nice, strong foliage. Another five percent or so have leaves, but they're kind of wimpy and light-colored, so I misted them a couple of days ago with Protilizer. I think they're perking up; we'll see."

"That's really good, Lil! I think I've got about the same so far," he said. "How's the rest of your day been?"

"Grocery shopping this morning; weeding after lunch," she replied. "How about you?"

"Very similar: Foraging for provisions, then tending the fields," he said, laughing. "I'm about to throw a burger on the grill. What are you having for dinner?"

She ran her fingers through her damp blonde hair and smiled. "I got lucky at Heinen's today; they actually had veal cutlets! I'm going to make veal Piccata, with mushrooms, capers, and Italian parsley from my herb garden, sautéed in olive oil with lemon juice. I'll put it over angel hair pasta and toss a salad with garlic, balsamic, olive oil, Romano and asiago cheeses."

"You tease! That sounds so delicious; I wish I were there to share it with you!"

"Yes, Gus, I do, too," she said. "Why don't you come for Labor Day next week and we can grill together again?"

*****

Sunday was warm and steamy, so Lillian served Häagen-Dazs vanilla ice cream topped with red raspberries from her garden to go with the after-church coffee in her air-conditioned kitchen. Brad chased the last berry in the sweet melted pool in the dish with his spoon, ate it and wiped his lips with his napkin. Then he looked at Micky.

"I'm *so pleased* that you're making *major* progress on writing your Fourth Step," he said. "Now that you've gotten your key relationships covered, the rest will be easier."

"Thanks, Brad . . . Sally's been a *huge* help . . . our sessions and that step really fit together."

Sally smiled and said, "The credit belongs to God and to Micky's willingness. I've just shared some of my experience, strength and hope in helping her fit the insights and perspectives she's gaining into the step's basic format."

"How are other things going in your life, Micky?" asked Lillian.

"Good," she said. "I'm actually playing decent beginner's-level golf on Saturdays with Paul and two of his friends, who are also my clients. We'll all be together tomorrow at the Club's cook-out. Work is going well . . . I have presentations in the works for two prospects in Columbus, and I'm researching companies in Toledo . . . that helps me stay out of the office and in good graces with my boss."

"Glad to hear it," Lillian said, smiling. "How about you, Brad? What's new?"

"Work is busy—I'm in the middle of a couple of really interesting projects. And I'm keeping to my meetings schedule, despite competing invitations from Oscar."

"And how are things going with him?" Lillian asked.

"We're going to a Labor Day barbeque tomorrow," he replied. "Mostly, I'd say things are okay, enjoyable. But I'm seeing hints of the old control rising to the surface."

"Such as?" Lil pried.

"Well, he keeps talking about wanting *us* to throw a house-warming party," he began. "I've told him I won't do that—but I *am* starting to plan *my* house-warming party, with *my* guest list: My co-workers, A.A. friends, clients I'm close to, a few long-time friends including some from New York. And a *few* people Oscar and I are/were close to—but *not* Oscar's clients, Oberlin pals and every gay man in Lorain County. Oscar will be my *guest*—*not* my co-host."

Lillian leveled her frank blue-eyed gaze at him. "Do you really think he could do that? Or would?"

"Well, if he doesn't, it would be a relationship deal-breaker—and I'll tell him that up-front," he said, then changed the subject. "And how are things with you, Lil? Particularly with your gentleman friend who's helping you with your roses?"

She blushed. "My feelings are growing for Gus. I invited him for the holiday; he'll be here in time for dinner tonight."

Brad got out of his chair and gave his sponsor a hug. "I'm happy for you, Lil! That's wonderful," he said. "He seems like a really nice guy."

"I thought so, too," Micky agreed. "He was eager to help me absorb information about roses, and answered all of my questions. And he was *totally* attentive to you, Lil!"

Sally said, "Lil tells me he's very talented in grilling. I've been invited to join them tomorrow for ribs—and I promise I won't grill *him*," she said, winking at Lillian. "*You*, however, are fair game. Have you called your editor, Ann, yet to tell her a new final chapter for 'Cat Hair' is in the works?"

*****

Shortly after lunch the next day, Sally quickly rinsed her plate and put it in the dishwasher. She then turned her attention to a classic urn-shaped vase on the counter next to a white five-gallon bucket overflowing with ferns, spikes of deep purple 'Hidcote' lavender, yellow zinnias, a few large blooms from her bright red climbing rose, 'Altissimo', and a few 'Olympiad' hybrid tea roses that were a closely matching shade of red.

These were about the only roses blooming in her garden just now, and she was grateful they would look good together. She was making the arrangement to take with her for dinner at Lillian's, and didn't think the two rosarians would appreciate any other flowers dominating the table. The small zinnias would be filler flowers, and they would add extra pop to the bright yellow stamens of the five-petalled 'Altissimo' blooms.

Her task was a labor of love, making this gift for her dearest friend, and she relished this form of relaxation on the holiday, which fell on her usual Monday day off. She created the greenery framework with the ferns first, then chose the largest red open flower to go closest to the lip of the vase, using its dark green shiny foliage to obscure the container's edge. She placed others of that type in a similar manner in three other places along the bottom, as the centerpiece would be viewed from all sides. Adding the hybrid teas and the smaller red blooms, she worked her way up to form the key elements of a cone.

Sally was filling in with the zinnias and lavender around the roses when a knock at her front door interrupted. Sighing, she removed her gloves and left them on the counter beside her floral scissors.

Opening the door, she saw one of her parishioners. "Ron! Hello! What brings you here on a holiday?"

His expression was somber, his face drained of color. "Sally, I'm so sorry to have to bother you. I'm the building host for the noon A.A. meeting, and one of its members told me about an apparently abandoned car in the back row of the north parking lot. He said he went to check it and saw the body of a woman inside with a syringe and a piece of paper next to her on the seat.

"I confirmed it, and I've called the police."

CHAPTER 27

A faded black Dodge sedan from the dawn of the new millennium was parked in the last row of the deserted lot, facing ragged pines and assorted volunteer trees, surrounded by weeds that stubbornly subsisted in the pavement cracks. Sally, wracked with sobs, clung to Lillian; Gus enfolded both women, an arm around the shoulders of each for comfort and support, both emotional and physical. All three were casually dressed in shorts and tee shirts, prepared for the hot, sunny holiday rather than a crime scene.

Ron, who had waited for the police at the entrance to the church's parking areas, now returned in the officer's patrol car. They got out and walked over to the group, where Ron introduced Sergeant Waters.

Sally did her best to compose herself. "I'm Sally Wise, rector of Grace Church. I live in the rectory there," she said, pointing to the Tudor house. Then her voice broke as she told him, "And that's my daughter, Shelley, in the car."

"I'm sorry for your loss, Reverend," he said. "Did she live here with you?"

Sally shook her head.

"Was she visiting you?"

"No. I didn't know she was here until my parishioner, Ron, knocked on my door a few minutes ago."

Sergeant Waters made some notes, then looked at the other two. "I'm Lillian Meadows. I live next door, on the other side of the church. My friend and pastor, Sally, called me and asked for my support in checking on this situation. And this is my friend, Gus MacGregor, who is visiting me for the holiday; he lives in Grosse Pointe, Michigan."

"Why did you feel the need for support from your friend, Reverend Wise?"

"Because when Ron told me there was a dead woman in the car parked here, I was afraid it was my daughter. She surprised me with a visit in February this year, stole my silver and sold it to buy heroin and then OD'd in my bathroom," she replied. "The paramedics saved her then. I offered to help her if she'd get treatment, but she refused."

"Is this her car?"

"She didn't have a car when I last saw her. She didn't have a job, either, so I sort of doubt that this is hers."

"Where did she live?"

"She told me that she was staying with her boyfriend in the Dublin area. And that she had just been released from the women's penitentiary in Marysville."

"Do you know the man's name? Address, or phone number?"

"No. I hadn't heard from her in five years or so, and she never returned any of my calls when she still had her cell phone. Then the number was disconnected," Sally explained.

"Has she ever been married? Have any kids? And was Wise her last name?"

"No to all of your questions," she said. "Her last name is Martin; Michelle Louise Martin. Can we get her out of the car, please?"

"The ambulance is on the way to take her to the coroner's office," he said. "I need to take a look at the scene before they can move her, though." He moved to inspect the car, noting the license plate and registration sticker. He then tried all of the doors, but they were locked. He took photos of the body and the car's interior through all of the windows, then walked away and took shots showing the car's condition and location. Then he called in the make and model of the vehicle and the plate number, attempting to identify and locate the car's owner.

The coroner's ambulance arrived. Two men got out and inspected the car with Sergeant Waters, confirming that all four of its doors were locked. Then he opened the front driver's side door with a lockout tool, noted the VIN number and called that in before unlocking the rear doors to deal with Shelley, who was stretched out on the back seat. He took close-up pictures of her face and arms, especially of the multiple needle marks, as well as the discarded tourniquet, syringe and a small bottle. After pulling on latex gloves, he put those items into an evidence envelope.

He also took photos of a note, written on a white lined pad that appeared to have slipped from her hand. It was just one page. When he had finished, he showed it to Sally, who was now standing next to the vehicle. "I'm sorry, Reverend. I know you'll want this, but the original will need to go into evidence, for now. Would you like to take a photo of it?"

"Yes. Oh! I didn't think to bring my phone," she lamented.

Lillian, who had followed her, said, "Here, Sally. Use mine." Sally tried, but her hands were shaking too much. Lillian took the phone back, and asked the officer, "Would you please hold the pad while I shoot the page?" He complied; Lillian checked the photo to be sure the words were legible before thanking him for his assistance.

He had turned to summon the ambulance team, but Sally grabbed his forearm. "Please. Could I have a few minutes with her? Privately? I don't know what the coroner will need to do, what shape she'll be in afterwards."

"Sure. Just don't touch her; they'll likely be checking her body for prints," he said.

"Fingerprints? For a suicide?"

"An apparent suicide, and yes, that's pretty standard," he explained. "It's important to follow all procedures to determine cause of death, no matter what things look like on the surface, to make sure the deceased wasn't murdered. And even if she did intentionally overdose, we need the toxicology report to let our officers know what's available on the streets."

"How long does all of that take? And whom should I call about having a funeral home pick her up?"

"Toxicology testing can take two or three weeks. I'll call you when the coroner is ready to release her body, and I can give you contact information then."

"Please, may I at least close her eyes?" Sally implored.

"Give me a minute," he replied. "I'll get you some gloves."

Sally prayed silently while she waited. "Dear God, please forgive Shelley for rejecting your greatest gift—life. Please, please forgive me for not teaching her to value it, to value you, your love and the life you gave her. Please forgive me for not showing her enough love to shield her from opportunistic people and the hell they took her to with the drugs they were providing."

Sergeant Waters returned and handed her a pair of latex gloves. "Five or ten minutes enough?"

She nodded. When he had left, she donned the gloves and reached inside the car, toward the light brown eyes so like her own, fixed in a stare at the car's slightly tattered headliner. With a quick, light stroke, she closed them and stepped back. "There," she said. "Now she looks at peace. Finally."

"Jesus, please grant her your peace. You died for all of our sins, and for hers—even this one. Please take your very lost sheep, Shelley, into your fold and grant her eternal rest. Amen."

Numb with shock and grief, Sally stood there looking at her daughter lying across the car seat but seeing instead a slideshow of images from happier times: Shelley's first birthday, her smiling mouth smeared with green and pink buttercream frosting; Christmas mornings through the years, with piles of torn wrapping paper and gifts lounging in their opened boxes all over the living room; Shelley proudly handing her a crayon drawing to tape onto the fridge-door gallery; helping her in the garden when she was old enough, and the wonder on her face when she saw a freshly-opened bloom; walking across the stage at her high school graduation; helping her decorate her first dorm room at Kent State; packing her graduation-present car and waving goodbye as she pulled out of the driveway on her way to her first job in Chicago.

Lillian gently laid a hand on Sally's shoulder. "Are you ready for them to take her now?"

She sighed. "Yes, I guess so. I can't do anything more here. But I don't want to watch them do that."

"I understand; let's go to your house, just you and me," Lillian suggested. "Gus has gone back to my place to start the grill."

The two walked over to the group of men waiting to get to work. Sally spoke to Sergeant Waters. "I noticed that my daughter is wearing a gold locket I gave her for her high school graduation years ago. I trust that will be returned to me?"

"All of her belongings will be returned. I'll make a special note of the locket," he said. "Again, Reverend, I'm sorry for your loss. I see way too many of these anymore."

"Yes. So many. Thank you." Sally turned away toward Lillian, who put her arm around her and led her dearest friend back to the rectory.

They entered by the side door, which opened into a small pantry. As they walked through the kitchen, Sally was jolted by the sight of the slightly wilting cut flowers strewn around the vase and oasis. "Oh, no!" she lamented. "I forgot all about these! I was making an arrangement for tonight's dinner table."

Lillian picked up the floral shears, deftly snipped their ends and returned the stems to the nearby bucket of water. "There; re-cutting will refresh them in no time. We'll finish up after we sit for a bit," she said as she moved to Sally's refrigerator and opened it. "I see a nice pitcher of iced tea. Would you like a glass?"

"Yes, please," Sally replied, retrieving two glasses from the white painted Shaker cabinet and placing them on the greenish black granite countertop. Lillian added ice and poured the tea, then followed Sally into the living room, where they reposed on the cushioned seat in the bay window. They sipped the refreshing, cold tea and rested for a few minutes in companionable silence, Lillian offering patient support until Sally felt like talking.

"I knew something like this would happen," she said. "I knew it when she turned away from me in that hospital room. I've heard so many parents, men as well as women, tell this story in Al-Anon leads or comments. So, when Ron showed up at my door this morning, I knew just from the look on his face. Before he even said anything. And when he said there was a dead woman in a car in the north lot, I was positive it was Shelley."

"I'm glad you called me, Sally. When you told me about the car, I was pretty certain of what we'd find, as well."

"But even knowing, it's still a shock. And even seeing her, even closing her eyes, it's hard to believe she's really gone," Sally admitted, shaking her head.

"Would you like to read the note she left?" Lillian pulled her cell from her pocket.

"Yes, if we can read it together, please?"

"Of course. You don't have to do this alone." Lillian turned on the phone and pulled up the picture from her gallery, enlarging it so the printing was readable.

She handed the device to Sally, who read aloud, "If you're reading this, you've gotten into the car. Hopefully, I'll be gone by then. I locked the doors because I want to die. No more Narcan!!! This is it.

"Sorry Mom, I couldn't think of any other place to do it. I don't belong anywhere. Never have. Sorry to cause you trouble, but there will be some I guess. I stole my boyfriend's car, but he stole it from someone else so I doubt if he'll come looking for it or will report it to the police! I also took some drugs from him to do the deed, but he won't report that either, I'm sure!" Sally looked at Lillian with a wry smile.

Then her voice wavered as she continued, "I screwed up my life so bad I can't ever fix it. And I don't want to get straight because the only time I feel good is when I'm high. I just don't want to do the things my boyfriend makes me do to get the stuff I need anymore. I don't want to go back to prison and it's only a matter of time before I end up there again. Like you said, I'm not a very good thief. So I'm going to die doing the thing I like best, and I just won't wake up so I won't be dope sick this time.

"Do NOT bury me anywhere. Like I said, I've never belonged anywhere and this is no time to start. Especially in your church. I don't believe in god. If there is one it hasn't ever done anything for me. So just cremate me and scatter the ashes or donate my body to science. Your choice. It doesn't matter to me.

"I also don't care if you tell my dad about this or not. He's always been such a nasty asshole that I didn't blame you for putting me in boarding school so neither of us had to deal much with him, and you probably don't want to have to deal with him now. OK by me if you don't!" Sally paused. "That's tempting."

Her expression turned wistful and her eyes misted when she read, "When I was little I used to wish we could live together without him, but I guess that wasn't possible. When I was with him, he always said how much you didn't want kids and that if it wasn't for him I wouldn't be here. Was that true? That's why I stayed away as much as I could. I didn't want to bother you." Sally's brown eyes darkened with anger. "That hurtful bastard! Why would he torment her like that?! Just to get back at me? No wonder she kept her distance all these years!"

She regathered herself to finish reading the note. "I certainly didn't want you to know about my prison time but then I had to visit to get money to pay for my stuff.

"By the way, that exclusive boarding school is where I started drinking and using. There were a lot of kids there like me. Like there were at Kent. And at my jobs. Lots more at Marysville. Partying was fun, getting high made all pain, disappointment, everything bad just go away. As long as I could stay in oblivion. That was the goal, to stay there as long as I could.

"The Life was really cool at first and for a long time but now it's too hard. Time to go.

Shelley."

"Interesting," Lillian mused. "She didn't address it to anyone, and she didn't use any closing. She didn't have much to say—and yet, she spoke volumes."

Sally hung her head. "I wish she'd have spoken up more. I wish she had asked me about not wanting her when she was alive, when I could've answered her. I could've explained that, no, I didn't want 'children' per se, but from the time I learned I was pregnant, I loved her! I stopped drinking to protect her during my pregnancy. I tried to give her a happy childhood. Later, I did my best to shield her from Phil's nightly wrath. When she begged me to divorce him to get away from his constant verbal abuse, I did it. And he still managed to abuse her, and poison her mind against me!"

"Are you going to contact him and let him know about her death?"

Sally sighed. "I don't know. Shelley didn't like him; she even gave me permission to leave him out of this. It's not like there will be any big funeral gathering. My parents are gone and I was an only child."

"Your friends in our church, in A.A. and in Al-Anon will want to be with you," Lillian reminded her. "We'll all want to support you through this, and afterward during your grieving process. That's what rituals are for. Many have been through very similar experiences, which they can share with you to help both parties."

"True. I just can't deal with all of that right now."

"Of course not. You can't make any plans immediately anyway, until you hear from Sergeant Waters," Lillian said. She looked at her watch. "The ribs should be ready soon."

"I'm not sure I'm very hungry," Sally protested. "And I don't want to spoil your time with Gus; he seems like a nice man, and I'm afraid I wouldn't be very good company."

"You need to eat. And Gus needs to be with you. The reason he came with us, and seemed to know just what to do—heroin took his only grandson two years ago," Lillian explained. "Come on; let's finish that arrangement and take it to my house."

Sally managed a smile. "Okay. I'm recalling that reading in the Al-Anon daily reader that tells us what to do when we're having a crisis: Do what we would be doing if there were no crisis."

CHAPTER 28

The next afternoon was so hot that the birds weren't singing and the squirrels were napping someplace cooler, but Sally and Lillian enjoyed the outdoors in the shade of Lillian's rear verandah. A large cut-crystal pitcher of iced lemonade sat on the small table between their chairs, with a matching plate of ginger snaps.

An antique reproduction ceiling fan stirred a lazy breeze that enhanced their comfort. Sally looked up at it and asked, "Is that new?"

Her friend smiled. "Yes, it is! A hostess gift from Gus; he installed it yesterday, right after breakfast."

"Oh, my! What a wonderful gift! It really makes it nice out here, despite the heat," Sally said. "He is so thoughtful. Talking with him last night did make me feel better, and I think it helped him process his feelings about his grandson."

"Such a waste, both of them," Lillian said, shaking her head. "Those evil drugs are sucking the hope out of an entire generation. No family is shielded, it doesn't matter what neighborhood a kid comes from."

"No, it doesn't. So, Gus went back to Grosse Pointe this morning?"

"After lunch," Lillian replied. "We wanted to share another meal."

"Very bonding. Jesus was always breaking bread with others; it is a powerful avenue for creating a family, a community," she said. "When will you see him next?"

"On the twenty-seventh. I'll be going to his place to present a program on my hybridizing results to his rose society. I'd better spend more time looking over the newbies in my test gardens by the raspberry patch."

"Speaking of the raspberries, I've been wondering whether that patch might be a good place to scatter Shelley's ashes? It's close to where she left this world, but isn't on church property," Sally mused. "Unless you'd rather not have her on yours, of course, which would be understandable."

Lillian smiled and nodded. "Actually, I was thinking the same thing. She certainly had many thorny times in this life, and I was touched by her words of never having belonged anywhere. Many creatures find refuge in the briars here, especially rabbits and birds; she'll be in good company. And during summer, birds eat many of the berries that are produced and then carry them elsewhere, so her spirit won't be limited to this place."

"That's a comforting thought, Lil. Thank you so much for offering this spot for Shelley!" Sally rose from her chair and hugged her.

"At least it's something I can do," Lillian explained. "So many, many people *need* recovery but don't *want* it. And I'm powerless to help them; I don't have the power to *make* anyone want to get sober, to want to live. And I certainly can't connect them with a Higher Power, or a God of their understanding. It's frustrating, and very, very humbling."

Sally's light brown eyes filled with tears. She tried to blink them away, then wiped her eyes with her fingers. "That's what hurts the most. My *job* is to connect people to God! And I couldn't do that for my own daughter. What a failure as a priest! I feel like such a fraud." Her trickle of tears increased to a flood.

Lillian took a tissue from her pocket and handed it to Sally. "Connecting people to God isn't in the ordination service. You're called to be a faithful pastor, a patient teacher and a wise councilor—and you are outstanding as all of those. You genuinely love and serve all of us in our congregation, administer the sacraments and powerfully preach about God's forgiveness to penitent sinners and the reconciling love of Jesus Christ. Those things *are* in your job description, and for the past fifteen years, you've consistently done them very well indeed!"

Sally dabbed her eyes with the tissue, then blew her nose. "Yes, but I *wasn't* able to pattern my *family* in accordance with the teachings of Christ. My own daughter didn't even believe in God. I can't possibly be a wholesome example to my people!" She shook her head.

"I don't buy that," Lillian objected. "Jesus' family didn't accept his ministry, either, nor did anyone else in his hometown. He could work no miracles there—the best he could do was to summon enough power to push back the crowd that was trying to force him over a cliff! Yet his example has shown billions of people a pattern for living and for worshiping God that has lasted for more than two thousand years."

"True."

"As you walk through this, I believe you will provide an inspiring example to those of us in your flock—many of whom, no doubt, deal with the pain and loss that results from addiction," Lillian said. "And when you doubt your ability to inspire anyone to turn to God, please recall what's happening with Micky. There's a real miracle!"

"Thanks, Lil. You're right—she is making great progress," she admitted. "Oh, dear! Today's Tuesday; she'll be coming at five-thirty for her counseling session. I've just got to pull myself together!"

"No, Sally, you don't. I'll text Brad to tell her what's going on. Why don't you take at least this week off from that? You really do need to take care of yourself right now."

She sighed. "Right again. Okay, we'll cancel this week. But next week I'd like to try to resume our sessions. It does feel good to see that I *can* help her, even if I couldn't help Shelley."

"Well, play that by ear," Lillian suggested. "I hope you'll be able to take some time off from your church duties?"

"The bishop is being very supportive, and said I can have three weeks off. This morning, I arranged for supply coverage," she said. "But I have no idea what to do—or not—regarding any kind of service acknowledging her death or laying her to rest. She would *not* want a funeral. And she didn't believe. I also don't know what to do about Phil."

Lillian refilled their glasses from the pitcher. "Regarding Phil: Pray about it. As for a service, you may need to consider handing it off to a different presider."

*****

It was even hotter by five-thirty that afternoon when Micky climbed the porch stairs and rang Brad's back doorbell. "Hi, Micky—come in! You look comfortable," he said, admiring her well-worn jean shorts, loose-fitting Cleveland Browns tee shirt and running shoes.

She laughed. "Well, ever since Sally told me to change clothes after work to relax . . . I've been taking that further and further. And it's too hot today to even wear jewelry . . . these are clothes I can sweat in!"

"The A/C should prevent sweating," Brad said. "But I did make a nice cool chef's salad for dinner. We'll eat in here—totally casual!"

Micky followed his gaze to the kitchen corner and gasped. "*Oh. My. God!* Brad, it's *beautiful!*" The object of her delight gleamed under a white, black and chrome triangular lamp shade swagged over a stunning square white porcelain-topped table with a black Art Deco design of double lines around the edges and Mondrian groupings of squares in each corner. Its four legs were tubular chrome, and it was surrounded by four chairs with a similar leg design. The chairs had slightly curved padded backs and plush-looking seats that were upholstered in shiny, soft vinyl that matched the burgundy accents in the floor, island and stove control knobs.

His face shone like that of a proud parent. "Look—it has a drawer here, great for storing place mats. And these two ends have sliding leaves if I ever want to seat more guests or put out more food for a party!"

"It's fabulous! Am I the first guest you'll serve here?"

He grinned. "You are! I'm so glad you *like* it!" Then his grin disappeared as he added, "Of *course*, Oscar *hates* it."

"You're *kidding* . . . Why?"

"Because it isn't the *same period* as the house—nineteen-O-three versus nineteen-thirties. Worse—the chairs aren't part of a set with the table, and in fact, are probably of even *later* origin, circa nineteen-fifties," he recited the décor sins of which he had been accused. "Finally, the chairs aren't even *original*—I had their chrome re-plated and their upholstery updated with custom-dyed vinyl."

"Your suppliers did *fantastic* work," Micky said, narrowing her sapphire eyes. "*I* think he's just *jealous* to see that you're so good at this!"

Brad took a large bowl of salad and set it on the soapstone countertop. "You're probably right—he always regarded decorating as his *exclusive* province. All those *degrees*, his *professorship*, his *presentations*, his *business*. Everything always had to be according to *his* standards."

Micky joined him at the counter and loaded salad onto a white Wedgwood china plate using the stainless-steel tongs in the bowl. "I think the table set *is* perfect in this kitchen . . . even the original owners of the house would've bought new furnishings if they'd lived here for long. *Especially* when new things came out that were easier to keep clean, like this *gorgeous* porcelain top!"

"This is why I moved out," Brad said as he sat down with her at the table. "It feels so great to be free to make my *own* decisions, in my *own* home." He set his plate and a basket of French bread baguettes toasted with garlic butter on the table.

"Brad, thank you so much for having me over this evening," she said. "It really hit me hard when I read your text about Shelley . . . I mean, I've heard in meetings about people addicted to drugs and alcohol killing themselves . . . actually, my own mother was one of them. I'm sorry about Shelley. But poor *Sally!* When someone close to you does this, it just leaves such a stabbing pain and . . . an emptiness. You know you couldn't have done anything to stop them, and, well . . . it *really* tears you *apart* to know you weren't important enough to keep them from leaving you behind." Her eyes welled up, and she dabbed the tears with her napkin.

"It's okay to cry, Micky," Brad said, touching her hand. "It's okay to cry for our friends. And it's normal for a similar death to bring up old, deep feelings about your own loss. So go ahead and cry—let it out. I'll go get some tissues."

He left through the archway next to the table and returned with a box of Kleenex. He handed her a tissue, placed the box in front of her, then moved his chair next to hers and sat down. Brad put his arm around her and said, "Cry as much as you need to, Micky. You're safe here."

*****

On Friday afternoon, Sally, who had been pacing her living room and clutching her cell phone, dropped into her favorite armchair by the fireplace and called Lillian.

Lillian answered after a few rings. "Sally, hi! Sorry I didn't pick up faster; I had to hunt for my phone. How are you?"

"Agitated," she replied. "I've been wrestling with prayers regarding Phil for the last couple of days, and, much as I'd love to follow the suggestion in Shelley's note about leaving him out of everything, it just doesn't seem like the next right thing. But I don't know how much to share with him. I really don't want him to come here, and there's nothing traditional planned."

"Hmm. I agree that you should at least call and tell him what happened. Basic human decency would seem to require informing a man that his only child has died. And that there are no plans for a traditional funeral, per Shelley's request. Ditto regarding burial, and specific request for scattering her ashes," Lillian said. "And right now, you don't know when the coroner will even release the body. You can tell him that.

"Then, depending on how he treats you after you've delivered the news, you have options: A) Ask if he'd like you to call back after plans are made; or if he's nasty, B) Tell him you just thought he should know that she's passed; and if he's demanding this, that or anything and insisting he be part of the planning and decisions, C) Tell him he's not welcome and that Shelley gave you that option. If you choose C, get his email address and send him the photo of her note.

"Try to avoid going off on him for telling Shelley you didn't want her. Pray about that before you call, because if I were in your shoes, I'd really need divine restraint to do that! Even though you and I know that no good would come of that discussion."

Sally exhaled a deep sigh. "What if he throws that at me without any prompting?"

"Just tell him that's not true and that you're going to hang up now. Then do so. And then leave him out of anything else. You are *not* obligated to suffer any abuse from him. Do you have his current contact information?"

"Just his work email and phone number from the firm where he works, and the company's address."

"That should suffice if any death notice paperwork requires it. It may be in your best interest to keep things civil, just in case Shelley created any debts or there are big expenses involved in putting her to rest; you may want to ask him to share those with you."

"I hadn't thought about that," Sally said. "I don't know if her hospital bill for last spring was ever paid. If not, I'm the one who checked her in. And I'm sure it won't be cheap, if an invoice comes my way." She rose from her chair and walked to the bay window, looking toward the raspberry patch.

"Lil, I've also been wrestling with thoughts about how best to lay Shelley to rest," Sally continued. "She pointedly did not believe in God or Christ, and I feel strongly that anything like a church service would be totally inappropriate for her. On the other hand, you, as the owner of the land where her ashes will be scattered—and as a writer—could use some spiritual concepts along with any additional thoughts you'd have. I could simply scatter her cremains, and perhaps say a few words about her.

"Would you be willing to serve as the presider? That way, I wouldn't be there as a priest."

"Of course, Sally. I think that's a wonderful idea, and I'd be honored to serve," Lillian said. "We can also host a luncheon at my house, if you like. That way, the church isn't officially involved in any way—but parishioners will have the opportunity to gather around you in support. You know they'll want to!"

Sally's voice caught with emotion as she replied, "Oh, Lil! I can't thank you enough—that would be perfect!"

"I'll make an announcement at Sunday's services, sharing the basic news," Lillian offered. "Would you like to write a note to go in the service bulletin and to share by email? Or should I draft something for you to review?"

"The announcements Sunday would be a great help," she said. "I'll write the note myself."

*****

Around four o'clock, Sally realized that her time for praying about the dreaded call to her ex-husband had morphed into procrastination that was only prolonging her agony. She closed with a simple prayer, "Please dear God, be with me in this call and guide my words and my actions, however it goes. In Jesus' name, I pray. Thank you, thank you, thank you. Amen."

Summoning her courage, she picked up her phone and placed the call.

"Phillip Martin's office," answered a crisp soprano voice. "Angela English speaking. How may I assist you?"

"My name is Sally Wise. I need to speak with Phil; is he available?"

"May I tell him the nature of your call?"

"I'm calling about a family matter," Sally said. "It's important."

"Please hold, Ms. Wise."

Family of Choice: Raising Each Other

Inside his ninth-floor office in Clayton, Missouri, Phillip Victor Martin III looked out of the expansive window, then at the clock. He hoped to get out early to avoid the Highway 40 weekend gridlock to reach his Frontenac home and the Absolut vodka waiting in the freezer. He grimaced when his assistant buzzed.

"Yes, Angela?"

"A call for you from a Sally Wise, Mr. Martin. An important family matter, she said."

"Put her through," he said, and after she clicked off, "Damn it!"

When he picked up the call, Sally was greeted with, "What the hell do you want?"

"I don't want anything, Phil. I just thought you should know that Shelley died on Monday of an intentional heroin overdose. In her suicide note, she requested that there be no funeral or burial, and instructed me to scatter her ashes. So, there's no need for you to do anything."

"*Monday?!* She died on *Monday* and you're just telling me *now?!*"

"I've been in shock, Phil," Sally explained. "She did it in a remote parking lot at my church in a car she stole from her unidentified boyfriend, her dope dealer with whom she's been living since her release last spring from the women's penitentiary. I hadn't heard from her for five years or so, when her phone had been disconnected. She told me she hadn't wanted me to know she was in prison."

"*Told* you? Told you when? Did you talk to her before she died?"

"February, when she showed up unannounced at my door in a snowstorm," she replied. "Supposedly for a visit, wanting to stay for a week or so to get her life back together; but, actually, it was to steal my silver, which I recovered in a pawn shop two blocks from my home. Then she shot up and OD'd on my bathroom floor. EMS saved her life and took her to the hospital for detox, but she refused my offer to pay for treatment to stay clean and sober. There was nothing I could do."

"*What* the *fuck,* Sally! Why didn't you call me then?!"

"What could you have done? Besides, I thought you two were in touch; she told me you were drinking, and had been for a long time."

"No. We *weren't* in touch," he snarled. "And of course, I drink. I don't *have* a problem—not like *you*."

"Phil, this conversation is over. I just thought you should know about Shelley."

"Just a *minute*—I'm her *father*. I have a *right* to decide how and where to bury my daughter!"

"No, Phil, you don't. She was an adult, and she put her wishes in writing, which I will honor. I'll send them to the email on your website as soon as I end this call, which is now. Good-bye."

Infuriated by the dial tone now screaming in his ear, Phil slammed down his phone. Too pissed off to drive immediately, he pulled open his desk drawer and took a swig of warm vodka. When he clicked on the email that pinged into his inbox, he opened the attachment and read the brief note. As he guzzled the remnants of the bottle, he realized that this embarrassing document now resided in the firm's servers.

"*Shit!*"

*****

Sunday, a bit after noon, Sally followed the path from the rectory's garden through the arbor connecting to Lillian's and around to the yellow Queen Anne's rear verandah. The weather had cooled enough that her sponsorship family's members were gathered in its shade.

Micky picked up a bouquet of fragrant white roses and lavender tied with a white ribbon and ran down the steps to greet her with a hug. "Sally, I'm so, *so* sorry about Shelley! Here, I made this for you—Lil gave me the flowers from her garden."

"Thank you, Micky! How sweet of you," she said, her eyes misting up. Sally enfolded her in a hug, which Micky returned. Both were crying, and they held each other tightly for several minutes.

When they stepped apart, Sally said, "I'm sorry that we had to cancel our sessions this week, Micky, and I'm afraid that I'm too drained to attempt counseling again this week. But I miss seeing you; would you like to come and visit me at home, as a friend? For tea, or maybe dinner?"

Micky smiled. "I'd love that! I can pick up French onion soup and whatever else you'd like from Dooley's, if that's okay?"

Sally smiled back. "That makes me feel better just thinking of it."

CHAPTER 29

By the following Tuesday evening, a Canadian air mass had slipped down over Northeast Ohio, and temperatures dipped below normal. Bright sunshine alternated with low-hanging, blue-gray clouds and cool, crisp air offered a prelude to the onset of fall.

Micky slid out of her Red Passion Cadillac and retrieved a large Dooley's to-go bag from the passenger's seat that she carried to the rectory's front door, which opened wide in response to her knock.

"I've brought comfort food!" she said as she hugged Sally in greeting. They went into the kitchen, where Micky extracted two insulated soup bowls and one large Styrofoam clamshell container. "It's so cold compared to last Sunday . . . I thought fettuccine Alfredo with chicken and broccoli would go well with our onion soup."

"Excellent!" Sally declared, taking plates from the cupboard for the pasta. "What about the soup? Shall we eat it from those bowls?"

Micky smiled and produced a small plastic container. "Dooley suggested we put the soup in oven-proof bowls, add this cheese blend on top and warm until it melts."

Sally nodded. She went to another cupboard and returned with two large ramekins. "These should do the trick!" She turned on the oven, prepared the ramekins and popped them in. "How was your day?"

"Good," Micky replied. "Two potential new clients in Columbus have put numbers from our proposed programs into their budgets for next year. Renewals for my current clients are starting to come in, and

I have presentations lined up for new prospects in Toledo in the next couple of weeks."

"Your boss should be pleased."

"He is. Thank God!"

"Have you had any more problems from him?"

"No . . . he hasn't tried *anything* since he was escorted out of the hotel in Dublin last month," Micky said with relief. "Still . . . I make sure he doesn't have a chance to, either. If I need to work late, I bring it home with me. And I *don't* tell him where I'm going in advance . . . I just file my call reports on time every Friday, and my numbers have made him back off."

"Sounds like a lot of pressure."

Micky shrugged. "I can handle it. For a while, anyway. And I'm going to a *lot* of A.A. meetings!" She picked up her plate of fettuccine and her soup and followed Sally into the dining room.

Sally said grace. "Almighty and ever-loving God, we offer you thanks for this time together. We thank you for your gifts of friendship and mutual support. And we thank you for this food and the people who prepared it, and especially for your daughter, Micky, who brought it here. Please bless it to our use and us to thy service. In Jesus' name we pray. Amen."

"Amen." Micky echoed. Picking up her spoon to dive into the soup's browned, molten cheese topping, she asked, "How are you feeling today, Sally?"

"Honestly?" She looked down and pushed aside a lock of red hair that was beginning to fade with grey. "Tired. I'm sleeping, but I just feel worn out."

"It's really sinking in now, isn't it?" Micky said. "I remember that in the shock of the news about my mother, it didn't seem real. Then, about a week later, I was just exhausted. I slept all the time, and I didn't want to do anything."

Sally attempted a half-hearted smile. "I don't want to do anything, either. But I have to make arrangements with a funeral home and make a few plans with Lil about the scattering and reception at her house," she said. "And then there's Phil—he's very tiresome."

"What's he doing?"

"Texting me nastygrams. Although the first one was somewhat amusing," Sally said. "I sent him the picture of Shelley's note that contained her wishes regarding her remains. It also said some very unflattering things about her father, and told me I didn't have to include him in any of this. He was incensed that I sent that to his company email, because now that 'awful information' is in the firm's servers."

Micky's eyes widened in disbelief. "*That's* his biggest concern? His daughter just killed herself, and he's worrying about it making *him* look bad . . . just in case anybody happens to dig through the jillions of bytes stored on the servers of a financial services firm?"

"I see you've got the picture." Sally enjoyed a healthy spoonful of onion soup and cheese. "He truly is an ass. And now, he's threatening to come to town and just stay until I do 'whatever I'm going to do with Shelley.' He says he has the right to be present."

"Do you really think he'd do that? Wouldn't that interfere with his business?"

"You're probably right," Sally concluded. "Even though much can be done remotely these days, he couldn't use his cell phone on the plane, and the rest of traveling doesn't allow time for much contact, either."

"You can't focus very well when you're out of the office," Micky said from her recent experience. "If he makes his money handling investment transactions or advising clients, it would cost him too much to come just to spite you."

"And he really doesn't care—as you so astutely pointed out," Sally agreed. "I think he just wants to put me on edge."

Micky finished her soup and started on the pasta. Sally followed suit, and conversation was set aside while they relished the warm, creamy dish.

Sally paused for breath when she was halfway through. She was smiling, and more color had returned to her face. "This was a wonderful choice, Micky! Plenty of protein, calming carbs—and the chicken breast in it is so tender! I must call Dooley later and give my compliments to the chef," she said. As she guided her fork back to the plate, she asked, "How are things going with Paul?"

After patting her lips with her napkin, Micky smiled and replied, "Everything's good . . . we've sort of settled into a routine. We go out to dinner most Friday nights, play golf Saturday mornings, usually with his friends Howie and Chet, who are also my clients and friends now . . . then after lunch, he goes to work at the dealership and I run errands, do laundry or whatever until time for Last Call with Brad. Unless there's an event at one of his clubs that we need to attend. We talk by phone most weekday evenings . . . sometimes we'll get together, but I need time for my meetings, and his dealership is open 'til nine."

Sally smiled. "That sounds nice, Micky. I'm happy for you," she said. "Is this the most time you've spent with any man you've dated?"

"Definitely!"

"How does that feel?"

"Comfortable. I like being with him . . . we're getting to know each other more . . . and we both have plenty of time to do our jobs and I have time for church and my program."

"Sounds like a good balance. You seem very relaxed and happy!"

"I am," said Micky. "And I feel particularly relaxed right now, full of onion soup and pasta."

"Me, too," Sally agreed. "This has been great, Micky. Would you like to come back on Thursday?"

"Sure. Let's do Chinese next time!"

*****

Sally's face beamed with delight as she spread hoisin sauce over the thin pancake and covered it with moo-shoo pork. As she carefully rolled up the package, she exclaimed, "I'm so glad you suggested this, Micky. I haven't had it for ages; Stromberg doesn't have a Chinese restaurant."

"Strongsville is great for its retail of everything, especially food," Micky replied. "And it really isn't very far away, you know."

"True. And I do go there to shop periodically. I just never think about seeking out a restaurant."

"Well, next time you're planning to come, call me and we can have a meal together . . . lunch or dinner. My office is there as well as my condo," she said. "Assuming I'm not out on the road, of course." Micky adeptly utilized chopsticks to take another bite of her cashew chicken on brown rice.

"How is your Fourth Step coming along?"

"Almost done. Thanks to our work together, I was able to put the major people or events of my life in perspective . . . and could see my part in them or what they affected in me," she answered. "Now I'm just reviewing past years in order, rummaging through my memories for any other resentments. And after that, it'll be on to fears and sex!"

Smiling, Sally noted, "We touched on those as well."

"Yes . . . and that made a *huge* difference in my understanding of what the Big Book says about them," Micky agreed. "I really appreciate the approach the book takes with sex . . . no judgments about it, just to be sure we don't do things selfishly or hurt anyone."

"Sound guidelines. Are you discussing the books' chapters on the Fourth Step with Brad?"

"Oh yes. He's really helpful," she said. "I'm thinking I'd like to ask him to hear my Fifth Step, when I finish my lists . . . as my sponsor, I think he should know everything about me to connect the dots when some current problem I call him about has roots in my past or a recurring character defect."

"Good idea."

"And you already know these things—you helped me discover them!" They laughed.

"Speaking of defective characters, it looks like you were right about Phil," she said. "His latest text started with threatening to hire an attorney to enforce his 'rights' concerning Shelly's remains. Then he claimed that since I had screwed her up so badly that she became a junkie, she was my problem. He decided he doesn't want any part of her now."

"Bet a major business initiative has come up," Micky surmised. "At least you won't have to worry about him being here. Any news from the police officer?"

Sally swallowed the last of her moo-shoo. "He called this morning. The autopsy determined there had been no foul play, cause of death was suicide by intentional overdose of heroin heavily laced with fentanyl. The coroner will release her body tomorrow, and I called the funeral home to pick her up and proceed with cremation. Sergeant Waters will bring me her personal effects."

"What are the plans?"

"We'll lay her to rest a week from Saturday, on the twenty-third at eleven o'clock," she said. "Lil will preside, since Shelly's ashes will go into her raspberry patch. And she'll host a luncheon at her house afterwards."

"The raspberry patch? In Lil's garden . . . why?"

"Because in her note, Shelley declared that she never believed in God, didn't want to be buried but preferred scattering her ashes. Anywhere except a church." Tears sprang up in Sally's eyes, and Micky reached out for her hand.

"Oh, Sally . . . I'm so *sorry*. That must hurt a lot!"

Lips pressed tightly together, she nodded. Then she confessed, "It hurts so much that I wasn't able to convey the love of God and Jesus Christ to my daughter. And that I lost her so early; in fact, it seems like I never really *had* a daughter. I kept hoping that eventually she'd come around, that we'd have a mother-daughter relationship. But now that can never happen."

Micky squeezed Sally's hand. "I know. Between her drinking and taking her life, I never really had a mother. Certainly no one who could show me how to live," she said, tears running down her cheeks. "But you're teaching me that now."

Sally hugged her. "You're helping me, too. Being here for me, like a daughter would," she said. She paused and took a breath. "Neither of them was able to be there for us; the disease was too powerful and they wouldn't allow God to help them. That's okay. And we're okay. We're sober. We have a program. We have a loving God we can depend on.

"And we have each other."

CHAPTER 30

Lillian, dressed in black jeans with a black cotton sweater and running shoes, stood next to Gus MacGregor and scanned the sky. She pointed south, beyond the yellow Victorian house where dark-bottomed, smoke-colored cumulus clouds were rolling toward the towering white columns currently overhead. "Looks like the forecast was right," she said. "I hope we can get the service done before the rain sets in."

Gus looked at his watch. "It's a quarter to eleven. Do you want me to go in and get Sally?"

"That's a good idea. I'll start getting people organized." As Gus ascended the verandah's steps, she moved through the crowd with a basket and handed each person a mesh bag of dried rose petals, created by Micky from spent blooms she and Gus had deadheaded from their gardens.

Inside, Gus knocked lightly on the doorway of the living room where Sally was sitting on a camel-back sofa with Micky. Brad was seated in a nearby needlepoint armchair. An elegant silk scarf with a naive print of blues, purples and greens draped over a small box on the coffee table.

"Are you ready, Sally?" Gus asked in a low, soft voice. "It's time to take Shelley out to the garden."

"Oh! Yes, I think so." She reached for the box as she rose, then set it back on the table and sat down again. "That's. That's my daughter," she stammered. "I carried her for nine months. But. But I can't carry her like this!"

Micky put her arm around Sally's shoulders. "Would you like me to do that for you?"

Sally dabbed her eyes with a tissue, looked at her and nodded. "Thank you, Micky. Thank you so much." The two of them stood up, and Micky lifted the box and its covering from the table.

Brad also rose from his chair, moved to Micky and tucked the corners of the scarf into her hands. "Try holding the package like this—it will keep everything together." He looked out the window. "It seems to be getting windy out there."

They went out by the back door and down the stairs to the group of more than one hundred people who had come to support Sally. Gus guided them around the crowd to Lillian, who then led everyone through the garden to its far, wilder area. All had followed the announcement's instructions to wear casual clothes with comfortable walking shoes.

Lillian stopped by the middle of the raspberry patch, and motioned for people to spread out around it. "Thank you all for coming to be with our dear friend Sally as we release the earthly remains of her daughter, Shelley, to return to the earth. Her spirit has already been released to the universe."

Sally, at Lillian's side, explained, "Friends, I'm not here as a priest to my parishioners today. I'm just a mother, giving her only child back to God in a manner and place that is in accordance with Shelley's wishes. She didn't want to be buried, but instead asked that her ashes be scattered. And she didn't want a church service, as she did not believe."

Lillian said, "However, Shelley chose to make her exit from this life over there, by the trees behind my raspberry bushes, in a secluded area

Family of Choice: Raising Each Other

of Grace Church's north parking lot. As a long-time member, I'm glad that Grace could provide a refuge for her then, and that these bushes will provide refuge for her from now on, as they do for many rabbits, birds and other wildlife. This resting place will not be static. Over time, she will commingle with the soil, nourishing the plants, helping them to form their berries. Birds will eat and carry the berries far and wide, so Shelley's former being will not be limited geographically."

Lillian paused, then continued. "Shelley stated that she did not belong anywhere, had never felt like she belonged anywhere, and so did not want to start now by being buried in one spot. But she had returned to her mother at her end. So, with this as her resting place, her mother, Sally, will have a tangible memorial and Shelley will have a place from which she may continue her travels."

Sally spoke again. "Shelley's path in life was not an easy one. Both of her parents drank. I got sober when she was twelve, and her father and I divorced a year later. We sent her to an excellent private school, where she fell in with other lost children and developed her own addiction to alcohol and other drugs. Despite that, she did well in school and pursued a promising career in her field during her twenties and early thirties. Then her phone was disconnected and she disappeared from my life. She turned up on my doorstep last spring, a heroin addict and ex-con. She overdosed during her visit, was saved by paramedics, but refused to go to treatment. The next time I saw her was on Labor Day. In a stolen car, parked where Lillian described with the doors locked, dead from an intentional overdose."

Tears quietly streamed down her cheeks. She looked around at the people in attendance. "I see so many friends here that I've made in A.A. and Al-Anon," she continued. "Many of us have had experiences with people we've loved who were or are like Shelley. There is no more *painful* form of powerlessness, in my opinion, than this. Please join me in a moment of silent remembrance of them and of Shelley."

Heads bowed. The silence was punctuated here and there by a sob or blowing nose.

Lillian began the Serenity Prayer, and others joined in. Then she checked the direction of the strengthening breeze, and asked people to line up behind her on the upwind side of the raspberry patch. Holding the scarf-wrapped box aloft, she implored, "Shelley, you are free from your earthly bonds. Be at peace with the Spirit of the Universe!"

She removed the scarf and handed it to Sally, who was standing beside her. Lillian opened the box and poured its contents over the bushes closest to them. Most of the ashes fell through their branches to the ground, some catching on the foliage. The wind carried the rest down the wide line of bushes, coating them along the way.

Lillian, Sally and Micky shook the rose petals out of their mesh bags over the bushes, and invited others to do so as well. Then Lillian led the procession back to the house.

Brad had returned there earlier to guide Dooley where to put the pans of fried chicken, green beans and potato salad he had prepared and to stage the service wear on the kitchen table, along with the first of several platters of fudge brownies that Lillian had baked. He steered people to the buffet as they came to the verandah.

Sally greeted everyone at the bottom of the steps, supported by Micky, Lillian and Gus. As the last of the guests went inside, a light patter of raindrops began and the four of them followed.

Brad turned to Sally. "Would you like me to bring you a plate in the dining room?"

"Yes, please," she said. "And bring one for yourself. Dooley's the caterer; he can take care of the food. I need my family with me."

Family of Choice: Raising Each Other

After they finished lunch, Micky left the table to look at the framed pictures of Shelley that were displayed on the sideboard. They showed her as a child of various ages in happy settings: At the Cleveland Zoo; on a carousel horse; wearing a party hat with a birthday cake in front of her; sitting on Santa's lap. But the child was never smiling. Her chin was usually lowered, and her light brown eyes stared out furtively, like a wild creature at the edge of a wood peering at the landscape to determine if it were safe to come out there. Then Micky came to an eight-by-ten portrait where Shelley was smiling, the light making her strawberry blonde hair frame her face like a halo and the eyes were looking out, connecting with the viewer.

Holding the photo, Micky asked, "How old was she in this picture? She looks beautiful!"

"Sixteen," Sally replied. "She was a junior in high school. We had a lot of fun together that year, talking about her hopes and dreams, looking at colleges. She was so excited when she was accepted into Kent State's fashion program." Sally joined Micky at the sideboard.

"This is her high school graduation. And then her graduation from Kent. In this last picture, she's modeling the first dress she designed that was produced by the Gap."

"That's *so* pretty," Micky said. "She was really talented!"

Sally smiled. "Yes, she was."

People started coming into the dining room to offer their final condolences and say their good-byes. Sally moved out to the front hallway to make their exits easier. Those who had planned ahead unfurled umbrellas as they stepped out from the covered porch, others made a run for it.

Micky and Brad cleaned up and put the leftover food into the refrigerator, then kissed Sally and Lillian goodbye and left.

The two old friends sat down on the porch swing, breathing in the rain-cleansed air. Instead of the storm that had threatened in the morning, they heard the soothing music of gentle, soaking rain on the porch roof and sidewalk.

Sally took Lillian's hand. "Thank you, Lil. For all of this. Especially for your wise and comforting words, and the beautiful ritual you created. It gave me the closure I needed, and it was perfect for Shelley."

"She's at peace now, Sally," she replied. "There's an old mountain saying: 'Rain on a casket means it's a happy corpse.' She's at peace."

CHAPTER 31

On Tuesday morning after the scattering service, Lillian's cat pouted by the kitchen's back door as she eyed the three suitcases parked there. She walked over and rubbed up against them, leaving her mark along with a few long hairs from her calico coat, then looked at her owner and voiced her discontent.

"Now, Pretty Girl, you'll be alright," she soothed, petting her. "Sally will take good care of you. And I'll only be gone for a few days." She picked up the cat as Gus moved the luggage out and loaded it into his blue GMC.

Lillian kissed the top of the feline's head and set her down in her bed in the corner. "You be good!" She grabbed her purse from its wall hook and locked the door behind her. Clambering up into the large SUV, she told Gus, "Even though it's been a few years since I went anywhere, that cat still remembers what suitcases mean. She began her lament as soon as I put them out on the bed to pack!"

He nodded as he pulled out of the driveway and headed toward the Ohio Turnpike. "Animals learn the signs that their routines are about to be disrupted. None of them like that," he said. "I don't think your lovely cat is fond of my visits, either."

"She'll get over it. Eventually!" Lillian laughed. "Do you have any pets, Gus?"

"Not now; I'm between furry friends. My dog died a couple of years after Maggie passed, and I haven't been sure I wanted to be that tied down just yet."

"It's hard to make decisions after you lose someone," Lillian remarked. "At least it was for me; my brain just didn't process things normally for a while. I wonder if Sally will go through the same grief phases, since she essentially lost Shelley years before this happened."

"I did when we lost Mark—my grandson. He hadn't been part of our lives since he was seventeen and went off to Ohio State. When he dropped out because of the drugs, he dropped the family, too. Even so, my world just stopped after he shot up and died just before his thirtieth birthday." He paused. "You know, Lil, you really did a great job with the scattering service. Your words gave renewed comfort to a lot of us there who've suffered losses to addiction, including me: Mark; his mother, Annie; and, of course, Maggie."

Lillian's right hand flew up beside her mouth in an expression of shock. "Oh, Gus! I'm so sorry; I had no idea. You'd talked about your grandson over Labor Day, which really helped Sally. But your daughter, and Maggie, too?"

"As we learn in Al-Anon, it's a family disease. Annie had one too many before getting behind the wheel and hit a tree a few months after Mark died. My beautiful Maggie drank off and on for all of the years of our marriage. Tried A.A. occasionally, but never committed to it. Al-Anon and God restored me to sanity and guided me to quit trying to control her and just love her for who she was, and enjoy her periods of sobriety. She did manage to rein in the quantity somewhat, most of the time. But the booze took its toll on her body. She had an esophageal hemorrhage and bled to death internally in her sleep one night."

She touched his arm. "I can only guess how hard all of that must have been for you. There but by the grace of God go I; and I do thank God every day for my sobriety, one day at a time."

They had reached the toll booth. Gus pulled up to the machine, took the ticket and drove toward Toledo. Then he looked over at her and asked, "When did you get sober, Lil?"

"October 13, 1971—in a couple of weeks, I'll celebrate 46 years of sobriety."

"That *is* something to celebrate! I'd like us to plan something special for the occasion—unless you already have plans, of course."

"Well, I usually have my sponsees over for dinner . . ."

"How about if I get us some prime steaks and grill them? And make a big salad and baked potatoes? If it's okay to invite myself back?"

She smiled at him, her blue eyes twinkling brightly. "I think you know you're welcome anytime now, Gus."

"Thank you. I never want to presume," he said. "So, what led you to A.A.?"

Lillian thought for a moment, looking back in time. "Well, it was shortly after my thirty-first birthday and my second divorce. Drinking was the main thing I had in common with my husbands, and since they both drank much more than I did, I was sure that *they* were causing all of our problems. Near the end of my second marriage, I started in Al-Anon, where it didn't take too long for me to recognize my *own* alcoholism—along with my mother's and that of others on both sides of my family.

"My pedigree includes English sots as well as Cherokees who couldn't handle fire-water and plenty of Scots-Irish who appreciated the efficiency of classic white lightning distilled in the mountain hollers of West Virginia. Both of my parents drank nightly; Dad didn't have a problem, but Mom usually wandered into a blackout at some point in the evening. But in Shaker Heights, where we moved when I started junior high school, it wasn't called 'alcoholism;' it was called 'cocktail hour' even though it lasted at least two hours, plus a nightcap.

The rule was to wait until after five o'clock—although holidays began with Bloody Marys before breakfast, and mowing the lawn or weeding the garden deserved a beer or two in the afternoon.

"Dad had no problem doing his job as president of a chemical distribution business and Mom was active in civic leadership positions. By the time I was in high school, I was drinking, too, with their permission. They said it was important to learn how to drink at home, before I went to college, because girls who don't know how to hold their liquor could get in trouble. I was good at that, so I thought everything was okay. I just followed in their footsteps, always made good grades, graduated college Phi Beta Kappa, landed a job in a large Cleveland ad agency and soon married its vice-president. Everything looked great on the outside."

"But everything wasn't great?"

"I'd always wanted a career as a writer, and that's what I thought the ad agency would provide, but women there could only be secretaries back in 1961. After I married, I couldn't work there anymore. So, I started taking some creative writing courses, which just gave my first husband another excuse to fight about. When the fights started to get physical, I filed for and got a divorce.

"But as the case dragged out, I drank more. And then I was drinking with my lawyer. And got involved with said lawyer, who became my second husband about a year after my divorce was final. That marriage wasn't much different from the first one. So, it didn't take me as long to end it, but it cost more.

"I had continued taking writing courses and wanted to go back to school full-time to pursue a master's degree, but that court fight really drained me emotionally. I drank even more, trying to cope, but then the booze turned on me and just made me anxious and depressed. By the time I was free from the marriage, my brain was so fried I had trouble connecting sentences. And I'd sit in my favorite bar, making notes on cocktail napkins for writing the great American novel, but I couldn't make out my scrawled handwriting the next day. The light bulb came on in one Al-Anon meeting when I heard another woman tell my story from the podium, and that she went to A.A. and got sober. I realized I had to quit drinking if I wanted a shot at having a happy, successful life."

"I'm glad you did," Gus said, smiling. "And I'm especially glad you succeeded in the publishing world; I recently read your first book and really enjoyed it!"

Lillian, bemused, raised an eyebrow. *Don't Get Your Tush Too Near the Toaster*? Thanks. But, really? My work has always been aimed at women like me, who grappled with unconventional jobs and navigating life in the changing era when I came of age and beyond."

He grinned. "Well, as the husband of an alcoholic wife, I could relate to your struggles with domestic chores for which you were totally unprepared. But I was surprised by the chapter 'The Best Thing I Make for Dinner is a Reservation'. You're such a fabulous cook!"

"Not back then, I wasn't. I got that title off of a tee shirt my mother gave me for my birthday. And that hamburger casserole I described really was a One-Hit Wonder. A neighbor's recipe, I must add. My mother didn't teach me anything about keeping house or cooking."

"Why not? I thought all women of the previous generation had skills in both."

"Not all women," she replied. "My mother was a MacAllister. Her father owned MacAllister Mining Supply in West Virginia. They lived in a glorious Victorian house in Bramwell, which had the highest per capita income in the country at that time. All of the coal operators, his customers, lived there, and competed for who had the most luxurious home. Their wives and daughters focused on finding the highest quality furnishings, the latest fashions, looking beautiful and being charming. Chores, including cooking, were performed by staff. The ladies of the house planned the parties, discussed the desired menu with the head cook and supervised the housekeeper, who handled the details of executing events as well as daily operations. That was how Mom was raised. And while Dad wasn't from money, he did well enough that we at least had a maid who cleaned and did most of the cooking. I was never encouraged to learn how to do any of that."

"Did you visit your mother's family often?"

"Lots, when we lived in Charleston. Bramwell was a couple of hours south, near Bluefield. It was a magical-looking place, full of homes built in the glory days of the Gay Nineties in the Nineteenth Century. My grandparents' house was a three-story Queen Anne that was on the higher bank of a bend in the creek that flowed through town. When I sat in the curve of the library's turret, I could hear the music of the water rushing over the stones; I thought the creek was singing to me."

"Ah. So that's where you got your love of Victorian architecture."

"Yes. My house reminds me of theirs, and I love that Stromberg has lots of beautiful old homes. I feel *truly* at home there."

"And your mother used her maiden name for your middle name."

"She was Mary MacAllister Meadows, so it was just natural to her that I would be Lillian MacAllister Meadows."

"So, how did Lillian MacAllister Meadows ever learn how to cook so well?"

"From my first sponsor, Sebastian," she said. "He taught me that cooking could actually be fun and creative—among many other things! Basically, he re-parented me."

"Your sponsor was a man?"

"He was gay, but discrete about it back in 1971," she said. "But since he was a professor at the Cleveland Institute of Art, no one thought much about it. Of course, some of the women in the program goaded me a little about needing a female sponsor, but his comments showed me that his brain worked like mine did. I felt like he was the big brother I never had; I always felt totally safe with him. And he was able to get me to open up about my feelings, admit what was going on with me—something that was *never allowed* in my family of origin."

"Nor in mine," Gus agreed. "That was regarded as a sign of weakness, a failure of self-control, especially for a man. It was also forbidden to talk about problems of any sort outside of the family: 'Don't air the dirty laundry!' But the family members didn't want to hear about them either, so the only option was to stuff everything inside."

"Indeed! Thank God for the liberation and cleansing power we get from the Twelve Steps—in A.A. and in Al-Anon. Where did you grow up, Gus?"

"Lots of places, really—Army brat. My father was an officer, West Point. At his insistence, I started college there, but after two years I realized I loved engineering much more than the military, so I transferred to MIT and never regretted it."

"When did you settle in Grosse Pointe?"

"I started my career in the Detroit area, working for automotive and defense companies. It took several jobs and promotions before we moved to the house where I've lived for the last twenty-some years."

The farmland that Lillian had been enjoying from her window's view began giving way to developments. They crossed the Maumee River and took the exit for I-75 north. Gus turned the conversation to plans for tomorrow night's presentation and the people he'd heard from who were expecting to attend. Lillian was relieved that she knew many of them.

The highway skirted along the Detroit River briefly before Gus exited and drove into Grosse Pointe's suburban neighborhoods. As they passed through streets lined with mature trees, Lillian saw well-kept yards and stately homes built in the late 1930s through the early 1960s. Architectural styles were mostly Tudor revivals, Georgian or Colonial. "This looks like Shaker Heights," she said.

"That's not surprising," Gus replied. "Both were well-to-do suburbs of industrial cities on the Great Lakes that prospered after the Great Depression and particularly post-World War Two."

He presently turned into the driveway of a soft orange-brown brick Colonial home topped by a grey shingled roof with a brown front door and matching shutters. A walkway led from the drive through some trees to the door, but Gus passed it by and proceeded to the garage. He cut the engine, popped the hatch and went around the car to open Lillian's door. "Welcome to my humble abode," he said as he extended his hand to help her down from her seat. "If you'd kindly open that door in front of the car, I'll put the plants you brought into the greenhouse."

Lillian followed him into a large, orderly space filled with high tables of healthy young plants growing in one-gallon black plastic containers on the right, and seedlings in tree slips on the left. An automatic mister came on and briefly spritzed the seedlings. She smiled and nodded her approval. "Very impressive, Gus. You've been quite busy out here!" She reviewed the tags on the larger plants. "Your cuttings of my introductions look wonderful. Thanks for getting them off to such a great start!"

"My pleasure," he said. "Would you like to stretch your legs in the garden for a bit before we take the bags inside?"

"Of course!"

The center aisle led to a door that opened into a smaller room with a desk, potting bench, tools and containers. Gus opened a final door and invited Lillian into the garden. A gravel path led to a rectangular patio of tan interlocking pavers. Gardens on either side of the path contained irregular plantings of young roses. Gus explained, "The nursery beds. I've culled heavily. I keep these close to the garage, because it's easier to water and to keep my records. Also, you don't see them from the house, so it doesn't matter if they sometimes look sparse."

Like her home, the yard was mainly gardens. But these were more scientifically organized: Hybrid Teas; Minifloras; Miniatures; and Floribundas were in dedicated beds, with Shrub roses in beds surrounding the house. A few Old Garden Roses infiltrated those areas.

"Where are your Climbers, Gus? I see lots of good spots along your fences, and a couple of empty trellises on the house."

He sighed. "I told you—it's tough to grow climbing roses around here. That's why I'm so excited about your roses. I'm hoping they'll work in our climate here."

He popped into the garage and got their bags out of the SUV. Lillian followed him along the driveway, in through the side door and up the stairs. He gestured toward an all-white room with a double bed buried in pillow shams and a white dresser. "This is the guest room," he said, pausing in the doorway. Then he set down the bags, looked deep into her eyes and continued, "Or, you're welcome to share my room. I don't mean to pressure you, Lil, but I also don't want you to think I don't find you attractive!"

She laughed and took his hands. "We've been seeing each other for three months now, Gus. I was wondering if we were going to move our relationship to this level! Why don't we have a little afternoon delight before dinner?"

With a smile of anticipation and relief, he took her in his arms and kissed her.

"Those steaks you're grilling smell heavenly," Lillian said from her chair at the patio table. "I really worked up an appetite!"

His white moustache twitched into a grin. "Yes, we both did!" He grabbed the long tongs and turned the meat.

She stood up and joined him at the grill, touching him on the shoulder. "I'm glad we waited until we could be here, on your turf. It felt perfectly natural to be with you in your bed."

"It felt perfectly wonderful to be in it with you," he replied with a wink. "And I'm glad we could both laugh about the inevitable awkwardness of first-time love-making, especially since we were equally out of practice!"

"And equally concerned that maybe our bodies wouldn't work anymore," she giggled. "Thank God for leisurely foreplay!"

"Yes. That's one of the gifts of age—being freed up from the bursting, insistent passion of youth," Gus said as he placed the steaks on plates. "There's time to enjoy just being close, and to explore one another, see what feels good, and how your partner responds."

She followed him to the table, next to a fragrant bed of apricot 'Honey Perfume' roses, and resumed her seat. They added salad and garlic bread to their plates, then Lillian held her water glass aloft in a toast. "To the joy and wonder of further explorations!"

They clinked glasses. "To wonderful explorations!"

*****

Lillian woke up alone in the king bed the next morning. She looked around at the gray walls and the 50-inch flat screen TV mounted above the dark wooden dresser opposite the bed, then at a matching highboy. The room's only bit of color was in the yellow, gray and white print floor-length drapes flanking closed white aluminum architectural mini-blinds.

The sound of rushing water indicated that Gus was taking a shower. She stretched and her hand hit the charcoal tufted headboard. Throwing her legs over the side of the bed, she hopped down to the light gray carpeted floor and padded into the bathroom, where the carpet gave way to 24-inch tiles of white Carrara marble with dramatic dark veins. Once she was past the threshold, the surface was pleasantly heated. After using the closeted commode, she washed her face in one of the rectangular sinks set into the white marble countertop. As she was drying off, the fogged-up glass shower door opened and Gus emerged with a white towel tied around his trim waist.

Lillian turned to him and smiled. "Well, aren't you a fetching sight," she said with a teasing leer. "A reminder of yesterday's fun is a great way to start the day!"

He grinned and raised his damp white eyebrows, dangling his hand near the towel's knot. "I could show you the full Monty, but then the day wouldn't start until lunch. I'm thinking you might enjoy a shower, coffee and breakfast now even more than my delectable self, though?"

Laughing, she admitted, "True. But I'll take a rain check!"

After reveling in the commodious white marble shower stall, she dried off with a fluffy Egyptian cotton terry towel like the one Gus had used as a fig leaf. Then she slipped on her well-faded jeans and a light blue V-necked tee shirt and headed downstairs.

Lillian was overwhelmed when she entered the vast open-concept kitchen/bar/dining room space, with its sleek white walls, industrial-size stainless steel appliances and quartz countertops that neatly defined the various areas. Her eye found a place to rest at the end of the room, where a picture window above the huge sink offered a view of the roses in the backyard garden. The smell of bacon frying drew her inside.

Gus deftly put the bacon on two plates, added scrambled eggs and toasted English muffins and led her to seats at the peninsula, where a pot of coffee, mugs and place settings awaited.

"You were right, Gus, I am hungry. This is perfect!" She looked around the area. "Your kitchen and dining area is stunning. I know you love to cook, but this seems like a lot of space for one person."

"Thank you. I had a lot of work done to update the house after Maggie passed. She liked early American furnishings, which were pretty tired after a few decades. And the formal dining room wasn't really comfortable to eat in alone, or even with a friend." He sipped his coffee. "So, I hired an architect and an interior designer and turned them loose. I like the clean functionality of everything, and eventually the changes will help sell the house, no doubt."

"But?" she queried, noticing a slight sheepish look in his eyes.

"But sometimes I feel like I'm staying in a luxury hotel. Or the set of an urban bachelor reality TV show."

Lillian laughed with relief. "Oh, Gus, I had exactly that reaction! It's all very well done, and great quality—it just doesn't feel like anyone really lives here."

After breakfast, they cleaned up together. Then he took her hand and led her through a doorway into the hall and a few steps further. "I really *do* live in here," he said.

"Oh my! Yes, this does look homey," she agreed. "It's still very modern and carries through the basic pallete, but that whole wall of panoramic windows brings the roses right into the room! And the washed terracotta bricks around the fireplace add some warmth, along with the rough mantle that matches the ceiling beams."

"I particularly like the skylights. They brighten the room regardless of the weather," he said as he ascended the curved brick steps leading to the bookcases on either side of the fireplace. "This is where I keep my gardening library, and a few of the crystal trophies from rose shows through the years."

"I love the rose photos everywhere. Are they pictures of your winners, or your photography class entries?"

"Both. Some were taken by friends who visited my garden, and were kind enough to share them with me."

Lillian walked over to the beige sectional seating area and patted its recliner portion next to an end table piled high with books, magazines and a remote for the huge TV recessed above the fireplace. "I'm guessing this is your favorite spot in the house?"

He nodded. "Yes. Other than the garden, of course."

"As I entered the kitchen this morning, I walked past a doorway and it looked like there's a grand piano in there?"

"A baby grand, yes. It's this way."

She followed him into a formal living room. The piano was at the end closest to the doorway; a wood-burning fireplace and original built-in bookshelves from the 1950s were at the other. Framed pictures of varied sizes covered the piano and the shelves. A gold-framed eight-by-ten of a beautiful young woman with thick wavy red hair spilling over her shoulders was the dominant one on the piano.

Gus told her, "That's Maggie, when she was young. Shortly after we were married. She was the pianist in the family; she convinced Annie to take lessons as a child, but she quit when she became a teenager."

"She was quite a beauty. I only knew her in later years, and she was certainly lovely then, too," Lillian said. She picked up a smaller photo of a blonde young woman. "Is this Annie?"

"Yes," he replied. "She got my coloring. And her mother's drinking problem, unfortunately." He looked over the frames, identifying Annie and Maggie at different ages and activities, as well as a few of his late grandson, Mark.

They moved to the photos in the bookshelves, most of which were of Gus' parents and earlier generations of his extended family. Lillian picked up a more recent-looking picture and asked, "Who's this?"

"That's my son, Bruce. He lives in Ann Arbor; he's a professor of mathematics at Michigan," he said. "Here are some other photos of him, as he was growing up."

As she looked over the images, she said, "He's a nice-looking young man. You've never mentioned him before."

"Well, we usually were talking about addiction or recovery, and Bruce has never had a problem. His name just never came up. He was always a good kid, responsible, made good grades, played sports, had good friends."

"Is he married? Does he have kids?"

"He married a couple of years after college, but it didn't work out. She fell in love with someone else, and they divorced. He's never had much interest in trying again, at least, not yet." He turned away from the bookcase. "Let's go out to the garden. It's supposed to be a beautiful day."

He led her back through the great room, then through a sliding glass door in the bank of windows that opened onto the patio. They strolled through the beds and discussed the plans for her presentation that evening.

"How many do you think will be there?" she asked.

"Probably around thirty or forty. I invited the Detroit Rose Society to join our Metropolitan Society for your program. People are very interested."

"It's been a while since I spoke in public. I'm excited, but also a little nervous," she confessed.

"Don't worry, they'll love your roses," he said. He cupped her face in his hands. "And I love you."

CHAPTER 32

"I'm so glad I was here for your first time back in the pulpit since your loss, Sally," Gus said from his seat at Lillian's round oak kitchen table after the October 1 service. "When you referenced Mark's Gospel about a man casting out demons in Jesus' name and told us how wretched and helpless you felt in being unable to do that with your daughter's heroin addiction, I was right there with you—and saw I wasn't the only one. Then you shared how you've lived out James' suggestion to submit yourself to God: When you draw near to God and resist the devil, God draws near to *you*, and the devil flees from *you*. Not from your daughter, but from *you*. That's worked for me, too. What a powerful, realistic message of hope!"

"Thank you, Gus. This *was* an emotional sermon for me today. It meant a lot to see your supportive face in the pew with Lil and Micky," she replied. "And it's a great blessing to be surrounded now by my *recovery* family." Sally reached beside her to touch Brad's hand.

He turned his hand over, twined his fingers around hers and gave a gentle squeeze. "That's what we're here for—to support each other."

"Oh yes," Micky agreed. "You've all helped me so much . . . especially *you*, Sally . . . I'm happy to have a chance to give back! I've never had anyone who loved and supported me before. Being a part of this makes me feel so much stronger . . . and *much* less afraid."

"You've grown a lot in these last eight months, Micky," Lillian observed. "Brad's done a much better job as your sponsor than I did."

"It's been a team effort," he insisted. "You've been the rock for all of us, Lil. Sally did the Third Step with Micky, and helped her with Four. And I'll hear her Fifth Step this Saturday."

Everyone smiled, and Lillian said, "That's wonderful, Micky! Step Five is a major springboard in recovery."

"I'm actually looking forward to it . . . Sally's counseling has taught me that I can't *change* my past, but I *can* put events in perspective. Brad says Step Five will fine-tune that, strengthen my foundation and guide us to create an action plan for doing Six, Seven, Eight and Nine." She paused, a bit embarrassed to be the center of attention. "So, how was your trip, Lil? How did your presentation go?"

"The trip was a breeze, since Gus did all of the driving—as well as most of the cooking," she replied, smiling at him. "And I was pleased that I hadn't forgotten how to handle PowerPoint and talk to a group of people."

Gus couldn't contain himself. "She's much too modest. She was a big hit—and so were her roses! I invited two societies, about fifty members, and everyone wanted her climbers as soon as they're available," he said. "I already had four trusted rosarians lined up with non-disclosure/non-distribution agreements and took their roses to trial in our area, along with me. But I also took two extra of each variety with the necessary paperwork, because I correctly guessed that we could turn the demand into a fundraising auction after her talk. We raised nearly five hundred dollars!"

"Wow! Congratulations, Lil. I'm so glad you convinced her to move forward with sharing her roses, Gus, among other things," Sally said with a wink at her friend, who blushed.

"My pleasure," he replied, a discreet smile beneath his neat white moustache.

Lillian turned to Brad. "You had mentioned holding your housewarming this month; have you set a date?"

He reached down to the slim leather portfolio leaned against the legs of his chair and produced envelopes, which he handed to each of them at the table. "Yes—Saturday, the twenty-first. You're all invited, of course. I hope you can make it—especially you, Gus. You're family now!"

The dapper gentleman grinned. "Thank you, I'm delighted to be included; in the family and on your guest list." He put his arm around Lillian and inquired, "As long as that's okay with you?"

She replied with a demure kiss on his cheek. "Of course, it is. But it's polite of you to ask."

Sally smirked at Lillian and reminded her, "You really need to call your editor."

Lillian reddened and quietly chided, "Hush!" To the others, she announced, "Remember, my anniversary dinner is coming up. Friday, the thirteenth—my lucky day! It'll be your lucky day, too: Gus has promised us prime steaks, and he's a master with a grill."

"I'll look forward to that!" Brad said, as he rose from the table. Sally and Micky joined him, and they carried their plates and coffee cups to the sink before saying their goodbyes.

Gus helped with the dishes then retrieved his bag from upstairs. Lillian accompanied him out to his GMC. Before he got in, he took her in his arms for a long, heartfelt kiss and lingering embrace.

She turned her bright blue eyes up to him before they let go. "I always hate it when you leave."

He smiled, wistfully looking back at her. "Me, too. But I'll be back in a couple of weeks for the parties—and more often after that, now that I've been adopted by your clan!"

"I'd like that!" she said as she released him to climb into the driver's seat. She waved and blew kisses as he drove off, then went back inside and straight to her office.

Seated at her walnut desk, she called her editor's cell. "Ann, I know 'stop the presses' is a phrase only used in old movies, but it applies now. We need a new final chapter—one that may give our readers an additional avenue of hope."

"Oh? What kind of hope? Can you give me a title—and a draft in a few days?"

"Yes to the draft. The title is 'Never Say Never,'" said Lillian. "Believe it or not, Ann, I've found love again."

*****

That evening after dinner, Brad was treading water in the capricious currents of his rekindled love life. He'd made Oscar's favorite dessert, orange soufflé, hoping to put him in a good mood. Encouraged by the relaxed expression in his lover's liquid chocolate eyes and satisfied smile as he blotted his lips with a napkin, Brad cleared the dishes and returned with an ivory envelope like the ones that had elicited so much joy a few hours earlier.

He sat down and handed it to Oscar with a smile and a slight flourish.

"What's this?"

"Your invitation—to be my most special guest at my housewarming party. On Saturday, October twenty-first, from two to five o'clock. The honor of your presence is most sincerely requested."

"It is? I've been sincerely requesting you to discuss plans for this event for the last two months, but you kept putting me off," Oscar snarled. "This is the first I've heard of it. And the engraved invitation suggests that it is a fait accompli."

"That is correct."

"But we're together again. We've always entertained together." Oscar's brow knit in perplexity.

"We're dating," Brad sought to clarify. "We don't live together, nor identify as a couple now. And when we *did*, our parties were always planned by *you*, using only *your* china and silver, to entertain *your* guests. I just cooked and served—your private caterer. We *never* entertained *together*."

"I don't understand."

"No, Oscar, you never did," Brad said. "This is *my* home, which I've decorated myself to reflect *my* taste. I'm welcoming *my* friends, my A.A. family, my clients, my suppliers into the comfort of my home. I'll serve them with my grandmother's china and silver—just as I did in the years before I met you. I get to be *me* again."

"But I *gave* you this house! You wouldn't have it if it weren't for me," Oscar insisted. "I would think that should entitle me to be co-host rather than just one of the guests!"

"Ah. *There* it is."

"There what is?"

"Your expectations—the *truth* behind your elaborate scheme to snatch the home I wanted so you could give it to me," Brad replied. "Sorry, but I won't allow you to control me anymore. I suggest you discuss this with your therapist. If you decide you can't be in this relationship without being in control, please RSVP with your regrets."

*****

Micky marveled again at the beauty of Brad's house as she drove her Red Passion Cadillac up the circle drive and stopped at the front door. Even though she had looked forward to doing this step, she wasn't sure about how it would go, and she noticed her legs were trembling slightly as she mounted the stairs.

Her apprehension evaporated as Brad met her at the door with a warm smile and a big hug. "Come in, come in, Micky! Thanks for being on time," he said as he looked at his watch. "You're even a bit early—which is good, since we have a lot of ground to cover."

As they cleared the vestibule, he guided her to the right and gestured toward the built-in window seat of the living room's bay, newly appointed with a gold-and-terra cotta upholstered cushion and a flotilla of pillows of various sizes, fillings and textures in complementary and contrasting colors. "Oh, Brad! When did you get this done? It really makes the room . . . and it's perfect with the sofa!" She sat down and noticed a large coffee table with ornately carved legs and an interestingly curved white marble top. "This is new, too . . . and I love the shape . . . I haven't seen anything like it."

"Thanks. The Victorians called it a turtle top. This is part of a set I found—there's a taller one in the dining room's bay."

"And you've buried this one in food . . . trialing things for your party?"

He grinned. "Well, I have experimented with a cocktail sauce for the shrimp. And a couple of dips for the veggies and chips, but the brie, Havarti and grapes are pretty standard," he admitted. "Once we get going, we won't want to stop for lunch—so I like to graze throughout the process. Food is always bonding and comforting. Plus, there are plenty of paper napkins that can be used as tissues, if needed."

"How long will this take?"

"As long as we need," he replied. "Did you totally clear the day and evening, as I suggested?"

"Yes. Paul went to Chicago to visit his kids."

"Then let's start with a prayer to invite God in to be a part of this." Micky nodded and bowed her head. "God, please be with us now and give Micky the strength, courage and honesty to admit the exact nature of her inventory findings to you, herself and me. Guide us to identify any recurrent patterns of character defects that emerge so that she may work on them in the coming steps. Amen."

"Amen," Micky echoed. "So, should I bring out my inventory now?"

"Yes. Let's start with resentments—they usually take the most time." He pulled a liter of LaCroix orange sparkling water from a tableside silver Champagne bucket and wiped it with a white linen towel. "Is this still your beverage of choice?"

Micky, organizing the pads she'd taken from her Coach bag, looked up and smiled. "It is, thanks!" She loaded a small bone china plate with a sampling of the smorgasbord while he poured her a generous amount of LaCroix in a crystal flute. She took a bite of brie, washed it down and said, "Okay . . . let's go."

Even though she had already talked to Brad many times about her problems with her parents—including while she was writing her Fourth Step—telling him everything now, all together, felt very different. And where she had timidly guessed at what her part might have been in the events she'd run by him previously, she now delivered a matter-of-fact statement of her own faulty attitudes and actions. Sally's counseling had helped her gain perspective and find her voice, and she'd dug even deeper about herself outside of their sessions in creating her step list.

Summing up her column regarding her father, she admitted, "Yes, I was terrified of him during his rage attacks and hated him for how he treated my mother. But I also quickly learned that after each of his fits, he was very remorseful and wanted to shower me with gifts to make up for it . . . and I took advantage of that. I'd ask for very expensive things . . . I thought I deserved them because of how bad he'd made me feel.

"I blamed him for making my mother kill herself. I never *said* that . . . but my total withdrawal from him probably made it clear. Now, in recovery, I realize that her alcoholism drove her to suicide. His abuse certainly didn't help matters . . . but neither did my just staying in hiding from him after her death. I feel bad now, knowing I intentionally abandoned him right after he'd lost his wife.

"The other result of my withdrawal is that I never developed a relationship with him. I made more effort to get to know the various women he brought in than I did with my own father; unlike other girls who resented their divorced fathers' new girlfriends, I was *relieved* because I didn't have to deal much with him when he was home from the road.

"I feel guilty about cutting him out of my life . . . I *had* to when I was working through my family background with Sally . . . and I don't know how close I can ever be to him . . . but I think I can probably do better."

Brad nodded. "I know. My family, *especially* my mother, made me feel unwanted when I decided against medical school—and my coming out as gay shortly afterward *really* cut what flimsy ties we *did* have. Except for my grandmother, God bless her!" he said. "But they did let me move back home with them when I drank away my New York culinary career. And then, I really treated them like dirt when

I left to move in with Oscar—still using their basement as my free storage locker. I think I can do better, too."

Micky closed her eyes, sighed and nodded. After a moment, she looked up at him with a faint smile. "Thanks, Brad . . . I guess I can try?"

He smiled back. "Yes. We can try. That's what your Eighth Step list is about—everybody who's on your Fourth Step also goes on Eight. So, keep your inventory papers!"

"*Keep them?* What if anybody ever *finds* them? I've heard lots of people say they *burned* theirs . . . you know . . . as an act of letting go of the past."

Brad shook his head. "Sorry, but that won't help you *straighten out* the past—that happens by working Steps Six, Seven, Eight and Nine. Applying Six and Seven to the defects revealed today will guide you to correct faulty attitudes and behaviors so you can *attempt* to repair your relationships. *That* is what frees us from the pain of the past."

She took a deep breath. "Okay . . . so . . . Mom. Her driving really scared me, especially coming home from modeling shoots. I really thought she had *coffee* in her stainless-steel travel mug . . . I couldn't understand why she kept crossing the centerline in the road in the *afternoon,* but not in the morning. I thought I was distracting her, somehow. That added to the deep guilt I carried for ruining her life by being born."

She paused as she grabbed a paper napkin and balled it up in her fist. "But that was *nothing* compared to the pain and responsibility I felt for her suicide . . . I wasn't *sure* because no one ever *talked* to me about it . . . but since she killed herself a couple of days after my last photo assignment, I believed that *I'd* done something *so terrible* that *I* made her do it. And I *hated* her for leaving me forever. I was stuck in this black muck of confused feelings . . . *guilt* and *hatred.* I didn't know what I did, but I thought my father was punishing me for it by stopping me from modeling."

"This was the revelation during counseling about the photographer's sexual abuse that you told me about?" She nodded and dabbed her eyes with the napkin. "Yes . . . I think so, now. At the time, when I was ten, I had *no idea* what had happened . . . and then I guess I just stuffed *everything, all of it* . . . until it came out with Sally's help."

"It's good that it did—things like that tend to affect us in multiple areas, but we can't deal with them if they stay buried." He scooped a shrimp through the Dijonnaise sauce, ate it and continued. "Still, Lil often laughs and says, 'More will be revealed. And usually, it's something you don't want to know!'"

Micky smiled and followed suit with the shrimp. "This sauce is *awesome*, Brad!" She returned the napkin to its intended purpose and wiped her fingers. "So, my *real* part in this . . . I was so intent on pleasing the photographer to keep getting jobs—like my mother had told me to—that I did whatever he told me to do. I really *didn't* know it was wrong, but it hurt me and my family."

They snacked through the rest of her recitation of resentments: Jack, whom they'd discussed many times; a girl in college who'd told lies about Micky getting the lead in a play by sleeping with the director, so she got even by stealing her boyfriend; and Ryan, a handsome guy she dated a few years ago who had dumped her for a former girlfriend, even though he'd said she always gave him shit.

"I was *so pissed* because we had tickets for the Sales and Marketing Christmas formal dinner dance, and I had to go by myself because it was too late to get another escort," she explained. "Over the weekend, I created an attractive gold-wrapped gift box containing droppings from a nearby dog park and had it delivered to his office on Monday, with a card inside saying, 'Because you only like girls who give you shit.'"

Brad couldn't help laughing. "So, would you agree these last two resentments show a bit of a vindictive streak?"

"Guilty. Something else to work on!"

"Indeed. And actually, all three lead nicely into the next section of your inventory. The Big Book tells us to examine our sexual attitudes and behavior; some need to make major changes," he said. "I know *I* certainly did!"

"I really don't have much for this section," Micky said. "As you know, Paul is the first man I've slept with *sober*. Most of my experience was in blackouts, coming to the next morning in a strange place with someone whose name I didn't know—like I did in Key West, the day I called Lil about coming back to the program."

"Did you go to bars intentionally to meet men?" Brad asked. "I did."

She paused and looked down with a furrowed brow. "I don't know about most times, but on the Key West night it was *definitely not* my intention . . . I really did just plan to have *one* drink and go back to the ship, since the Top Dog winner was being announced at the banquet that evening, and I knew my numbers were good enough to win."

"Okay, that one we chalk up to alcoholism," he conceded. "But what about the rest? How often did you go out?"

She looked up. "Most weeknights . . . weekends, guys were with dates, so no one was free to buy me drinks. Oh! So, yes . . . I guess I *did* primarily go to bars to meet men—to buy me drinks."

"But you've always made pretty good money, Micky. You didn't *need* guys to buy your drinks," he pointed out.

"I don't know," she replied. "I think maybe I just needed guys to *do something* for me . . . show me that I was wanted. But I never wanted anything to come of it . . . I never gave them my phone number. They'd often give me their business cards and invite me to call them, but I never did . . . I had a small dresser drawer where I stashed the cards, and every so often I'd dump the cards in the trash. I didn't *want* to know them."

"And you really never remembered having sex with *any* of them?"

"No. One week, I must've brought guests home with me . . . when I stripped my bed to do laundry, I found two pairs of jockey shorts in different sizes." She raised her indigo eyes to meet his green ones. "That I did put on the list. But I don't know if they were together, or were there on different nights. Whenever it was, neither were still there in the morning."

"Any boyfriends?"

"A couple, in college. I usually wasn't blacked out with them, but we certainly weren't sober during sex. In both cases, we were both too busy with working at the TV station along with our other classes to be a couple long enough to even move in together. Neither ended badly . . . they just ended. No hard feelings." She shrugged.

Micky helped herself to more brie, and Brad ate two more shrimp. Then he said, "I wonder if your childhood introduction to sex is linked to your anonymous encounters with men during your blackouts. There's a common theme with you really not knowing what's going on, liking the physical feeling enough to participate, and having no emotional connection afterward."

She pondered that for a moment. "It's possible. I can bring that up in my next session with Sally."

"I'm seeing a pattern in my own life," he said. "I was just a little older than you were—eleven—when my parents and brother went out of town to look at colleges, and had my sixteen-year-old cousin Joe stay at the house and watch me. He invented a game at bedtime that ended in him sodomizing me, then threatening to beat the crap out of me if I ever told anyone.

"I've had a lot of unhealthy sexual relationships, especially in my teens and early twenties—with men who really hated that they were gay, so they'd beat me up, after. Oscar, for all of his faults, is actually a step up in my history. And now that I'm sober, I won't tolerate any more abuse or dangerous situations."

She shuddered. "I'm lucky nothing bad happened to me! I was always so terrified when I woke up and didn't know where I was or how I got there . . . or how to get home. But I always did . . . so I forgot all about that fear as soon as I turned into my driveway, and switched over to fearing I'd be so late I'd get fired and lose my job. That would've killed me."

"Why are you so afraid of that?" Brad asked.

"My *biggest* fear is not being able to support myself . . . of having to go back and live with my father."

"Because of his raging verbal abuse?"

"Yes . . . but also because he'd insist on running my life. Like my college major . . . communications instead of theater . . . then steering me away from broadcasting and into sales, where I'm constantly afraid of not making my numbers and getting fired."

"So, you're afraid of losing a job you didn't want to begin with," Brad noted. "Why do you stay in that field?"

"Because I make a lot of money. And now I don't have any background to do anything else." She dropped her eyes.

Brad laughed. "Micky, I'm living proof that you *can* change careers—radically, even! And sometimes, life provides experiences that can lead you in a new direction. Trust me! Or, rather, trust God—He's *much* more reliable." He ate another shrimp. "So, any other fears in your inventory?"

"I'm still scared that Jack will force himself on me . . . it's getting tiring to have to keep orchestrating ways to avoid being alone with him. Another fear is of being alone. But I'm also afraid of being married—although, I think I'm getting over that one, now."

Brad narrowed his eyes. "Is *that* why you don't want to look for another job to get away from Jack?"

She looked away, then admitted, "It's a possibility . . ."

"Okay—an addition to your sex list: Consider your relationship with Paul and ask yourself if it's selfish or not. Per the Big Book. Page sixty-nine."

She thought for a long moment. "Maybe a little . . ."

"I know you'll do what you want, Micky," he said. "But keep this old saying in mind: Women who marry for money *earn it*."

"I've never heard that."

"Well, you have now. And since a key pattern of behavior that's emerged from your inventory is using men, I'm suggesting that you be careful of what you wish for—you just might get it.

"The other key pattern I see is your reliance on money instead of relying on God, or reaching out to earthly friends for security, help and support. All of your fears result from this. As you work on these character defects in Steps Six and Seven, those fears will diminish and lose their power over you." He then opened the Big Book and showed her the instructions to follow immediately when she returned home.

She hugged him. "Thank you so much, Brad . . . for being so non-judgmental. And for sharing your own stories . . . it made me feel better to know I'm not the only person who has done these things!"

"We're not bad people trying to become good, Micky—we're sick people working to get well," he replied. "As long as we stay sober, we don't have to live that way anymore."

CHAPTER 33

The afternoon of Brad's housewarming was cool with bright sunshine that highlighted the reds and oranges of the fall foliage. A brisk breeze rustled the leaves, and coaxed a few of them to take flight briefly before floating to the green grass below.

Guests had been arriving steadily since two o'clock, and Brad had opened the front and vestibule doors to ease entry. He had stationed himself on the living room sofa, enabling him to welcome them without standing sentry.

Micky brought a plate laden with shrimp coated in Dijonnaise sauce and sat down next to him. "You've addicted me to these," she chided, as she set the plate on the rose inlay of the coffee table.

He grinned, grabbing a shrimp and a napkin. "I thought it was just nervous eating during your Fifth Step," he said. "I was *not* inviting you to another deck chair on *The Titanic!*" He popped the shrimp in his mouth, then noticed a pleasant-looking brown-haired fellow in a maroon sweater over khaki Dockers and topsiders enter and look around.

Brad waved at him. "Ben! Good to see you—come join us!" Ben smiled and sat down in one of the barrel armchairs by the gold tufted sofa. "Micky, this is Ben, a friend from my gay men's meeting in Strongsville. Micky is my sponsee—she's accusing me of hooking her on a shrimp addiction last week during her Fifth Step." He handed Ben a paper cocktail napkin and gestured toward the mound. "We have to save her from herself!"

"Those *weren't* all for me," she protested, laughing. "I saw Brad sitting here and thought he looked hungry! Please . . . help yourself!"

Ben complied, and his face lit up. "These are great! I'm glad you have plenty." He reached for another. "Thanks for inviting me, Brad. Your house is stunning!"

He smiled. "Thanks—I'll be happy to show you around after you've had some food."

Micky asked, "What do you do, Ben?"

"I'm partner of a boutique law firm for technical start-ups and university research departments," he replied. "I specialize in intellectual property protection and licensing; my partner handles the corporate formation side of things. You?"

"Sales. For an incentives company that helps clients sell more."

Brad was about to encourage Micky to elaborate, but his gaze shifted to the center hallway and his countenance darkened. "Excuse me." He rose and walked to the doorway, where a tall, dark, handsome man had arrived with a short, moon-faced, balding one.

"It's three-thirty, Oscar—I thought you weren't coming," he said. "And *you—you weren't* invited."

"Since I'm not your co-host, I thought I could come to your open house at any time," Oscar explained in silken, haughty tones. "Baxter is my plus-one. I thought he'd like to see what you've done to the place."

Brad's face became white with anger, but he kept his voice modulated. "That's none of his business," he said, jerking his chin toward the intruder. Then he looked directly into Oscar's flat black eyes. "And it's a very cheap shot from you. Please leave. *Now.*"

A twisted, triumphant smile crossed Oscar's face. "Of course. Come, Baxter, we can certainly find better things to do."

As they swept out the door, Brad glanced at the crowd around the dining table, relieved to observe they were engrossed in the food and their conversations. Micky and Ben, however, looked aghast. "I'm sorry you had to see that," he said as he rejoined them.

"Was that *Oscar*?" Micky asked. "And who was that with him?"

"Yes—*that* was Oscar. And the other one was that *double-dealing* unprofessional real estate agent who really put me through the wringer to bump up his commission on selling the house to Oscar—who then *gave* it to me to pry his way back into my life. Which he'll no longer be a part of, after this."

Ben shook his head. "I remember the pain you shared during the meeting when you thought you'd lost the house. I don't know what led up to what just happened, but you deserve better," he said. "You're a good guy."

"He's right, Brad, you *are* a good guy," Micky agreed. "Oscar may look like a movie star, but pretty *is* as pretty *does*. You're better off without him."

"Thanks," he said, a smile returning to his face. "Would you like to see the rest of the house, Ben?"

"Of course!" The two stood up; Ben just slightly taller than Brad.

"I'll take the plate to the kitchen," Micky said, picking it up from the table. "I need to go; Paul's taking me out to dinner."

Ben laughed. "You'll be a cheap date after filling up on all of those shrimp!"

She smiled. "That's why I'm quitting now. It was great meeting you!" She headed down the hall toward the kitchen. Brad led Ben into the office, as the first stop on the house tour.

"This was built as a sunroom, but I decided it would make a great office."

"It does. I can see why you faced your desk toward the back doors; awesome view!" Ben paused to admire the antique oak roll-top desk and chair. "From your family?"

"Yes. It was my grandfather's—my grandmother left it to me. He was a lawyer, descended from the town's founding family, the Stroms."

"Cool! It's a beauty," Ben said, as he followed Brad out of the room.

After a quick peek into the lavatory under the stairs, they proceeded to the kitchen. Brad pointed out the original elements versus his updates.

Ben inspected everything, nodding approval as he went. "I really appreciate your explaining what you've done here," he said. "I have a nineteen-twenty-three bungalow in Berea that needs to have some modern-day conveniences added, and I want to make sure I don't destroy the home's integrity in the process."

Brad grinned. "I *knew* there was a reason I liked you so much—that's what I do! I'm an architect for Classic Homes Construction, the lead designer and—my boss just told me *today*—a partner in the firm. We'd love to help you!"

Smiling, Ben admitted, "This is the main reason I came today. I knew from our after-meeting chats in the parking lot that you were doing some things to your home, and I wanted to see them."

Brad cracked the swing door from the butler's pantry and saw a crowd around the dining room table. "That room is completely original; we can see it a bit later, when people have cleared out," he suggested. "The other major project was adding a shower to the master bath—would you like to see that next?"

"Of course! That's one of the things I'd like to do in my home, if possible."

They returned to the hall and climbed the stairs to the second floor, Ben admiring the carved banister and wall sconces along the way. He gasped upon entry to the master suite's beamed cathedral ceiling and fireplace in the TV room. "This was originally the bedroom, but I thought it the perfect private space for relaxing—I don't mind having the flat screen over the mantle up here," Brad explained as he led Ben into the room on the other side of the house. "This was the dressing room, but since the master bath is here, and there's plenty of space, I decided to make it the master bedroom."

"Oh, yeah, there's plenty of space," Ben agreed, looking around. He followed Brad to the door and into the bathroom. "Wow. Look at the size of that tub!"

"Everything you see here is original," Brad said, then gestured to his right. "And *there* is the shower I created." He described his hunt for the period frosted glass for the shower door and for the matching hex tiles and ceramic baseboards.

"I love it! Especially the frosted door; it looks like the window, and hides the updated fixtures and nooks inside," Ben said. "So, where did you find the space to add this?"

Brad walked him out and around to the cedar closet, and pointed to the shoe rack. "That used to be the same depth as the hanging portion next to it. As you can see, there's ample room for my clothes without it, and it's more organized for my shoes."

"Brilliant! I *would* like your help for my place," Ben said. "Do you have a card?"

As they left the bedroom, Ben paused by the French doors. "Where do these go?"

Brad opened them and invited him out on the balcony.

"This is wonderful!"

They sat down on the cushioned chairs beside the wrought-iron café table, and enjoyed the view of the neighborhood below. Then Ben said, "I'm really glad we finally got to know each other a little. We've been going to the same meeting for years, but you were always quick to leave afterwards."

"Well, I used to have a longer drive home," Brad explained. "And then I was working *and* going to school, so I was lucky just to *get* to the meeting."

Ben looked at him with solemn, clear gray eyes. "I'll call your office on Monday to set up a meeting about my house. And I'd like to get to know you better, when we can talk for more than fifteen minutes standing out in the weather," he said. "But I definitely don't want to get in the middle of whatever is going on with you and Oscar. I'm *not* into drama."

Brad smiled. "Neither am I—but it does seem to get foisted upon me sometimes," he said. "I think I'm seeing things more clearly now, and can complete the break I initiated last January. In the meantime, would you like to get together for lunch—as friends?"

Ben smiled and shook hands with Brad. "Lunch sounds good."

CHAPTER 34

The day following Brad's party was much warmer, and Lillian had the back door open in hopes of getting some breeze through the screen door. The after-church group had already had plenty of coffee, and Micky was about to bite into her second blueberry muffin when she saw Brad, face flushed, scrambling up the steps to the verandah.

She put the muffin back on her plate as he burst through the door and into the kitchen. "Brad! We were wondering where you were! It's not like you to be late . . . and you look upset. Are you okay?"

He paused to catch his breath. "Sorry—I just had a *bizarre* phone call. From Oscar, of course. Are there any muffins left?"

Micky offered hers, but Lillian was already up and heading to get him one along with a mug of black coffee.

Sally asked, "What happened, Brad?"

He filled her in on what had transpired the day before, which she said seemed unnecessarily hurtful. "And what was so upsetting about today's call?"

"He asked me how my party had been, and I told him it had been *great*—until *he* had arrived *with Baxter*," he recounted. "But Oscar *insisted* he hadn't *been* there! *Denied it* when I repeated that he was. And he *did* sound honestly confused—how can that *be*?"

"He really *was* there, Brad," Micky assured him. "I *saw* him . . . and so did your friend, Ben."

"Was there anything *different* about him yesterday?" Sally asked.

Brad thought for a moment. "Yes. His eyes looked totally *vacant*—no expression. I couldn't see into them, they were *flat*—even an unusual shade of brown. And that *twisted smile* and *condescending voice*—but I've seen those *before*, when he's attacked me."

"Did he appear to have been drinking?" Lillian wondered.

"No—neither did. And I didn't smell any alcohol."

"Those could be symptoms of Dissociative Identity Disorder; it used to be called Multiple Personality," Sally said. "The memory gap, without some other explanation, is particularly telling. It's estimated that around seventy-five percent of people will have at least *one* episode during their lives, as a reaction to some trauma or stress. But for the rare people who have chronic episodes, it's a deep-seated mental illness."

"You know, Brad, all of those times in the past when I was around him, I'd think, 'There's *something wrong* with Oscar,'" Lillian said. "But I never said anything, because I couldn't *identify* it. It was like having a noise in your car's engine that shows up occasionally. You can't describe it, and the shop can *never* find it—but you *know* it's there."

"Well, we'll see. Oscar said he'll ask his therapist about it," Brad said.

Lillian smiled. "So, other than that, Mrs. Lincoln, how did you like the play?"

Brad laughed, and relaxed a bit. "It was so much fun to entertain like I used to! Lots of people came all through the afternoon. You all, of course, and others from the program. Most of my clients, suppliers and co-workers also showed up. My boss was impressed, and chose the occasion to offer me a partnership in the business! And, I got a new client, too."

"Your friend, Ben?" Micky guessed. "I really like him!"

Brad blushed slightly, which she noticed. "Yes. He said he'd call the office tomorrow to set up a meeting. He has a Craftsman bungalow in Berea that needs updates."

Micky gave him an innocent smile. "I'm sure you two will work *very well* together."

"Gus really liked your house, Brad," Lillian added. "Of course, he says your back yard needs a rose garden!"

Sally asked, "When will Gus be back next?"

"Thanksgiving," she replied, blue eyes twinkling. "I'm finally going to do the feast again. You're all invited, lovers, friends, and family members welcome!"

Her announcement was met with claps, cheers and raised coffee mugs.

"That's wonderful, Lil, thanks!" Micky said. "I've invited my father to lunch next Saturday . . . it's time to try to connect . . . let him know who I am, and what's going on in my life. About being an alcoholic in recovery, and you guys. And about Paul. Depending on how that goes . . . could I invite him? I really don't want another stiff holiday meal in a restaurant."

"Of course," said Lillian. "And what about Paul? Does he go to his kids' homes in Chicago?"

"I don't think so . . . his ex lives there . . . I think the three of them do holidays together, without him."

"Then he's welcome, too," Lillian declared, smiling. "I'll leave that up to you."

"I'd love to have the comfort and security of being surrounded by my *real* family," Micky said. "I'd really like them to meet you!"

*****

Micky arrived at Don's Pomeroy House twenty minutes early in order to get settled into her favorite library booth and relax well in advance of her father's arrival. She sipped her Coke and studied the menu for a few minutes, deciding on her order. Then she set it aside, took a deep breath and closed her eyes in prayer. *God, please be with me here today. Please take away all of my fears and resentments and help me to make a human connection with my earthly father. Guide us both in creating a new beginning that we may develop a relationship. Strengthen me to admit my faults and to behave differently toward him going forward. I ask this in the Name of your Son, my savior, Jesus Christ. Thank you. Amen.*

She felt a warm peace flow through her, and she opened her eyes just as Mike McHale entered the library dining room. She stood up, smiled and waved. "Dad! Over here!"

He reached her in a few long strides and gathered her in a hug. "You look wonderful, Micky! Whatever you've been doing these last months, it seems to agree with you."

"Yes . . . there's been *a lot* going on," she said as they slid into their seats. The waitress appeared and took Mike's drink order. Micky picked up the menu. "Let's get our orders in when she comes back . . . I'm starved." He complied, and they got that out of the way when his seltzer and lime was delivered.

"Okay . . . first, I need to apologize for avoiding you recently," she began. "And, actually, I've realized that I did everything I could to keep you at a distance for my whole life . . . especially after Mom died. I began some intensive therapy in May that dug up a lot of very *painful* memories I'd tried to keep buried . . . but they were there anyway . . . sabotaging me.

"I didn't realize that I'd been using alcohol as a means to deal with them. And when I got sober last January and started working the steps of recovery in A.A., it became apparent that I needed professional help to face these issues and *really* neutralize them so I could stay sober. Some major ones were about my fear of you . . . your rages at Mom scared the living *bejesus* out of me . . . I was terrified and spent most of my time *hiding* from you. So, it wasn't emotionally safe for me to be involved with you during that period while I was digging those things up and looking at them as an adult."

Mike's chiseled brow bunched in a confused frown. "A.A.? Why are you in A.A.?"

"Because I'm an alcoholic, Dad."

He shook his head. "No, you're not—you never even drank!"

"Oh boy . . . Dad, *think* about it," she said. "How many of the days in an average year were you actually *at home?* And even when you *were,* how much time did we spend *together?* I drank through most of high school, and was a daily drinker by the time I went to college."

Normally composed and in complete control, Mike was flustered and lost. He ran his fingers through his iron-grey hair. "But you always had great grades! Activities! Then you got a great job, and have been winning awards for your performance ever since! Alcoholics can't do those things."

Micky couldn't help smiling. "Oh, yes, we can, Dad. As you just stated, I *did*. Many of us are super-high-achievers. And when we screw up, we're smart enough to get out of a jam. Actually, I *first* went to A.A. seven years ago . . . after I got a DUI."

"*What?!* You got a ticket for drunk driving? How could I not know about that?" The color had drained out of his face.

"I had a company car. You had nothing to do with it," she explained. "Because of seeing how you berated Mom about her drinking, there was *no way* I was going to tell you. Besides, *I* didn't really believe that I was an alcoholic then, I just had some bad luck. As a first-offender, I had to complete a weekend seminar and get signatures on a court paper that proved I'd attended three A.A. meetings a week for six months. Then I stopped going, and started drinking again."

Quietly, he asked, "So why did you go back in January?"

"Well, as you said, I won all of those awards . . . and I won my company's Top Dog award, best sales rep for the whole previous year! I thought I had a good chance at it, but wouldn't know until the ceremonial dinner on the company's top performers' cruise. But I stopped in Hemingway's favorite bar in Key West for *one drink* . . . and missed the dinner *and* the ship. *That* convinced me."

They sat in silence for a couple of minutes. Finally, he broke it. "I don't know what to say. I guess I shouldn't be surprised; your mother and my father were both alcoholics. I've heard it runs in families. I'm glad you're sober now. And that you're working on stuff—God knows you had a lot of hard, nasty things thrown at you at a young age! I was always so proud of how well you came through it all. Or, I should say, how well you *appeared* to have come through it.

"And you're right—I was never home. Never there for you. I didn't know how much I hurt you when I went off on your mother. I didn't know I scared you, and I'm sorry for doing that. I can't blame you for avoiding me; I guess I never provided anything positive for you when I *was* around.

"Sometimes, I did sense that I'd gone over the line, and I tried to make it up to you. But I realize now that I should never have behaved that way in the first place."

She smiled slightly. "Thanks, Dad. And I'm sorry that I took advantage of your peace offerings . . . I made a point of asking for things I knew were *really* expensive ... not because I *wanted* them, but because I wanted to really make you *pay* for hurting me.

"We don't really have a relationship," she said. "But I'd like to try to start one, if you're interested."

He nodded and said with a wistful smile, "Yes, let's try to start over. You never had much of a family life, and I'm to blame for that. It's amazing that you've become such a strong young woman. How did you possibly manage to do that?"

She shrugged and smiled. "Because I'm now part of a very strong, loving and supportive A.A. family. I don't have to do anything alone anymore ... we have each other's backs."

The waitress delivered their meals without speaking. As they ate, Micky filled her father in on Lillian, Sally and Brad, as well as her spiritual life from the program and from her joining Grace Church.

Mike was impressed. "They sound like good people. A writer, a priest and an architect—all professionals. I can't believe you connected with all of them in A.A.!"

She laughed. "Dad, people in A.A. didn't all crawl in from Skid Row," she admonished. "In fact, Alcoholics Anonymous was founded in nineteen-thirty-five by a stockbroker and a surgeon, and the third member was an attorney! There are *a lot* of people like us." She reached for a roll from the bread basket.

Noticing her ring, Mike said, "I really do like that emerald, Micky. I was glad I could find the pendant for you last year." He looked up into her face. "And I see you have emerald earrings now, too; when did you get those?"

"My boyfriend gave them to me for my birthday in August."

"Boyfriend? Those look serious; tell me about him."

"Yes, I'm in a serious relationship, Dad . . . for the first time," she said. "At least, I think it is. He's told me that his intentions are honorable.

"His name is Paul Price. I've known him since March. He owns five luxury car dealerships in Elyria. Mid-forties, divorced for five years . . . two grown kids who live in Chicago."

"How did you meet him?"

"He's a client . . . and before you remind me about how I should *never* get involved that way with clients, I have to tell you that this began when he told his friends about the great program I created for him. Then he asked me to his country club to meet them on Memorial Day. That was the business event I had to go to. I thought it *really was* just business, and I *did* get two additional new clients from it. Then, he insisted on paying for golf lessons . . . and we started dating in June."

"Will I have the opportunity to meet Paul?"

"How about Thanksgiving? Lillian is hosting us all at her house, and says all of our family and friends are welcome. That would be a nice, low-pressure way for you and Paul to meet each other . . . and my family."

*****

Brad had taken the afternoon off from work on Friday, November third, as the appointment Oscar had made with his therapist in Oberlin was scheduled for two o'clock. He didn't know if it would run longer than an hour, or what shape he'd be in at its conclusion.

The sun was already lower in the sky than it was just two weeks ago. Brad grabbed his gold-tinted aviator sunglasses from their case above the driver's side visor and planted them on his face to fight the glare as he drove due west. The hue from the lenses warmed the vista, which had been looking bleak; recent storms with high winds had stripped the bright fall leaves off of the trees. The seasons were on the brink of change. All of the corn had been harvested from the vast fields he passed, exposing bare soil between rows of faded stubble. It was time for northern Ohio to prepare for winter.

The polite male voice from his GPS app guided him to a medical office building at the eastern edge of Oberlin. He noticed the black Mercedes sports car in the parking lot. Brad found the suite on the first floor. He sat down by Oscar, who reached out and shook his hand.

"Thanks for coming."

Brad nodded. "Hope I can help."

The interior door opened, and a tall, whited coated man with cropped steel-grey hair and round titanium-rimmed glasses emerged to greet them. "I'm Dr. Staunton. You must be Brad. Hello, Oscar, it's good to see you."

They followed him down a short hallway to his office, and settled into hunter green leather armchairs that were separated by an end table. The various shades of green and simple, classic furnishings created a professional yet calming space.

"Brad, Oscar told me last week that he had apparently gone to a housewarming party at your home and caused a disturbance by bringing an unwanted guest, but that he has no memory of that event," Dr. Staunton began. "Can you please tell me what happened, and what you observed about Oscar that day?"

"Of course." Brad recounted what he had shared at Lillian's.

"And you say that you've noticed this demeaning tone of voice and sneering facial expressions before, during previous disagreements with Oscar?"

"Yes. Especially in the ones that were nasty or violent enough to make me leave. He didn't normally treat me like that, or I wouldn't have been with him in the first place."

"Were you aware of any memory lapses that Oscar experienced with those?"

"I can't be sure—I *do* know that he would never discuss the incidents afterwards, which meant that nothing was ever really *resolved*," Brad said. "He would always make some lavish grand gesture and *apologize*. He always seemed so *sincere*, and was his most charming self, that I'd cave and get back together with him."

"You've been a couple for about eight years, correct?" Brad nodded. "Roughly how many times has this happened?"

"Just the times I left? Or the number of unpleasant disagreements?"

"Think of the times you left, but don't tell me yet," the doctor instructed. "Oscar, you go first. How many times did Brad leave home—not necessarily moved out—but left the residence at least for overnight?"

"Oh, there weren't many," Oscar declared. "Overall, we've had a very good relationship. I'd say, maybe four. Or five."

"And what were their durations?"

"Usually just a night or a weekend."

"I see. Brad, does that describe your experience?" The doctor stroked his trim beard.

"Not at all—wow." Brad looked shocked.

"Tell us your recollections, please."

"The total number was more like twenty," he said. "Most *were* a night or a weekend—I'd make them into pleasant get-aways, like a weekend at the Ritz-Carlton in downtown Cleveland or at the Cedar Point hotel. Sometimes I'd use a week of vacation to stay at a bed-and-breakfast in Amish country. Doing enjoyable things kept me from feeling like a victim, I made the best out of a bad situation.

"But one time, early on, I went back to New York for two weeks and stayed with a friend—I looked into possibly moving back there. A year or two later, I spent *a month* in Paris with another friend. And when I went to Kent State to study architecture, I rented an apartment for my final year and lived there during the week—I just came back on the weekends to work my part-time construction job. It made taking all of my classes and studying easier—but it also gave me breathing space from Oscar. He wasn't happy about my new career. And of course, you know that I moved out for good last January. His move into violence convinced me that it wasn't safe for me to stay with him any longer."

"Oscar? Do you remember any of that?"

"No, except for January's move. The Kent thing, I thought he just stayed over some nights if he was too tired to drive home."

Dr. Staunton paused to look through his notes in a manila file folder. "Oscar, you've made good progress since we've been working together, and that Brad is even here today speaks to that. But that was working on making the good side of you better.

"Unfortunately, it appears that you alternate between an intelligent, creative and very charming identity and another darker, vindictive, abusive, controlling and violent one. The span of time covered just in Brad's experiences with you and the frequency of the incidents shows it is chronic in nature. The memory lapses associated with them, coupled with our earliest discussions about your total lack of early childhood memories or any memory of your father or anything about him also fit with Dissociative Identity Disorder, famously illustrated in the play about Doctor Jekyll and Mister Hyde."

"So I'm *not* crazy to have spent all of this time bouncing *in and out* of this relationship," Brad said. "I really *have* been dealing with two *different* people!"

"Yes, and you've responded appropriately to both," the doctor told him.

"Is this treatable?" Brad asked.

"The condition is treatable with intense psychotherapy and medications, and many patients are able to live healthy and productive lives," Dr. Staunton replied. "However, finding an effective treatment plan can be difficult, and there are no guarantees, particularly for someone who has been living with this for many decades. Oscar has managed to build an impressive career and has maintained many friendships. But the level of intimacy involved in a romantic and domestic relationship may be beyond his psychological comfort zone. I do recommend that Oscar pursue treatment, but you need to make your own decision about what's best for you."

Brad looked down at his hands, clasped in his lap. "A dear friend, who is a priest and a licensed clinical counselor, already guessed your diagnosis and told me about the disorder," he said. "Thank you for confirming it."

He turned in his chair and looked at Oscar. "This has been a *wild ride*—much has been *wonderful,* thank you for loving me and for taking me in when I was a broke student trying to start over after drinking away my career.

"Unfortunately, much has also been *horrible.* I'm grateful to know that it's not your fault, that you have a mental illness that caused you to treat me so badly. That makes it easy to forgive you—and myself for repeatedly coming back. But it also tells me *clearly* that your behavior is out of *my* control *and yours,* and that I can't reasonably hope for a life with you that is steady, drama-free—or safe in any way."

Brad stood up, pulled Oscar out of his chair and threw his arms around him in a long hug. Then he looked into Oscar's remarkable deep brown eyes and told him, "I will *always* love you, in some corner of my heart. But I can't *do* this anymore. And I won't."

CHAPTER 35

Micky jumped up from her seat beside Paul on the sofa in Lillian's living room to answer the front doorbell, and greeted her father with a quick hug as he entered. She led him inside and said, "Paul, this is my father."

"Hi Paul, I'm Mike McHale," he said, and firmly grasped Paul's outstretched hand. The two displayed practiced sales pro smiles as they sized one another up during the greeting.

"Great to meet you, Mike. I've heard a lot about you."

"Not much that's good, I'm guessing," Mike said with disarming candor. "I just recently heard about you, and I look forward to getting to know you."

Micky laughed and turned toward the elegant redheaded woman in a carved chair with needlepoint upholstery. "And this is Mother Sally, my priest and an important part of my sponsorship family."

"It's good to meet you, Mike," she said as he shook her hand much more gently. "And please just call me 'Sally.'" Micky sat down by Paul and showed Mike to a matching needlepoint chair next to her.

"Our hostess, Lillian, and two others are in the kitchen, preparing our feast," Sally explained.

"You don't cook?" Mike asked.

She laughed. "I cook well enough to feed myself, but it's not my strongest talent. Lillian cooks as an outlet of her creativity and spoils us regularly, especially with baked goods and pasta; her gentleman friend, Gus, is a wizard on the grill; and Brad is a graduate of the Culinary

Institute of America and had a career as a chef before becoming an architect. I help most by staying out of their way in the kitchen!"

"And I keep her company." Micky added.

Brad emerged through the swing door and placed a silver gravy boat and tray of rolls on the cloth-draped dining table. "It's time—please come and serve yourselves from the buffet in the kitchen. Lil will be at the head of the table, with Gus and Sally on either side of her. The rest of us will take the other four places."

They filed past the sideboard, which offered a preview of the pumpkin silk pie, apple pie, and spice cake dessert options, and entered the kitchen where the bounty beckoned from silver serving pieces: Sliced turkey separated into white or dark meat; dressing cooked inside the bird or in a casserole dish; mashed potatoes; a bowl of gravy; sweet potatoes; cranberry salad; broccoli casserole; and roasted root vegetables. They piled their Spode china plates high and took their seats at the dining table.

Micky introduced her father to Lillian, Gus and Brad, and Lillian asked Sally to say grace.

"Just a quick one," she agreed. "Gracious God of all mercy and blessings, we thank you for this food and those who prepared it. Bless it to our use, and us to your service. In Jesus' name we pray. Amen."

Everyone echoed amen, and Sally continued. "While we eat, let's go around the table, and each of us tell the *one greatest* thing that happened in the past year for which we are grateful. Lil, will you please start?"

"Wonderful idea, Sally. For me, I'm most grateful for getting back into living life. The process of writing my latest book forced me to take all of the actions I'd postponed that enabled me to climb out of the black hole of grief and be *myself* again."

Gus said, "And one of the things she did, hosting her open garden, connected her and her wonderful hybridized roses with me. Greatest joy I've experienced in years!"

"My turn?" Paul asked. Everyone nodded. "Definitely this beautiful, smart woman coming into my life." He smiled at Micky.

She hesitated. "Just *one*? Well . . . I guess I'd have to say I'm *most* grateful for sobriety and recovery . . . *everything* good flows from that . . . including Paul."

Mike looked at Micky. "The best thing for me is the chance to build a new relationship with my daughter."

"Wow—there've been *a lot* of good things this year," Brad said. "But I think I'm *most* grateful for one of the hardest ones—learning the truth about Oscar's mental illness. It gave me the clarity and closure I needed to finally, completely free myself from an untenable situation. I feel like I really have a bright future now."

"I'm glad you said that, Brad," Sally began. "The hardest thing in my life happened this year, when my daughter died by suicide in a stolen car in one of the church's parking lots. The shock and searing grief are still raw." She paused, then continued, her voice catching at first. "But the previous five-year void was hard, as well. Not knowing if she was still alive, or if she was, where she was and what she was doing. That was *torture*. I'm grateful that she did come to me at the end, so at least I know she is now in Lillian's raspberry patch and she is finally at peace."

Small talk dominated the rest of the conversations while the piles on the plates diminished. Paul and Mike chatted about business and economic forecasts for the coming year; Micky and Brad talked about his breakup; Sally caught up with Lillian and Gus about progress with patenting her roses.

As they finished dessert, Micky said to Brad with a sly smile, "That burnt orange sweater and hunter green cords look pretty sharp ... are you going somewhere after this?"

"Maybe—a client invited me to join his family and friends to watch football games after dinner. It's their Thanksgiving tradition."

"A client named *Ben*, perhaps?"

He reddened, and Mike noticed it. "I always used to warn Micky about socializing with clients," he teased. "But I see now that maybe that can work out."

Paul smiled. "Indeed, it can! Mike, this was a great opportunity to meet you, but we really didn't have a chance to talk. I always say you can really get to know somebody on a golf course. Do you play?"

"A little."

"Micky says you're usually on the road. How long are you here?"

"I fly out Sunday afternoon. What do you have in mind?"

"Well, the course at the Elyria Country Club is still open, and Saturday's weather is supposed to be decent. How about nine holes with a mid-morning tee time, and we can have lunch in the Grill? Micky can join us for lunch."

"Sounds good. Text me the time."

*****

Blue-grey clouds hung low in the sky, and the temperature had warmed to fifty degrees by nine-thirty when Paul Price and Mike McHale climbed into their golf cart. A gust of breeze swirled fallen oak leaves on the cart path before them.

"It's a little nippy, but it's not supposed to rain," Paul said. "Pretty good for this time of year. We'll play the back nine so we can finish at the club. Just a short stroll to lunch that way." He put the cart in gear.

"I hope you're not the kind of guy who insists on betting," Mike said. "I can't even remember the last time I had these clubs out of the closet."

"Not a problem, I prefer not to make bets myself. I just enjoy the game," Paul replied. "Do you not like golf?"

"It's not that I don't like it. I just never have time to play or practice, so I'm pretty lousy at it," he explained. "I work all the time, and when I'm not in meetings, I'm in the air."

Paul nodded in understanding. "I get it. I work all the time, too—including on the links and at my clubs' social events. This is where most of my best customers spend their precious free time; most of the cars you saw in the parking lot came from my dealerships." He swerved slightly to avoid a small tree branch on the path. "When it comes to luxury cars, people want to do business with people they know and like. They trust that I'll take care of them—getting exactly the car they want, keeping it performing at peak with a total lack of inconvenience. Treating them to a round of golf, sending over drinks from the bar or picking up a couple's dinner tab now and then helps to strengthen those relationships."

"Speaking of strengthening relationships, those emerald earrings you gave Micky for her birthday make a statement," Mike observed. "She says you told her your intentions are honorable?"

"I did. I also promised I wouldn't rush her," Paul said. "She's said several times that she'd never wanted to marry. But recently she's been making comments about being more open to the idea."

Mike looked away, out at the view of the course over his right shoulder, then turned his head back to look at Paul. "I'm sorry about that. I didn't provide a positive impression regarding marriage and family life."

311

"She's told me," Paul said. "But she also told me that you instilled a strong work ethic in her and coached her a lot about selling. She's a marvel—just blew me away the first day we met!" His face lit up with a smile at the memory. "I even asked her to teach my reps more about prospecting and research. And the program she put together for us is surpassing previous sales records at all five dealerships. The ones she created for my two best friends are killing it, too."

He pulled up at the tenth tee and they both extracted their drivers, balls and tees from their bags. As they approached the tee, Paul explained, "This is a long par four. Four hundred forty yards. Try to place your tee shot to the right side of the fairway, otherwise, you'll have a tough second shot due to trees on the left. Also, a stream runs along the left side." He stepped up, teed up his ball and demonstrated with a well-practiced swing and clean, long drive.

Mike remembered how to tee up and assume the proper stance, but he rose up during his swing and topped the ball, which dribbled off of the tee. The next swing hit the ground behind the tee, sending a large divot five yards. After replacing the aggrieved sod, he collected himself, slowed his swing and smoothly connected, finishing with good follow-through and a successful drive down the center of the fairway.

"That last one looked nice," Paul said as they walked back to the cart. "I'll give you a couple of mulligans on the others."

Mike flashed a movie-star grin. "I appreciate your generosity. I'm also glad Micky won't be with us until lunch. I'd hate for my daughter to see how truly terrible my game is."

Paul returned the smile. "Yeah, she's coming along really well. Been taking lessons for six months now, and can play a creditable round. She has good potential."

"Do you play together a lot?"

Family of Choice: Raising Each Other

Paul shook his head. "Every couple of weeks or so, she'll join me with our two buddies, also clients of hers now. Just for fun. Nobody's serious, so there's no pressure. While she's still learning the game, I think it's best we not play as a two-some; she's got a great pro, and I don't want to screw anything up with my pointers."

They parked and walked out to Paul's ball. He'd chosen a three iron, which delivered a long shot with low loft that landed in a good position for his approach to the green. Mike tried a seven iron, as he had to take a shorter shot to get around the trees Paul had warned him about. But he put too much power behind it, and landed in the right rough.

"Shit! Oh, well. At least I hit it. Hey, Paul, any pointers you want to pass along to me are most welcome."

"Okay. I'd use a nine iron for your next shot. Just try to get it out of the long grass and position it in the middle of the fairway. Don't try to hit it too hard, and don't try to lift it out. The club will do the lifting if you just keep your head down and swing through the ball."

Mike followed the instructions and was elated by the results. "You're a genius! Thanks!"

"Try your five iron for the next shot. Don't try to get it on the green, just keep it straight, get it near the green and stay clear of the bunkers." Mike complied, and again was successful, his ball landing in the vicinity of Paul's.

Back in the cart, Mike asked, "Micky told me you were divorced. Did your ex-wife play golf with you?"

"No, she had no interest in the game. So, between my long hours at the dealerships and out on the links, we really never spent much time together," he said. "So, when the kids went to college and started careers in Chicago, we split up and she moved there to be near them."

He took his seven iron from his bag, and Mike followed suit. Paul's third shot sailed over the slight elevation and landed neatly on the green, some five feet from the pin. But the seven iron in Mike's hands carried a greater wallop from his taller stature and he overshot the green.

"You've got a lot more power than I do," Paul noted. "You should probably use one higher numbered iron than I would, except for chip shots, which you'll need to do next."

When they parked beside the green, Paul took out his putter and advised Mike to use his nine iron. Paul strode confidently to his ball, assessed the slope of the green and putted. Mike lifted the flag just before the ball rolled straight into the hole. He then walked to the back edge of the green and climbed down the embankment to his ball, once again in the rough. He did manage to launch it up on the edge of the green, then two-putted to finish the hole.

Paul handed him a score card and a pencil, then recorded four strokes on his own card. "Great! I made par. What did you have, Mike? Just count from the drive that made it."

Mike hesitated. "I really can't remember; I was so busy trying to figure out what I was doing."

Paul counted on his fingers. "Your drive. Second shot into the rough. Third was the chip out onto the fairway. Fourth got near the green, fifth overshot, sixth onto it, and two puts. So, eight. Not bad, for not having played in a long time."

"Thanks, Paul. You're a good guy. I think Micky's found a keeper."

They returned to the cart and headed to the next hole. Paul grinned and said, "Hope so! And I'm glad you think that, Mike. Any fatherly advice for me?"

"Yeah. Don't make the mistake I made with her mother. I married a good-looking, successful career woman and insisted afterward that we have children—which she didn't want. Worse, after Micky was born, I made her stop working to be a full-time mom; even though she was an account supervisor at a big ad agency, I never realized how much her job meant to her. Our marriage effectively ended then, but she soldiered on for ten more years, drinking more and more until she took her own life."

Paul nodded. "Micky told me. I know she doesn't want kids, and I already have mine. And I know how she feels about work. That's the biggest thing we have in common," Paul said. "She's too professional to say it, but I get a strong feeling that she's not happy with her current job. She's so talented! I'm hoping that maybe she'd come and work in our business, assuming that she accepts my proposal. When we get to that."

CHAPTER 36

Brad and Ben had chosen the overcast Saturday of Thanksgiving weekend to explore for vintage architectural pieces to use in Ben's renovation. The low inky clouds made the exterior of the architectural salvage business look especially bleak as Brad pulled up in front of a dingy stucco two-story warehouse protected by steel window mesh and an eight-foot chain link fence topped by three barbed wire strands.

He texted their arrival, then laughed at his client's apprehensive expression and darting, questioning grey eyes. "Relax—they'll come out and escort us inside. You'll be amazed at the breadth of materials they offer. It really *does* require a warehouse, and you won't be paying retail prices with mark-ups to cover rent for a more fashionable address."

The rust-red steel loading dock door rolled up. They climbed out of the Mini Clubman and walked toward the sales manager, who greeted Brad with a wide smile. "Back again already, my friend? What are you after this time?"

Brad returned the smile with a familiar handshake. "Tom, this is Ben, my client and friend. We're renovating the kitchen and master bath in his Craftsman bungalow—we want to look at doors, windows, plumbing fixtures, cabinets and hardware. Maybe flooring, too. And lighting. We're at the idea-starter stage—but you never know!"

Tom shook hands with Ben and laughed at Brad. "Yes, with you, we never know. Somehow, things from all over our warehouse just come together for you."

Brad, laughing, shrugged. "What can I say—I like to design around found objects."

Inside the dock, Tom pressed the button to open the man-door into the main warehouse. A great cavernous space full of Nineteenth and Twentieth Century goods sprawled before them. "Where do you want to start?" he asked.

"Probably plumbing," Brad replied. "Both projects will need fixtures."

Tom nodded. "Gutting?"

"Oh yeah," Ben said. "A previous owner modernized, so everything just looks really out of place and very outdated now."

"Anything we might want?" Tom asked Brad.

"Possibly in the kitchen. That looks mid-Century, especially the sink and cabinetry. I doubt you can use anything from the bath—looks like a do-it-yourselfer job from the seventies."

"Send me some pix of the kitchen. If anything looks good, we'll pay for that part of your demo." He had walked them to the plumbing area. "Happy hunting! Text me if you need any help or pricing."

"Remind me where your doors are; we'll be looking for some kind of cool opaque or textured glass for a new shower stall. That could guide our bath fixtures."

Tom pointed. "Right over there. But let me take you now. We have a few that would work, one in particular I think you'll want to see."

They followed him to a vast wall of stalls where vintage doors of various types leaned against sturdy partitions. Tom pulled out one with light green opaque half-inch squares of raised, beveled glass topped by tiny square pyramids arranged in solid rows. On the other side, the green glass was smooth. The door's glass was edged in stainless steel. "Factory doors. We have twenty of them, so you can be picky about any nicks or blemishes. But they're all pretty clean."

Ben slowly ran his fingers across the raised pattern and smiled. "This is really cool! And I love the color; this shade works well with Craftsman designs elsewhere in my house."

"Great! The stainless will hold up to water, too," Brad said. "Tom, do you have any that are set in the original frames with the hinges? And maybe handles?"

"Let me look while you go explore the fixtures. I'll come and get you."

The two returned to the sea of toilets, tubs and sinks, focusing first on the bathroom rather than kitchen. "What type of sink do you want, Ben? Pedestal? Wall-mount, or do you need a vanity for storage and counter space?"

"No vanity. I don't use much grooming stuff; everything can fit into a medicine cabinet."

"Ah. We'll need to add that to our list. So, let's look at wall and pedestal sinks," Brad suggested.

Ben was overwhelmed by the inventory. Sinks in all shapes and sizes competed for attention, some in white but most in shades of pink, blue and yellow, with a few in black or green. While he struggled to find a focal point, Brad had quickly scanned them and looked beyond to an area where a few matched sets were showcased. He hailed Ben to join him.

"Eureka! Pay dirt!" Brad exclaimed. "*Everything* we need—a very cool wall sink, with a toilet and tub in this light jade color that will be *perfect* with your green shower door!"

Ben's eyes lit up. "Yes! And look—chrome towel bars on the sides of the sink. They'll look good with the stainless door trim. I love the simple efficiency of having them mounted on the sink. And I'd really like just a couple of hooks by the shower for my bath towel and robe."

Tom had returned. "Oh, good choice. Nineteen twenties era Crane set: shelf-back sink with cut corners, two-piece toilet and matching tub. Late Art Deco, very appropriate for your home's time. These fixtures will look great with your shower door. I did find one with the full frame. Only adaptation you may want would be to take out the latch, or you could use it as-is."

"Thanks, Tom—can you please mark these as sold and start writing up the prices for us? We'll move toward the kitchen stuff now."

As they walked, Brad advised, "Try to look over the whole group as a snapshot first and see if anything jumps out at you—once you're in the middle of the goods, everything seems to blur and you have to look at each piece to see anything."

They paused accordingly. After a couple of minutes, Ben said, "You're right. Much better. In fact, I think I see my sink and main kitchen countertop." He walked directly to a stainless-steel vintage industrial kitchen countertop with stamped-in drain board creases designed to direct flow from each end into a pair of double sinks. He flashed a triumphant smile at Brad. "How do you like this beauty?"

"Impressive! Let's measure it." He stood at one end and pulled his laser from his Dockers pocket. "Eight feet by twenty-five inches. Great working space and practicality, and it'll fit nicely." He looked at the black simple cube-like cabinets holding it up. "These won't look right. I see you gravitate to industrial, and we can certainly go in that direction for your faucets. And we can probably find some fantastic vintage industrial light fixtures here. But I'd advise some simple Craftsman style cabinets under these. Quality reproductions are readily available, often in a range of colors. For both upper and lower options."

"Yeah, I guess I do like the industrial feel. Like the shower door," Ben realized. "I'm okay with Craftsman cabinets to support the long counters, and that should be plenty for my cookware, silverware and cleaning stuff. But I'd rather use open shelves for dishes and glassware, I think."

"What about the sides of the range? You need counter space there—and some of the space under the stainless drainboard will be taken by a dishwasher. Waste receptacles will need to go in that area, too," Brad reminded him.

Ben thought for a bit. "Could we find more vintage stainless to use as countertops by the stove?"

"Let's look for stainless," Brad agreed. "Industrial-quality stainless cleans easily and you can put hot things directly on it."

"Cool. You okay with the open shelf idea?"

"Well—they're really not period-correct. Craftsman design is all about creating decorative storage spots," Brad explained. "But *you* live there now. As long as you understand that the open shelves look is the 'in' thing now, and *will* look dated in time—and that everything on them will get dusty and even splattered, we can do it. If you decide later that you don't like it, we can always take the shelves out and install cabinets."

Ben grinned and clapped Brad's shoulder like he'd just made a touchdown. "Right! Let's do it!"

Brad smiled and nodded. He grabbed his phone, texted the order for the sinks/drain-boards counters to Tom and asked the locations of lighting, wood, brackets, flooring and windows. As they walked toward their next objective, Brad said, "Thanks for inviting me over after Thanksgiving dinner—I really had a good time, especially meeting your family and friends. And watching football."

"They liked you, too," Ben replied. "But none of us could figure out why you never played football. With your height and build, you'd have been a natural."

Brad shrugged. "Maybe. I did pretty well in wrestling. But with my dad being an orthopedic surgeon and mom a nurse—football was off the table even for discussion."

"And you probably didn't want to risk your pretty face," Ben teased.

"I think I would've looked really *hot* with the glare-reduction paint." Brad winked.

"Oh yeah. Plus in the pads and pants, you'd have been hard to resist. I definitely would've recruited you for my off-field team," Ben said. "I'd still like to, if you're eligible."

Brad looked up into the buff young man's clear gray eyes. "I'm very interested—but I just left my last team a couple of weeks ago. I need to discuss this with my agent."

"Understood. What's her name again?"

"Lil. She never tells me *what* to do—or not—but she does voice what she sees as possible issues. And she digs to get me to talk about what I really think and feel."

"She sounds like a great sponsor. Mine knows you from meetings, thinks this could be really good," Ben said. "So, I can wait. Lunch after we finish here?"

"Sure. There are lots of good restaurants in Ohio City."

*****

Micky, who'd been steering clear of the office for the last four months, had to be there for most of Friday, December first. The three weeks between Thanksgiving and Christmas were always crazy busy, as everyone wanted to wrap up all business before the holidays began and the year ended. She was on the phone and waiting for call-backs all day, finalizing kick-off details for programs beginning January one, signing contracts for renewals and new customers, and dealing with multiple technical contacts to unsnarl an issue with November's award points for Chet's distributor sales reps. At five-forty, she was hurriedly trying to finish up her call reports and was so intently focused that she didn't hear footsteps in the hall.

She screamed when she felt hands on her shoulders.

"It's just me," Jack Benson said. "You've been working so hard all day. You look like you could use a massage."

"No thanks. *You're* making me tense. Please don't touch me." She rolled her chair back into his legs and stood up, moving him away from her. She grabbed her cell phone from the top of her desk, quickly pulled up Paul's cell number and called.

Jack, unaware of that, moved toward her to trap her in the corner. "I've been waiting a long time to catch you here. You shouldn't be such a stranger. We used to be much closer; I miss that." He reached out for her, and she ducked.

Paul picked up and she put him on speaker. "Hi, Paul! I'm still in the office. Can you swing by and pick me up here?"

"Sure. I'm on Royalton now, almost to your building."

"Perfect! First floor, end of the hall, *remember?*" Her voice, higher than usual, trembled.

"I know where it is, but why don't you meet me outside? Are you okay?"

"Not really, *please hurry!*"

"Be right there. Should I call the police?"

"I hope you won't *need* to . . . but please stay on the phone until you get here."

Jack, recognizing the voice of their client, looked puzzled but backed off.

"I'm in the parking lot, Micky. Getting out of the car now, and in the door."

"Thank God! And thank *you*, Paul!" She smiled with relief as she heard their main office door open, then footsteps coming toward them.

Entering the office, Paul saw Micky's pale face and shaking hands, still in the corner, and her boss standing awkwardly by the edge of her desk.

"Everything's fine, Paul," Jack said, attempting to sound assured. "We just had a little misunderstanding."

Paul shot him a dark, glaring look. "Oh, I think I understand very clearly. And I want you to understand—in no uncertain terms—that harassing Micky in *any way* is off-limits. I'll make sure you pay for this." He gestured for Jack to step aside, moved to Micky and assisted her out of the office, his arm around her shoulders.

Outside, he settled her into the passenger's seat of the Jaguar S-Type he had driven for the evening. "We'll pick your car up after dinner. Pomeroy House?"

She nodded. "I need comfort food . . . their French onion soup will be a good start."

He pulled out of the parking lot and headed toward the restaurant a few blocks away. "What happened, Micky?"

She recounted her day and the incident with Jack, concluding, "My phone was on my desk, so I was able to call you . . . I'm *so glad* you were already so close!"

"Has anything like this happened before?"

She told him about her August scare at the hotel in Columbus. "Since then, I've worked out of my condo and from the road. But the office is much easier for all of the year-end mayhem . . . I guess Jack took advantage of that."

"You need to get out of there."

"I know. But I'm *not leaving* until late January . . . I have a *ton* of bonus money coming. I've worked my ass off . . . actually *exceeded* the ridiculously high quota Jack hit me with. I won't go until I collect!"

Paul pulled into a parking space at the restaurant, turned to look at Micky and smiled. "I admire your spirit. And your sound business sense. But I don't think you'll be safe at that office. Let's move you into one of mine. You can forward your office phone to your cell, and you'll have access to our copier, scanner, fax and overnight shipping. Okay?"

Her beautiful face lit up with a smile. She looked up at him and said, "*Okay* . . . you're my hero, Paul! I love you!"

CHAPTER 37

Sally sat slumped over the desk in her rectory office, chin supported between her fists and elbows digging into the wood in front of the monitor. Tomorrow was the first Sunday of Advent, the beginning of the church year, and she just could not come up with a sermon that felt right to her. Normally, she would preach about the Gospel. But the passage appointed by the Lectionary, Mark 13: 24–32, spoke of Jesus telling his disciples about his coming again at the end of the earth and of heaven to gather his elect.

"I wish we could focus on preparing for the Nativity rather than the other Christ the King of the Second Coming!" she cried out in frustration. "Why did this passage have to be selected to kick off this season?" Looking back again to the beginning of that chapter in her Bible for context, she shook her head. "No help there—the temple will be thrown down . . . wars, earthquakes and famine are just the beginning of the suffering . . . woe to those who are pregnant and to those who are nursing infants in those days—in our secular *human* calendar, your innocent Virgin Mother is carrying you now! Everywhere we go, Christmas carols are blaring from speakers and unneeded merchandise spills out from shelves telling us to buy, buy now, only so many shopping days left until we must out-do the wise men who brought gifts to honor your birth! You tell your disciples that they must proclaim the good news to all nations, but then they'll be hated by all because of your name and be put to trial. Parents will betray children and children will rise against parents and have them put to death. And you say only God knows when this will take place, so we are to beware and keep alert, presumably so we can be the ones who endure to the end and be saved? Saved for *what?* Both Heaven and Earth will be gone in this Gospel—we don't hear about the new Heaven and New Jerusalem until the book of Revelation!"

The Old Testament reading from Isaiah seemed to her a little more in keeping with the Advent theme of preparing oneself for the coming of the Lord. While not cheerful, the prophet beseeches God to tear open the heavens and come down to earth again, because it has been so long since he made himself known to his people that they have all forgotten him and have become sinners. "Because you hid yourself we transgressed, we have all become like one who is unclean, all our righteous deeds are like a filthy cloth . . . there is no one who calls on your name or attempts to take hold of you, for you have hidden yourself and delivered us into our iniquity." She sighed. "Yes, I can work with that."

Silently, Sally asked God to work through the words she would put together, and began typing. After a couple of hours, she had combined her thoughts about both pieces of scripture.

She felt relief at completing the sermon, but the effort had exhausted her. And the negativity had enveloped her like a second skin. The themes of pregnancies began colliding in her tortured brain: Those of the women in the end of time; of Mary and her cousin, Elizabeth, mother of John the Baptist; and of her own. Pregnancy once was referred to as "expecting," and Sally cynically thought that no one ever expected that the child she delivered would be lost to a gruesome death. Babies born into a world in the process of ending; a son who was crucified for working miracles, loving and healing people; or his cousin who was imprisoned for bringing people to God and then killed to satisfy a fearful king's daughter's birthday wish of his head presented on a platter. Or her own daughter destroying herself with drugs and preferring to kill herself rather than quit and recover to end her pain.

Realizing that she was going down a dark hole, Sally began to pray. "Mother Mary, I don't often pray to you, but I need the strength and solace that only another mother who has lost her child can give." Her words dissolved into tears and racking sobs. As she wailed and gasped for breath, it came to her that she needed to talk to an earthly mother or father who had also lost a child to heroin.

When she had allowed calm to reclaim herself and dried her face, she called Lillian and told her what was going on. "All of my Al-Anon friends' addicted children are still alive, thank God, and I don't want to ask them if they know anyone with my loss. Do you have any ideas, Lil?"

"I don't know any mothers, but Gus certainly has experience, strength and hope in that situation."

"Oh, yes. And he was so very helpful to me when . . ."

"I'll call him now, Sally. Why don't you come over here? I'll put the kettle on for tea."

"Thanks, Lil, I'll be right there."

She arrived just as the kettle was screaming. Lillian invited her in, shut off the burner and poured boiling water into mugs with Constant Comment tea bags waiting. She looked at her guest. "Kitchen or living room? And would you rather talk to Gus in private, or should we put him on speaker?"

"Let's sit on your loveseat and put the speaker phone on the coffee table," she decided. "I'd just be telling you all about the conversation anyway, so this will save the energy."

They made their way to the front parlor and settled in. After a few sips of tea, Lillian held up her hand with the cell phone and raised an eyebrow at Sally, who nodded. Lil tapped the number, touched speaker and placed the phone on the coffee table in front of them. When it was answered, she said, "Hi, Gus, Sally and I are here in the living room. You're on speaker; is that okay?"

"Of course. Sally, Lil told me you hit a rough patch of grief this evening. I'm sorry to hear that, and sorrier to say that it goes with the territory. Would you like to tell me about it?"

"Hello, Gus, thanks for being willing to talk to me about this. And thanks for saying it's not unusual to be ambushed by a rush of negativity.

"I've been struggling for the past few days, trying to write my sermon for tomorrow. I don't like the Gospel appointed for the day, and I just got absorbed into this dark muck over it—I just feel stuck there. I mean, I do feel better coming over to be with Lil and talking to you, since you've also lost a child and a grandchild to addiction. But I'm afraid of how that despair came out of nowhere and overwhelmed me . . . what if it happens again? I still can't get that vision of her staring up at the ceiling in the car out of my mind."

"Yes, those things stay with us. Over time, they move more to the back of our minds, but your experience of seeing Shelley like that is still very fresh, just three months now. I can see how those scriptures and others used in the season of Advent could gang up on you. But the underlying emotional trigger is the holiday season, with its unrealistic focus on the perfect families no one has, and the gaping holes in the family portraits for those of us who've lost members of our younger generations. It's not supposed to be that way. But that's the way it is."

Sally sipped her tea, then set the cup in the saucer on the table. "I don't understand; it's been many years since Shelley spent any holidays with me. As a teen, she split the time between me and her father, then by college, she went to friends' homes."

"My grandson, Mark, was never around, either. But there was always a chance that maybe he'd stop by on Thanksgiving or Christmas. On the other hand, his mother, our daughter Annie, was always with us—and was the center of chaos. She and her mother would be well into their cups before the meal was served, and something would always set one or the other off. Our son, Bruce, and I often had to finish the cooking. Sometimes, we'd just eat the feast by ourselves while Annie and Maggie went at it. But there was always the hope that sometime, we'd have a nice holiday dinner together, with peace on earth and goodwill between women. But it never happened. And now, it can't ever happen, because all three of them are gone."

"And that's where the pain is?" Sally wondered.

"Yes, it comes from the finality of what might've been now will never be."

"How do you deal with that?"

"I expect it," he answered. "I don't dwell on it. But when it does show up, I say, 'Oh, there you are.' Then I allow myself to just feel the feelings and let them go. That works for me; you might try it."

"Okay, I will. Anything else?"

"I always make plans with the people who *are* in my life. For example, my son, Bruce, and I always spend Christmas Day together, watching football games, playing cards and eating Christmas dinner. That's special to us; we don't get together very often, but our Christmas tradition is important to us."

Lillian leaned toward the phone. "When and where will *we* celebrate Christmas? Our service at Grace Church is Christmas Eve. I was hoping you could come."

"Well, there are twelve days of Christmas," Gus said. "I was thinking it would be best if I came on Boxing Day and stayed through New Year's, if that's okay?"

"What if I drive up on Christmas Day to your place?"

"I don't want you to be on the road in who knows what kind of weather, Lil. And while I would like you to meet Bruce, Christmas Day really isn't the best time for that. That is our special time. As the quiet, sane member of the family, Bruce sort of got overlooked in the midst of the ongoing drama of the other three. I hope you can understand."

She paused for a moment. "All right. Boxing Day it is," she agreed. "I'll make Christmas Dinner for Sally and me, and there'll be plenty of left-overs for your visit. And, of course, I'll be baking!"

*****

Sally, looking rested and relaxed, smiled with delight as she bit into one of Lillian's warm frosted cinnamon rolls. After dabbing her lips and licking icing off of her fingers, she complimented the baker. "Thank you for making these today, Lil; they're my favorites," she said. "And thanks so much for your help last night!"

"Apparently, it worked. You hit that sermon right out of the park this morning!"

Micky nodded in enthusiastic agreement. "I'm *so glad* you apologized for the spooky Gospel . . . and I thought the *same thing . . . wait.* Mary's pregnant now. In a few weeks, she'll be riding on a donkey to deliver God's son in a stable in Bethlehem. To *save* the *world . . .* so, why is Jesus now with his disciples, telling them the world will *end*? And then you tied it to today's craziness of Christmas carols starting before Thanksgiving and all of the merchandizing madness . . . we were *all* laughing at the absurdity and were *definitely* with you when you declared it was time for us to straighten our own *personal* paths, and to be ready for *God* to set things right in the world, since *we clearly* aren't able to do that *ourselves!*"

Family of Choice: Raising Each Other

"That's what I love about Grace Church," Sally said. "I don't have to act like this perfect priest who always knows everything. I can be just as baffled as everybody else, and lead us into looking to God for the answers." She paused before changing to another church subject.

"The bishop is planning to visit us at Grace on February eleventh, the last Sunday before Lent. I'd like to get a group of our new parishioners who are interested in being baptized, confirmed or received in the Episcopal Church prepared for him to administer those sacraments in that day's service, and I think starting a class this Thursday evening would be a good Advent exercise, as well," she said, looking at Micky. "Would you be interested in officially joining us, dear?"

"Oh, yes! What do I need to do?"

"We'll meet in the Vestry Room at five-thirty for the four Thursdays of December, then have two final preparatory classes on February first and eighth. We'll read and discuss a book that explains our Episcopal faith and practices," she replied. "And you'll need to find your Baptismal certificate, if you were baptized. Were you confirmed in any Christian church before?"

"I'm pretty sure I was baptized as a baby, but I wasn't ever confirmed," Micky said. "I'll have to check with my father about my baptism and that certificate."

"Good! I look forward to having you in our class." Sally tried but failed to stifle a yawn, then got up from the round oak table. "Excuse me! Even though I slept well last night, I feel an afternoon nap coming on. Thanks again for everything, Lil!"

Micky also pushed back her chair and stood. "I need to go, too... I have to organize things in my office to be ready for tomorrow... 'tis the season when everybody wants everything yesterday so they can wrap up before the year's end."

Brad, who'd been quietly enjoying the pastry, looked at Lillian and asked, "Do you have time for another mug of coffee?"

"Sure." She smiled. "I'll get the pot. Another cinnamon roll, too?"

He savored the fragrance and grinned. "You know me well."

She returned with the goods and sat down, leaving the coffee pot on a placemat on the table. "Yes, I do know you, Brad. What's on your mind?"

He bit into the warm, sweet bun and poured coffee into his mug, then took a swig to wash the bite down. "I've been spending some time with a friend from my LGBTQ meeting, Ben, who's also become a client. He's said he'd like our friendship to become something more, and I think I'd like that, too—but I'm wondering if it's too soon after Oscar to start a relationship?"

Lillian licked some excess icing from her cinnamon roll. "That depends on how you look at the timeline, and more importantly, how you feel," she said. "It's been about a year now since you moved out of Oscar's home. And even though you let him back into your life (and your bed), you never really committed to him again. You always had one foot emotionally out of that, you didn't act like you two were a couple. And you made that very clear when you had your housewarming party."

Brad thought for a moment. "You're right—I enjoyed the courtship, but I never felt I could trust him. And, as it turned out, I couldn't. Can't. When I learned his diagnosis, I accepted that trusting him is not possible, for a condition beyond his—or my—control."

"How do you feel about that?"

"Relieved! And free."

"Free as in enjoying being solo? Or as in free to be with someone else?"

"Good question," he admitted. "Short answer—I don't know."

"So, when did things start heating up with Ben?"

"We've been talking in the parking lot after meetings since last January, but nothing more until I invited him to my open house," Brad explained. "He mainly came because he's been considering making some updates to his Craftsman bungalow and wanted to see what I'd done to my house. Then he saw Oscar—and his bizarre behavior, which led to his diagnosis and the end of our relationship. We started having lunch shortly after that, and he invited me to his family's house after Thanksgiving dinner to watch football."

"Football?"

Brad blushed. "Yeah—he's a jock. He played in high school and at Baldwin Wallace. Still hangs with his teammates."

"Nice to know that he has good relations with his family and with friends. Oscar was a lone wolf, even though he knew lots of people and threw those huge parties. You were the only person he was close to, which is likely why he was so driven to totally control you," she observed. "It sounds like Ben has a broad emotional support system; he'd be much less likely to try to dominate you."

"Which means—what?"

"That you could allow this relationship—you do realize you're already in a relationship, right?" She stopped at the change in his facial expression.

Brad had raised his eyebrows in surprise, and attempted to protest. "No, we're just friends! And we also have a business relationship. We're just two guys who like each other and go to lunch sometimes."

Lillian smiled and emitted a patient sigh. "Brad, friendship *is* a relationship. I was just saying I think you can be safe in letting this grow naturally and see where it goes without fear of being taken captive like you were with Oscar. You've been sober for eight years now. And you've had some good practice with setting boundaries in these last months. So, if you want to, give this new relationship with Ben a chance to grow. It will be up to you to know when you're ready for it to include sex."

*****

Micky was tired after her first day at her new office, in one of the sales cubby holes with doors bordering the showroom of Price Cadillac. She stretched out on the black modern chaise lounge in her living room, and took a moment to admire the antique Chinese silk oriental area rug in the center of her seating area's sectional grouping. Brad had been taking her antiquing, and she'd fallen in love with what he identified as "Chinoiserie." A striking rug had stopped her in her tracks, and he had convinced her that this sapphire-blue floor covering with its gracefully curving green stems attached to golden yellow lotus blossoms and vivid red rose blooms would work with her black minimalist furnishings and light gray carpeting. She'd liked it so much that, on her own, she'd augmented the theme with a good reproduction ginger jar vase, which she'd placed on her black glass-topped dining table and filled with silk flowers picking up the rug's hues. She had also replaced the stark modern chandelier with an antique brass and enamel Chinese-style fixture. Brad had helped her install that.

She knew she needed to bring him up to date on the recent happenings in her life. She picked up her phone and tapped his number.

"Hey Brad, it's me," she said when he connected. "Sorry I had to cut out early yesterday."

"Hi, Micky. That's okay—you'd said something about needing to organize your office?"

"Yes... I moved my active client files of things wrapping up now out of the firm's office on Saturday and took them to an empty office at Paul's Cadillac dealership. I spent yesterday over there setting up, and worked there today."

"*What?* Why did you do that?" Brad realized he was screaming into the phone, and sought to tone it down. "I'm sorry for yelling, Micky—but that bombshell came out of nowhere! Why didn't you mention it yesterday?"

"The why is Jack waited until everyone else had left last Friday, then snuck up on me and grabbed me and wouldn't let go until I bashed into him with my chair," she explained. "But he was blocking the door and had me cornered in my office."

"Oh my God, what did you do? You looked okay yesterday."

"Luckily, Paul was on his way to pick me up and was almost to our office building when I called his cell... I put the phone on speaker so Jack knew not to try anything more, and let Paul know I needed help ASAP," she said. "He rescued me, thank God!"

Brad was confused. "I thought you were staying out of the office since that incident at the hotel last summer."

"I *have been*... but the work volume is so crazy now, I really need office support. Paul understands I can't quit *now*... I have *so much* bonus coming, but need to stay with the company until everything gets paid in mid-January. It's just for a few weeks," she concluded.

"Why didn't you call me after your boss assaulted you?" Brad asked in an agitated tone.

Micky shifted on the chaise, and pulled her knees up to a semi-fetal, seated position. "First, I was in shock. And then I was with Paul non-stop until early Sunday morning... I just had enough time to drive home, shower, dress and get to church... and after that, I've been with him or working out of the dealership until I just got home now. So, *now*, I *am* calling you."

"You're right—sorry, again," he apologized. "So, you'll be looking for a new job in January?"

"That's the plan . . . I'm *way* too busy now, but I agree with Paul that I have to get out of there . . . he says he has some ideas to discuss soon, after the holidays," she said. "Still . . . I've got to admit, working there today felt weird . . . I may go back to mainly working from home, and just go in if I need teleconferencing or FedEx . . . again, it'll just be this way for a few weeks."

Brad sighed. "At least you're safe. *Please* keep in touch! I really *care about* you!"

"I care about you, too. So, enough about *me* . . . how are *you?*"

He recounted his discussion with Lillian regarding whether it was too soon after ending things with Oscar to start a new relationship. "And she insisted that I was *already in* a relationship with Ben—even if we weren't having sex yet."

Micky giggled until she was gasping for breath. When she could breathe again, she wiped the laughter tears from her eyes and declared, "*I* could've told you *that,* silly boy!"

CHAPTER 38

Sun streamed in the bay window of Lillian's small parlor on the east side of her Queen Anne house, giving a false impression of warmth on this early December day. Just a few minutes ago, it was cloudy and eddies of small snowflakes had danced around the same window. She enjoyed the changing scene from her chaise lounge, under a heavy afghan throw and her overweight calico cat. She sipped a mug of coffee and directed her gaze back to the *Wall Street Journal* editorial she'd been reading when her phone rang.

"Oh, blast! Where did I put it now? It's supposed to be so convenient to always have your phone with you, but I never had this problem with my landline; I always knew where the telephone was!" She attempted to rise from the chaise, but the cat had no intention of stirring.

"Get up, Pretty!" she commanded. "Even though I'm sure it's not for you, I need to answer the call." She managed to slide out from under the lush-furred feline, who remained on the afghan. Once standing, Lillian saw the phone on a marble-topped table near the door and trotted over to take the call.

"Good morning, Lil! I have great news!" declared the woman's cheerful voice.

"Ann! How are you? And what good tidings have you heard?"

"Well, despite our slight delay due to your late-add final chapter, your book still shipped to stores just before Thanksgiving," her editor told her. "So, after its first week of availability, *Cat Hair in the Bidet* made the New York Times Best Seller List for nonfiction memoirs!"

"*It did? Wow!*" Lillian leaped with joy, startling the cat. "That's *wonderful* news, Ann! Thank you!"

"You deserve it, Lil. That book really resonates with a lot of people, especially women," she said. "But surprisingly, a lot of widowers are buying it, too. That wasn't the case with your previous works, but it's gone viral on social media and is catching on fast. Marketing wants to capitalize on the wave and get you out for signings to increase pre-holiday sales; our publicist will be emailing you a schedule for the weeks of the eleventh and eighteenth."

"Oh, my! That fast?"

"They wanted to start this week, but I told them you'd need to get your ducks in a row."

"You were correct, Ann. When will I be able to decorate my house for Christmas? I don't have a tree or anything yet! And I need to shop for making Christmas dinner! I have company coming."

Ann snickered. "By 'company,' do you mean the gentleman of the final chapter? How long is he staying?"

"Yes. And he's staying through New Year's."

"Perfect!"

"Why is that so perfect?" Lillian inquired.

"Because you'll be back on the road January third."

"Not really! But I guess you wouldn't kid about a thing like that," she conceded. "It's been a few years since I had a book launch; I forgot about all of the traveling for promotion."

"You've always been great at it, Lil," Ann said. "You're a trooper. Now go buy that tree, plan your menu, throw that tinsel around—and then pack. It's on!" She ended the call.

Stunned, Lillian just stood there for a few minutes. Eventually, she staggered back to the chaise and sank down on it, next to the cat who had now claimed possession. After staring out the window at additional snow showers, she collected her thoughts enough to call Sally, who shrieked with excitement at the news.

"Congratulations, Lil! I *told* you the book could be your best yet. Looks like it is!"

"But, Sally, I'm really overwhelmed," Lillian protested. "How am I going to get everything ready for Christmas *and* prepare for the tour in just six days?"

"The Lord created the world in that timeframe," she replied. "And he didn't have friends to help!"

*****

Brad leaned forward from the padded bench back of his seat in Fahrenheit and clinked his water glass with Ben's over the crisp white tablecloth. "To our first real date," he toasted.

"And to many more," Ben replied. "I'm so glad your sponsor pointed out that we already *are* in a relationship. And even gladder that it's evolved to dating."

"Speaking of levels," Brad began. "I think we need to wait until late March before we elevate ours much further. That would be six months after the last time I might've had relations with Oscar—and in light of his diagnosis, I can't be sure he hadn't been with anybody else. I'd like us to both get tested for HIV then—just to be safe."

Ben nodded. "That's reasonable. And responsible. I've never been a fan of condoms," he said. "Were you always so careful?"

"Not during my drinking days," Brad admitted, with a slight eye-roll. "When I got sober, Lil passed along the warning of her late sponsor, Sebastian, who died of AIDS: 'You don't want to risk cutting your life short for twenty minutes of fun.'"

"Wise words to live by. Literally."

Their appetizers arrived. The waiter delivered grilled avocado with sweet Thai soy sauce, lime, goat cheese and crispy grilled toast to Brad; black truffle meatballs to Ben.

"Oh, these are great!" Ben declared after his first bite. "I've heard of this place, but I've never been here before."

"The menu is very innovative—it changes every six weeks, based on what's in season from local or regional farms," Brad explained. "I thought you might like it, and it's close to the gallery opening—thanks for coming with me to that. The owner is one of my suppliers."

"It was okay, fairly interesting," Ben said. "Although I usually prefer more active entertainment. And fine cuisine is very nice, especially for special occasions like this, but I'm more into discovering great diners, delis and ethnic food."

As if on cue, their waiter cleared their places and returned with their entrées. Brad smiled as he inhaled the aroma of his. "I have nothing against those types of eateries—but I *love* the sophisticated subtlety of dishes like this: Kobe beef short ribs with a ginger-soy-apple glaze," he said. "So—what do you mean by 'active entertainment?'"

Ben looked up from carving a bite from his rack of lamb. "You know, sports. Going to games. I love football, of course, but I also like basketball, baseball, hockey, soccer. I have season tickets to the first three. The Cavs will be back in town soon; we should go."

"Sure, let me know when," Brad said. "I don't know that much about sports, but I'm open to learning. What else do you like to do?"

"Hiking. Some camping. A little bird-watching. There's a program at Ohio Raptor Education that I'd really like to do some weekend in the spring," he replied. "They teach you the ancient sport of falconry. You learn by actually working with the birds."

"Hiking is good. I run to stay in shape, so that would add scenery. And I really think it would be cool to try falconry!" Brad's green eyes sparkled with excitement. "But *camping*—my idea of camping is staying at a Holiday Inn without a pool."

Ben laughed. "The kind of camping I'm talking about *has* a pool. And showers. Plus, a full-service restaurant and pool-side food and beverages. A group of my friends rents a luxury motorhome—the kind that has multiple pull-outs for extra bedrooms—and we drive to this great facility in central Ohio where we rent a space for a weekend. It has electrical hook-ups for the A-C and water. It's a blast!"

"I could get into that." Brad agreed. "How about theater, the arts, museums? I usually buy a package of tickets to Playhouse Square, and I like to take in new exhibits at Cleveland museums—Art, Natural History, the Rock Hall, Crawford Auto. Plus, I belong to several architectural restoration societies and go if they're having good programs or social functions."

"I'd definitely like the restoration events," Ben said. "And I'd try the others. I don't know much about classical music, but I've usually liked what I've heard. Just *no opera*. I draw the line at that!"

Brad made a sour face. "I agree. Especially *Chinese opera*—to me, that sounds like cats in heat! What about travel? I haven't gone *anywhere* in the last nine years except places where my ex had business. I'd *love* to go back to Europe—Paris, to introduce you to my friends, but also to see lots of places I didn't get around to visiting when I lived there."

"I love traveling! Just haven't made time or plans to do any for a long time," Ben said. He looked into Brad's eyes. "And I haven't had anyone to share the experience with. It will be wonderful to do that with you."

*****

Micky smiled in anticipation as she hovered her hot spoonful of Dooley's French onion soup above the bowl, then looked up at Brad. "I can't believe it's been almost a year since we first had soup and burgers together here!"

"And you had your moment of clarity regarding your alcoholism," he said, smiling back. "When you connected the dots between that *one* drink you'd intended to have and waking up with a *stranger,* having missed your cruise ship and the big *awards dinner,* you declared that you *never* wanted that to happen again. Now, here you are, just a few weeks away from your first anniversary!"

"Thanks to *God* . . . and to *you,* Lil and Sally." She put the cheesy spoonful of broth in her mouth, savoring the rich flavors. "Along with meetings and the Steps. I brought my Fourth Step list like you said. Does *everyone* on it go on my Eighth Step list?"

Brad swallowed his mouthful of soup. "*Theoretically*—yes. But as for using it as a list for your Ninth Step *amends*—no. For instance, there's no need to track down your high school mean girl nemesis whose boyfriend you stole in revenge. She probably wouldn't even remember him—or you—by now, so there's no point in reminding her of that pain.

"What *is* important is for you to remember your tendency to punish people who hurt you. Instead, to be more discerning in choosing the people you let into your life to begin with—and to exit the association early if you see or experience bad behavior by them. In cases where you can't do that immediately, you need to watch your *own* behavior *closely*—or you'll generate *more* trouble and increase your resentments. Your best choices there are to limit your exposure or to try to improve the relationship, if possible."

"I am working on *that* . . . I took my father to lunch last Saturday. I needed to ask him for my baptismal certificate . . . Sally said I'll need it to get confirmed in the Episcopal Church."

"Oh, yeah—I remember her talking about holding classes for that," he said. "How's that going?"

"It's good . . . I like the classes and the other parishioners taking them," she replied. "I worried a bit at first about adding one more thing to this *incredibly* busy time right now . . . but I feel *calmer* after each one. They're making me feel *closer* to these people, and *especially* to Sally . . . helping all of us really seems to have brightened her up. She'd seemed really depressed about the upcoming holidays.

"And I'm feeling closer to my father than ever before . . . he really *cares* that I've found sources of support and stability *now* that he never could give me. He said I was baptized in a Catholic church in St. Louis, where he and my mom were from. He'll have to track that down and request the certificate, because it's not with his papers. He said my mom probably had it with hers, but he was so upset when she died that he just threw her things away without going through them. We actually *talked* about that . . . her suicide . . . how we *both* kind of came unglued. First time *ever!*"

Bridgett, their waitress, cleared their soup bowls and replaced them with burgers and fries.

"So, is my father on my Eighth Step list, or am I already making Ninth Step living amends?" Micky asked.

"Both. *Living* amends are *ongoing*. So he goes on the list, and you can put a check mark by it rather than crossing it off." Brad picked up his portabella and brie burger. "Another one for your list would be your boss—what's the status there?"

"I'm taking care of business from my Price Cadillac office," she said. "I'm emailing him my call reports, keeping him apprised . . . he'll make plenty of bonus from my work, and so will I . . . I *might* even win Top Dog again this year."

"Are you still planning to leave the company?"

"Yes. As soon as I receive all of the bonus money I have coming. That should happen in late January," she said.

"What then?"

Micky shrugged. "Not sure . . . my father said he played golf with Paul after Thanksgiving . . . Paul told him his feelings for me are serious, intentions are honorable . . . and asked for my father's approval, when the time comes. He didn't say when that would *be*, but it seemed like it would be soon."

Brad returned the French fry he'd just picked up to his plate. He looked Micky straight in her deep blue eyes. "Are you ready for that?"

Her gaze didn't waver. "I think I am."

CHAPTER 39

Ben Gates pushed his chair back from Brad's elegant table with a contented sigh. "My compliments to the chef! Everything was wonderful, especially that rolled chocolate cake thing—what did you call it?"

Brad grinned. "Bouche de Noelle. It's a traditional French dessert for Christmas dinner.

Excuse me—I'll be right back!" He disappeared briefly behind the swing door to the butler's pantry and emerged with an unwrapped cardboard box, which he handed to Ben.

"Merry Christmas! I hope you'll excuse the presentation, but I couldn't think of a way to wrap this without causing damage."

Ben pulled back the loose flaps on the top. "Oh, wow! I think I see a very cool lamp shade. Now, how do I pull it out?"

Brad leaned over to assist. "You hold the sides of the box, I'll lift it." Aided by his slow, steady pull, the amber art glass shade rose, and the bronze craftsman lamp's base followed. "I thought you might like this for your living room or your study."

"You're right! We'll have to take it back to my house and try it to see where it looks best." He stood to take the lamp and kissed Brad. "Thanks!" After admiring the lamp for a minute or so, he set it down and pulled a flat rectangular box from his inside jacket pocket. "I can't take credit for the wrapping. They did it at the store," he said, handing it to Brad. "Hope you like it."

Brad opened the box and smiled when he saw an eighteen-karat gold necklace in a small but masculine flat chain design. "Thank you, Ben—nobody's ever given me jewelry before!"

"Well, I wasn't sure, since I've never seen you wear any," he said. "But it's not just a gay thing anymore. Heck, most of the pro ball players in any sport wear bling on the field these days! And this size is good if you'd rather wear it under your collar."

Brad handed the necklace to Ben and turned his back to him. "Put it on for me?"

Ben complied, and as he closed the clasp, he nuzzled Brad's ear. "I know we're waiting until March, but there are a lot of intimate pleasures we can enjoy without *exchanging* body fluids."

Brad reached back for Ben's hand and led him toward the staircase.

*****

Micky made French toast and bacon for their breakfast on Christmas morning, and they lingered a while over coffee. Paul wiped his mouth to remove some confectioner's sugar and cinnamon on his lips. "This was delicious, Micky," he said with some surprise. "When did you learn how to cook?"

She smiled, her blue eyes sparkling. "I'm glad you liked it! Brad taught me," she said. "It's handy to have a sponsor with a background in pastries . . . and he was right, this was easy! How did you like the service last night? I especially enjoyed the string quartet and the trumpets."

"Very nice, yes. You certainly know a lot of people there."

"I do . . . of course, Mother Sally and Lillian, whom you've met, are family . . . but many others are becoming friends, too. It's so wonderful to be part of this parish . . . to *belong*."

Family of Choice: Raising Each Other

"I thought I made you feel that way, don't I?"

"Of *course* you do, Paul! This is *in addition* to you." She smiled at him. "You can't have too much love in your life!" She looked across her living room at the Christmas tree, its twinkling lights beckoning, then looked back at Paul. "Now?"

He leaned over the table and gave her a light kiss. "Okay. Let's have at it. You've got quite a pile under that tree."

As she sat down on the blue Chinese oriental near the packages, Paul picked up a large box in glossy green wrapping paper with a gold ribbon and bow and handed it to her. "Here, open this one first."

She untied the satin ribbon and carefully peeled open the taped seams. Lifting the box's lid revealed a heavy silk robe, in deep red with a classic paisley pattern. "I thought you could use that now," he said. "You look a little cold in just your pajamas."

She laughed. "Yes . . . you're right! Thanks!" She took the robe from the box and put it on. "It fits perfectly! And it *is* warm . . . and so *luxurious*." She leaned down and selected a gold wrapped box of similar size and handed it to Paul, who promptly ripped off the paper.

"Ah, great!" he said as he inspected the Ralph Lauren olive golf slacks with light olive logoed shirt. "You must've noticed me ogling them in the pro shop."

She giggled. "Busted! I also thought the color would bring out your eyes."

He held the shirt up to his shoulders. "So. Does it?"

"Oh, yes! Hazel is such a subtle color . . . that shirt does brighten them up."

They spent the next forty-five minutes turning the pyramid of gift boxes into piles of wrapping paper and cardboard. The loot included more clothes for each other, along with golf gear. Micky received a wok and Chinese food cookbook from Brad; *Doctor Bob and the Good*

Old Timers, a book about A.A.'s founding and early days in Akron and Cleveland Heights, Ohio, from Lillian; and from Sally, a signed copy of Lillian's first book, *Don't Get Your Tush Too Near the Toaster*. She laughed. "Everybody is having fun highlighting my unfamiliarity with the kitchen! There's nowhere to go from here but up!" She opened an envelope from her father, and held up a gift card for Morton's The Steakhouse. "See, my dad knows my cooking will *never* approach what we can get here!"

Micky scrambled up from the floor and pulled a large box from behind the tree and dragged it to Paul. "Here's your big gift from me."

His face lit up with delight. "An Optishot simulator! Wow! How did you know I wanted this?"

"I overheard you, Chet and Howie talking about golf simulators," she said. "And I know *the club's* is much, much better . . . but in the winter, I thought you might like to practice at home sometimes."

He jumped up and grabbed her for a deep kiss and embrace. "Thank you, Micky! I've got a big gift for you, too." He handed her a Christmas card with an itinerary inside. "I made reservations to stay in Honolulu for New Year's and a couple of days before we board the ship for the Cadillac cruise to Tahiti. We fly out on Saturday. Will you be able to get things tied up and packed by Friday?"

Micky clapped her hands and jumped up and down. "I'll make *sure* I do! Thank you, Paul!" She hugged and kissed him.

He pulled a small gift-wrapped box from his robe pocket. "One more."

Her heart pounded with excitement and she caught her breath as he handed the box to her. She waited, expecting him to say something.

"Open it."

The wrapping paper revealed a dark blue velvet jewelry box. She looked at him, with a question in her eyes, but he remained silent.

She lifted the lid and got goosebumps when she saw bright white diamonds. But they weren't in a ring; instead, they were earrings. They were stunning, but not what she had expected.

She picked one up, and saw a one-and-a-half-carat round diamond that would cover her ear lobe, from which a two-carat emerald-cut diamond dangled, accented by two small pear-shaped diamonds on either side. The clarity and cut of the gems caught the tree's lights and flashed white lightning. "Oh, Paul, these are *fabulous!*"

He smiled. "They'll look more fabulous on you. And they'll go with everything—especially more diamonds," he said. "Put them on for tonight's Christmas buffet at the Club. I want your father to see them when we take him there for dinner."

*****

"I hope you don't mind leftovers, Gus," Lillian said as she led him to the sideboard with the remainder of the meal she and Sally had enjoyed on Christmas Day. "But they really are appropriate; Boxing Day in seventeenth century Britain was when the wealthy gave their servants the day off and sent boxes home with them filled with gifts, bonuses and leftovers from the manors' Christmas feasts!"

He carved a more well-done slice from the other side of the rib roast, and helped himself to the side dishes. "Your table looks lovely, Lil, as do you."

She smiled. "Thank you, Gus. I did put out fresh napkins."

He nodded and began eating. She decided to skip the blessing, since he hadn't waited. Instead, she broke the silence by continuing her tutorial. "Boxing Day was special to everyone in England and its territories as the second day of Christmastide, which also was the same date as Saint Stephen's Day. Today in England, it's a day for giving gifts to the poor, shopping and major sporting events. The top football and rugby teams all have matches, and the second-most-prestigious steeplechase, the King George the Sixth Chase, is held. It's also one of the main days of the season for mounted hunt clubs."

"I know. It's a holiday. But it's not Christmas, is it?"

"I understand that you had another obligation, Gus," she said. "You can't be in two places at the same time."

"No, I can't. And Bruce is my *son*—he's not an obligation. He's the only family I have left; as I am for him."

"It's a tough time for anyone who's experienced loss," she acknowledged. "Sally is still really struggling, and I still miss decorating the house and the Christmas tree with George."

When they finished the meal, they went into the living room and exchanged the presents they'd put under the tree. He gave her a royal blue turtleneck cashmere sweater that he insisted made her eyes look even bluer, and a gold rose pendant on a fine chain. "It's not as beautiful as the real ones you hybridized, but it can serve as a reminder of what brought us together," Gus said.

"That's lovely," she replied. "The rose as well as the sentiment. And I love the sweater, thank you!"

He opened his gift, a large green wrapped box with two books inside. The first was *Classic Roses*, an encyclopedia of species and old garden roses. "I thought you might like to learn more about some of the key roses in my breeding program," she teased. "Might give you some ideas!"

The second was an advance copy of her book with an inscription over her signature. *Thank you, dear Gus, for inspiring the extra chapter by reawakening love!*

He paused, and his eyes brimmed. "Thank you, Lillian. I do love you, and I'm honored you wrote about that in your book," he said.

"But Bruce is very cool to the idea of me becoming seriously involved with you—or anyone else. He said he's had to wait all his life to get any attention from me. And he's right; I was always so preoccupied with the drama of all of the alcoholics in our family that he got overlooked."

"Isn't he in his forties now? Hasn't he dealt with that yet?"

Gus shrugged. "I don't think there's an expiration date on pain. Or a statute of limitations," he said. "Bruce told me he doesn't want me to even consider selling the house and moving out of town."

"Um, we've never discussed that," Lillian said. "How do you feel about that possibility?"

"I don't know," he admitted. "I've thought about it, some. But now, it doesn't look likely."

She put her arm around his shoulder. "Let's just enjoy the next few days together and put thoughts of the future on the back burner," she suggested. "I'll be flying out again next week. I'll be on promo tours for the next month or so—and you don't need to be driving on winter highways. If I have a book signing in or near Detroit, I can come to see you."

She hesitated. "If you'd like that, of course."

CHAPTER 40

A light breeze off the Pacific Ocean just 350 feet from their table rustled Micky's black hair, but it didn't disturb the brilliant diamonds suspended from her ears. She and Paul had finished dinner and were lingering on the patio overlooking Kahanamoku Beach, watching the dramatic dance of the clouds' changing colors with the sun's reflection on the sea as it descended toward the horizon. Blazing shades of yellow, orange and crimson that had started out as bright hues while the couple had enjoyed dessert now intensified and were growing darker while the sun became a red ball hovering just above the water.

Micky was mesmerized. The golden path on the water's surface narrowed as it led to the sun, then turned blood red until it spread out along the horizon in burnt orange, like fire raging across a prairie. Suddenly, the blazing wide line collapsed to form a small, fiery pool surrounding the now barely visible sun—which immediately vanished with a flash of green light.

She gasped. "That was *incredible* . . . I've never seen anything like it!"

Paul put his arm around her shoulders and kissed her cheek. "It's been an incredible year. Now the sun has gone down on twenty-seventeen, and there's one more thing I'd like to do to tee up an even happier New Year."

She turned to look at him. "What's that? I thought you got everything tied up with the calls you made this afternoon."

"I did. But I'm not talking about business, Micky. I'm talking about *us*. When you came into my life last spring, *everything* improved. I fell in love with you that very first day, and it's grown every day since then." He reached in the pocket of his gray casual slacks and pulled out a small box.

"Here are the diamonds that go with those earrings," he said as he lifted back its lid. "I'd like to put them on your left finger. Micky, will you please marry me?"

"Oh! Oh yes, Paul . . . *yes*, I will marry you! I love you, too!" They kissed and held each other tightly. When they relaxed their embrace, she teased, "I'd *really* thought *this* was in the box you gave me on Christmas Day . . . and when that wasn't a ring, I thought maybe you weren't going to propose after all."

He slipped the ring on her finger. Then she lifted her hand with a flourish and admired the white light that flashed with the movement. "It fits perfectly! How did you know my ring size? And it *does* match these fabulous earrings!" Micky was dazzled by the emerald-cut three-carat center stone flanked by one-carat pear-shaped baguettes whose points merged with a band of smaller channel-set white diamonds.

He grinned. "One of our friends knows a jeweler. Howie's brother Bob does custom work, and Howie's been around him enough to guess a woman's ring size. I worked with Bob to select the stones and create the designs."

"You really *did* have me going at Christmas!"

"Yeah, it was fun watching your expression! I could tell what you were thinking, but I knew it wasn't possible to be too disappointed with those gems," he admitted. "Still, I didn't want your engagement ring to be a present, and I wanted to keep Christmas separate. We'll always remember getting engaged every New Year's Eve."

"And I'll *always* remember this spectacular tropical sunset," Micky said. "When do you want to have our wedding?"

"I'd like to have it as close as possible to the date I first met you, in late March," he replied. "That really was special to me, and I don't want to waste any time before we're together."

Her smile rivaled the diamonds. "Me neither! We'll have a lot to do when we return from all of our travels, but I'm sure we can handle it."

*****

In the much colder climate of northeast Ohio, Brad and Ben snuggled in a collection of pillows and chenille throws on the carpeted floor in front of the fire while they watched the descent of the Times Square twenty-eighteen crystal ball on Brad's flat screen above the mantle.

When it was closer to its destination, Ben said, "There was something I wanted to give you for Christmas, but wasn't sure how to go about it. Something big for us to do in the coming year."

"Oh? What is it?" Brad asked. "Because I had an idea like that, too—but I didn't know how it would work with your schedule."

Ben grinned. "Maybe we're on the same wavelength? I was thinking of plane tickets to Paris. Maybe some other travel while we're over there. You?"

Brad laughed. "*Yes—definitely* the same wavelength! I'd like to see if we could stay with some of my friends in Paris, and then take a river cruise to see cities in several countries. We'd need to discuss where we'd like to go, how long we can travel, and what we want to spend."

"Let's get started next week checking our vacation days and schedules," Ben suggested. "Then we can think about priorities, budgets and research cruises and plane fares."

"Sounds good to me—let's aim to get our plans together in January so we can book by Valentine's Day," Brad said. "That will take care of our gifts for that holiday!"

"I'm in!"

As they laughed and kissed each other, the ball on TV came to rest amidst a deluge of confetti, horns and fireworks. Together, they shouted, "Happy New Year!!!"

CHAPTER 41

Micky and Paul spent New Year's Day on the beach. After snorkeling, they had sandwiches from the snack bar, then napped under a cabana. When she awoke, she rummaged in her beach bag for her phone.

"Well . . . it's time to make our New Year's calls and announce our engagement," she said. "I think I should call Sally first and get our date scheduled, so we can pass that along with the news."

"Good idea," Paul agreed. "They'd be asking anyway, and we want to get on everyone's schedule."

She tapped Sally's home number from her contacts list and the call was answered on the second ring. "Aloha, Sally! Happy New Year!"

"Happy New Year to you, too, Micky! Are you on board for your cruise yet?"

"Not yet . . . we board tomorrow afternoon," she replied. "I'm calling with great news that concerns you . . . Paul proposed last night, and we'd like you to marry us."

"That's wonderful, Micky! I was just telling Lil how happy you've been looking lately," Sally said. "Do you have a date in mind?"

"Hello, Sally, it's Paul. We have you on speaker; and yes, we have a date: I first met Micky on March twenty-third last year. Best day of my life! That's a Friday this year, and I—I mean, we—are hoping to have our rehearsal that evening and the wedding the next day, either late morning or early afternoon. Would that be possible?"

"That's just before Holy Week begins, so I know we don't have anything scheduled then," she said. "But the timing will be tight. Morning would be better, so the altar guild can change things back to Lenten colors and clear away the wedding flowers to set up for Palm Sunday the next day. Also, we'll need to have four premarital counseling sessions. When do you two return from your travels?"

Micky answered, "We fly back on Sunday evening, January twenty-first. But that week will be crazy, catching up on everything."

"Tuesdays are best for those sessions," Sally said. "Especially since we'll be resuming our confirmation classes for the first two Thursdays in February. I'm looking at my calendar now. It will work if we start on January thirtieth, then meet every week after that, finishing on February twentieth. Will five-thirty be a convenient time?"

Paul looked at Micky, who nodded. "We can make that work. Thank you, Sally."

"Yes, Sally . . . thank you *so much* . . . for everything!" she added.

"My pleasure. Thank you for the great news to start off the year; congratulations!"

Micky ended the call and they kissed. "Whew! I'm *so glad* that worked out. Now I can call Brad, Lillian and my father."

"I think I'll take a walk on the beach to make my calls," Paul said. "Including the Club to book the dates for the rehearsal dinner and the reception. Is that okay with you?"

"I hadn't thought about that . . . but it probably would make the most sense," she said. "You don't think it's too far away from the church in Stromberg?"

"Not really. And there will likely be guests who just attend the reception, especially business invitees."

"Oh! I really hadn't thought about a guest list yet . . . you're way ahead of me!"

Paul grinned. "Well, I've been thinking about this for a while. You just started last night."

"I've been *thinking* about it . . . on and off . . . but only in *general*, no details," she said. "What about attendants? I really only have Brad and Lillian, since Sally will be performing the ceremony."

"I'll ask Howie and Chet. But what about Bill and Betty Eldridge? He's been like a father to me since my dad died, and you've gotten pretty close to Betty, haven't you?"

"I guess that would be okay," she said. "And it would be great if they could help organize things that will take place at the Club. I'm going to have my hands full. But I want Brad to be my Gentleman of Honor and Lil and Betty can be brides-matrons."

"That sounds good. See you in a bit." Paul rose from the lounge and left the cabana.

*****

The senior Gates' living room erupted in roaring cheers, fists pumping toward the ceiling and arms raised in tandem, with their owners having leaped from their burnt umber leather La-Z-Boy sectional seats. Brad guessed that the team favored by the home crowd had scored a touchdown. Ben noticed the empty bowl with green smears and alerted Brad. "Is there any more of that guacamole you made? It went fast, along with those chopped jalapeno peppers you had on the side."

"I'll make a fresh batch," he replied. "I brought a sack of ingredients. I didn't know how well it would go over—does your mom have any more chips?"

"I put five bags in the bottom cupboard to the right of the stove. My usual contribution, since I don't cook much and they go with everything," Ben said. "You don't mind missing the game?"

Brad smiled. "Not a problem—cooking is *my* contribution!" He grabbed the bowls and retreated to the kitchen, grateful for the refuge. As he reached for his paring knife to peel the first avocado, his phone sang the opening bars of "Pretty Woman." He traded the knife for the phone and swiped to answer. "Happy New Year, Micky! How are you—and how's Hawaii?"

"Happy New Year to you, too, Brad . . . Hawaii's great, and so am I . . . I'm *engaged!*"

"Congratulations! When did he pop the question?"

"Last night, right after the most *incredibly beautiful* sunset. He wants to get married on the anniversary of our first meeting, and we just set that up with Sally." She gave him the dates. "I'm hoping you'll be my Gentleman of Honor?"

"The honor would be mine—*of course* I'll stand up with you. And do anything *else* I can to help you with planning—and I *don't* mean just the *wedding*. You'll be making a *huge* transition in a *short* timeframe," he noted. "When do you get back?"

"Not until the twenty-second, effectively."

He whistled. "Wow."

"I know. *Very* little time!" she sighed. "Well . . . I have more calls to make, like to Lil. Thanks for *everything*, Brad!"

Brad returned his attention to the avocadoes. After enjoying the momentary escape from the gathering maelstrom, he called his sponsor, who answered immediately.

"Happy New Year, Lil. I assume you've heard the news—our Micky is getting married."

"Yes," she said. "Dear God."

*****

The port in Honolulu was near their hotel, so Micky and Paul were among the first guests to board the ship. They proceeded to their stateroom on Deck Seven and stood outside on their verandah, watching bustling deliveries of supplies for the voyage being loaded on board below as well as a peek of the open water beckoning from beyond the bow.

"This is *so* exciting, Paul! I'm glad we're taking this trip together ... although I never *imagined* that I'd be *with you* when I pitched the program to help you win it last spring!"

He laughed and kissed her. "Well, I did envision it. And here we are!"

A soft knock announced the arrival of their luggage, and they set to unpacking and stowing everything away. As she claimed the storage shelves beside the sink for her toiletries, Micky remarked, "You know, we've never lived together, just spent parts of weekends and usually at my place ... these next two weeks will give us a preview."

"Yes. And please remember that I will need one of those shelves for my razor and grooming kit."

"Oh ... sorry!" She moved her shampoo and conditioner to the shelf below the vanity.

They were just finishing up when the captain announced the safety drill and instructed all passengers to report to their muster stations.

Back in their cabin, she stood by the open closet. "How dressy is the Cadillac Welcome Aboard Dinner?"

"Dressy, but not formal; save that for the Dealers Round Table Awards," he replied. "And you were right: I did achieve that, thanks to our incentive program."

Family of Choice: Raising Each Other

She smiled. "You're welcome!" She chose her emerald green wrap dress with matching jewelry and kitten-heeled gold strappy sandals. She examined her reflection in the full-length mirror on the inside of the closet door. "How does this look? You may remember it . . . I wore it to one of the celebrations at the Club."

"Yes. That gave me the idea for your birthday earrings, which do look great with it." Paul stepped in front of her to knot his tie. "You need to share the mirror, too. These staterooms are designed to economize on space."

They exited and made their way to the third deck dining room at the stern, where a receiving line was set up for the Cadillac award guests. A member of Micky's company's travel operations staff gave each of them a lanyard with the program theme and their names, and steered them to meet Cadillac's CEO and the National Sales Manager. The next hand they shook belonged to the owner of the incentive company, who introduced himself to Paul, then looked at her with surprise.

"Micky! You look lovely as always, but what are you doing here? This isn't one of your programs," he said.

She gave him her best dazzling smile. "You're correct, Mr. Cordero . . . but one of *my* programs helped Paul win this trip."

"And she won my heart," Paul interjected. "Micky is now my fiancé, which is why she's here with me."

"And why Paul will be with me at our awards trip at La Costa in two weeks," Micky explained.

Alonzo Cordero broke into a broad smile and pumped Paul's hand again. "Congratulations!" He kissed Micky's cheek and said, "May I present my wonderful wife, Lana. Lana, Micky is one of our best sales representatives, who has just become engaged to this gentleman, Mr. Paul Price. They met through work on one of our programs."

"As did we!" Lana Cordero took Micky's hand to admire her engagement ring. "How beautiful! He has very good taste; but of course, he chose you!"

"Do you play golf, Paul? Because if you do, I'd like you to be my guest at the course on our first port."

"I'd like that very much, thank you! And I did bring my clubs."

"I'll make the arrangements and the information will be sent to your stateroom. Congratulations again to you and Micky; enjoy your cruise!"

*****

Micky and Paul did some serious relaxing during the next five days as the ship sailed to Tahiti. They'd agreed to not buy satellite cellular access, and for the first time in their relationship, they were unplugged from day-to-day business responsibilities. They enjoyed a couples massage in the spa, swam in the pool, practiced on the driving range on the top deck, worked out in the gym, and relished being mostly free from any schedule.

Resting in Paul's arms after delicious, leisurely sex, she sighed with contentment and said, "This *feels* like our *honeymoon* . . . I'm *so happy* just being with you!"

He smiled and kissed her again. "Yes, it does. We've really needed this time away together."

The fourth day at sea was a formal night for everyone on board, and a portion of the main dining room was reserved with maroon velvet ropes for the Cadillac Dealers Round Table event. Paul asked Micky to wear her best floor-length gown, a midnight blue halter sheath overlaid with layers of tulle for a skirt, accessorized by her diamonds. Paul looked very handsome in his tuxedo, and beamed with pride as his installation was announced.

During the days at sea, Micky and Paul encountered the Corderos in passing around the ship or on the jogging track, and sat with them in the theater watching a musical review. They also saw each other on the dance floor at the blues lounge and in the audience for the classical piano performance.

On day seven, they woke up to a vista of sandy beach with palm trees in the port of Papeete, Tahiti, the capital of French Polynesia. Paul stretched, yawned, kissed Micky and got out of bed. "I've got to get moving. I'm meeting Alonzo at eight-thirty in the second-floor lounge near the gangway to make our tee time, and I want to have breakfast first. What are you doing today?"

She sat on the edge of the bed. "I have a tour of the island that starts at nine and takes five hours. Then I hope to do some shopping. I'll get up and go to breakfast with you."

Micky's tour included walking on the black volcanic sand beach at Plage du Taharu and hiking through the jungle at Fautaua Valley, where a waterfall plunged one thousand feet into a shimmering pool. Returning to the city's very French urban center, the group visited the Robert Wan Pearl Museum, where Micky bought a black pear-shaped pearl pendant with matching earrings and a round black pearl ring in a simple gold setting. After lunch in an outdoor café, the tour ended with shopping in the central municipal market. Micky couldn't resist buying a tropical floral-print sarong and a shark tooth pendant.

Back in the stateroom, she put her new jewelry into the safe, looked at her watch and decided she had time to find the "Friends of Bill W" meeting listed in the activities published in the ship's daily bulletin. Brad had told her about the importance of attending the on-board meetings during the trip, and since Paul hadn't returned from his golf game, now was her chance.

The ten people in the room on Deck Three had been attending the meeting since the start of the cruise, so Micky briefly shared her story of getting sober and where she was in her program. She concluded her comments by explaining her absence at the start of the voyage was due to getting engaged on New Year's Eve. "These past few days are the first time we've had to just be with each other," she said. "It's been great . . . and it's also great that I've been able to come here today." Everyone congratulated her, and a couple of the women admired her ring.

After the meeting, a sixtyish-looking woman introduced herself to Micky. "My name is Barb. I've been on many cruises during my sobriety, and these meetings are a Godsend," she said. "Is your husband-to-be also in the program?"

"Oh, no . . . he drinks, but he doesn't have a problem."

"Does he have any problem with you going to meetings?" Barb asked. "As I recall, it took my husband some time to really understand and accept that."

"I was upfront with him as soon as we started dating . . . and it hasn't been a problem so far."

"Good! Well, I have to get ready for dinner. Here's my cabin number if you need to talk—it's hard to reach our sponsors back home, and there's booze everywhere you look on the ship!" She handed Micky a small slip of paper, and they walked to the elevators.

As soon as Micky opened the cabin door, Paul exclaimed, "There you are! I wondered what happened to you. I was getting worried."

"Oh . . . I went to the four-o'clock A.A. meeting . . . very nice people. I just need to put on a nicer pair of slacks to go to dinner." As she started to change, she asked. "How was your golf game?"

"My game showed that I haven't been on the links since Thanksgiving, but my main purpose was to get to know Alonzo and make friends. I think we did," he said. "He certainly said many nice things about you. And don't worry—I was careful not to let anything slip about your plans to leave the company. Didn't want anything to affect your chances of winning the top sales award or getting your bonus money delayed."

"Thanks!" She smiled and headed for the door, but Paul intercepted her and put his hands on her shoulders.

He gave her a light kiss, then said, "I'm glad you're alright, Micky. But I was concerned when you weren't here and I didn't know where you were. Next time, do me the courtesy of leaving a note, okay?"

"Oh! Sure . . . sorry."

*****

During the next two days, Micky and Paul took excursions on Raiatea and Moorea, followed by several days at sea. On January fourteenth, they arrived at New Zealand's Bay of Islands, an area on the east coast of the Far North District of the North Island.

Paul and Micky took their golf bags to the celebrated Kauri Cliffs Golf Club there, once described by a PGA Tour star as "Pebble Beach on steroids." Ranked in the top one-hundred in the world, the par 72 championship course provided the couple with ocean views from fifteen holes. They lost several golf balls, as the long greens sloped sharply toward the sea, and both were greatly challenged by deeply-seated sand traps.

As they sat down for a late lunch in The 19th Tee, Micky laughed and said, "That was *fabulous* . . . and so beautiful that I didn't even *care* that my game is nowhere near being worthy of this course! I hope the one at La Costa isn't as difficult."

"Probably won't be, although I've heard it's very good," Paul said. "I'm glad we got some practice in before the couples scramble at your company's trip in a couple of days."

After returning to the ship, they again checked for messages. Micky moved to the balcony to return a call from Brad.

"Happy Anniversary! I think it's the fourteenth where you are, isn't it?"

"Thanks, Brad! You're right . . . it *is* January fourteenth here in New Zealand," she said. "Thank you for remembering!"

"What's *important* is that *you* remember—this milestone is a big deal! You've had *a lot* happen in your first year of sobriety," he said. "Your anniversary date is your flag in the ground from which you move more and more into becoming the person you were created to be. That flag—that touchstone becomes more *valuable* with each year."

"What do you mean?"

"After eight years, I have *much more* to lose *now* if I pick up a drink than I did when I first came crawling into the program," he explained. "And my life continues to expand as I experience more and grow more over time."

"Thanks, Brad. I'll remember that. I can't wait to celebrate when I see you in person!"

She ended the call and returned to the cabin, smiling. "Brad called to celebrate my first anniversary of sobriety, which is today!"

"Oh. Well, if we're celebrating, I'll order a bottle of Champagne," he responded. But seeing the storm clouds gather in her eyes, he added, "Kidding."

The lightning flashed. "That's *not* funny, Paul."

He turned serious, too. "It's just that I regret I won't ever be able to share drinks with my wife."

Micky narrowed her eyes. "Did you drink with your first wife?"

"Of course!"

"And how did that work out? Maybe trying other forms of togetherness would be a better idea," she snapped. Then, in a softer tone, she added, "I get it that you don't understand that this date is important to me . . . I'm going to the meeting now to be with people who do."

CHAPTER 42

The ship sailed to Auckland, New Zealand, for two days of port time before disembarking on January 18. On the first day, Micky, a J.R.R. Tolkien fan, insisted on taking a day trip to the Hobbiton movie set created for filming *The Hobbit* and *The Lord of the Rings*.

When they returned to the ship, they took advantage of the available free wi-fi. Micky checked her online banking account, and turned to Paul with a wide smile. "Good news! My paycheck was deposited yesterday, as usual . . . along with my year-end bonus money! I'm relieved it was paid so promptly."

"Was the amount what you expected?"

"Yes . . . *that's* a relief, too . . . I was worried that maybe Jack would try to play games to delay it," she admitted.

"Like he did with your Cadillac lease last year?"

She looked down and nodded.

"Remember, when we left your office that night, I let him know that he'd better leave you alone," Paul said. "I think he got the message."

They kept the second day's sightseeing simple, only going downtown to see Auckland's iconic Sky Tower and lounging in a sidewalk café, as they needed to pack for a grueling day of travel to the site for Micky's award trip for her company.

The next morning, Micky and Paul were in the first group off of the ship, and their luggage was loaded on the chartered bus taking the Cadillac participants to the airport. Even with the expedited departure, they had to scramble to make their flight after clearing customs and security.

They flew to Honolulu to catch their flight to San Diego on a U.S. airline. It was early evening before they arrived at the Omni La Costa Spa and Resort. Fortunately, when they checked in, their bags were loaded on a cart for delivery to their Spanish mission-style villa and they were directed to the casual welcome area for the company's award winners, where they could relax with hors d'oeuvres and libations.

Although exhausted, Micky enjoyed reconnecting with her fellow winners, whom she hadn't seen since the previous year, and introducing them to her fiancé. Then someone she hadn't seen recently walked up to them, looking a bit puzzled.

Paul acknowledged him with a curt nod. "Jack."

"Hello, Paul," he began. But before he could ask what he was doing there, the ring on Micky's left hand flashed like a beacon. "Oh! I see congratulations are in order."

"Yes, thanks," Paul replied.

Micky lifted her hand with a flourish that she knew would make the reflected light pop. "Beautiful, isn't it?"

"Wow," was the best Jack could manage. Then, after an awkward pause, he added, "I wish you both much happiness." He turned and made his escape.

*****

On Friday, they played in the couples' golf scramble, paired with the Detroit rep who handled the Cadillac account. "Jason, this is Paul Price . . . of Price Cadillac in Elyria, Ohio. Thanks again for helping me with my pitch last March! My program helped him win the Tahiti trip, which was *fabulous* . . . and now we're engaged!"

Jason noticed Micky's ring, and whistled. "I'll say! You certainly are," he said. "And this is my wonderful wife, Jennifer."

"Nice to meet you both. Congratulations!" The petite redhead smiled, then said, "I'll apologize in advance; neither of us are very good golfers."

"That's okay," Micky replied. "I just started with lessons last summer, and really haven't played very much . . . let's just go have fun!"

Paul kept things moving, reminding the other three whose shot it was and dispensing suggestions as needed. He and Micky did well enough to compensate for Jason's and Jennifer's errant strokes and missed putts that their foursome came in third when the winners were announced at the dinner that evening.

"Wow, I never thought we'd have a chance to win anything," Jason marveled. "Thanks for pulling us through! Speaking of winning, Micky—I'm hoping to give you a run for your money tomorrow night for Top Dog!"

She smiled. "We'll see about that! But your Cadillac program was *huge* . . . plus, I don't think anyone has ever won Top Dog *twice*, have they?"

*****

All of the company's winners who had earned the trip to La Costa were pampered with a Swedish massage that used citrus and jasmine essential oils, a manicure and pedicure, and a hydrating facial. Micky let go of her stress, once she got used to being among her female peers without any makeup or competitive outfits. The spa-issued white robes, sandals and coral-colored towels wrapped around their heads served as equalizers. At first, she was unnerved by the novel situation, but eventually found herself able to converse with the other women openly with no pretense or posturing. It reminded her of how comfortable she felt at A.A. meetings; perhaps because she had learned there how to interact with others on a simple, human level.

Nevertheless, after this Kumbaya experience, she paid out-of-pocket to get her thick black hair styled in an up-do at the salon. She wanted to leave a lasting impression at her swan song awards dinner.

Paul was in the shower when she returned to their villa, and she was just finishing dressing when he emerged. She was wearing the same gown that she had donned for his Round Table dinner, but the formal hairdo upped the stun power exponentially.

It stopped him in his tracks. His eyes moistened like they did the first time he saw her dressed up, and once again, he had trouble speaking. Finally, he said, "You look sensational!"

He moved to her side and embraced her. She smiled to thank him, but saw his expression darken when he saw their reflection in the mirror. "Oh, no. That hair makes you look taller than me," he complained. "Can you fix it? Take out the pins and brush it out?"

She broke out of his embrace and moved away from him, just in case he might grab for her hair. "No! I just spent two-hundred-and-fifty dollars, plus tip for this! No one *cares* about our relative heights—*I* never have," she insisted. "Except when you act like this. This is *my* awards night . . . I supported you for *yours* and now it's my turn. You just said that I look sensational, and I'm going with that . . . and with *this hair!*"

Sullen, he relented. "Okay. Point taken. But please don't choose that type of hairstyle for our wedding, okay?"

"Fine . . . I'll remember to tell the stylist then." They headed to the cocktail reception.

Heads turned when they entered the room. Alonzo Cordero greeted them with enthusiasm and a wide smile. "Micky! You look like a movie star!"

"A star arriving on the red carpet for the Academy Awards," his wife, Lana concurred.

Micky responded with an appropriate, gleaming smile. "Thank you ... you are too kind! But it *is* fun to get all dressed up sometimes!"

"Well, you certainly look like a winner. Doesn't she, Paul?" said Alonzo. "Enjoy the evening, we'll see you later."

After greeting colleagues and introducing them to Paul, Micky found their place cards and they took their seats at a round eight-top near the front, by the head table. "I hope this is a good omen," Micky said to the others, crossing her fingers.

"I think it is," said her Detroit buddy, Jason. "They know who the winners are, and I doubt they'd want to slow down the show by waiting for people to hike from the back of the room."

The tablemates made small talk, trading stories of major sales and occasional humorous disasters they'd dealt with during the year. They admired the presentation of each dish and enjoyed the food while they waited with thinly disguised excitement for the main event. Micky quickly ate her double dark chocolate mousse and fled to the ladies' room to check her teeth and fix her lipstick, returning just before the lights were dimmed and Mr. Cordero stepped up to the microphone in the spotlight.

The screen beside him had the company logo and headquarters photo showing while he thanked and congratulated all of the winners for their efforts and productivity, making this a record year. The slide deck advanced showing various statistics, then moved to showing the names of winners from each region, with applause. Then the showcase began for the runner-up's achievements, showing numbers for the competition's metrics while Mr. Cordero described the winner's outstanding accomplishments before inviting the recipient to the platform. A young woman from the table behind theirs gasped with joy, left her chair and hurried forward to receive an engraved plaque from him and pose for a picture.

After she had returned to her seat, the process resumed for the Reserve Champion. By the second slide, Micky whispered to Jason, "Does this sound like you?" He nodded, and prepared to move, smiling with glee as his name was announced.

While everyone applauded, Paul quietly asked Micky, "Were your numbers higher than the ones they showed for him?"

She nodded. "I think so . . ."

When Jason was seated and everyone congratulated him, Micky bit her lip when the next slide displayed the final set of numbers. "Oh my God . . . those look like mine!"

Mr. Cordero told the audience, "I said earlier that we set a new record this year, and we're setting a new precedent for our Top Dog honor as well. A big part of our company's record was due to this year's Top Dog setting a record in her territory—following her record-setting performance *last* year that made her Top Dog then! We've never had a repeat winner, usually because it's nearly impossible to repeat a larger percentage of growth on a greatly enlarged base.

"How did she do it? Well, I'll admit I thought her boss was crazy for setting a *huge* quota for twenty-seventeen. But she *expanded* her territory, gaining new clients in Columbus, and west of her Cleveland territory to Toledo and points in between. All while increasing the programs run by her existing clients. Hell, she's so good that one new client sold two of *his friends* on our company—Micky McHale, come up here and claim your *second* Top Dog trophy!"

Micky radiated star quality when she stepped into the spotlight and received the engraved silver tray, basking in the cheering and applause of the standing ovation.

But Mr. Cordero wasn't finished. When the crowd quieted, he continued. "That new client I just mentioned is here with us tonight, because the program Micky created for his five luxury automotive dealerships helped him earn our Cadillac Trip to Tahiti that Jason sold. And he fell in love with our Micky, and proposed to her, so she accompanied him to Tahiti, and they flew directly here to share her award. Paul Price, please join us up here! I want a picture of all of us. Lana, my sweet bride, please come join us, too!"

*****

Micky and Paul had accepted Alonzo Cordero's invitation to join him and Lana for brunch the next day before departing, and the couples were enjoying the view of the golf course from inside the dining room. Congratulating Micky again on her spectacular performance, he asked, "What's next for you?"

"Actually . . . I have a *lot* of personal changes to handle when we get home . . . the wedding will be March twenty-fourth," she said. "I hope you and Lana can save the date?"

"We'd be delighted to attend," Lana replied, with a happy clap of her elegant hands. "But that will come up very quickly—you'll have much to arrange!"

Micky laughed and nodded. "Oh, yes! Besides planning the wedding, I'll need to put my condo on the market and prepare to move."

Paul spoke up. "Micky and I have discussed her possibly handling all marketing for my dealerships, as an in-house agency, and perhaps also taking care of that for my two friends' businesses as well; I've run the idea by them, and they'd be on board," he said. "This would also include our incentive programs with you."

"Oh? What would that look like?" Alonzo was intrigued.

"She would continue to interface with us, monitor our programs' progress, suggest tweaks as needed and work with your internal teams for execution. She also would create our plans for next year," Paul explained. "But she would do that directly, without dealing with Jack Benson or being your employee. She's already been working out of my office for the last month, and never skipped a beat."

"Really? Why was she working out of your office?"

"Because I had to rescue her from Jack's unwanted advances," Paul said, grimacing. "I was coming to pick her up for dinner when she phoned me and asked me to come get her at the office instead—and to hurry. She sounded scared, and when I got there, she was cowering in the corner of her office behind a Ficus tree, with Jack lurking beside the door."

Alonzo looked at Micky, his face growing red with anger. "Is this true, Micky? What happened?"

"Yes." She recounted the events of August and December.

"That scum! He's history!" Alonzo Cordero was livid, veins dilating around his dark eyes. "I'm so sorry that happened to you, Micky; but why didn't you tell me?"

She looked down and sighed. "Jack kept threatening to fire me. That was why he gave me the gigantic quota. He has admitted that and thought it was very clever. See, he said he knew he couldn't fire me after I won Top Dog last year, but as soon as I didn't make my numbers, he could do anything he wanted."

Lana laughed. "So, you sold your way out of his trap! Bravo! And I understand why you didn't want to go over your boss' head to report him. We've all known women who did that, and even when they could prove what they said was true, it wasn't appreciated. And their careers suffered."

The waiter appeared with their meals. As Micky started on her eggs Florentine, Lana continued. "I can see why you'd like to start your own business; I started mine so I could focus on helping customers without dealing with bosses," she said. "Mine is a corporate travel agency, and Alonzo was one of my customers. As our business dealings grew, so did our feelings for one another." She looked at her husband with affection.

"And when we married, she effectively became head of my company's travel business, but she still owns her part. I added staff on my payroll to operate trips at our necessary scale, she moved her office into our headquarters building, but she bills me for her work—and she has other customers, too."

"Micky, I'd advise you to set up your marketing agency along those same lines," Lana said. "I love my husband dearly, but I wouldn't want him to be my boss. This is healthier, for both of us!"

Laughing, Alonzo agreed. "Paul, what my wife says is true! I think I get much greater care and attention as her client! We both think it's great that Micky wants to work as your marketing arm, with you as her main client. Micky, consider this month as your last with my company. And we'll figure out mutually agreeable compensation for you on this year's programs for Paul and his two friends." He extended his hand to Micky, then to Paul.

"Thank you, Mr. Cordero! For *everything* . . . yours is the only company I've ever worked for," she said, her blue eyes glistening. "I'm so grateful for the experience to serve you, and for all that I've learned here."

"Please, call me Alonzo now," he insisted. "And I still owe you a new Cadillac lease for your second Top Dog year."

Before Paul could say anything, she replied, "What I'd really prefer would be for you to buy my current car for the residual value when the lease ends in March, and put it in my name. I love this car; it's my first big trophy and I want to *keep* it . . . and it will always remind me of our work together."

"I'd be happy to do that. But why does the lease expire in March? Shouldn't it be this month?" Alonzo was confused.

"Another one of Benson's games. He delayed giving Micky the car she'd earned," Paul said. "So, she prospected my nearby Cadillac dealership, pitched me on the incentive program—and included a trade agreement for the car lease! I fell in love with her that day. And if you'd like to tie everything up this month, we can terminate the lease early."

Alonzo kissed his fingers toward the new couple in salute.

CHAPTER 43

Paul's alarm clock jarred Micky out of a deep, dreamless slumber. She groaned and rolled over, hoping to go back to sleep, but Paul nudged her.

"Sorry, but it's Monday, and we're back to reality. Time to go back to work," he informed her. "Why don't you shower now and I'll make the coffee and breakfast."

"Okay . . . that's a nice enticement . . . thanks." She rifled through her carry-on bag for shampoo, conditioner, deodorant, comb, brush—and realized she didn't have a hair dryer. All of the hotel rooms and the cruise ship had furnished those.

"Paul? Do you have a blow-dryer?" she shouted.

"No."

She repacked the shampoo and conditioner, and found a shower cap from one of the places where they'd stayed. She was really looking forward to going home at the end of the day.

After a quick shower and application of minimal makeup, Micky put on the winter outfit she'd packed for this occasion and carried her luggage downstairs. The grueling air travels, all of the excitement and post-experiences let-down collided with the lost hours and jet lag. She felt like collapsing in a heap, and hoped the coffee would prop her up. She wished she could main-line the caffeine.

As she gulped the first mug and shoveled scrambled eggs into her mouth, Paul spied the suitcase and garment bag in the hallway.

"I thought we'd take things back to your condo this evening, after dinner," he said.

She looked up from her plate with effort. "Paul, I'm not sure how long I can last in the office today," she replied. "I'll make sure everything is on track with everybody's incentive plans, and will leave early if there aren't any issues. I'm exhausted . . . and I don't want to have to unpack late tonight. I'll put those in my car and drive it to work."

He looked disappointed. "Well. I'll shower and shave. Can you be ready to go in fifteen minutes?"

"Sure."

When they arrived at the Cadillac dealership, Paul insisted on walking Micky around to greet everyone and to inform them of their engagement. Congratulatory shouts, enthusiastic pumping handshakes and oohs over the ring abounded. Micky was heading into her office afterwards, only to have Paul insist they repeat this at the four other facilities as well. By then, it was time for lunch, so she finally got to her desk around one o'clock.

Mercifully, she found that all was well with her clients' programs. She made her escape by three and dragged into her condo thirty minutes later. She unpacked directly into the washing machine, put her toiletries away in their accustomed spots and dropped her body onto the living room chaise.

It felt good to be alone.

*****

Having told Paul that she'd be working from home most of the week, Micky didn't set an alarm for Tuesday morning, and slept until seven-thirty. After a long, refreshing shower followed by coffee and an English muffin, she wrote out a to-do list and began making calls.

The first was to Brad, who volunteered to take her shopping for her wedding dress later that week, and to advise on staging her condo to put on the market, including what she wanted to move over to Paul's, offer for sale with the condo, donate, or put in storage.

Then Sally called and invited her to come for lunch, correctly guessing that Micky hadn't yet restocked food. Over chicken salad sandwiches in the rectory, Sally offered to help her with some of the typical mother-of-the-bride duties.

"I can book our organist for you and arrange a meeting for you and Paul to discuss music," she began. "I also know several photographers who've done good work for other couples who got married at Grace; I can call and see who'd be available and send you links to their websites. Ditto for the florist. Have you given any thought to colors you'd like for flowers? Or dresses for your attendants? The two need to work together."

Micky shook her head. "I confess I haven't had a chance to do *any* planning . . . and I know we don't have much time!"

"Well, what are your favorite colors?"

"For clothing, I usually like colors that look good on *me* . . . but *I'll* be wearing *white*," she replied, laughing. "Brad will be my gentleman of honor, so I guess his tie and boutonniere can pick up whatever colors we come up with. I also don't want Lil and Betty to have to buy dresses, especially matching ones!"

"Good thinking. Let's brainstorm colors you like, that most women have in their wardrobes."

"And then we can *ask* them which ones they *do* have . . . or would like to buy, and decide with their input," Micky suggested. "I like Kelly green, and this *will* be the week after Saint Patrick's Day!"

"Good start. We can emphasize foliage, but we'll still need some other color or group of colors," Sally mused.

"Oh! Could we do your palms for the altar, use them on the floor at each end of it for the wedding, so the altar guild can just put them up there when the florist removes the wedding flowers?" Micky wondered.

"I like that idea; we could repeat palms in some other areas of the church, which would be a great help to the guild."

Micky chewed her chicken salad while she pondered flowers, then took a drink of water. "I like deep blue . . . and strong pink, although other shades of pink are okay, too . . . with some white accents. And *fragrance* . . . I'd *really* like to fill the church with *fragrance*."

Sally smiled. "Blue hyacinths would give you both color and fragrance. Roses come in many shades of pink, including deep pink. Most florist roses lack fragrance, but the hyacinths will make up for that. Fragrant white lilies, used sparingly, could provide accents in both color and aroma. When you choose your dress, it may guide the design style for the flowers."

"Brad and I are going dress shopping this week. We'll see when he has a light schedule."

"Wonderful! I'm sure you two will have fun doing that," Sally said. "The last big item to do immediately is to choose your invitations, then get your information to the printer soon, as that can take some time—and you'll need to mail them no later than six weeks before the wedding." She consulted the calendar she had put on the dining table. "That will be February ninth, which is just two weeks from this Friday! We'd better go to the stationary shop after lunch."

Micky drove them to a print shop up the street, past the square near the far edge of Stromberg. The January day was clear and cold, with a biting wind, and her body hadn't adjusted yet from her tropical travels. When they got there, she let Sally do all of the talking, as she was totally unfamiliar with wedding protocols and the various types and styles of invitations.

Sally queried her as she talked with the portly white-haired proprietor. "How many guests do you think you'll invite? And do you plan to have plus-ones? Children?"

"I'm not sure . . . all of my close friends will be in the wedding, but Paul thinks we'll need to invite clients and business friends," Micky said. "How many people will the church seat?"

"Easily one hundred in the nave and another forty in the balcony," Sally replied. "If you need to invite a larger number, especially if they're mostly business contacts, you might save invitations to the wedding and reception for family and intimate friends and invite the rest to the reception only."

"Oh, yes . . . I remember Paul said many people would only be at the reception at the County Club. And I think plus-ones would be a good idea . . . but I don't think we'll need to include children. Unless Paul wants to . . . I'll ask him."

"You'll also need RSVP cards and envelopes; will you be serving lunch? If so, will there be a choice of entrées?"

"Hmm . . . another question to discuss with Paul," Micky noted aloud and on her phone's notepad. "I'm thinking yes, especially if we're having a lot of clients. If we do, we'd need the offerings on the reply card, right?"

"Yes, but you don't need a full description," Sally explained. "You could just go with 'Beef,' 'Chicken,' 'Fish' and 'Vegetarian.'"

"These days, I think we'd better specify 'Vegan' or else we'd be getting calls to clarify," Micky said. "Are there price breaks for the invitation packages at different quantities? And could we see the paper and design options, please?"

"And show us those that also include thank you notes and envelopes," Sally added. "Micky, you'll also need to decide if the invitations are coming from your father—and get *his* guest list ASAP—or if you and Paul will be extending the invitations. Is your father giving you away, and paying for the wedding and reception? Also, you'll need the name for the return address for the thank you envelopes; are you planning to take his name, or keep yours?"

"Wow . . . so *many decisions* to make in such a short time! I'm taking my father to lunch on Saturday, so I'll get some of those answers then," she said. "I'd *prefer* to keep *my* name, especially since I'll continue doing business with some of my clients."

Micky looked at the dozen paper options and the sample fonts list. "I want white versus ivory paper. I *don't* want the lacy or frilly designs, or the overly curlicue fonts that you can't read," she told the proprietor. "Could I please have samples of these three and a copy of the fonts list to show my father and my fiancé? Also, do you offer fulfillment services to handle assembly and mailing if we provide spreadsheets with the guests' information?"

"Certainly," he said. "And we do offer fulfillment for quantities of one-hundred-fifty or more. When is the wedding?"

"March twenty-fourth."

"In twenty-nineteen?"

"No, this March. In about eight weeks," Micky clarified. "Can you handle that?"

"If I get your deposit and all of the wording by next Monday; with the spreadsheet two weeks from today. We need time to make sure there aren't any issues with that," he said. "And there will be rush charges of ten percent on everything."

*****

"Micky—I've found a dress you *must* try on!" Brad rustled tiers of tulle outside the changing room door.

His mischievous tone made her skeptical. She opened the door a crack and peered out, immediately hooting with laughter. "*No* . . . oh, no, no, no, no, *no*," she protested. "Besides, I don't think the hoops under all of that fabric would even *fit* into this room!"

Slipping into a very fake Southern accent, he persisted. "Oh, now *come on*, Sugah. You'd look *just like* Scarlett O'Hara at the barbeque at Twelve Oaks, surrounded by beaux *vying* for your attention!"

"I don't *need* any more *beaux*. I'm *engaged*," she retorted.

"But you look so much like Vivien Leigh," he teased. "You'd make a *perfect Scarlett!*"

The bridal consultant, thinking he was serious, agreed. "That is one of our most popular gowns, and you'd really do it justice," she gushed. "Try it on; it's much more comfortable than it looks."

Micky laughed and said, "He's kidding . . . and I've already found my dress."

She stepped out from the fitting room and walked across the room to the three-way mirror like a queen processing to assume her throne.

"Oh. My. *Goddess*." Brad struggled to find words. "You're right. That's *it*. I've never seen anything like it—but it does evoke vibes from Twentieth Century glam movies."

Micky swiveled back and forth, examining views of the dress from all angles. It was shimmering white crepe satin, floor length with long sleeves that she thought would keep her comfortable in late March temperatures. The neckline was a striking bateau off-the-shoulders shape that was interrupted in the middle by plunging into a deep, narrow V where the fitted bodice gathered in four folds at its termination point. The luxurious fabric draped gracefully into a slender columnar form that flared toward the back to produce a slight train effect. Lace panels from under the arms to the tops of her hips modestly accentuated her hour-glass curves and formed the back of the dress. A light flesh-tone fabric inside the V lent structure to the neckline, so she wouldn't have to worry about a wardrobe malfunction.

"That is *stunning* on you, and it's a perfect fit," marveled the saleswoman. "Bring in your shoes and we'll adjust the hem, if necessary. Now, what about a veil?"

"Do I have to wear one? I'm thinking this would look best with just a simple, sleek hairstyle . . . maybe a French twist, with white flowers or a clip," Micky said. "I don't think a veil would really look right with this dress."

"I like the flower idea," Brad agreed. "But maybe you should also get a clip as a fallback, in case the flowers don't work well."

"Great idea! That would probably be the way to go for travel after we leave the reception."

The sales consultant hurried back with a tray of options, and Micky chose one with small white roses and another with understated rhinestones. "When's the wedding?"

When Micky told her the date, she advised coming back with her shoes in a week or two at the latest. "Good thing the only alteration you'll need is the hem!"

*****

Micky had invited her father to their usual library booth at Pomeroy House, but he suggested bringing Chinese to her place instead. When he arrived, he handed her a bag still warm with their food, saying, "I'm glad we're doing this here, Micky; I don't want to worry about how long we tie up a table, and it would be better to talk privately, without interruptions."

He looked around as he followed her to the great room. "It's been some time since I was here last. It looks nice."

"Thanks, Dad . . . Brad is going to help me stage it for sale . . . and I have a meeting with a real estate agent on Monday."

She had set the table with notepads as well as placemats and eating utensils. The invitations samples were also within reach. After they spooned contents of the white cartons onto their plates, Micky launched into some of the questions Sally had raised, using the text on the mock invitations as a guide.

"Since this is your first wedding, it is appropriate that I extend the invitation to the wedding—or reception for the wedding—of my daughter, Mikhaila (Micky) McHale and Paul Price at blah, blah, blah. Reception and luncheon to follow at blah blah. Be sure to include addresses for the church and the club.

"Speaking of addresses, since I travel so much, your address should be used on the invite and RSVP cards. And I know you're worried that the condo might not sell quickly, but keep this as your legal address until after you return from your honeymoon. I'll explain in a bit.

"Yes, I will want to invite some friends and clients. Only close friends will come to the wedding; others to the reception—and just long-term ones at that.

"Of *course* I will pay for your wedding and reception, and all of the things that go with that. Have you found your dress yet?"

She smiled. "I have . . . it's *fabulous* . . . and kind of expensive," she replied with a note of apology in her voice.

He waved that off with his hands. "Not a problem, Micky. I'm glad to be a part of your life again—or rather, finally—and I'm honored that you'll let me walk you down the aisle." Mike McHale choked up a bit and wiped a tear or two away from his gray-blue eyes.

Micky raised her teary eyes to meet his and smiled. "I'm glad, too, Dad. And thank you for giving me the wedding." She reached out and touched his hand.

"Are you and Paul going to choose china and silver? If not, would you like to have the things your mother and I chose? I haven't used it for a couple of decades, and doubt if I ever will."

"I'm trying to remember what it looks like . . . kind of clean, simple design, ivory with a gold band or two around the edges?"

"Yes. The inner band is very fine, the outer one is heavier. The silver pattern is also simple and classic," he said, sizing up her décor. "I think it would blend well with your taste."

She laughed. "Brad says I'm still figuring out what that is. But my dress and these invitations are a clue; nothing frilly! Yes, I would *love* to have Mom's china and silver . . . I only saw them on holidays, and they were part of what made the occasions *special*."

"Good. I'll give those to you now, even if you'd rather store them at my place for the time being, since you're about to move."

"As a wedding present?"

"No. They're yours; family heirlooms, so to speak," he said. "As such, they are *not* marital property. Nor will your new business be. Besides the wedding costs, my gift to you will be the services of my attorney to get your business incorporated—in your name, at this address—and to draw up your prenuptial agreement, listing all of your assets and liabilities that will remain separate from your marriage."

"*What?!*"

"Trust me, Micky, Paul will insist on a prenup, and it's actually in both of your best interests," he explained. "You told me on the phone about how the Corderos have their individual businesses, and she bills him for her services, and pays his company when she uses those resources for her outside clients. Like you, she married *into* an *existing family business*. While they work closely together, and apparently both businesses have prospered, they are *not* building a business *together*."

"What about . . . well, the *emotional* aspect of getting married?"

"From that aspect, establishing these legal distinctions is even more important," he replied. "In addition to becoming your *husband*, Paul will remain your client—he will *not* be your *boss*."

"Ah . . . I see. You're *right*. I couldn't deal with that!"

"My attorney will also draw up some basic contracts you'll need for your marketing agency, which you'll need to have all of your customers and suppliers sign—including, and especially Paul. You'll need to keep your cash from the sale of your condo to borrow from to keep your cash flow intact. And you'll have to insist on keeping retainers current. Marketing is *always* the first place that gets cut when things get tight at a firm. And you'll be responsible for paying all of your suppliers per their terms, or you'll lose your commission discount—and you'll still owe the money."

"You really think I'll need to worry about that with Paul?"

"Micky, I ran a D and B on him, like I would for any potential new client we'd pitch for media placements. He has a very sizeable private company with five operating units, all of which are highly leveraged. His funds are more like ocean tides than the steady cash flow of a river. Your agency will enable him to maintain his marketing presence consistently—for which you are compensated by the commissions you earn. And you'll be billing him, like all of your customers, directly for other work you do. The average hourly rate for business-to-business agencies in this market is a hundred-and-fifty to two-hundred dollars. I'll also set up an appointment with my accountant to teach you how to bill your hours, keep your books and pay your quarterly taxes. Use your *own* service professionals—not Paul's."

"What happens when we get married and I officially move into an office in one of his dealerships?" she asked.

"First, you simply change the address of your business," he said. "You may want to agree on a rent and do a trade agreement, where a certain dollar amount of billable services will be provided in lieu of rent payment. But check prevailing office space rents first. I don't think it would be much. And it really would be cleaner to pay monthly with a check. Oh, you'll need to set up a business banking account once you get your corporate tax ID number."

"Wow. Okay . . . this is *a lot more* than I thought I'd have to do before my wedding."

"Lastly, I'll have the attorney also draw up a contract for the use of your name, image and likeness in any marketing," he advised. "I'm sure Paul will want to feature you in ads."

"Yes, he's already upset that I want Mr. Cordero to buy my current leased car for me. He wants me to be seen driving all of his other models," she noted. "Dad, thanks for all of this. I would *never* have thought of these things . . . but I understand now how *important* they are!"

He smiled at his daughter. "You're welcome, Kitten. I wasn't a good father or a good example as a husband, but my multiple marital mistakes taught me a few things. This gift is the *least* I can do for you!"

*****

A tall, round cake with white frosting decorated with a many-hued buttercream rose garden commanded the center of Lillian's oak kitchen table. The family gathered around it, laughing as Micky leaned over to examine it and realized its green writing was honoring her: Happy First Anniversary, Micky!

"Oh! This is *so beautiful* . . . *thank you*, all of you," she said with a cracking voice that ratted out her emotions. "I couldn't have done it without you . . . and *especially you*, Brad!"

"Well, you put in the work, dear," Lillian said. "But we couldn't have had this cake without Brad; he created this masterpiece, and decorated it from his memories of my garden."

Micky looked up at him and smiled. "You're the *best* . . . but this looks way too pretty to eat!"

"We will, though," he insisted. "I'm starved—and if you think this *gateau* is all about looks, wait 'til you *taste* it!" He picked up the cake knife and offered it to Micky, who demurred with a wave, shaking her head.

"Okay, I'll do it," he said as he cut and plated perfect slices for each of them. Lillian brought the coffee out, and they all sat down and held hands for Sally to say grace.

"Dear Lord God, we thank you for your daughter, Micky, who has grown with us over the past year and has grown nearer to you. We pray that you will continue to bless her with increasing sobriety, wisdom and grace, especially as she begins her second year with many important changes in her life. Thank you also for your servant, Brad, who was her closest guide and sponsor, and whose artistry produced this lovely cake to honor her. We pray that you will bless it to our use, and us to thy service. In Jesus' name we pray. Amen."

"Amen! Let's eat!" Brad proclaimed.

Everyone agreed that the cake tasted even better than it looked. They all congratulated Micky on her anniversary, her engagement, and were excited when she described her plans for her new business.

"I'm so grateful to the program and your help for all of the *incredible* things that have come into my life in the past year," she said. "The greatest gift has been Steps Four through Nine . . . they helped me build a new relationship with my dad." She described yesterday's guidance and his wedding gift of the legal fees to create the documents. "It will add a *lot* more items to my to-do list, but I can see the importance of his advice . . . and his *love* in sharing it with me."

Sally pointed out, "Yes, you'll be carrying an extremely heavy stress load. Be sure to take care of yourself, and we'll all help in any way we can. God will give you the strength and will continue giving you guidance through these transitions, one day at a time."

"Indeed," said Lillian. "And even though you'll be crazy busy, make time to get to meetings. When my career took off, my beloved sponsor, Sebastian, told me, "Never let what the program gives you take you away from the program."

Brad reached into his pocket. "One more thing, Micky." He took her hand, placed his over her open palm then curled his fingers so she made a fist. "Your first-year medallion. Hang onto it through everything that comes in this next year of your sobriety. This is the one Lil gave me for *my* first anniversary—then she told me, 'Now the *work* begins!'"

CHAPTER 44

Micky was comfortably settled in the armchair by the fireplace in Sally's office, glad for the warmth from the gas logs on this cold January thirtieth evening. In the matching chair beside her, Paul was looking pleasant, wearing the slight smile and focused gaze he used when customers entered his office. His right arm, draped around the back of Micky's chair, emphasized their unity.

Sally was seated across from them, behind the small coffee table. "Shall we start with prayer before we get started?" she suggested.

The couple bowed their heads. "Lord God, Heavenly Father, we invite you to be with us as we begin our discussions of the ways in which the Episcopal Church will support Micky and Paul in the sacrament of marriage that they make with you. We thank you for their love of one another, and pray for your guidance in our talks that they may prepare a solid foundation for their married life together. In Jesus' name we pray. Amen."

"Amen," they echoed.

"Note that I said that *you* make the sacrament with each other and *with God*; the wedding ceremony that we will celebrate on March twenty-fourth is where you make your vows before God, the Church and those present, and receive God's grace and blessing to help you fulfill them in your life-long union.

"To perform the ceremony in the Church, I must get permission from the bishop. We're required to have at least three pre-marital counseling sessions to make sure your marriage starts off on firm footing. While the Church permits divorce, we strive to avoid it—in these sessions, we'll cover areas that are the most common causes of failure, and will seek to address any potential issues that may emerge. I also insist on a fourth session to answer any other questions, but mainly to review the mechanics of the ceremony and confirm your choices of music, scripture passages and names of your readers and witnesses."

She paused to hand them both draft copies of the service with options of scriptures typically used in various sections. She also gave them a single sheet of documents required by the Church and also by the State of Ohio for the marriage license, urging them to apply for the latter as soon as possible.

Referring to the documents required by the Church, she said, "Micky, I already have your Certificate of Baptism, and will get your Confirmation in a couple of weeks. Paul, I will need those from you, please, along with your previous date and place of marriage and a copy of your divorce decree."

He nodded.

"You'll also need to complete this questionnaire regarding the end of your previous marriage." She handed him a four-page folder.

He quickly scanned the first few questions, frowned and balked. "This is personal. It's nobody else's business!"

"Actually, it *is* the Church's business," Sally explained, remaining calm yet firm. "It's important to be certain that there are no outstanding issues that would imperil the new marriage, such as kids, money, or other things; and evidence that the reasons the marriage ended aren't likely to be repeated."

Micky touched his hand and told him, "Divorced people get married in the Episcopal Church all the time, Paul . . . the questions on that form can't be that bad."

He sighed in acquiescence. "When do you need this?"

"Please bring it to our third session," Sally replied. "We'll be discussing some of the same topics then."

She turned their attention to the sample service brochure. "Let's walk through this, and I'll make some notes on things we know so far. We'll need to use your full names at the beginning, then just your first names for the rest of the service. Micky?"

"My birth certificate name is Mikhaila McHale . . . no middle name," she said. "But could we put 'Micky' in the middle in parentheses, and use that?"

"Of course."

But as Sally was writing this down, Paul interrupted. "But Mikhaila is such a beautiful name! Much more feminine. It's a shame you don't use it."

She looked at him with surprise and a bit of annoyance. "Yes, I agree it's a pretty name, but it's never been used by me, except on documents. I have *always* been called Micky . . . and if you were to insist on using that *other* name in our wedding, I'd feel like *I* wasn't being married."

He was about to pout, but Sally asked for his full name.

"John Paul Price."

Micky jumped on that. "Now, if I were to call you 'John,' would you answer?"

"No," he admitted. "Point taken. I know you and love you as Micky."

Sally proceeded to read the service. She paused after the requirement to confess any lawful reason why either of them could not be united in marriage. "I'm assuming there aren't any, but if there *are*, we'd better disclose them here, rather than during the service, right?"

They laughed and said, "We're good."

She laughed with them, and continued through the declaration of consent. "Is anyone presenting either of you to be married? In other words, is anyone giving you away?"

"Yes," Micky said. "My father will walk me down the aisle, and will give me away."

Sally smiled. "That's lovely, Micky! I know what that means to you."

She read the prayer following that, then stopped at the list of scripture readings options. "You'll need to take some time to look these up, choose at least one of them, usually one from the Old Testament and one from the New. And you'll need to ask lay people to read them from the lectern during the service."

"Okay . . . Paul, would you like me to narrow the list and show you my favorites to make the final choice?"

"Please."

Sally said, "If you'd like to include Communion in the service, you'll need to choose a Gospel reading, too, but I would read that one."

Paul fidgeted. "Do we really need Communion? Won't that take a long time?"

"How many guests do you think you'll invite to the wedding?" Sally asked. "For a typical Sunday service with about fifty people, between the prayers and administration of the sacrament, it can add roughly fifteen to twenty minutes. If you have a large crowd, I'd say easily half an hour, a bit more if there are guests in the balcony."

"Not many of the guests are likely to be churchgoers," Paul noted. "And those who are, are probably Catholic, so they wouldn't take Communion here. Plus, other than Christmas Eve, we've never gone to church together, so it's not part of *us*."

"Well . . . it would be nice if we *did* . . . but I agree Communion would only be important to *me* . . . so, okay, we'll skip that," Micky said.

Together, they read through the vows, the prayers on pages noted in the Book of Common Prayer, and the blessing of the marriage to become familiar with their meaning and the general flow of the service. After they concluded, Sally invited Paul to the confirmation service to be held on the coming Sunday. "It will start at ten-thirty, but Micky will need to be here at nine. The bishop likes to have a private talk with the candidates as a group beforehand. But they'll all sit with their families during most of the service."

"When I was confirmed in seventh grade, nobody made a big deal about it," he said.

"But it *is* a big deal, especially for adults who are making a very personal decision to join the Episcopal Church," Sally replied. "And I'm sure your parents and family were there, weren't they?"

"Yeah, I guess they were."

"Well, you're going to be part of Micky's family now," Sally pointed out. "Wouldn't you like to be there for her?"

*****

At the end of the last day in January, Micky's employment with the Cordero Incentives Corporation concluded. That evening, she was relaxing in her favorite spot, reclining on her chaise with her laptop open. She checked her online banking, smiled broadly and exclaimed, "Yes!"

She closed the laptop and FaceTimed Paul. "Well . . . I'm now officially a free agent, and my Top Dog prize money has been deposited in my account! And I got a sweet email from Alonzo thanking me for my years of service in growing his company, the outline of his proposal for my compensation arrangement in our new relationship,

Family of Choice: Raising Each Other

and telling me that the written proposal will be delivered tomorrow by FedEx, along with the title to my car!"

"Congratulations. But I still wish you wouldn't have asked him to buy out the lease on that car for you," he grumbled. "And you didn't even do me the courtesy of consulting me first. I'd have advised you to take the cash value of the new lease instead, but you pitched it on the spot to the Corderos, so I couldn't say anything."

Her jaw set in a determined line. "This is what I wanted, Paul. Sorry you're not happy with that."

"But I'd planned for you to be driving a different luxury car all of the time—I want you to be seen in them," he complained.

"I'll drive them in ads and to certain functions . . . my dad's lawyer is drawing up paperwork on compensation for use of my name, image and likeness in my marketing services for the dealerships. Remember, I worked for years as a paid, professional model. There's a standard industry scale for talent fees—which you'd have to pay if you hired someone else," she said. "But I need to have a car that is *mine*."

He saw the determination in her hot blue eyes staring him down through the phone's screen. "You win."

*****

Micky and Paul joined Sally a week later, returning to the chairs by the cheerful fire in her office for their second premarital counseling session.

Sally began with a quick prayer, then consulted her checklist. "Have you applied for your marriage license?" They nodded.

"Paul, do you have the documents we need?" He handed her his paperwork.

"And, any decisions on your readings?"

Micky answered, "Song of Solomon second chapter, verses ten through thirteen; and Colossians, third chapter, verses twelve through seventeen. I haven't asked any readers yet."

"Good! So, this evening, let's talk about your relationship. I know that it began a year ago as a business relationship and moved into a more personal one a couple of months later. Paul, can you tell us how that came about for you?"

He laughed. "Well, Micky is a *most* impressive woman! Her beauty hit me immediately when she entered the dealership that first day, but her brains, poise, preparation and professionalism put her in a class by herself. I was sold on her proposal because it made good business sense. But I'll admit, I was entranced; I couldn't wait to see her again."

They smiled at each other. Sally prompted, "And then?"

Paul described the various extra activities that allowed him to spend more time with Micky, including promoting her to his friends, who also became clients after he made introductions at the country club's Memorial Day bash.

"After that first meeting, the guys started razzing me, pointing out that I was obviously head-over-heels in love with her," he said. "They encouraged me in that. You see, I hadn't dated *anyone* during the five years since my wife divorced me. I'd just buried myself even deeper into work."

"Why was that?" Sally queried.

"First off, it was easy to do. I just invited a lot more customers and their friends to play golf or took them to dinner, which filled my waking hours and kept me from feeling lonely. Sold a lot more cars, too. And I wanted to avoid the frantic desperate dating I'd seen so many divorced guys do, which looked pathetic, empty and caused them a lot more problems than it was worth. So, I just didn't look at women as potential partners, and I politely declined offers to introduce me to any."

"How about you, Micky?"

"As you both know, I also kept myself super-busy with work. I told Paul at that first lunch that I hadn't dated much and that I didn't ever plan to get married, since my parents' relationship didn't make that look appealing! So, I *definitely* wasn't looking at Paul that way, but he made me feel very comfortable... I did feel that he appreciated my expertise and valued my opinion and insights into his business. But I really did just think of his invitations to club activities as networking opportunities. It took Lillian's friend, whose husband is the club president, to clue me in on the fact that Paul and I were *more* than just business colleagues.

"I'd been raised to *never* get involved romantically with clients, so I had to wrestle with the concept of dating him," she admitted. "But I'm *glad* I did! He was very respectful of me, and supportive... always treated me like a queen."

"And when did you feel that the relationship was becoming serious, with long-term potential?" Sally asked.

They both answered, "In August."

Paul continued, "On her birthday, I told her that my intentions were honorable, but that I understood her reservations about marriage and would wait until she was comfortable with the idea."

"I was glad he added that qualifier, because while it was *exciting* to hear him say he wanted to be with me always, it was also *scary*. I did need some time to get used to the idea, but somewhere around November, I was liking it... even hoping for it!" She laughed, taking his hand.

"So, Paul, tell me some of the things you love about Micky."

"Well, I already covered a lot of them. Her beauty is real, in jeans without makeup or dressed up to receive an award. And she's sincere. Generous. Competitive, but can laugh at herself. Her intelligence and honesty. Her maturity, she seems older and wiser than her age. She's open to trying new things. Her general capability. And she's very loving and loveable."

"Micky, what do you love about Paul?"

"The way he treats me. He's kind . . . generous . . . protective of me . . . polite . . . is respectful of me and of others. He's honest and dependable. Balanced, solid. A very good businessman with a good reputation. Also very handsome, and ditto on the loving and loveable attributes!"

"All wonderful things," Sally said. "Now, how about things that annoy you about each other? Paul, what does Micky do that really gets under your skin?"

"Nothing," he quickly replied. "She's perfect just as she is."

"Surely there are things about her that you don't like. Or maybe things you wish she didn't do, or that you wish she did do?" Sally prodded.

His hazel eyes scanned the priest's face, reading her expectation for him to look further. "Well, I like that she's independent. But sometimes I'd prefer that she consult me before she makes a decision; maybe that's due to her being a bit younger than me. My ex-wife never did anything that we hadn't discussed, which was kind of the norm for our times," he explained. "And it would be nice if she could cook a little. Although she did make wonderful French toast on Christmas morning!"

"Micky? Any response to what Paul said? And what annoys you about Paul?"

"I've been on my own for all of my adult life, so I'm accustomed to making my own decisions, especially about my own property or things that are important to me," Micky said. "I do ask his opinion on things we do together, and I think we arrive at solutions well. Brad is trying to teach me a bit about cooking... I admit I have a lot to learn!

"The second question... I said that I like how Paul is protective of me... but sometimes I feel like he goes a bit overboard... it can feel more like controlling, which hits a wound from my childhood observances of my parents' issues."

"Paul, do you think you and Micky can work through tempering these things?"

"Of course. I'll have to remember that we do have a small generation gap," he said. "But nothing that we can't deal with." He smiled and put his arm around Micky, who smiled back.

"Good. Now, I know this may seem intrusive, but sexuality is a key part of marriage, and issues with that can break the union," Sally said. "So, I need to ask: How is your sex life?"

Paul grinned. "No problems there!"

Micky agreed. "It's wonderful! Not only physically... which is *great*... but I also feel a strong emotional bond when we make love."

"Frequency is okay for you both? Style, timing is good?" Nods to all questions.

"Have either of you not felt like it for any reason? If so, was that okay with the other?"

"Once I had a killer headache," Micky said. "Paul brought me some ibuprofen and a glass of water, and gave me a massage instead."

"Very thoughtful," Sally said. "Last questions: What do you two have in common?"

"We both work a lot," they said in unison.

"Also, golf," Paul added. "Micky just started playing last summer, and she's already pretty good!"

"We also like to dine out, and to dance at club functions," Micky said. "We enjoy meeting new people, and dressing up to attend charity fund-raising events."

"And what things do you do without the other?"

"I go to my A.A. meetings, meet or talk with Brad, and go to church on Sundays . . . including my family time at Lil's after," Micky replied. "And I see my father for lunch occasionally. Although the three of us also get together sometimes."

Paul said, "On Sundays, I usually play golf with my two best friends. Three weeknights, dealerships are open until nine, so I usually stay late. That gives Micky time for her evening meetings."

"Have you ever gone to an open meeting with Micky, to learn what A.A. is about?" Sally asked. "Or given any thought to checking out Al-Anon?"

Paul was surprised by the question. "No, I haven't. She's never asked me to, and since she's not drinking, why would I need Al-Anon? But I do understand that A.A. is important to her."

*****

Paul arrived at Grace Church at ten sharp for the morning service during which Micky would be confirmed. One of the ushers remembered him from Christmas Eve and gave him a warm greeting and handshake. Handing Paul a service bulletin, he reintroduced himself and pointed to the pew where Lillian, Brad and Ben were waiting. They welcomed him and advised that he sit on the aisle, so that Micky could easily leave when the candidates for confirmation were called to come forward. Brad introduced Paul to Ben.

Family of Choice: Raising Each Other

As Paul scanned the bulletin, he saw to his dismay that along with Micky, a total of fifteen people, including two infants, would be baptized, confirmed, reaffirmed, or received in the Episcopal Church. Before he could make up an excuse to leave, Micky hurried to the pew and sat at the end.

"How was your meeting with the bishop?" Lillian asked her.

"It was wonderful . . . he made all of us feel *special* . . . and also perfectly at ease. He asked that each of us take a couple of minutes to describe why we were taking this step, and what it *means* to us," she replied. "I told him how important it is for me to truly *belong* here, about the friends I've made during our classes, and how we support each other. I also talked about how much I've grown *spiritually* here at Grace in this past year, and how I look forward to continuing on that path."

The organ voluntary began, and Paul looked at his watch. Right on time, he thought; a good sign.

He watched the others and followed suit when they stood or sat, but did not attempt to sing the hymns. Presently, the bishop called all participants and their sponsors to come forward together. Waves of candidates emerged from the pews, including Lillian and Micky.

Brad and Ben were as clueless as he was, so he felt better about struggling to keep up with the responses to the questions the bishop posed to the congregation. He watched as Micky knelt at the altar rail with her classmates, Lillian standing directly behind her. The bishop placed his hands upon her head and said, "Strengthen, O Lord, your servant Micky with your Holy Spirit; empower her for your service; and sustain her all the days of her life. Amen."

Paul checked his watch again. Maybe he'd still have time to join Howie at the club's golf simulators.

Although he did not understand what the church or this ceremony meant to Micky, he could see it in her face and bearing as she rose and returned to the pew at the bishop's dismissal. Her face was radiant and her sapphire eyes glowed in a way he had never seen before. When she sat down beside him and he took her hand, he could feel a power or some odd kind of energy pulsing through her.

After the service, when Lillian invited the group to celebrate Micky's confirmation with cake at her house, Paul realized that he needed to follow along.

CHAPTER 45

Sally exclaimed, "Just five more weeks before your wedding! Is everything coming together on schedule?"

"Pretty much," Micky replied, with a hopeful smile.

"Except for a hiccup in the flights we had scheduled for our honeymoon," Paul said. "Our initial flight out of Cleveland got canceled, and the replacement leaves ninety minutes earlier. So, we'll have to cut our time at the reception accordingly, but I think we can squeeze everything in."

"Where are you going?" Sally asked.

"We'll board a cruise ship in Santiago, Chile, that will sail up the coast of South and Central America, Mexico, BaJa California and end in San Diego," Paul replied. "A nice twenty-one-day getaway with no interruptions or business activities for a peaceful start of our married life together."

"We'll be ready for that," Micky agreed. "It's been *so* hectic managing all of the details in a short time . . . I'll *really* be ready for a long rest!"

"Yes, there is a lot to organize before getting married—especially with two mature adults with businesses, properties, assets and children," Sally noted. "That's why our Church has us discuss these things in this premarital session, to make sure both people are on the same page and that the appropriate paperwork is in place."

Paul reached into his portfolio on the coffee table. "Speaking of which, here's my completed form regarding my first marriage." He handed the folder to Sally, who took a few minutes to read it.

When she looked up, she said, "You and your first wife were very young when you married. Had you known each other long? And why did you decide to marry then?"

"We grew up together, dated in high school," he replied. "It was always assumed we'd marry and start a family, like our parents. I had graduated from college and was working in our family's business so I didn't have to worry about employment. My wife was in school as an education major, but never really wanted to work. So, we got married and had our son, Peter, ten months later and our daughter, Paulette, two years after that. It was an old-school, traditional marriage: I provided for the family, and she raised the kids."

"You've written here that when your son started college and you were on the cusp of an empty nest, your wife, Elizabeth, asked you for a divorce. You state that it was because you worked all of the time, and that she considered her job in the family was basically done. Also, that counseling was not sought.

"What had happened during the intervening nineteen years that the two of you had apparently no interest in remaining in the marriage?"

"Well, in the early years, she had her hands full caring for two toddlers, and I only worked at the Cadillac dealership. Then Dad bought out a neighboring Pontiac dealership when the original owner retired, and did the same thing with the Oldsmobile store on the strip. Our workloads didn't change much, since we kept all of the existing employees.

"But in 2004, when GM gave Oldsmobile and Pontiac dealers the option of selling other brands or operating as independent car lots,

I turned those stores into pre-owned luxury cars businesses. Those successes and the contacts I made helped in later obtaining franchises for our other current dealerships. In the midst of these transitions, my father died of a massive heart attack. I had to move into high gear, dedicating all of my waking hours to running these businesses. My wife had never been interested in my businesses and never got involved at the Club with me. She did take the kids to the pool, and they all played tennis, but none of them wanted to play golf or socialize.

"So, the kids were the only thing we had in common, and since we had no argument about my paying for their college educations and support, giving her the house, plus generous alimony, I was basically no longer part of her life. When Peter started school at Northwestern University, she sold the house and moved with Paulette to Chicago, where they all still live."

Sally looked at Micky. "How do you like Peter and Paulette?"

"I don't know . . . I haven't met them yet."

Sally was visibly taken aback. "Why not?"

"We've all been too busy to get together," Paul said. "I took a weekend trip last fall to tell them about Micky in person, and that the relationship was serious. But we weren't engaged yet. I called them the morning after she accepted my proposal and gave them the news, along with the wedding date and told them I hoped they would attend. Both said they wanted me to be happy, and that they'd tell their mom. Paulette put the date on her calendar; Peter was said my getting remarried was okay with him, but that it didn't affect his life and he'd rather not be at the wedding."

Micky looked at him. "Oh . . . you didn't tell me that . . . I sent him an invitation!"

"I'm glad you did. I'm hoping he'll reconsider."

Sally asked, "How does his decision to not attend make you feel, Paul?"

"Honestly? Like I got kicked in the guts, initially. I told him that was his choice to make, but it still hurts—more like a smoldering burn now. As busy as I was, I always took time to be there for his baseball, soccer or basketball games."

"How involved have you been in your children's lives since your divorce?" Sally inquired.

"We talk on the phone nearly every week, or text," he said. "I always send cards and gifts for their birthdays, Christmas and Easter. Holidays, of course, are spent with their mother, which is natural since she lives nearby and always was the one who did the decorating and meals. Occasionally, they come to visit friends and they stay with me."

Micky was confused. "Oh . . . I didn't know you had that much contact with them. You never talk about them . . . I thought they weren't a very big part of your life."

"Of course, they are. I'm their dad. We just live in different cities that aren't next door, so we don't get together often," Paul explained, looking a little uneasy.

"Yes," Sally said. "Even after they're grown and have their own careers and abodes, they'll always be your children. That's why it's so important in a subsequent marriage to have all of your wishes spelled out in legal documents—that you discuss with them—exactly who is responsible for what. Often, parents who remarry haven't thought these things through and find they need to update their plans before the ceremony.

"For example, Paul, who is named as your healthcare power of attorney to make decisions for you in the event you are not competent? Ditto for your power of attorney, who would have access to your assets and the authority to pay bills and make legal and financial decisions for you in that case? Or the executor of your estate, who can tell your surviving wife how long she can remain in the home? Or, are you making your home jointly owned with right of survivorship? And where do you plan to be buried? Is there a family plot, and if so, would your ex-wife also be buried there? How do your children feel about that? You'd be amazed at the trouble this can cause in an emotional time of grief and loss if everyone isn't on the same page."

His face flushed red as he snapped, "That's none of your business!"

Sally was undaunted. "Actually, it is my business. Not only am I performing the public ceremony that celebrates your spiritual union with Micky, but I also act as an agent of the State of Ohio who *legally* joins the two of you in marriage. So, however you choose to arrange your affairs, I *am* responsible to make sure you *both* are aware of and in agreement with those arrangements. And as a priest, I've had to deal with the burial arguments, and they can be brutal." She leveled her light brown eyes at him and maintained contact until he looked away.

Micky broke the silence. "Um, Paul. We did our prenups that covered our businesses . . . but we *haven't* discussed any of this. My dad said I do need to make a will, and I have another appointment with my attorney on Friday . . . maybe you should come with me, and bring what you have so he can review that and advise us regarding any necessary updates?"

"Mine are more complex," he replied. "There's a revocable trust in addition to my will. It would be easier to handle those with my attorney. I'll make an appointment for both of us to see him. You can still draft your will and your POAs with your counsel."

"So, I take it updates will be needed?" Sally asked.

"Yes, now that I think about it, Micky's name should replace my son's on my healthcare and durable powers of attorney, and also on my living will," he admitted. "It made sense when I got divorced, since he was studying to become a lawyer and is now working for a large Chicago firm. But it would be less than ideal to have the person in charge of my affairs be in another city, versus my wife who'll be by my side. And yes, I will need to update beneficiaries in my will and trust, although Peter will still remain a trustee."

"Thank you, Paul." Micky placed her hand on his.

"Finally, I know the plan is to have Micky's office in one of your dealerships," Sally noted. "But I'm wondering if perhaps there might be friction with working together?"

Paul answered quickly. "That will avoid the pitfall that broke up my first marriage. We're good on that!" He smiled.

Micky added, "Technically, my business address will be my home address, which will change when I move to the house in Avon. My lawyer said it would be confusing to list the address as that of another, existing business that belongs to someone else. I'll probably be spending some time at the dealership office, especially when I'm working on Paul's projects. But otherwise, I can work from home . . . or wherever."

*****

Sally hurried to the rectory, lit a fire and called Lillian.

"Sally! It's nice to hear from you. How's everything back home?"

"Mostly good," she began. "But I do need my sponsor's input on some weird but strong vibes I keep getting from Paul in our premarital counseling sessions."

"What do you mean?"

"I can't share any specifics, of course, but I'm troubled by feelings I've had in all three meetings."

"You usually have pretty reliable instincts, Sally. Can you describe what you're sensing, what you're picking up beyond the spoken words?"

Sally furrowed her brow and paused for a minute or so. "Not without breaking confidentiality."

"Do you have any more sessions?"

"One more, next week," Sally said. "But we usually just go over the mechanics and flow of the ceremony, check all of the boxes regarding music, readings, stuff like that.

"Now is usually when I write my letter to the bishop, stating I believe the marriage should be performed and requesting permission to do so. But I confess my heart really isn't in it."

"Could you postpone that until after the last session, and maybe work in a summing up? Like, asking each what they've gotten out of this? Any surprises? Did they learn anything to help them better understand their partner?" Lillian suggested.

"That's a good idea, I could try it," Sally replied, but she was still worried. "However, what if I'm still stuck with these feelings?"

"Are you certain enough to recommend against the marriage?"

"No. And I'd hate to put the kibosh on Micky's wedding without some *solid* reason," Sally admitted. "I'm also not comfortable waiting until the last minute to send my letter. The deadline is Friday, the twenty-third, only two days after I'll talk with them."

"Well, ask for God's guidance and compose the letter," Lillian advised. "And if you still feel unsettled, maybe we can all ask Micky some questions during our last Sunday coffee in my kitchen before the wedding."

*****

The next evening was Valentine's Day, and Micky and Paul spent it at ECC's gala dinner, sharing a table with Betty and Bill Eldridge. Per the theme, all of the ladies wore red dresses; Micky's had a straight bateau neckline and long sleeves.

Betty leaned toward Micky to admire a magnificent diamond necklace. "What a stunning piece! Is this new? I don't recall seeing you wear it before—and trust me, I'd remember that!"

Micky smiled and blushed slightly. "Paul put this on me just before we came here tonight . . . I barely had a chance to look at it in the mirror!"

Paul grinned in triumph. "It's her wedding gift, about a month early. I thought Valentine's Day was a good time to give it to her, so she can make sure it will work with her wedding dress."

"Very practical," Betty observed. "And sentimental."

"It matches my engagement ring and earrings," Micky explained, raising her left hand between her ear and her collarbone to demonstrate.

Betty nodded in approval. "Quite a set! Wherever did you find these?"

"Howie's brother created the design, obtained the stones and made them," Paul replied. "He does excellent work."

"Indeed he does. Well, Micky, will they go with your dress?" Betty asked.

Micky gave her a Mona Lisa smile, then answered. "Perfectly."

"Your invitations are lovely; very chic and understated. We received ours yesterday," Betty told her. "Please pass along your RSVPs as you get them, so I can start planning seating charts. I'll need to give the kitchen a final count by March ninth."

Micky nodded. "Thank you *so much* for agreeing to coordinate the wedding reception and luncheon, as well as the rehearsal dinner!"

"My pleasure, my dear. Bill and I are so honored to be in your wedding party!" she gushed. "Paul, have you decided on the menu for the rehearsal dinner? Micky gave me the selections for the luncheon last week. But she said you hadn't decided on the cake flavors yet."

"I'll be happy with whatever she wants," he said. "I'm really not a cake guy."

"Who's doing your cake?"

"My Gentleman of Honor, Brad, is a former pastry chef . . . he's interviewing bakers, since he doesn't have a commercial-size oven and will be busy with the rehearsal and wedding," Micky said. "Paul, do you want me to just work with Brad on the flavors? Or at least bring you samples to approve?"

Paul smiled. "I trust your judgment. And Brad's. Why don't you two just handle it."

*****

Brad and Ben had just finished the rack of lamb, wild rice pilaf and Greek salad that he'd prepared at his house. They cleared the table together, then piled their research notes and calendars in place of the plates.

"I've checked with my friends in Paris, and everyone will be in town the last two weeks in April through mid-May," Brad began. "And it looks like Viking has some intriguing river cruises in early May. But most of the ones that start in Paris just tour France, primarily the Chateau country along the Loire River."

"Don't they have any cruises that would let us see cities in several countries?"

"They do, but we'd have to travel to other places where those cruises embark," Brad said. "However, train travel is *very* easy throughout Europe. And there are four major stations in Paris, so we can catch trains to virtually the entire continent."

"I checked with my partner at work, and there's nothing on the books or pending in that time frame," Ben said. "And since I've never taken a real vacation—just a long weekend here and there—he's cool with my taking whatever time we need. Even the whole four weeks, if we want to."

"Great! I've got the same situation with *my* firm. Although I'm now a partner and the lead architect, I'm not the *only* architect or project manager," Brad said. "I'd like to spend at least a week in Paris. Let's go to my office, check out the cruise options and decide what we want to book!"

*****

Lillian had been on tour for most of the past six weeks. As she sat in the empty green room before going on the set for her "Morning in America" interview, she pondered how she wanted to handle the question she always faced regarding the newfound love life she wrote about in the final chapter of her best-selling book. So far, she'd been coy in her replies, evading a direct answer with, "I don't want to give away my possible next book!" But she hadn't heard from Gus since his visit that ended on New Year's Day. Now, she wasn't sure she was being honest with her readers with that verbal sleight of hand; it was seeming less likely that a book based on that romance would materialize.

There was a knock on the door. A slight, dark-haired young woman entered to beckon her. "Ms. Meadows? We're ready for you in five. Please come with me."

Family of Choice: Raising Each Other

She prayed silently. *Please God, guide me through this interview and give me the words you want me to say; words that would be of help to people watching this program. Thy will be done. Thank you, thank you, thank you.*

She followed the young woman to the marker on the floor, just off stage and waited for her introduction cue to enter. "This morning, we're *so* happy to have with us the *author* of the number one *Best Selling* memoir, *Cat Hair in the Bidet*. Please welcome Lillian MacAllister Meadows!"

Flashing a practiced smile at the red light illuminated camera, she carried herself gracefully within the spotlight to the conversation corner and sat down opposite the show's latest blonde ingénue hostess.

"Lillian, you've written several highly successful humorous memoirs sharing your experiences through many phases of contemporary women's lives, dealing with topics such as breakthrough professional jobs, unsuccessful marriages, divorce, and finally marital bliss. And now, widowhood. How did you come to write this book? And what's been different about writing it?"

"As you mentioned, I'd kissed a lot of frogs, who, rather than becoming princes, became ex-husbands," she began. "I wrote about those things in retrospect, after getting through them, and it was easy to see the humor then. Writing them was fun. It was a way of putting my experiences into perspective and moving on to my own happily-ever-after. Many women have gone through those same things, and my readers had a good laugh because they could relate to my words of anger, frustration and eventual joy.

"In my book *Hairs in the Sink and Other Signs of Love*, I chronicled how even in a happy marriage, there will be humorous annoyances of daily life with another human being. It's part of the deal—and very much worth it!

"Then George, the love of my life, died. Suddenly. With no warning. We'd married in our sixties, so we knew our time together on this earthly plane was not unlimited. But I'd expected *more*. I was in shock. I moved through the initial things that had to be done in a blur, and then I cocooned in the wonderful house we'd renovated together ... and three years went by. Until my publisher coaxed me out of that and back into the world with a book deal that I couldn't refuse.

"However, this time I wasn't writing in retrospect, but rather in real time. I hadn't done *anything* to move on. So, goaded by deadlines and by my best friend and priest, I made a list of all of those tasks and wrote about the experience as I did each one of them. Writing this book was *a lot* harder—especially since I had to actually *do* the work that I had procrastinated!"

"Yes, and some of them led to unexpected good things, didn't they?" her interviewer teased. "Like the Open Garden reconnecting you with the widower! So, this being Valentine's Day, I'm *sure* our audience is *dying* to know: How is your love life *progressing* with the gentleman of your final chapter?"

Lillian paused and looked pensive. "I'm not really sure. I've been in constant motion since the holidays, traveling a lot. So, I guess I've been pretty hard to catch up with."

"Oh! So, you haven't heard from him since the holidays?"

"No," Lillian replied. "But no matter how this turns out, I don't regret opening myself up to love again."

Back in her hotel room that evening, Gus called.

"I watched your interview this morning," he said. "I thought about it all day. Thought about you, about us. I love you, Lil. And I realize that I don't need to figure out our future—I just need to see you again, to be with you whenever we can be together."

Family of Choice: Raising Each Other

She teared up, sniffed and admitted, "I love you, too, Gus. And I agree, we don't need to know how this will work, what our future will be. I just want you in it, however it unfolds."

"Do you have any promos near Detroit?"

"Not yet. But I'll be in Chicago for three days next week. Want to meet me there?"

"Of course! Let me know when, and where you'll be staying."

"Then I'll be back home for the month of March, which is good, because Micky is getting married on the twenty-fourth. I'll be one of her attendants, and she sent the invitation with your name on it as well as mine. May I RSVP that we'll both attend?"

"I wouldn't miss it for the world!"

*****

The first Sunday morning in March still retained February's chill, but the sunlight shining through Lillian's kitchen window reflected the cheerful spirits of the gathered friends. As she topped off coffee mugs, Lillian declared, "I'm so glad to finally be home again and to be with all of you! It seems like I was on the road forever."

"We're glad you're back, too," Brad agreed. "I've really missed your coffee cake—but I missed our family meetings most of all!"

"Thank you for agreeing to read the Old Testament passage at the wedding, Lil . . . in addition to being an attendant! I'm so glad you and Betty both have dresses that will work," Micky said.

"Well, I had to spruce up my wardrobe for the book tour," Lillian replied. "It's good to get more use out of my new clothes."

Sally finished her cinnamon crumb cake and smiled. "I'm so glad your book is such a success, Lil. Remember, I predicted it might be your best one yet! I see it's still on the Best Sellers list, so your travels were worth it. But it's great to have you back home!"

Micky said, "Brad and I are going to my place to discuss Step Ten . . . and then to take my summer clothes over to Paul's. My condo goes on the market this week!" She crossed her fingers as she waved goodbye and edged to the door.

Brad grinned. "The timing is perfect. She'll be married in three weeks—and she'll *definitely* need to have that step handy then!" They all laughed as he joined Micky and left.

*****

"So, Micky, by this time next week, you'll be boarding a cruise ship, starting on your honeymoon," Brad teased her. "Are you ready for that?"

She shrugged, palms up. "How do *I* know? I *think* everything is in order. And thanks to you, my condo is already under contract, and most of my things are over at Paul's," she said. "I keep checking my lists, and nearly all items are now done."

Sally asked, "How many people are coming to the wedding at Grace?"

"Eighty-six . . . all of whom will also attend the reception. Another one-twenty-eight will attend the reception only. The deadline has passed for RSVPs, so those numbers should be firm," she replied. Then she rolled her eyes. "Except, *of course* I never received one from Peter Price, and Paul asks me about it every single day. It's become an *obsession* with him! I keep asking why not just *call* him and tell him how important his presence is to you . . . but *noooo* . . . he refuses to *grovel* to his own son."

Family of Choice: Raising Each Other

Sally looked down, bit her lower lip, then decided to go for it. "Micky, I've been very uncomfortable about Paul's inconsistencies when he talks about his children. He claims everything's fine, they talk every week, it's okay that he seldom sees them—and then we have a situation like this. How do *you* interpret it? And how do you think you can manage to develop a relationship with them?"

"Yes, I've noticed that, too," Micky agreed. "I *don't* think he has a very good relationship with *either* of them, so I'm not worried about trying to create one myself. I am *so glad* you brought up the advance directives topic, though . . . we went to his attorney and got things squared away so I have the customary rights and decision-making power of a wife to take care of her husband's affairs, if necessary."

"That's another thing," Sally began. "He was defensive, almost hostile, whenever I asked any of the standard questions required for these sessions. I must say, I've never encountered that in all of my years as a priest. Yet once he realized he had to answer, his responses seemed reasonable. What do you make of that?"

"I did ask him about that . . . he said he was caught off-guard, had never expected to be asked about those sorts of things," Micky explained. "As you pointed out, he was very young when he got married, and his wife was a Baptist. They didn't have pre-marital counseling. Also, since it was a first marriage for both of them, and they were just starting out in life, none of the issues we've discussed applied to them. And these really are very private matters we've been discussing, so his initial reaction was to protest the intrusiveness. He's really not so bad, once you get to know him."

"The two of you do appear to be coming from different pages on a number of things, but you seem to be able to get him to come around to your point of view," Sally observed. "Does this happen frequently?"

"I don't know . . . I guess I never thought about it," Micky replied. "I think he's just accustomed to running his businesses his way, and has lived alone now for five years and hasn't had to consider anyone else's ideas. He can tell when I really care about something and knows I'm going to do what I want, so he gives in. Like getting my own car. The latest is he doesn't want me to bring my black chaise, blue Chinese Oriental rug or those accent pieces, which are the only décor items that are important to me. He says they don't go with his daughter's interior design . . . she did the house. I pointed out that I will be the *lady* of the house, and he realized that they're coming. I'll put them in my home office."

Sally, Lillian and Brad looked at each other.

Brad tiptoed into the thick silence. "You've been making major life decisions at the speed of light for the past three months now, Micky. See if you can chill a little this week—let's take in some meetings together. You need them now more than ever!"

She sighed. "You're right . . . I'm getting married, I've quit my job and am starting a business, my condo sale will close a week after I return from our honeymoon, and I'm moving. I guess I *am* a little stressed out!"

CHAPTER 46

The evening of March twenty-third was cool and Grace Church's thermostat wasn't programmed for full heat mode at that time, but Micky thought that would be good for keeping the flowers fresh for the morrow's ceremony. The florist had done an even better job than she had imagined, and she delighted in the aromas of the hyacinths, roses and lilies.

She shivered a bit in her pink wool dress as people arrived for the rehearsal. Sally, Brad and Lillian were already there, along with the organist. Betty and Bill came in and gave her a hug, followed by Howie and Chet as well as Mike McHale.

Her father greeted her with a bear hug. "I thought I'd never have the opportunity to do this," he said, his baritone voice breaking slightly. "Thank you for inviting me back into your life and letting me give you this wedding. Everything looks beautiful!" He looked around the Gothic church, pews adorned with flowers leading up to magnificent arrangements on the altar, flanked by fresh green palms standing on the floor like sentries. "Where's the groom?" he wondered.

As if on cue, Paul emerged through the front door leading a young woman with red-gold hair on the arm of a tall, gangly young man. They approached the McHales, and Paul introduced Paulette, who then introduced her boyfriend, Andy. "Sorry we're a bit late," Paul apologized. "Their flight was slightly delayed."

"No problem," Micky assured him. "Nothing has started yet."

Sally hailed Paul to the front of the nave to give directions to him and Howie. Micky took Paulette's hand and said, "It's so nice to finally meet you! I'm glad you could come."

"I'm not sure why, though, since I'm not even in the wedding," Paulette complained. Then she looked down at Micky's hand. "Wow! What a ring! No wonder our Christmas gifts were skimpy this year," she said. "Can I try it on?"

Micky was aghast and quickly withdrew her hand. "Of course not! It's my *engagement ring* ... it has a *special meaning!*"

Paulette pouted. "I understand why Peter wouldn't come. He didn't want to have to deal with any of this!" She grabbed her date's arm again and dragged him off to look for an out-of-the-way place to sit.

Sally approached and welcomed Mike. She guided the attendants on the timing of their entrances, walking speed and where they were to halt, then did likewise with Micky and her father. She walked everyone through the ceremony, music, vows, readings, blessing and recessional. After a couple of run-throughs, everyone was comfortable with their parts and Paul invited the group to follow him to the club for the rehearsal dinner.

At the club, Micky was thrilled to see that the florist had done an equally exquisite job in decorating the main dining room for the reception and the smaller hall for this evening as he had done in the church. "Betty, *thank you* so much for organizing everything here," she said. "It all looks *gorgeous,* and you knew all of the areas where flowers would be needed ... *I* wouldn't have had a *clue!*"

"My pleasure, Micky," she replied. "I've done quite a few events here! And you and Paul are *special* to me!"

When the guests were seated, before the waiters began serving the salads, Paul stood up to address the group. "Thank you all for coming to share in the joy of our wedding. *I chose the date, because this date,* today, is very special to me. It's the anniversary of the day I first met Micky, when my life changed."

Before he could continue, a waiter wheeled in a cart with a large sheet cake and placed it in the front of the room. Paulette jumped up and exclaimed, "This day's special for me, too! It's Andy's birthday today! And here's the cake!" She clapped her hands, oblivious to the fact that everyone was staring at her in shock.

Betty was livid. "Get that thing out of here this instant! Take it back to the kitchen," she snapped at the waiter. "Paulette, I've known you since you were a small spoiled brat, and you haven't changed since then! Believe it or not, *this occasion* is *not about you!* Sit down and shut up, or remove yourself if you can't behave."

Glaring at Betty, and at her father, Paulette grabbed the hapless birthday boy and told him, "Come on, Andy. We'll have cake for dinner in our hotel room!" She stomped off with her boyfriend in tow.

Mike McHale leveled a stern look at Paul, whose face was bright red with shame. He showered Micky and the guests with apologies, who were all relieved to turn their attention to the salad course.

*****

Brad and Lillian stayed with Micky in Grace Church's Guild Room the next morning, helping her into her designer wedding dress and adjusting her glittering diamond jewelry. At first, she had thought this would be unnecessary, but was glad they had insisted when she discovered that the fitted bodice and heavy drapes of the satin skirt prevented her from reaching her feet to fasten the straps of her white kitten-heeled sandals.

She sat in a wing-back chair and lifted the hem past her slender ankles while Brad knelt on the carpet, slipped the delicate shoes on her feet and secured the fastened straps through their keepers. "I feel like Prince Charming with Cinderella," he said with a wry grin.

"You *are* a prince, Brad, and you're certainly *charming* . . . but, obviously, you can't be *my* prince," she replied, laughing. "Too bad!"

For a final touch, they played with the selection of adornments for her French-braid hairdo, trying the options with her standing before the antique ceiling-height peer mirror. "While I *love* the fragrance of the white lily, it's a bit overpowering this close to my face," Micky admitted.

Lillian added, "It's also too large to be worn on the side like that; it looks unbalanced. And you have plenty of flowers in your bouquet."

"The rhinestones are okay—but try these," Brad suggested, as he produced a handful of white seed pearl flowers on hairpins from his jacket pocket. "They were my grandmother's. So, you'd have something old that's new to you, and something borrowed—to go with your blue garter."

She hugged him, with tears welling up in her eyes. "Oh, Brad . . . they're *perfect . . . thank you!*"

He put the tiny ornaments in a row to accent the edge of the twist in her glossy black hair and kissed her cheek. "I'd better go now and help the other male attendants seat the guests. I'll send your father to knock on the door just before the processions begin, and Lil will lead you to the narthex unseen."

Micky smiled as he left, then checked her mascara in the mirror as she dabbed her eyes with a tissue.

"You know, it felt really right to hand you over to Brad for your sponsor," Lillian reflected. "The two of you have both grown so much over the past year. You truly have become a woman of grace and dignity, Micky—we get to be the women God made us to be by staying sober and living this program."

Micky smiled. "One day at a time!"

"Of course! That's how it works," Lillian agreed. "Now, you're about to embark on a new life, personally and professionally. We'll continue to walk those paths with you, too—no matter *what* you encounter."

There was a knock on the door and her father's deep voice announcing, "It's show time."

Lillian led them down a sloping hallway, through the undercroft and carefully up a narrow staircase that opened in the narthex, where the attendants were gathered. The organ voluntary finished. After a pause, the processional music began, "Rondeau" by Jean Mouret.

The double doors opened. Brad and Howie entered together, followed by Lillian with Chet, then Betty and Bill. Paul had entered from a door on the right side of the nave and stood near the steps, in front of Sally. Howie joined him, and Paul's other attendants lined up next to the Best Man. Brad anchored the bride's side on the left.

When the attendants were in place, Micky and her father stepped into the doorway, and began their walk down the aisle. She reveled in the fragrance of the flowers, concentrated from their overnight stay, and the sun had popped out from the clouds, brilliantly illuminating the reds, golds, blues and greens of the stained-glass windows that she loved. The photographer clicked away, capturing images of the stunning father and daughter. The music she had chosen was the theme used for public television's *Masterpiece* series, and the guests later said that in her elegant dress on the arm of her tall, handsome father, she truly looked like a queen. She felt regal, too. It was the most exciting experience of her life, and she felt goose-bumps along with joy.

As she got closer, she saw Paul's eyes fixed on her, filled with love and admiration and overcome by seeing her in that stunning dress, adorned by the jewels he had given her. She smiled as she locked eyes with him when she and her father had nearly completed their journey.

Paul suddenly broke his gaze away from Micky and looked to the left side of the church, loudly crying, "My son!" He bolted from his place and ran to embrace the young man whom no one had noticed sneaking down the side aisle when the guests all rose at the bride's entrance.

Mike McHale boomed, "*Paul—what* the *FUCK?!*"

The music ceased. Everyone froze.

McHale continued, "*What* is *wrong* with your *kids?*"

The young man grinned and waved, which was shut down by Howie, who had arrived to try to handle this mess.

Quietly, Mike asked, "Micky are you sure you want to go through with this? You really want to be part of *that* family?"

She was in tears and in shock, looking like a deer in the headlights after being run over by a previous truck. "I don't *know* . . . our flight leaves at five-thirty . . . the reception . . . everything is *all arranged!*"

He looked down at his distraught daughter. "And so is your paperwork, Kitten. If you want to continue, don't worry—if it doesn't work out, you can always get a divorce."

Everyone was waiting. Howie had installed the errant son next to his equally self-centered sister and had returned Paul to his proper place, who now apologized profusely to Micky and begged her to marry him.

She looked up at her father and nodded. They walked the few remaining steps and stopped in front of Sally. Mike couldn't remember whether he was to sit down now or after giving her away, but decided he wasn't going anywhere right now. She needed his support.

Sally began the ceremony. "Dearly beloved: We have come together in the presence of God to witness and bless the joining together of this man and this woman in Holy Matrimony. The bond and covenant of marriage was established by God in creation, and our Lord Jesus Christ adorned this manner of life by his presence and first miracle at a wedding in Cana of Galilee. It signifies to us the mystery of the union between Christ and his Church, and Holy Scripture commends it to be honored among all people.

"The union of husband and wife in heart, body, and mind is intended by God for their mutual joy; for the help and comfort given one another in prosperity and adversity; and when it is God's will, for the procreation of children and their nurture in the knowledge and love of the Lord. Therefore marriage is not to be entered into unadvisedly or lightly, but reverently, deliberately, and in accordance with the purposes for which it was instituted by God.

"Into this holy union Micky McHale and John Paul Price now come to be joined. If any of you can show just cause why they may not lawfully be married, speak now; or else forever hold your peace."

Sally allowed a long pause.

Everyone was on edge about the question. Heads tilted towards one another, and the church was filled with the hum of muted murmuring. Brad, through his pasted-in-place smile whispered to Lillian, "There's no *bigamy* or anything like that—but isn't there a law of *common sense* that's being violated here?"

Hearing no objections voiced, Sally continued, asking the couple if either of them knew any reason why they could not be united in marriage lawfully and in accordance with God's Word. Then they each declared their consent to have each other as their spouse; to live together in the covenant of marriage, and to love, comfort, honor and keep each other, in sickness and in health, forsaking all others and to be faithful to one another as long as they both lived.

She then asked the congregation, "Will all of you witnessing these promises do all in your power to uphold these two persons in their marriage?"

And when they followed the program and answered, "We will," Sally thought, *"I hope they mean it."*

Next, she asked, "Who gives this woman to be married to this man?"

Mike McHale answered, "I do." He then stepped back to the front pew.

After a short prayer, she invited the people to be seated, motioning for Micky and Paul to take the chairs in front. After the readings, homily, and a brief musical interlude, the couple followed Sally up to the altar where they made their vows and exchanged rings.

Sally joined their right hands and said, "Now that Micky and Paul have given themselves to each other by solemn vows, with the joining of hands and the giving and receiving of rings, I pronounce that they are husband and wife, in the Name of the Father, and of the Son, and of the Holy Spirit.

"Those whom God has joined together let no one put asunder." She couldn't help looking pointedly at Peter and Paulette Price.

Prayers, the blessing of the marriage and passing of the peace concluded the ceremony. The couple and attendants recessed to Ludwig von Beethoven's "Ode to Joy", and piled into the limo that drove them to the Elyria Country Club. Once there, they assembled at a spot Paul had selected for photos of the wedding party.

In the interest of time, the attendants were spared the rigors of the receiving line, so they filed into the dining room for refreshments before the luncheon. Micky and Paul took this opportunity to personally greet all of the guests, since most were business contacts and the couple would have very little time for informal mingling due to the revised flight schedule. They made the most of it, though, giving each guest due attention and conversation.

Micky was glad to finally be seated at the head table, and it was fun hearing the toasts. Betty had thoughtfully made sure that Micky's glass was filled with her special non-alcoholic drink. She also appreciated the expedited service and the club's cuisine, as she was famished.

Then they needed to move into the photo-op activities: Cutting the cake and eating the first pieces (at Micky's insistence), the father-daughter dance and first dance as a married couple; the tossing of the bride's bouquet (Lillian caught it) and of the blue garter (caught by Brad).

Micky did take time to tell Gus how glad she was that he was there. "And don't worry about Lil's catching the bouquet . . . I don't think there's any expiration date on that!" Likewise, she said to Ben, "Interesting that Brad got the garter . . . I hear you two have quite the trip planned this spring! Who knows what might happen . . ."

Then she had to disappear and change into traveling clothes. Betty planned to take care of her wedding dress, getting it cleaned and put into a proper storage bag. Paul had loaded their luggage into the car the day before.

The band was playing and guests were dancing when the couple re-entered the dining room. Paul and Micky stepped up on the bandstand and he took the microphone. "Thank you all for sharing this day with us! We're so sorry that flight snafus shortened the time we have to spend with you, but we've got to run. Have a wonderful time!"

Everyone showered them with baskets of rose petals as they left, including a gauntlet outside from the doors to their car.

Micky's family huddled together, piles of fallen petals underfoot. Brad said, "It's too bad they had to have that runaway exit—after all of that planning, she didn't even get a chance to enjoy her own party! Hope the photographer can capture all of the memories she'll miss."

"We'll have to dance enough to make up for her," Gus suggested with a wink, his arm around Lillian, who looked up at him and smiled.

Ben said what they'd all been thinking. "I can't get over those unbelievable brats Paul spawned! I hope she doesn't have to spend much time around them."

"Amazing," Mike McHale said. "I mean, our family was admittedly messed up, but Micky didn't turn out like that. That guy doesn't deserve her."

Sally shook her head. "This doesn't bode well. I should have stopped it."

"I think she'll find that family isn't as nice as ours," Brad noted with sarcasm.

"I don't think she realized there *was* a family there," Lillian replied. "If the behavior we just witnessed is their best, she'll need to cling tightly to her program and to us."

"That's why we form families of choice," Sally added. "Some born of blood ties offer no comfort and can prosecute gory civil wars. But not all families of choice are healthy, either: Shelley chose drug addicts and criminals. Mercifully, our family is based on recovery, spirituality and God's love."

Brad looked at Lillian. "I'm glad sponsorship doesn't mean planning her life for her."

"No, that's above our pay-grade," she agreed. "As Sally said, the couple made the marriage sacrament with God—he'll have to figure this one out!"

To Be Continued . . .

There's more to come in the story as our family members' lives continue to unfold, one day at a time. But what's in store for them?

Will Micky and Paul have a happily-ever-after marriage? Will she be able to create a place in his family . . . or want to?

Will Gus' son accept his father's love for Lillian? Can they sustain their long-distance relationship? Will Lillian get another love story for a next book?

How will Brad's romance with Ben develop? Will Ben remain in his Craftsman house Brad is renovating, or will it go on the market?

Sally has added remorse for performing Micky's marriage ceremony despite her forebodings and the ominous spectacles Paul's children displayed to the guilt she carries for her failure to impart God's love to her own daughter. She wrestles with doubt: Is she fit to be a priest?

Sally knows God will sort all of these things out. But how that will appear for all of them on this earthly plane remains to be seen—and the God of her understanding has a divine sense of humor!

More will be revealed as this Family of Choice deals with Life on Life's Terms.

Acknowledgments

Family of Choice: Raising Each Other began in a novel-writing workshop taught by Scott Lax. Scott is an award-winning novelist, playwright, screenwriter, journalist, and producer as well as a fulltime Senior Professor of Practice in Creative Writing at the Cleveland Institute of Art + Design. I am grateful to Scott for his instruction, support, and editing of the completed manuscript.

Heartfelt thanks to the Rev. Vincent Black, the Rev. Leah Romanelli DeJesus, and Kathleen R. Ashton, Ph.D., ABPP, who enthusiastically praised the overall story and characters, and provided detailed feedback on the manuscript, particularly in their areas of professional expertise. Dr. Ashton also urged me to consider self-publishing.

My friend Fred Leick recommended I read a book by his former colleague at Proctor & Gamble, Peg Wyant, titled *One Red Shoe: The Story of Corporate America's First Woman*. I was so impressed by the book that I looked to see who published it, and was surprised to learn that Gatekeeper Press specializes in self-publishing. As Peg Wyant was renowned for her due diligence, I felt safe in choosing them for my project!

Gatekeeper Press Co-Owner Tony Chellini, my Author Manager Eden Tuckman, and Olena Tkachenko and the illustration and design team all provided warm, personal and professional service and guidance. Thank you for your help in creating a finished product that I'm proud of, and especially for handling all of the necessary details and distribution to make it available to readers. This relieved me of a great deal of stress, and allowed me to move forward with promoting it and beginning the second novel in the series.

I thank my friend Bill Rice of RBR Associates, Inc. for helping with marketing and for putting me in touch with storyteller Roy M. Griffis, who kindly shared his experience and advice in self-publishing.

Thanks also to many other supportive friends who liked the novel's concept or enjoyed reading some initial chapters. The familiar passages used in the wedding scene in the last chapter are from the Prayer Book.

Loving thanks to my husband, Jeff Sommer, for his understanding when I was busy writing. Not a fan of fiction, he did not read the manuscript; however, he enjoyed the story when I gave him a detailed verbal synopsis. I thank him for his delightful sense of humor, especially for some ideas he offered for the novel's ending. He keeps me laughing every day; I married him for the free entertainment!